ISTRIA GOLD

First published in Great Britain in 2022 by MPress Media

A CIP catalogue record for this book is available from the British Library

ISBN 978-1-7398906-2-9

Designed by: Mpress Media
Set in Adobe Caslon Pro 11pt
Printed and bound in the UK using 100% renewable electricity

This book is printed from independently certified FSC™ paper to ensure responsible forest management

For more information visit:
calmproductions.com or www.mikedowney.eu

'Endlessly surprising. Mike Downey has a truffle dog's nose for a good story.'
Lee Hall, writer of Billy Elliot

'Mike Downey's debut novel, Istria Gold, skilfully braids three stories of gladiators in the Roman occupation in AD 81, partisans in the Second World War, and the contemporary return of a failed cop to his Croatian homeland. Downey, who fell in love with Istria forty years ago, shares his infatuation of this landscape steeped in conflict, history and glorious food – especially, the truffle. This precious tuber is both a real and narrative mycelium, embedded within the Istrian soil, connecting Downey's fascinating characters through centuries of turmoil - characters as rich and complex in flavour as the truffle: from the father and daughter team of ex-gladiator Severus and Lucia who discover how to preserve them in oil, to Nino, a young Partisan in the Resistance whose passion for truffle hunting almost gets him killed, and his grandson, Marco, who reconnects to his family – and himself – through a hunt for a dangerous truffle cartel. Downey is a passionate tour guide as well as a nimble story-teller. He had me Googling maps of Istria and looking up plane ticket prices. Here is a classic adventure story, sparkling in the Istrian sun and best read with a glass of Istrian walnut brandy, goat's cheese with turmeric, and, of course, truffles.'
Melanie Finn, author of Away From You and The Gloaming

'Downey has the uncanny ability to switch between wildly different storytelling eras, leaving us longing for the one left behind, only to find ourselves instantly immersed in the next. Clearly, I've never spent much time in either the Roman occupation of Istria, nor the Nazi occupation years later, so my assertion is entirely indefensible ... but his depictions are so grippingly authentic, the man must possess a time machine.'
Michael Kalesniko, author of Pucker Up and Howard Stern's Private Parts

'Mike Downey and his Istria Gold is a novel that is at once epic and startling!'
Rebecca Lenkiewicz, writer of Oscar® winning movie, Ida

'Downey's prose is sharp, engaging and entertaining - so much so that before you know it, you've arrived at the end of the book and want to start all over again. His protagonists are alive and vivid on the page, and his ability to submerge the reader in multiple and concurrent historical periods makes this book a winner!'
Bob McLeod, Good Reads

Also by Mike Downey

Non-fiction

THE FOOL ON THE HILL
Low Altitude Thinking

THE FILM FINANCE HANDBOOK
A practical guide to film financing for European producers, Volume 1

THE FILM FINANCE HANDBOOK
A practical guide to film financing for European producers, Volume 2

THE SELF MANAGING SCREEN

MAGNOLIAS
Berlinale – Film – Memories

For the Theatre

IN SEARCH OF ARTAUD

THE BIG SLEEP (adaptation)

Translation

HAUTE SURVEILLANCE by Jean Genet

Anthologies / Compendia

INTERNATIONAL DICTIONARY OF FILMS AND FILMMAKERS: FILMS VOL. 1 (Contributor)

INTERNATIONAL DICTIONARY OF FILMS AND FILMMAKERS: FILMS VOL. 2 (Contributor)

SCREEN INTERNATIONAL YEARBOOK 1985-1990
(Contributing Editor)

ISTRIA GOLD

*****

Mike Downey

mpress (MEDIA) LIMITED

'Activism is my rent for living on the planet.'

Alice Walker

'You have asked the scholars what this tubercle is, and after two thousand years of discussion, the scholars have answered the same as the first day: 'We do not know.' You have asked the truffle itself and the truffle has answered you: 'Eat me and adore God.' To tell the story of the Truffle is to tell the history of the world's civilisation.'

Alexandre Dumas

'The treasure which you think not worth taking trouble and pains to find, this alone is the real treasure you are longing for all your life. The glittering treasure you are hunting for day and night lies buried on the other side of that hill yonder.'

B. Traven

'In battles of gladiators, and in the case of men of the very lowest class and condition and fortune, we are accustomed to dislike those who are timid and suppliant, and who pray to be allowed to live, and we wish to save those who are brave and courageous, and who offer themselves cheerfully to death... we feel more pity for those men who do not ask our pity, than for those who entreat it.'

Marcus Tullius Cicero

'Think well about this, dear brothers and sisters, and you will see that we should have been in a state of terrible chaos, in a fratricidal war, in a country which would no longer be Yugoslavia, but be only a group of petty little states fighting among themselves and destroying each other. But our people do not want that to happen.'

Josip Broz - Tito

For Marijana

Contents

Part One

Chapter I
The Return of the Prodigal
London/Istria: December 23rd, 2019

Blocking out the endless customer service announcements, he jostled gently for position – in that very British way – on the current of people that flowed in a smoothly moving wave along the underground corridor from King's Cross to Saint Pancras. If you were prepared just to go with the flow it was like surfing a wave. But if you had somewhere to get to it was all too easy to get bogged down in the bottlenecks and eddies of human tide that seemed to have taken so naturally to the subterranean world in the last 150 years. He looked like someone who had nowhere particular to go. But looks can be deceptive. A very specific appointment awaited him this crisp London winter morning, its beauty thrown into relief by his abrupt descent into the bowels of the capital. Public transport in London continued its century-and-a-half-long tradition of being a very real assault on the senses. This feeling was accentuated so much more following his most recent mission, deep undercover with a hard-core anarchist/environmentalist group, Resist the Global. It was this assault on the senses of humble PC Marco Mihailić that he found not only offensive; it inspired in him an uncharacteristic meanness of spirit, and he, commensurately, lowered his usual flag of tolerance to all men to at least half-mast.

Sliding down the escalators to the clatter and creak of the Hammersmith & City Line his mood was not improved as he went over in his mind the events of the last two weeks. They flashed before his eyes like a movie montage. The attack on the animal experiment unit in Oxford by him and his animal rights protest buddies. The dawning of the realisation by the crew that the Thames Valley Police must have had had a tip-off. The subsequent rounding up of the usual suspects and questioning of all the group at Saint Aldates Police Station; court, bail, and release on Monday morning. Then, worse than that. The worst possible thing that could happen. The sense of shameful expectation that when he got back to the 'camp', a seedy squat in the old power station in Osney, he would have been discovered as the rat. The rat that had betrayed them all for the last three years. And just when it really couldn't get any worse, the person who discovered that he was the undercover spook, the one who had found the passport – his genuine passport, with his real name of Marco Mihailić, real date of birth and real status – was Janey. The woman he told he loved. The woman he had loved. Still loved. The woman who had carried and lost his child. The woman he had deceived outright and who had allowed him to go free before informing the rest of the squat.

And now here he was on the way to Paddington Green Police Station, ostensibly to hear the final decisions regarding his fate as an undercover operative working for the National Public Order Intelligence Unit. And it wasn't looking good. He looked at his reflection in the window behind the empty seat opposite him. How had it come to this? He stared deeper and deeper into his own eyes across the empty carriage.

There was nothing genuine about him. He wasn't even a genuine Brit, yet here he was in the middle of Brexit Britain defending British values on behalf of the great British public. They loved nothing more than their animals and their animal rights. Sometimes, he thought, more than humans and their human rights. He looked at himself again.

'Who actually are you, Marco Mihailić? Will the real Marco Mihailić please stand up?' said a small, slightly irritated voice in the back of his tragically dreadlocked skull.

When Marco and his Serbian mother, Maja, left the former Yugoslavia – now Istria in Croatia – following his father's death in the Croatian Homeland War in 1995, it was under a cloud. Recriminations, misunderstandings, old family feuds turned into a flare-up. Maja was bitter and furious with her father-in-law, Nino, for she blamed him for the death of her husband – his son, Ivo. With his military connections he could have got Ivo out of the draft had he wanted to. One night she took Marco and left Istria behind. A few humiliating and degrading years later at the hands of the UK's Home Office she finally managed to claim refugee status, wiped the slate clean, and their new life together began. Away from the madness and the old feuds, the age-old story of many a refugee or migrant, determined to start over, forget the ethnic hate, and move on. There were far fewer on the move across the world back then.

Maja and Marco took their chance together, away from the mess that was the Croatian homeland and the family she felt had betrayed her and her husband. Maja threw herself into living, working and surviving in her new country with a passion. She cleaned every office in the Square Mile for as many hours as there were in the day and, more often than not, night, to give the boy a decent life and a decent education. The only time she used her philosophy degree from the University of Belgrade was when she was issuing advice to Marco. Advice he always listened to.

This was the first day since her death, three years earlier, that Marco was glad that she wasn't alive. Equally, it was the first time he admitted to himself that perhaps his decision to go undercover had a direct link to her death. Escape. Anonymity. Denial of the past. Avoidance of guilt. He went into hiding in more ways than one.

Not a great reason to be cheerful, but something to hold on to, as the day wasn't likely to get any better.

He looked back into his reflection. Further reasons to be cheerful sprang to mind. The nose ring and the bolts through his eyebrows could go, along with the empathetic nose stud. If he was being honest with himself, he'd started to look like a macrobiotic Frankenstein's monster. He could finally get rid of these ridiculous white-boy Rastafarian dreadlocks, grown to blend in sympathetically with his fellow anti-globalist crusaders.

Marco was awoken from this particular trance as the train jolted momentarily to life before stopping again after another wheezing 50 metres of track was consumed. Par for the course on the Hammersmith & City. The old red light. It was during this return to reality that he realised that the only other occupant of the carriage had switched his phone to speaker and was singing along to some inane lyrics of the rapper *du jour*. Assuming it was a mere headphones error, Marco let it ride for a minute, then realised that the youth was seriously into sharing his music. Marco made a conciliatory, palms down 'chill, dude' gesture, which was summarily ignored.

'Hey, fella, take it easy with the speaker. I'm OK with it – but other people will be getting on at Edgware Road,' lied Marco semi-convincingly.

The kid in question was white, angry, late teens, dressed (again, ironically) like a black rapper; he came over and sat in front of

Marco, turning up the volume and multiples of 'motherfuckers' as he did, directing each one of them at Marco. Bang on cue the Hammersmith & City boneshaker lurched into action the last 100 metres towards Edgware Road. Marco simultaneously surged out of his seat. The cut-glass Received Pronunciation vowels of the loudspeaker announcement sliced in above the motherfucking din: 'Next stop Edgware Road. Connect to the District Line for Earl's Court. Mind the Gap. Mind the Gap.'

Marco had the kid in a straight-arm bar take-down. In two or three prestidigitatory seconds he'd also handcuffed his fellow-traveller to the handrail by the side seat next to the carriage door. The kid had absolutely no idea what had hit him and by the time the poor wee thing looked up he saw the doors slowly closing on cue and Marco on the platform, demonstrating clearly with a thumbs up to the lad that he's dropping the phone in this particular bin. As the train pulled out, Marco gave a gentle wave accompanied by a gentle goodbye smile. Goodbyes were not his strong suit, but lately his life seemed to be a long litany of them.

★★★★★

The meeting at Paddington Green Police Station went exactly as expected. No surprises there. Marco had always been a bit of an outsider in the force, not just because of his Yugoslavian origins but because, even as a naturalised Brit, he had never quite come to terms with England's class-ridden social hierarchy; not only in civvy street, but also in the Metropolitan Police – as well as in the anti-globalist underground.

After leaving college he thought that by joining the Met he would finally be able to integrate, assimilate, become one of the guys and live quietly, anonymously outside the confines of any tribe. He wasn't counting on the depth of British exceptionalism that he would ultimately find. When that didn't go according to plan – and with the loss of his mother to a very virulent form of lung cancer those three years back to spur him on – he thought he would ingratiate himself further with the establishment by offering to risk giving up his very identity by going underground, and in doing so infiltrate the presumed domestic enemy facing the British state. More specifically, the anti-blood sports, anti-fascist, anti-animal experiments brigade. So he drove himself further underground, further away from his original goal of being the best of British; of integrating and being quasi-invisible. He had no immediate family in London, no ties, and had always been by nature a loner, so he had nothing to lose.

He first understood this when he began to feel that the underground organisations that he was infiltrating were much more of a home, more of a friendly place for him than the Met. The goals and objectives of the tree-huggers were things he really believed in, and he supported them in their desire to effect change and create a better, more sustainable world. He would transport himself back to his childhood memories of walking the truffle woods of Istria with his grandfather, Nino, and his dogs. That was truly a natural world with ancient traditions worth fighting for. And then there was Janey. The Janey who had opened her heart and soul and mind and given him a real home, a real safe place for the first time in his life. Only in real life it wasn't that. It was a home whose foundations were built on the shifting sands of deceit. A turning point came for him when he saw the poster outside the Everyman Cinema in Hampstead for a documentary about Alice Walker. It had a quote on it which went, 'Activism is my rent for living on the planet'. It struck a chord somewhere deep inside Marco and he turned. In the three years that he had been serving Queen and country as an undercover operative Marco had infiltrated a number of protest groups, including anti-racist campaigners and anarchists. His daily work often went beyond that of a mere passive spy, becoming himself a distinct activist. He thus left himself open to the claim, by both the Met and the activists, that his role in organising and helping to fund protests meant he had turned into an *agent provocateur*. Damned if he did, damned if he didn't.

The long and the short of it was this: the Met was about to hang him out to dry as the scapegoat for a failed infiltration, uncovered by his victims, discovered by a gleeful press, for which they needed someone to carry the can. The final upshot: there was no going back to either of his old lives. The whole thing was made worse by these repeated accusations of being an *agent provocateur*, as well as his two-year-long love affair with Janey, whose pregnancy, miscarriage, were now all a matter of public record. Alongside the fact that the tabloids, ever keen to find a bad apple and vilify the boys in blue, had now found one who was not only a shit, bastard, love-rat, and a copper: he was also a dirty unwashed hippy to boot. And a filthy, unexceptional, all used-up foreigner – the worst of crimes in the current anti-immigration mood of the nation.

Not one to dwell on things, and being a practical soul at heart, Marco now had to consider his options: hang around in the UK under yet another assumed identity half-heartedly provided by the force – and eventually be hunted down by the men in Guy Fawkes masks *sans* protection of the force; or try something different. Or, like his hero Ronald Biggs, escape to South America via the Antipodes with a new name, cut-price Parisian plastic surgery, and a sack-load of cash. The only thing stopping him was that he didn't have the cash.

Like his grandfather, his father, his mother, and his ancestors before him across the Balkans, he knew deep in his mind that however good things were looking, something very bad was always bound to happen; some kind of an escape route was *de rigeur* for those of the Balkan diaspora, never mind their creeds or nationality. His mother had drummed this into him over and over again. It was ingrained into her DNA, her inherited national psyche. Even though you didn't think you needed an escape plan it was probably best to have one. Both the history and the meteorology of their former region had a terrible habit of allowing the winds to change. He didn't need a new life. Why did he need a new life, a new identity, a new place to live? He had a very old one to go back to. His original one. Having fucked up both of his assumed ones, maybe he could make a go of the one he left behind in 1995?

★★★★★

Why they'd chosen Paddington Green, Marco couldn't be sure, but he suspected that in doing the dirty deed away from his unit's base down by the river they would allow a certain anonymity to his disgrace and allow morale within the unit to remain unchallenged. Why rub his colleagues' noses in the fact that an undercover officer just like them had been thrown under the bus, with protection neither from potential revenge from the eco-warriors nor from the toxic press that had been plaguing him and anyone they could get to admit to knowing him. Again, for the second time that day, he felt blessed that his mother wasn't around to see this happen. And then he had another wave of optimism, clutching at whatever small mercies could be salvaged from what wasn't his best day so far on the planet. Marco had been a devoted servant to the Met for nigh on a decade and a half, almost one-third of that on the front-line underground. Meanwhile, Chief Superintendent Cassidy, who was running Marco's 'early retirement' meeting, was generous to a fault. He had made it clear that no officer of the Met would be facing charges over this incident. Gross misconduct was as good a reason as any for 'early retirement'.

The Commander asked him to hand over his warrant card and his handcuffs. It was only when he reached into his bag that he realised he could only fulfil one of these obligations and had a little smile to himself.

'It's no laughing matter, Mihailić,' barked the Commander, demonstrating his relevance to Chief Superintendent Cassidy.

'I can't guarantee, however, that there won't be any civil charges brought,' added Cassidy. 'You left quite a mess with Janey Foulkes. This is something we can't help you with. You are aware of that, aren't you? This is the main area of your misconduct. You crossed the line, Marco.'

And crossed the line he had indeed.

Cassidy leant across the desk.

'I don't like this any more than you do, Marco, but we have to follow procedure. It didn't have to turn out like this, son.'

'It didn't what?' replied Marco, starting to lose his cool, mimicking his superior. 'It didn't have to turn out like this, son?'

A silence descended on the room. Marco filled it. 'You really have no idea, do you? You have no fucking idea what it is we do,' continued the soon-to-be ex-PC Mihailić. 'You put the squeeze on me to go in faster, deeper, further into the Resist the Global group, so desperate you were for results to keep the tabloids at bay. And when it goes tits-up, it's "Oops, nothing to do with us!"'

'That's not how it was Marco, and you know it,' said Cassidy.

'And there's me – the honest cop in the middle caught out as the Judas to both sides. Well, Chief Superintendent Cassidy, you weren't there, and you haven't got a clue.'

'That's enough, Mihailic!' cut in Cassidy, trying to keep things on an even keel.

'Do you really want to know what made me sick of you lot? It wasn't the kickings or the beatings that I took from your bully boys in the Territorial Support Group – they all added to my cover. It's that you had no fucking idea what a good policeman I was. What a good policeman I *am*.'

'At risk of repeating myself, Marco,' said Cassidy, 'you brought this on yourself. You were sleeping with the enemy. Fucking the enemy. There's no way back from that, and you know it.'

Another chasm of silence descended. Marco broke it with: 'Can I ask you a question, Sir?'

'Go on.'

'Have you ever been in love?'

And once again, the silence.

In truth, it was the pressure from his handlers that had forced him to go deeper, stay longer, build the relationships to get a better result. In the end these relationships represented the impossible position in which he felt he had been placed and as he spent more and more time with Resist the Global the more he began to sympathise with their causes. The merits of sabotaging experiments on live animals were as clear to him as fighting against sweatshop labour around the world or exposing the role of drugs companies and their global monopolies. As time went on Marco began to see how internationalism, eco-socialism and anti-capitalism were a way of opposing imperialism, nationalism, materialism, and militarism.

And each dawning realisation had brought him closer to Janey. The reality was that the Resist the Global activists in the squat in Oxford had become his friends. His family. He genuinely was in love with Janey, and he wanted her to have their child. He was closer to his comrades in the gang than he had ever been with anyone in the Met. They loved him. Janey loved him. Now the likelihood was that she would be obliged to show her allegiance to the family, to the resistance by dragging him through the courts in a civil case. The bloodthirsty tabloid press would have a field day and he would deserve every prick that he had to kick against.

'Mihailic! Mihailic? Now. Sign these papers,' said Cassidy, bringing Marco out of his reverie. 'And then we're finished.'

Marco looked back long and hard into Chief Superintendent Cassidy's eyes and coldly stated: 'My name is Mihail*ich*,' emphasising the correct pronunciation; and, after a pause, adding as a distant afterthought, 'Sir.'

These bastards, he thought to himself as quietly, and unremarkably, he walked down the steps of Paddington Green Police Station and into the rest of his life.

As he waited to cross the ever-bustling Harrow Road he realised that he had already made the right decision. A decision based on family. He couldn't stay in London. He'd be torn to shreds on a daily basis for as long as the whole débâcle lasted.

He had no choice. All he could to do was pack up and jump on a plane. Home to Istria. Recently he had become sentimental. Not about Istria, but about certain words. One of them was 'home'. As he thought about it he checked a tear back into its brimming duct and made for the other side of the road.

'Taxi!' he called out as the vehicle hit the intersection with the Edgware Road. He strode towards it with a spring in his step garnered from the decision that meant he would soon be out of England. Hopefully, for good. And back in the bosom of his eccentric and natural family down by the Adriatic.

The taxi pulled up at the lights.

'Tredegar Square, E3, please.'

'Hop in,' said the chirpy cab driver. Marco jumped in and the door slammed shut. Immediately the driver started: ''Ere, aren't you the cop geezer who got nicked knocking up the hippy bird? Good on you, mate, she was quite a…'

Before the cheeky cockney cabby had time to finish his sentence Marco jumped out of the other side of the taxi and skipped away down the Edgware Road to the Central Line at Marble Arch. Hoodie up, scarf in place. He wouldn't be making that mistake again.

*****

As he breezed up the escalator at Mile End Station and into the turnstiles, off went the alarm denoting a non-functioning Oyster card. They hadn't wasted much time between signing him off and stopping the card: less than an hour. Emergency call to a mugged pensioner at home – waiting time three hours. The Met could be slick when it wanted to. He lined up at the excess fares cash desk, paid his dues and walked out of the station, somehow feeling like a freer man having paid his own way. He made a beeline against the lights straight across the Mile End Road and into the safe haven that was Tredegar Square. He wasn't a cop anymore; why should he obey the rules?

Tredegar Square was probably one of the most beautifully preserved Georgian squares in the whole of London. One of the advantages of undercover work meant lots of overtime and no living expenses. Hence, he could afford to live in a small basement flat in the conservation area. Or rather, as the last three years had taught him, it was a wonderful place *not* to be living.

Turning into the square from Zachary Mews was when it became apparent. There they were in all their glory – the protestors, about 30 of them, either sporting the Guy Fawkes mask of Anonymous or the anarchist full-face motorcycle headgear. Marco thought it ironic that his final day as a cop would find himself under siege, pilloried and drummed out of the country by the very people he had been 'turned' by. It was inevitable that they would find out where he lived. But it was not just the protesters that were the problem. In letters two-feet high across the front of his house were scrawled the words:

'SUPER GRASS-FED RAT!!'

Ironically, it wasn't even his part of the house. He lived in the garden flat. They'd painted Terry's place upstairs.

Then the chant began. First as a murmur. Then gradually growing and growing until the whole neighbourhood rang with the slogan: 'Super grass-fed rat! Super grass-fed rat! Super grass-fed rat!' endlessly into the frosty early evening of the magic hour. What a pity, he thought, that having taken so long to get to know the characteristically reticent British neighbours, he would be shunned; on the other hand at least those whom he hadn't managed to get to know – and there were quite a few – would now actually know who he was.

Doing a full 180 on his heels Marco retraced his steps back to the Mile End Road into his local, the Purple Anteater. If there was anyone there who would still serve him. Fortunately, none of the papist gunpowder plotters spotted him come into the square. He could lie low in the idiosyncratically named Purple Anteater for a couple of hours and, if necessary, hop in to his flat over the back wall from Coburn Road.

Sometimes spending a few hours in the pub is the antidote to everything that adversity can throw at a man. Especially when faced with an aggressive team of Guy Fawkes mask-wearing activists in front of the homestead. As Time-Warner clocked up more royalties on the global sales of their leering visor franchise, Marco had worked his way through the cocktail list of the Purple Anteater. It was now closing time. Hoping against hope that the perpetrators of the gunpowder plot would have returned to wherever it was they all came from, Marco stumbled out of the Anteater, retraced his steps to the square and made a discreet entry to his home without further disturbance.

He sat in his empty flat. A flat that had been home just for the occasional weekend over the last three years – but a retreat that had provided him with shelter from the storm. A place of refuge from the multiplicity of orthodoxies that clamoured for his soul. A place in which, for right or wrong, in good conscience or bad conscience, he could always make peace with himself. And that is what he did for the rest of the evening. Make peace with himself on the last ever night he would spend in his haven, his sanctuary – his port in a storm. He logged on to the Ryanair website and booked himself on the first flight the next day to Trieste. It being the night before Christmas Eve he was lucky to get a seat at all, and willingly paid the equivalent of a BA business fare for a meagre Ryanair middle seat. Beggars, after all, couldn't be choosers.

While he still had the energy, he finished his packing, and booked an Uber for 07.00 the next morning. Enough time to get to Stansted, make a few Christmas purchases, and get on with the rest of his life. With his family. *Home*. There it was again. The trigger word. This time he let go. Tears came easily, unforgivingly. He cried for himself, for his mother, for his still-born child, for Janey, for his other self, and for his father. The order didn't matter. The fact that he finally allowed himself to cry did. It tore him apart and it freed him at the same time. Temporarily, at least. And in the aftermath, he concluded his packing.

There were two last things he needed to pack. These two objects that were intrinsically linked to the family and keeping memories alive as time began to erase traces of his past, slowly but surely. Firstly, the sole photograph of the only moment of collective familial happiness in the archive: his mother, father, grandfather and grandmother, with himself in swaddling held in front of the group in a wicker basket. In the bottom left-hand corner was a handwritten note: 'Alba, 1989'.

If you looked even closer it was possible to see that Grandfather Nino, with an impish smile, had raised Marco's white embroidered coverlet to reveal a treasure trove of tubers. *Melanosporum*. The black truffle of Istria – hidden deep within his traditional wicker cradle.

Early pictorial evidence of the side-hustle of his old Yugoslav Communist family and his part in the success of their entrepreneurial schemes carried out in Tito's socialist workers' self-management paradise: truffle smuggling.

Umbria produced the best truffles in the world. But the Piedmont was more famous and therefore the prices were better there. Thus began Marco's maverick outlaw life of crime – at the age of eight months being employed in the forbidden truffle trade of the former Yugoslavia. Having crossed the border to Italy with his nappies lined with the turd-like droppings that were *melanosporum*, *aestivum* and *macrosporum* – not forgetting the rare and wonderful *magnatum pico*. The appearance of a nuclear family confused the sniffer dogs at the border and achieved their goal of a safe haven in Italy laden with illicit mushroom life – and with Nino's ill-gotten cash gains stuffed in the very same white terry-towelling nappies that carried the truffles. With this extra cash infusion everyone lived the good life: studies, apartments subsidised and, most of all, for Nino himself; after a life of intrigue and politics he could finally think about building the truffle restaurant of his dreams in the not-so-distant future. From that photographic moment when this criminal team had been immortalised on the GDR's finest ORWO black and white film stock for eternity.

The second thing he needed to take into consideration was his legacy, bequeathed to him by his father after his disappearance in the Croatian Homeland War of the nineties. It was an unusual thing to leave a child but not inconceivable, given that his father was a learned archaeologist. The single piece of *Murmillo* gladiator *manica* arm guard from the forearm armour had been left to him, aged 10, in case his father did not return from the war. Marco held it up to the light. He studied the strange runes marked into the metal on the reverse side. As a ten-year-old the *manica* filled his imagination; it reminded him of the times his father took him to the ancient Vespasian amphitheatre in Pula and told him stories of the games, the gladiators, the animals, and the brave dogs that fought alongside the *venatores* in the bloody sand of the arena. It was his father who first taught him where the word 'arena' came from: it was the word for 'sand' in Latin – and still is in Spanish. The sand that soaked up the blood and guts and gore from the games, the sand that could be swept away and replaced in an instant as if nothing had happened. All Marco knew was that the *manica* was his most prized possession and it was coming with him.

He took the photo from the frame, scrolled it carefully, inserted it into a paper tube taken from the kitchen roll, and placed it safely inside the nigh-on 2,000-year-old arm guard. He put both into his hand luggage for travel in the morning.

He lay his head on the pillow and waited for sleep to come. He was ready for the next phase of his life. Come what may, it had to be better than the living hell of the last few months.

★★★★★

Needless to say, the great river of un-mindfulness that is Lethe failed to arrive on schedule. None of the old tricks worked. Usually, he had no trouble at all in nodding off as soon as he closed his eyes. In real life he was a champion sleeper; he could represent Yugoslavia (if it still existed), the UK – and, for sure, plucky and much diminished little Croatia. But this night, his last in England, was different. He hoped it wasn't the beginning of yet another new phase. Could it be a part of the profound guilt he was feeling for letting down just about everyone who had been important to him? Longing for dreams of redemption, he tossed and turned as he struggled to drift off. Nothing worked. His relentless brain flickered at a steady 24 frames per second and the slumber he desired more than anything else eluded him. He tried everything – the one technique the weightlifting coach of his teenage years taught him always worked: tensing all his muscles in one go for as long as he could hold them. Nothing. Then the standard police training method: relax the face, the shoulders, deep breath – and say 'stop thinking, stop thinking, stop thinking' over and over again to yourself. So, the advice from the Police Napping Manual was similar to the advice they gave for waking coppers – the less you think the better. Gave a whole new meaning to the idea of sleeping policemen.

He couldn't remember if it was Erwin Rommel the Desert Fox or Sun Tzu the Taoist philosopher strategist who advised never to fight a battle that you can't win. But it didn't really matter. He took their advice and gave up. As he eased his way out of bed and into the bathroom, he muttered to himself: 'Wise is the man that knows when to fight. Wiser is the man that knows when to just shut the fuck up.'

They had to read Sun Tzu at Hendon Police College as part of the required reading. He knew all the gags. His favourite was his own composition: You shall not win a war by reading *The Art of War* alone. You must also assemble an army, do some fighting, that sort of thing.

He looked at his reflection and did a double take. And came to a realisation. The kind of realisation that can only take place in the dead of night, alone, in the silence of an empty house. This, he finally understood, was what his subconscious was telling him to do: get a haircut. No. More than that. Half an hour later the stinking dreads are on the floor, his septum is sore, bloody yet free from stainless steel. The three bolts from his brow clattered into the sink below him. The nose stud was trickier. It was infected. He cleaned it up the best he could and finished his ablutions with a hot, freedom-inspiring shave. An actual 'close shave' as opposed to the metaphorical ones that had filled his life in recent times.

His new look could only be described as 'straight'. A regular suit jacket completed him. Straight as a die.

As he settled down in his favourite armchair for his last cup of Yorkshire builder's tea in Tredegar Square, dawn came up over Mile End Road and he imagined the dawn he would see in Istria on the following morning – and was filled with inspiration.

'Home,' he thought, and his eyes pricked again at the memory. In a good way.

So, it was back to his roots. Back home. Back to Nino and Faida, the grandfather and grandmother that his mother, Maja, had worked so hard to deprive of his presence. His summer holidays with his grandparents and cousins had kept him close to his family and his language so that now, when it came to be creating a new life, going back to the old one could prove as good as any.

He grabbed his bags and headed for the door, stopping only to pick up the hand-addressed envelope that lay on the mat beneath the letter box. Instinctively, he knew what it contained. He put it in the inside pocket of his jacket and walked out into the morning.

*****

Nino Mihailić is on his early morning walk in the truffle forest beneath the village of Vrh. He loves nothing better than to be out just after dawn with his precious dogs, enjoying the damp, which never seemed to affect his old nonagenarian bones; and he loves the snuffling sound of his beautiful animals as they edge through the forest led by their sense of smell.

After his stint in the Partisans during the Partisan War of Liberation, Nino was a respected public figure, a famed ex-Partisan in Buzet who served in Tito's administration after the war in the Foreign Office. After 'retiring' – as he put it – he became head of tourism for the county of Istria. This allowed him to pursue his hobbies on a more regular basis: especially his truffle-dealing hobby. Not without certain risks in the Communist period, but there were enough people in the chain and enough cash changing hands for a blind eye to be turned. It was a discreet habit he developed after the war as a side-line. A thinly disguised predilection for dog walking in the woods between Motovun and Buzet yielded enough truffles for him to sell on the black market in Trieste and Alba, with enough truffles to provide his family with the little extras that, in the early days of socialism, were difficult to come by. But this was the joy of Yugoslavia. Nestled between East and West, capitalism and communism; truffles could always be found in Hungary, Romania, Albania, and Bulgaria. Identical species to those of neighbouring Italy and France. But the borders were open only to Yugoslavs. That was Nino's advantage. A little Zastava car; friendly faces at the passport control and customs. These added up to an apartment in town, some extra land around the family home in Draguć, decent medical care, and a Zagreb education for his son, Ivo – Marco's father, the archaeologist – now dead. Of course, it didn't hurt that as a hero of the revolution he was a former military man at the foreign office, making him the prime choice as commissar for tourism for Istria. These jobs brought their rewards in the old country. And similar to the post-Homeland War Croatia, good, loyal service to the state was well rewarded back then.

The silence is disturbed: his mobile phone rings out. 'Hallo? Hallo?' shouts Nino Mihailić down the phone. 'Who is it?'

'Grandpa? Nino? It's me, Marco! Grandpa, yes – it's me.'

'Marco – my boy! Where have you been? It's been three months at least. You know how old I am? Ninety fucking years old! Do you know how old I might be if you leave it so long next time?'

'No, grandpa, I don't,' Marco replies, patiently playing along with the ritual.

'I might be dead. At my age you never know. Did you ever think of that, Marco?'

Marco chuckles down the phone: 'Come on, Nino. You'll outlive us all. Calm down and tell me how you are. Are you OK? Is Faida well?'

'She is the one who will outlive us all and have many more husbands than me. You wait and see.'

'Nino, she's 93 years old. You need to keep a lid on your jealous thoughts. It will eat away at you and before you know it will be just you, alone with your stinking old truffles. A sad old fart…'

Laughs. 'Yes. Perhaps you're right.' Shouting: 'Betty! Come back, you stupid dog – over this side.'

'Listen, Nino. I'm at the airport. I'm coming home.'

Silence. Unusual for Nino, thinks Marco.

'But we rented out your room,' pipes in Nino, not terribly convincing.

A longer silence.

'Ha, ha, ha, ha! I really had you there my boy. One up for the old man!' So, beside himself with laughing, he starts to cough a rickety-rackety old smoker's cough, assuaged only when he sparks up a fresh cigarette from his pack. 'It's wonderful, my boy. Home for Christmas. What could be better? Zvonko is here with the kids. And Emina. It'll be just like the old days… when your father was alive. Hurry up – we have the feast tonight. And the *badnjak*. If these white truffles I have planned for the dinner don't set a fire in your pants again for

Emina I don't know what will. I will call Faida to make up the room. Bye, my boy. My son. Bye!'

Marco hangs up, smiling to himself at the old man's continued cussedness who, even at his great age, shows no sign of slowing down or losing his sense of humour.

★★★★★

Joining the classic, endless security queue at London Stansted Airport; it was littered with wailing children and put-upon and beset parents, as well as a thuggish Essex security detail with their consistent tendency to be over-intimate on the frisk. There are those that say that Stansted isn't an airport – merely a maximum-security, second-rate shopping mall with execrable piped music and the odd plane. Marco had an informal league table of 'Shithole Airports of the World'. In first position, the jewel of the Hertfordshire and Essex borders: Stansted. Marco hated Stansted so much that it was his second-, third- and fourth-placed shithole airport on the planet. Fifth was Juba in South Sudan. Which, when he visited a few years ago as an electoral monitor for the EU, was a tent by the runway. Marco wasn't so far off the mark in his bigotry. Stansted Airport had been named last year (not for the first time) one of the worst in the world, coming second from last in a global league table. Only Kuwait International was considered a bigger flop in a damning report that saw three UK airports languish in the bottom ten.

Stansted represented a veritable cornucopia of musical bad taste, inappropriateness and aural ugliness that, as far as Marco was concerned, was as great a danger to the planet as mining lithium. He grew up with music. Classical music had been his life; it had been the thing that attracted his first love, Emina, to him all those years ago when they met at the International Musical Youth Summer School in Grožnjan. And tonight he was going to see her again. There probably wouldn't be trumpets – more like an atonal meeting on the borderline of cacophony and disharmony where Pierre Boulez meets Arnold Schoenberg, but at least he would get to see her again.

A whistle-stop breeze through the terminal, scooping up Christmas presents for everyone, as well as some spares for anyone he might have forgotten. As he ambled down towards the gate, confident with his priority boarding pass for his middle front row seat, he mused to himself that Stansted seemed to have been designed with such ruthless ugliness as to suggest a loathing for the human race and a sadistic desire to inflict suffering on it. He resolved to find out who the architect was when he reached Istria and to begin a concerted vendetta.

★★★★★

With the on-time take-off at 11.00, and it being an hour later in Istria, Marco thought that midday on Christmas Eve was a respectable enough time to start the festivities. Not that he had anything to celebrate. He just needed a drink. The letter he picked up on the way out of his flat had been burning a hole in his jacket pocket and he sure as hell wasn't going to read it without some anaesthetic. In parallel with his present-buying spree Marco managed to multi-task well enough to slip into duty free to pick up a decent bottle of screw-top Domaine la Sarabande Misterioso 2015, 'A rather fine and beautifully crimson red from the Languedoc and with a spicy-type blackberry aroma imbued with raspberry hints,' apparently. He took a long healing draught, via a paper cup purloined from a swift detour into Prêt A Manger, and steeled himself for the worst.

The letter was from Janey.

He'd recognized the girlish curlicues of an unsteady hand on the envelope straight off. No one understood better the level of betrayal that had taken place more than Marco. But it still wasn't enough to know what it had done to Janey. Deep down in her being, this level of betrayal meant that she would never be able to trust another human being again. Ever. He took another slug of the Misterioso, fastened his literal and metaphorical seat belt, and dug in for what was going to be a bumpy flight. He opened the envelope and pulled out the lined A4 sheet.

Dear Matt:

Actually, I don't know what to call you because I have been in a relationship with a completely different person for the last two years.

In all this time you have been the centre of my world, my alpha and omega, my everything – and yet you didn't really exist.

I suppose this is what they must mean when they say that life is an illusion.

The weird thing is I can't stop loving you. But I know I must. Because of what you have done to me, I can now never trust my own judgement about anything ever again.

Can you even begin to imagine how that feels?

I know you as Matt and if you are the same person as Marco or whatever it is your real name is, I know that nothing I say can hurt you as much as you will be hurting yourself about this. And believe me. I would really like to hurt you.

Matt, I had nothing to do with what happened at your place tonight. This is something that the guys have started, and they will persecute you until they feel they have had their pound of flesh and have ruined your life as best they can.

I will stop loving you. I just don't know when.

Never contact me again.

Nothing can come of nothing.

Janey

Then the tears came freely, like a silent rain. No noise. Not tears of self-pity. Just loss. A gaping sense of emptiness came over everything.

With tears.

The blue-uniformed Ryanair stewardess whisked past him.

'Another one in the Mile Cry Club,' she quipped loud enough for him to hear, and went on her way to the galley.

She returned two minutes later with tissues.

'Here you go, my darling,' she said quietly in his ear, 'take a deep breath. Have another glass of wine and try to stop before we land in half an hour. I can lend you some of my make-up if you want.'

Marco looked up and smiled. Sluiced back the tears and slush. And pondered on the moment. A moment made more magnificent by the fact that in a quarter of a century flying on Ryanair, man and boy, this was the first genuine act of human kindness he had ever received from anyone working in the fleet. It made him almost want to cry again. But, as was often with Marco, he turned adversity into humour, saw the funny side, and pulled himself together. And had another glass of red.

★★★★★

'ENGLISH MOTHERFUCKER!!!!'

The first words that Marco heard above the din of arrivals in the terminal as he came through customs and out on to the welcome area at the Friuli Venezia Giulia Airport.

'Where have you been, you dirty English Serb Motherfucker!!!'

At once he was lifted into the air by a bearded bear of a man, spun round in a sweeping jive-like dancing movement, and put down again with three very large kisses on the cheeks, followed by, quite literally, a bear hug.

'Three times for Serbs!' boomed Zvonko, Marco's best friend from childhood, as he presented three more loud, smacking kisses on his friend's cheeks. His brother, his minder, his keeper. His only friend. The only man he ever loved. And when he wanted to be (which was often) a complete and utter lovable pain in the arse. His parents had wanted to call him Zeljko – the child that is desired – but after the first 48 hours he was so noisy and larger than life that his parents changed it to Zvonimir, or Zvonko – loud like a bell.

'Good to see you, brother,' said Marco, catching his breath.

It was turning out to be an eventful morning.

'How did you know I was coming?'

'The old man. He called me. I was in Motovun sleeping one off at Kaštel. And how could I resist coming to pick up my little baby brother from the airport?!' He picked Marco up again and spun him round. A small crowd was gathering.

Marco stood back to take in the full scene that was Zvonko. Three-piece suit. Grizzled beard. Two metres tall. Big sunshine smile.

'Let me look at you,' said Zvonko, giving Marco the once over.

'Let me look at you!' said Marco, looking him up and down. 'Zvonko: is there something you want to tell me? Are you going to make me an uncle? Twins, maybe?'

He lunged for Marco, who neatly sidestepped. Zvonko brought himself up to his full height and extended his not inconsiderable belly to its maximum girth. He looked at Marco, pointing. and swung his hips, as much for the crowd as for Marco, and said: 'Girl, this isn't a beer belly – it's a fuel tank for my love machine!'

'Right,' interjected Marco, 'it's time to get out of here. Where are you parked?'

'Out front. Come on, move it. I got your bag. We're just in time for drinks in Grožnjan, lunch in Motown, and dinner back home. It's about time you and I had a proper catch up. There's lots to tell. Not all of it good.'

*****

Signposts on the road. Markers of his existence. Marco knew this road like the back of his hand. He and his family had travelled it more times than anyone could care to imagine. War, peace, communism, capitalism, blue jeans, coffee, banned books, foreign language newspapers and, more than anything else, truffles. And more truffles. Nino's way of life. Now he would be back again, seeing it all again first hand in the new EU-branded Croatia. No more borders, no more black market, no more smuggling for the people. Low-level larceny across the population would from hereon in be replaced by corruption at such extraordinary levels and on a scale hitherto unknown and unrivalled in this nascent state. And presumably, he thought, as they edged towards the land of the Black Diamond, more truffles. Maybe life in this new world order would be boring for his grandfather after his colourful cross-border existence.

As Zvonko swung his brand-new Mercedes down around the corniche of the autostrada above Trieste and beneath the massive twin towers of the Cattinara Hospital, they saw the Trieste of James Joyce, Fulvio Tomizza and Italo Svevo laid out before them, part-industrial wasteland, part-historical monument, and formerly the most strategic part of the Austro-Hungarian Empire. Along with Fiume on the other side of Istria it was the lifeline to the world, its only southern link to the sea, and was pivotal to the survival of the Habsburgs. For the moment, though, it just looked like a long grey series of oil storage dumps, made fragrant by the odour of the roasting of beans at the Illy coffee plant just down the bay. The blend was intoxicating.

'So, tell me, little brother, how long are you planning on staying this time?' asked Zvonko, not without mischief.

'That depends on you, big brother. Depends on how long you can resist the temptation to be a complete pain in the arse.'

'Heh, heh,' chuckled Zvonko to himself. 'Speaking of pains in the arse, how come you are looking like my bank manager these days? The pictures we saw of you over here in the papers – dear "Mr Super grass-fed rat" – are a bit different to the ones we saw in the *Sun* and the *Daily Express*. Bolt through the neck, white-boy dreadlocks – hey, dude! – that was a pretty good look. The girls over here are in for a big disappointment.'

'It will be a while before I am back in that game. Girls I mean,' said Marco.

'Pretty bad, eh?'

'Yep. You could say that.'

'But it doesn't mean you didn't look like a total idiot,' he said, trying to cheer Marco up a bit.

'I guess I was living proof that a leopard can change its spots.'

They laughed.

'It was work. It was a costume. It was like – I don't know. Play acting. You remember the shows we used to do at school? Same thing. But the bullets were for real. Anyway, all that is over now, and I've come back here to get away from it. I was hoping to get some support from my friends. But if that's not the way you see it then I can get out here and get the bus. I didn't ask you to come and pick me up.'

'Hey, hey, hold on there! I wasn't criticising. Take it easy, man. I'm your buddy. I know I'm a fuck-up. But it's also OK for you to be one, too! Ha! I don't mind you treading on my turf!' said Zvonko, winking and taking Marco's hand. 'Good to know that finally I am not alone. I can't imagine what it was like for you, and especially the girl. And for it coming out in the British press like that – they really are animals. But you need to know it's been out here too. It's no biggie. The Croatian press love it when something happens in the world with a Croatian in it. You know the kind of thing – famous Croatians. Maybe you'll get a spread in *Gloria* magazine. Like Nino. He was in there a few months back. I still think you're one of the good guys. But you need to talk with Faida and Nino. And Emina.'

They smiled at each other and drove on holding hands in a single clenched fist, only releasing the hold as the Mercedes slowed down to pass the border crossing at Dragonja when they reached for their passports.

Cruising up above the borderlands to Buje, the sounds and smells of his former homeland filled his senses and Marco began to relax for the first time in months. He was just falling into a deep sense of peace and well-being when Zvonko cursed loudly to the car, yanked on the brakes, and swung it over left into a sharp turn and revved it up the hill from Buje to Grožnjan.

'There's something I forgot.'

'Thanks for the advance warning,' said Marco.

'To turn.'

The sign to 'Grožnjan/Grisignana' appeared wide and large in front of them.

'I thought we should have a drink at Ladonja. For old times' sake.'

There were various places in Marco's world that were marked 'significant' in his metaphorical notebook of childhood memories. None more so than in Grožnjan. The small town abandoned during and after the Second World War, the properties being re-allocated to visual artists, painters and sculptors from all over the former Yugoslavia in the fifties. Not only that, but in the sixties an international music school: the *Jeunesses Musicales Internationales* was founded there. It was there that Zvonko and he decided to sign up for the summer school in 1999. Their desire was not so much driven by their love of music (though it was certainly a part of it), but by their love of girls. It was here that Marco had met Emina, the almond-eyed, Bosnian soulful pianist sweetheart of his musical summers. Zvonko also met Maria, Olga, Jennifer, Sarah, Sun Min and a number of other international beauties; and at the drop of a hat he would give full details of all these friendships in explicit detail, even almost 20 years later. With Marco and Emina it was different. She was the pianist; he was the vocalist. What a couple they had been. And how she had been loved by his family. Especially by Faida, his grandmother, who reminded her of the little girl she was herself over 70 years ago in Tuzla, Bosnia, who watched the Germans kill her mother, father, brother and sister in cold blood, from the cupboard in which she had hidden herself.

But those days were long gone. And Grožnjan, the town of artists, was a very different place in 2019 from what it was in 1999.

*****

'Fuck Ladonja,' says Marco, 'there's nobody there that we know any more. And it's not open out of season. It's not even called fucking Ladonja anymore. Follow me.'

They walk through the winding medieval streets of Grožnjan, a town that from Venetian times had lived a sort of charmed life. Back then the Doges encouraged settlers from the Veneto to move to Istria where they were given free land and were exempt from fiscal duties and work obligations for 20 years; the only condition was that they were obliged to cultivate the land within five years. Yet even in depths of winter the town had a soul; the community of artists with their *bijou* galleries and stalls for artisans had provided a steady income year-round for the artists, the shopkeepers and a few bars and restaurants. That's probably how so many stray cats managed to survive there. These and the ever-present Catholic church, whose bells rang out hourly just to remind everyone who in the new Croatia was really in charge of things.

'You see what I mean?' comments Zvonko, moving into pontification mode. 'When Comrade Tito gave the houses for free to artists in Grožnjan he wasn't just giving away houses – he was giving the town back its soul. It would be hard to see any of the right-wing pricks running the country now do anything with vision, beyond having the foresight to steal as much as they can before the country is completely bankrupt. Maybe Croatia can be OK now that everything of value has been stolen by the crooks.'

'Who would want to be a politician in this shitty country if there was nothing left to steal?' says Marco.

'People with ideals?' says Zvonko, turning it into a question.

'OK. Let's not start on that,' says Marco, entering a café on the south side of the town. A view of Motovun and the surrounding Venetian hillside municipalities, olive groves and vineyards spill out before them, shimmering resplendent in the thin winter light. 'It's a conversational dead end. Yes: those on the right who are currently running the show are the lowest form of political pond life. We know that. And admire as much as I do Josip Broz Tito and his magnanimous support of artists, you also need to consider why the houses were empty in the first place.'

Zvonko flashes his wide grin to Marco in a minor admission of defeat. He then turns it up a notch as the waitress approaches the table to get their order.

'Two *medenicas*, *due caffè espresso*, and two glasses of water for two old men, beautiful young lady,' says Zvonko, upping the smile voltage a couple more notches before finishing off with a stage wink and saying, 'And I guess you should then bring the next two *medenicas* at the same time because we are thirsty old boys from the Jeunesses Musicales.'

The waitress goes in to get the drinks.

Marco says, 'You really can't help yourself, can you? It's like a reflex. A kind of Pavlovian response. Fertile woman under 40 equals man acting like dog with two dicks.'

'I'm not sure you should be the one giving me lectures right now about attitudes to women.'

Silence.

'I guess you're right. How are things with Marina and the kids?'

'Business as usual. She has been sharpening her hate on the whetstone that is her very expensive attorney and getting ready to move in for the jugular to try to finally bleed me to death.'

'That's weird; I would have thought she would have gone for a rusty knife. And the testicles. Or a blunter instrument. Like a sap or a baseball bat.'

'She already bludgeoned me into submission. And it's a matter of public record that I have no balls.'

'OK. Fair enough. What about the kids?'

'The kids? The kids are just great. One weekend in four, and a night midweek. We have a blast. We are experimenting with exotic cuisine at the moment. Last week we did *nadan kozhi varuthathu* with *iddyapam* and *Malabar parotta* – and Marina hates me for that as well. You know I used to have a girlfriend from Kerala?'

They smile; the waitress arrives with their drinks, and a toned-down Zvonko thanks her. Without winking.

'See? That wasn't too painful, was it?'

Even bigger smiles. Eye contact made; they toast.

'Here's to life, my friend. In all its forms,' offers Zvonko.

'To life! And to family!' adds Marco.

'And home. Home sweet home,' says Zvonko, gesturing to the green Istrian hills encircling them.

They take a short time out and take in the extraordinary panoramic view to the south and to the Adriatic. A sweeping sea of green below and a crisp azure winter sky above told them they really were at home and that the prodigal had finally returned.

'There's something I need to tell you about Nino,' says Zvonko. 'I don't think it's anything serious. But recently he hasn't been himself. Even Faida asked me to keep an eye on him. It's not just forgetting things or the usual senior moments. It's weirder than that. He keeps disappearing for long periods. No one knows where he is. And when he comes back, he's silent. Which is completely unlike him. Everything is going OK at the restaurant; Faida makes sure of that. But according to Nino it was a bad truffle season, and the pickings are slim. Which is not what Adriano in Montona is telling us or Dino in Buzet. I think we need to keep an eye on him.'

'He's probably just getting old,' says Marco, 'it's a miracle he's still so active.'

'In his head,' says Zvonko, not without a certain grudging admiration, 'in his head he's 35.'

'He still has the Partisan spirit; so does Faida,' remarks Marco.

Whilst the aftermath of the Partisan War of Liberation was good to Nino, in many ways it was in the aftermath of the Homeland War that it all took off for him. The new Croatia. New money. New ways. His truffle business had flourished in a way that made him one of the main players in the region. It had given him a new lease of life in his seventies. A tough businessman, he was known for playing fair but driving a hard bargain and not suffering incompetence or stupidity gladly. And, as with all new economies, he had to learn to deal with the new influences in 'business' that were operating at every level in the newly-composed state of Catholic Croatia. In any case, his restaurant was in its fifth year and had become very much a highlight on the gastronomic fault line of Istrian cuisine. But new forces were coming into play in the truffle business and, as Marco was well aware, for people like Nino it was adapt or don't survive.

Maybe coming home now wasn't a bad time.

'Come on, fat boy,' says Marco, knocking back the second *medenica*, leaving a wad of notes on the table and grabbing Zvonko's car keys. 'I'll drive.'

And hit the road they do. Marco takes the wheel and heads down the back road to Ponte Porton, up through the rolling verdant valleys of central Istria, intoxicated by the green hillsides and mountains; mother Učka in the background keeping guard, the Julian Alps and Marches beyond, their crisp white slopes etching a silhouette against the clearest of deep blue winter skies. What was not to like? He was back in his element. He swings the car round the corners with the confidence of a man who knows these roads and these hillsides intimately. They are part of him. Who he is. Soothing, yet harsh at the same time; healing yet demanding.

As the punchy little Mercedes makes a left turn up towards the karst hills overlooking Buzet, Zvonko is awoken from his post-*medenica* siesta. 'Maybe you'd like to tell me where we are going and why I am not safely in the Luna Restaurant in Motovun having a little livener and a lovely post-hangover pre-Christmas snacklet treat of *fuži con tartufi*?'

'Because, my dear friend,' retorts Marco, 'we're going on a little adventure. In fact, we're almost there. In actual fact, we are here. I think.'

The car comes to a halt in no-man's-land on the stark windswept road above Buzet, or Pinguente as it's known in Italian. Famous as *the* truffle town of Istria. Getting out of the car Marco leads Zvonko over to a field which looks like a normal field – but when you look carefully there are karst limestone pits with various depths going – as some speleologists will confirm – down to 100-plus metres.

'So, Mister Istria. Mister "I know everything about Istria",' starts in Marco, 'Here's your starter for 10 points. What's Buzet famous for, then? Apart from truffles, paragliding, parasailing and *biska*? I'm sorry. Time is running out. Five, four, three, two, one…Bzzzzzzzzz.'

Zvonko: 'Go on, illuminate me.'

'The "foibe", my dear, the "foibe",' says Marco. 'You know: one of our dark little secrets. My dad used to bring me here from time to time. I had no idea why. It just seemed to be another place to come and look at the paragliders. But for him it had a special meaning. It wasn't till later in life when I started to do a bit of reading that I worked out why. He was an archaeologist, so I expect that had something to do with it. But you didn't need to be an archaeologist to work out what had gone on here and when.'

'Go on, go on. Let's see how you can pour cold water on what was turning out to be a perfectly lovely day.'

'No, I don't mean to do that. But have you ever asked yourself? About Grožnjan? Those art colonies set up under Tito. What happened to those people? Where some of those people went? The foibe have been pretty much forgotten in our part of the world. God knows how many victims were thrown down the pits around here in those days. Enough, I think. But he used to take me up here. It's called the *Foiba Bertarelli*. Reports from the inhabitants of the time saw a whole bunch of people being marched up here by the Partisans, and no one ever came down. I was only little, but he always repeated the mantra "history never forgets".'

'It's amazing those right-wing HDZ bastards haven't got around to putting up a memorial,' says Zvonko, 'you remember the story of that idiot in Split a couple of years ago who bust his own head trying to pull down an anti-fascist memorial? Serves the little prick right.'

'I know. It's extraordinary,' says Marco. 'But I think the problem here is local. They say that hate is local. And, just like Grožnjan, things are neither black nor white. Which is why I suspect there is no marker honouring the dead and murdered Italians who used to live here. Like so many things in this fucking godforsaken part of the world. Swept under the carpet.'

'Come on, that's a bit extreme; we've always been very multi-denominational in Istria. Romans, Franks, Venetians, Habsburgs, Orthodox Montenegrins, Croats, Serbs, Gypsies, Albanians; even those funny buggers, the Ćići from Romania, all the colours of the fucking rainbow.'

'For sure. And it's a matter of fact that this area has always been bilingual and bicultural – Croatian-Italian, but nothing was exclusive. Mussolini's guys weren't much help. These foibe were a kind of knee-jerk reaction to his anti-Slav policies. The fact was – is – that the cultures are interdependent, and love for Istria can only be expressed in some kind of co-existence of the cultures, wouldn't you say?'

'Oh, that's way above my pay grade, governor. Can we talk about something more interesting? That waitress, for example. Did you see the way she…' Marco cuts him off mid flow.

'OK, OK. I would like to invite you for a glass of champagne in Vrh before we get back to face our various bits of Christmas music at the homestead.'

And that's what happens. They hop in the Mercedes and make a beeline for Vrh and the *konoba* there that is just closing for the holidays. The local *méthode champenoise*, for which the village had become notorious, fizzed up the afternoon no end as they drove on to Draguccio, so much so that as they approach their destination, and the cypresses around the twelfth-century graveyard come into view, Zvonko swings the car right and down into the village of Draguć. Home. At least for now. With a little macho screech of the tyres the car halts on the drive of the Mihailić family home: 'Stancija Mihailić: Restoran'. A good-looking young woman wearing leathers stands out front, next to a mighty Triumph motor bike, smoking. She looks at Marco.

'Good of you to turn up, dickwad. Only about 12 years too late,' she says, stubbing out her cigarette on the wall and not even looking at him as she walks back into the restaurant.

Marco smiles. 'And a very Merry Christmas to you, Emina. Actually, I didn't think people of your persuasion celebrated Christmas.'

Chapter II

Bread and Circuses

Colonia Pietas Iulia, 81 AD

The nights before the games were always difficult. No matter how many times she and her dogs went through it, for Lucia – who at the tender age of 18 was the chief dog handler for the games – it didn't get any easier. She lay half-awake, deep in the bowels of the newly completed mighty amphitheatre of Colonia Pietas Iulia, one of the most impressive arenas outside of Rome. Her loyal charges were stirring, sentient to her anxiety. Unlike the other animal handlers, and because of man's special relationship with the canine, Lucia always spent the whole day with her hounds on the eve of combat. Of course, they too could feel the growing tension as they approached the inevitable hour. Dogs were such sensitive beasts, even the most brutal of them, and their powers of extrasensory perception were not lost on Lucia. She recognised that their ability for precognition went far deeper than her own mere human 'instinct'.

To keep them occupied prior to the hour of combat she'd take them on a good run down the Consular Road, the Via Flavia, for a couple of furlongs before they turned off down towards the sea path in the direction of Vasanium. At this point she would allow 20 or so of her best fighting dogs to have their head and run free for a few hours or so: swimming or splashing in the surf, just playing tag, or chewing on random bits of flotsam. And today, on the eve of the opening of the brand-new arena, this is exactly what she had done, along with her assistant handlers, Philumena and Thelos, who were now joining in with the dogs' games. These two youngsters, brother and sister, were only children themselves, but occasionally Lucia, who, like them was an orphan, allowed them to enjoy some moments of real childhood that their life on the road with the gladiatorial show rarely afforded them. It was a lot more than she had growing up on the road. But she wasn't complaining. She was far luckier than many in this outpost of the empire: she could earn a living, such as it was, and sleep warm and safe at night.

Some of the dogs loved nothing more than to gallop along the stony beach, fighting over driftwood and splashing around in the shallows.

Others favoured the windswept olive groves in which to scamper, play chase and be the animals that they actually were, pursuing the elusive lizard or play-fighting with a sibling; a brief vacation away from the killer dog inside that was trained to maim and slaughter in the arena. It was time out of life for both human and canine.

Looking back down the bay from the little peninsula she saw Colonia Pietas Iulia Pola stretch below her, built around a sturdy-looking, well-protected bay where, legend tells, Jason found shelter from Colchis while escaping with the stolen Golden Fleece. And so the city became known as Polai, the City of Refuges, by the Illyrians who came here first. Whether the legend was true or false, to Lucia it didn't really matter. She loved the old stories, and this particular story of betrayal and vengeance was one that was close to her heart: it had been told to her by her father over and over again on the long journey from their home on the far reaches of the empire to Mother Rome.

As she breathed in the crisp, moist and gently warming air of early spring coming off the *Mare Adriaticum* she thought to herself that there were worse places to live. She looked down at the long inlet that protected the harbour at Colonia Pietas Iulia, one of the safest places in the whole of Illyricum for any fleet – even two fleets, should the need arise. The excellent anchorage, depth of water, and the fact that the fourteen islands of the Pullariae Archipelago provided extra protection from the winds that buffeted the harbour – the warm and wet southern wind called the *Jugo*; the *bora*, cold and dry and hailing from the north; and then the stable summer weather – the north-westerly *Mistral* and a soothing night breeze from the shore called the *Burin*.

And now, after what seemed like a lifetime on the road travelling from city to town, from makeshift wooden fighting rings to huge stone arenas, playing funerals and exhibitions, Lucia hoped that, somehow, one place could become her home and she could finally settle and know what living could be like without the endless travails of the nomadic life. A safe harbour was what she yearned for. Being on the road had its advantages, of course. But she was tired, and though a nomad at heart she yearned for a kind of stability. Like knowing that her loved ones, be they canine or human, would be alive at the end of the month; that would be a good start to normality.

Colonia Pietas Iulia Pola (to give it its full name, Colonia Pietas Iulia Pola Pollentia Herculanea), had come a long way from the days of Jason and the Golden Fleece; it had *colonia* status, the highest status that a Roman city could have. With 30,000 inhabitants it was one of the larger outposts of Rome – within striking distance of the *Urbs Sacra*, the Sacred City itself. It was thus a key trading post – especially for its wines and olive oils, as well as the *amphorae* that these delicacies were stored and transported in – at this most strategic position on the Mediterranean. It was on the route of the sea currents to Parentium, Venetia and the great shipping centre that was Ravenna, and onwards south to the whole of the Roman Empire. Equally, these liquid treasures were also needed by the Roman settlements to the north, especially the Danubian Limes, the military frontier that marked the furthest edge of the empire in the north at this time, and the excellent road systems made this possible.

She wrapped her woollen cloak around her and clasped it at her neck with a brooch, a brooch whose pin had been dipped for luck and good fortune in the blood of the two soldiers-turned-gladiators who had saved her life. She looked back to the town where she could see in the distance the merchant vessels of the busy port, where a couple of *oneraria* and a *corbita* were being loaded and unloaded. From there her gaze followed the Corso leading to the Arch of the Sergii and onwards to the Porta Herculea and the Porta Gemina through which one entered to find the forum and the Temple of Augustus, father of the contemporary city. It was on the magnificence of the arena that she held her gaze for a few moments as Philumena arrived at her side.

'Are you alright? You don't seem happy.'

'You know what it is, Philumena: it's always the same the night before the games.'

'I know. We never know who's going to make it and who isn't.' They exchanged a look. A look of world-weariness that went far beyond their tender teenage years.

'All we can do is prepare them the best we can. Be ready to face the worst of the injuries. Do what we have to if they need any help to get to the other side,' said Lucia, strengthening her resolve and, in doing so, bolstering the courage of her young charge. From the age of six Philumena, like Lucia herself, had become familiar with the brutality of the world of the gladiatorial arena.

'I didn't mean that,' said Philumena, with an authority far beyond the lightness of her years. 'I was referring to Severus and Nasica. Remember? Humans?' They burst into laughter at the gallows humour of Philumena's response.

It was at this point that they heard a cry and a splash, followed by peals of unrestrained laughter. Thelos, Philumena's younger brother, had been pulled over into the chill of the late spring sea water by Britannica, Lucia's favourite dog; she and Brutus were her house dogs and she loved them more than any of her dog tribe. They rushed over to pull him out. His teeth were already chattering in the cold Adriatic, but the brisk *mare superum* that filled the young lad's lungs was knocked out of him by a few powerful whacks on the back from Philumena, while Lucia wrapped the young boy in her woollen cloak.

'Tough love, little, brother,' said Philumena as she whacked him again, 'that'll teach you for going in too far.'

'She just came charging towards me,' spluttered the young lad, 'and by the time I saw her it was too late – I was five cubits under. I can't wait to see her in the arena tomorrow. She'll be the pride of the pack.'

'If you don't give it a rest very soon, you shrimp, I'll show you who the pride of the pack is!' said his big sister.

Lucia grabbed Britannica by her not inconsiderable ears, and she stood on her hind legs, resting her giant paws on her shoulders. 'You little minx. That was very naughty. But you know I can't resist you,' as the giant of a dog licked Lucia's face, Philumena called the rest of the dogs together and they prepared to re-enter the city and the arena in an orderly fashion, representing the *familia* and acting as a walking advertisement for the games on the next day.

It was always a sad day for Lucia because she knew that for many of her charges it would likely be their last. These were seriously trained dogs, and would do their mistress's bidding, including laying down their lives for her. Some dog handlers counted success on how many dogs they had lost, and how many of their carcasses would be fed to the lions and tigers. Lucia was the opposite. Success for her was measured in skill and strategy in the arena, not the amount of blood spilled. This was also how she had become one of the most skilled healers and surgeons on the tour. The experience she picked up from saving her own dogs from their injuries could be used to save other beasts as well. Humans included. This made her very much in demand. A valued commodity in a world in which life was cheap.

As she looked over the short sea passage to the beautiful *Insulae Pullariae* she thought about her home back in Britain, her dead mother – and then back to the present, and her lover, the young gladiator Nasica, who she knew was doing his final exercises for the games the next day. She wondered if she and her dogs and her lover could ever know any sense of peace. Live a life as if it were not lived under a permanent death sentence. And then there was Severus. What was she going to do about old Severus?

When they arrived back at the amphitheatre it was quiet. The gladiators, fighters and assorted other humans had gone off to the pre-match dinner, the *cena libera*. It was then that she, along with Philumena and Thelos who were like family to her, got down to preparing the dogs' own *cena libera*, the opposite of that of the humans: a light supper in case it should ruin their appetite for the fight tomorrow. Not too much meat, but some tasty morsels that Philumena had got from the incoming fishing boats. She knew the dogs were fond of such treats.

It would be in the early dawn that Lucia's two favourites, Britannica and Brutus, would feel her anxiety and would nuzzle her awake. Then she'd lie there wondering how much longer she could go on with this cycle of canine birth, training, and death, with these animals that she loved more than anything else in her whole life, more than her own eyes. But this was not the time to be dwelling on such things, as both she and her canine charges had other things on their minds. They were, after all, *canes belli*, the dogs of war.

*****

Severus the *murmillo* had studied nights at the school of hard knocks. A former foot soldier, he had retired with full pension after his service in the army. He didn't know what else to do, so when Lefty Albanus, his marching buddy from the legion, suggested he try out for the well-known *lanista* Decimus – who, coincidentally had also served with them – he thought, 'Why not? Give anything a shot once.' That was ten years ago. And he hadn't looked back since. A punctured lung, three days in a coma and a knife wound to the throat missing the jugular by about half a *uncia* was about all he had to show for his ten years in the ring. But he was, compared to most Romans of his age, quite well off.

Having been a career soldier Severus had seen service all over the empire since joining up 20 years earlier in the mad, bad days of Emperor Nero. He'd never been in love and never been married. Kids? Who knows? There was the camp follower in Spain who in the throes of passion one night swore she had been impregnated there and then: 'Fill me with your little babies,' she had screamed. And then demanded support on the spot for the as-yet unborn child. By the time the child could have come around Severus was already in Caesarea fighting alongside his brother, Festus. But that was all behind him. He was heading for one of his last fights, and for the first time in his life he knew he had to face up to his responsibilities and take care of Lucia. Family was the most important thing.

Ever since the time of Augustus, and even before, gladiators were able to amass a good deal of wealth from their performances – if they survived the arena. The more money they made for themselves, the more money they made for their *lanista* and the *familia gladiatorius* – the gladiatorial family led by their *lanista*. It was no coincidence that the word 'lanista' was derived, appositely enough, from the Latin word for 'butcher'. For convicts and criminals the very first sentence they longed for was to be sent to a gladiator school as punishment for their crimes: *damnatio ad ludus*. This meant survival – and a brand-new lease of life was the prize. There was a chance that after two years of training and making it through three years in the arena they would win the *rudus*, the wooden sword that was the symbol of liberation. However, the common perception that to be a gladiator one had to have come from a motley tribe of criminals, slaves, prisoners of war and condemned men was not entirely true. In fact, often the opposite was the case. Gladiators were the glamorous stars of the ancient world: pin-ups, with their fan clubs and big pay days. The business even had free men queuing up all over the empire to get a piece of the action, the glamour, and the cash. And it was the free-born gladiators, the *autorati*, that were prized for their consistent performances and high morale. Their nerves must have been good to take the vow to be burned, beaten, and killed in combat. But a good *lanista* was the key to where the big *denarii* were hidden. The *lanistae* were the entrepreneurs, the proprietors and impresarios of the troupe of the *familia gladiatoria*. They purchased or contracted gladiators and managed their careers in the arena. Shrewd, powerful, but often cruel and uncompromising, what they lacked in social status they made up for in earnings potential; and some were among the richest Romans alive.

For Severus it was just a job. Just like his time in the legion in Britain, Caesaria, and all over the burgeoning empire, it had been a job. The blood and guts of the arena weren't much different to the brutality and madness he'd seen when putting down Boudicca and her tribe twenty-odd years back, and from there moving on to Britannia Superior to the Ordovices and Caractacus. It was a dirty job, but someone had to do it, thought Severus. And that's how he found himself in Colonia Pietas Iulia on a cold early spring evening getting ready for the big opening of Vespasian's masterpiece – albeit completed by his sons: Titus, whose reign as emperor was a short-lived two years before dying of a fever and being succeeded by Domitian. An unusually peaceful death for a Roman emperor. Nevertheless, Jewish tradition spices up the legend in time-honoured fashion and says that Titus was plagued by God for destroying the second Temple Mount and died as a result of a gnat going up his nose, causing a large growth inside of his brain that killed him. Whatever it was – the gnat or the sweats – Titus, like his father and his brother, were men of the arena, the Flavian amphitheatre, whose inaugural games lasted 100 days and marked the gold standard for the great games of the future. At the closing of the games Titus officially dedicated the amphitheatre and the baths in what was his final recorded act as emperor. That and having had 9,000 human lives destroyed in the games itself. Domitian had big *caligae* to fill.

Severus's training at the Capua elite school just outside Pompeii went on for what seemed like a lifetime. It was only, in fact, two years. One hundred years before Severus became an alumnus of the Capua school Caesar had 5,000 gladiators in training there. A dozen years earlier Capua's most famous alumnus, Spartacus, led the uprising in which 70 gladiators escaped and started a slave revolt with an army numbering in the tens of thousands. He defeated Roman forces over half a dozen times, marching his people up and down the Italian peninsula until the movement was brutally put down by Crassus.

Eventually Severus passed out and became one of the most in-demand *murmillo* gladiators on the circuit. Decimus may have been head of his *familia gladitoria*, with power of life and death over the whole crew, and fabulously wealthy; socially, however, he was on the same level as a pimp or butcher and other notorious chisellers and ne'er-do-wells.

On the realisation that Decimus, the old trusted ex-*Praefectus Castrorum* of their legion, was in fact an out-and-out crook, he and Lefty managed to get their contract bought by 'Pretty Boy' Oceanus, one of the most powerful men in the fight business. He was an ex-grunt-and-grapple man himself, and back in the day known as 'Barmaids' choice' when he was still fighting. Severus and Lefty's careers looked set to take off. Unfortunately, Lefty was killed in his first fight – killed, in fact, by his very own best friend Severus on a thumbs up, thumbs down decision. Oceanus paired them at the very last minute. They never asked themselves the question what would happen if this draw came about. It just did. Severus did what he had to do. The truth of it was that Lefty ran onto Severus's sword to make it easier for him. When the sword snapped off inside his best friend and he watched the life ebb from him as the crowd went wild, something inside Severus also died that day. His heart was broken. When the call came from the *summa rudis*, or referee, to walk out of the arena through the *Porta Sanavivaria*, the Gate of Life, he couldn't move and his feet. He remained rooted in the bloody sand of the arena until his best friend and fellow legionnaire, Lefty, was carried out through the Gate of Death. Severus still wasn't over it. Probably never would be.

It was for that reason that he took on the added responsibility of looking after Lefty's daughter, Lucia. She was a worry to him. For obvious reasons. But ten years are a long time in the gladiatorial business. He still hadn't told Lucia how her father died. It had been preying on his mind. Especially since the fight in Colonia Pietas Iulia Pola came up. Severus thought that tomorrow's outing would probably be one of his last fights. Either way. Just a feeling in his waters. Hope springs eternal in the life and death world of the professional fighter.

Before fighting, every good gladiator was bound to take the gladiator's oath: 'I will endure to be burned, to be bound, to be beaten, and to be killed by the sword.' Severus had no problem with doing this, so long as he got a good dinner beforehand as was his right as a gladiator of the highest order. The reality was that Severus the gladiator knew that his life expectancy wasn't great – and when the end came it was almost guaranteed to be nasty and messy. So you had to take the perks when you could get them. And while Oceanus may have been a complete ass in many ways, as a former fighter he knew and respected the importance of the public dinner, the *cena libera*, and he knew how to push the boat out when required. Tonight would be a special occasion. They would go through the motions in the town square for the public meal, but he had invited the whole troupe afterwards to a slap-up after party at the home of Lapidus, a wealthy local trader with whom he had been billeted for the duration of the games.

No doubt about it, the sign writers had certainly done their job on this one – Oceanus was no slack when it came to publicity: the whole of Colonia Pietas Iulia was buzzing with life in anticipation of the games. Severus and the entire gladiatorial school who would be fighting tomorrow were paraded in their finery along the streets of the city. They were a sight to behold – and not without their fan clubs, male and female. Many was the time in the past when Severus and Lefty had let their guard down and fallen into the old trap of going off with one of the arena camp followers the night before a fight. No longer: he had responsibilities. And he wanted to get out of there alive to some other life. What that life was, he wasn't quite sure. But getting killed in the arena for a living didn't promise a great future.

But right now, walking through the crowds – around the *colonia*, through the bustling port to the forum – these gladiators, who had come from all walks of life to live, entertain, and possibly die in the arena, were the toast of the town. Severus was at the peak of his celebrity. Children would run up and offer greetings, then rush off into the crowd with their wooden swords in mock combat, imitating their heroes. It was a day of celebration: there was no training and the parade at the forum was a way to advertise the event. Afterwards the *familia gladitoria* of Oceanus would retire to the private *cena libera*, an unrestricted meal at which they reclined on couches and ate their fill in a kind of a not-very-morbid last supper. The break from training was a welcome one. If anything it was a moment to sit, take stock, and put one's affairs in order; to hope for the best and fear the worst over a couple of glasses of decent wine. It sure as hell beat the gladiator's high-energy drink that was a blend of ash and vinegar which they drank on a daily basis. A working boy needed to get his calcium and magnesium from somewhere.

Meanwhile, the beauty contest of masculinity took precedence in the forum. People went about their usual business of buying and selling all manner of things, both games-related and non-related. Trinkets for the wife, small weapons for the kids; the big names on the gladiator roster were commemorated as small effigies to take home as gifts to children which they could put on a shelf above their beds. But the public really turned out to check out the bare-chested, oiled-up musclemen who might just be preparing for their last supper, and to feel slightly better about themselves – that it wouldn't be them whose guts would be spewed out on the sand in the arena. A kind of dark 'there but for the grace of God' curiosity in the mob, and there was a crowd of a thousand or so who wanted to see them in the raw flesh for the last time before *rigor mortis* set in.

★★★★★

The noise is almost unbearable as hawkers, merchants, stallholders, and sellers of tat tout their wares in the open forum and in the alleyways down to the harbour.

Beneath the din two young girls come up to Severus and check him out disdainfully.

'All right, grandad?' says the sharper of the two. 'I hope you're not frightened of dying?'

The girls think this is hilarious. Nascia, the junior gladiator walking beside Severus, sniggers. Severus gives him a black look, turning back to the girls and responding with sweetness and light: 'No, girls, not a bit of it. I'm not frightened of the *mortifer*. Because I will die undefeated! *Morior Invictus*!'

This creases them up even more. With the gladiators' parade it is always a bit like a bad night in comedy. Nevertheless, the least a gladiator can do to save his dignity is have a whip-smart response ready for the habitual hecklers. And Severus usually has one. After all, having been in the game for so long he's heard most of the heckles before.

'Oh, what about this one?' says her friend, coming up close to the newbie gladiator, the tyro Nasica. 'How old is this beardless wonder, then? Twelve? Thirteen?'

Her friend lifts the skirt of his tunic and blurts, 'Twelve *polices* more like,' before bursting into laughter and running into the crowd like it was the funniest thing they had ever heard. Nasica blushes as they disappear into the growing throng.

'Is it always this humiliating?' asks Nasica. 'This really wasn't the kind of thing I signed up for. I mean, they must have been 13 years old, no more.'

'I know you are a posh boy, Nasica, but where I come from girls get married younger than that. Welcome to the big, bad world,' says the fight-weary Severus. 'All forms of human life are here. And we are just their public playthings.' Severus looks around him. 'Just be thankful that the lads from Pinguente aren't here. They're the worst. They usually just come in for a bit of a punch-up, but last time they started to have a go at me. They were yelling "Severus is a shithead." I had to go and teach them a lesson. Bit of a warm-up for the next day it was. I suspect that's why they aren't here tonight.'

After the parade the team is ushered by the doctors and the *medicinii* down to Lapidus's place for Oceanus's special dinner party. Severus made sure he had a seat next to Nasica at the lavish and extravagant table provided by Pretty Boy Oceanus. He needed to have words with this young tyro, who just happened to be chasing after his stepdaughter, Lucia. However, no sooner are they all seated than Oceanus starts on one of his thuggish *lanista* motivational speeches.

'Gentlemen: why are we here?'

The gladiators respond as if in unison: 'We are here to fight!'

Oceanus stands, his cup of *malvasia* spilling on the table. 'Why do we fight?'

'To the glory of the *familia* and to the honour of Oceanus!'

Severus leans in to Nasica and whispers, 'You're a newcomer. I'd pretend to join in if I were you.'

'But I don't know the answers,' replies Nasica.

Oceanus: 'Who are we fighting for?'

The *familia gladitoria* respond as one: 'The Emperor Domitian.'

'Money!' whispers Severus into Nasica's ear.

'Now, eat, drink, make merry,' shouts Oceanus in high spirits, 'for tomorrow we – or rather, you – may die.'

Only Oceanus laughs at his own joke. A chill runs round the rest of the table as Oceanus sits down and sluices back another goblet full of wine.

Life had been good to Oceanus. Living proof that bullies and criminals can thrive in a system that protects its own. Good in the sense that he was still alive. He had traded up his less-than-average gladiator skills and his baby-face good looks by taking advantage of the new possibilities in the gladiator management business. His own unofficial school with its small-scale troupe of gladiators had grown into quite a *familia*. He was known to be one of the coming men, favoured by the Flavian emperors Vespasian, Titus, and Domitian. Outside the main games he did freelance shows here and there for wealthy patrons, as well as the odd security detail, but now he was about to hit the big time. Following on from the changes made in the latter years of Augustus, and picked up by Domitian, government officials were now taking over the duties of *lanistae* in towns with arenas the size of Colonia Pietas Iulia's. Word had it that Oceanus was in line for the job as procurator. The extra powers as procurator would give him more financial control and *carte blanche* as to what happened to his men and animals both inside and outside the amphitheatre; it would also make him one of the richest and most powerful men in the whole of the province.

It is no wonder Oceanus looks so smug, carelessly slapping the backside of one of the serving girls as she makes a beeline back to the relative safety of the kitchen. He takes another drink. Maybe it was the booze that was making him fat and soft around the gills of his reddening face? Maybe it was a dose of the pox. At that moment he cared little. Life was being good to him, and though age was withering his Pretty Boy looks, despite the make-up, he meant to enjoy it while he could. Rome was fickle. The time is now.

The food is served by a team of hand-picked lusty wenches, not forgetting a few good-looking young lads chosen by Oceanus to cover every eventuality. The men, reclining on couches, make the most of the luxurious surroundings, which is what they are compared to their regular life of gruel and ground bones in the training camps. They get stuck into the various sweetmeats that are brought in and replaced constantly over the next couple of hours.

Severus leans over Nasica in as menacing a way as possible, crushing a bread roll with his left hand. 'I know what's going on between you and Lucia, and I don't know if I like it. You with your fancy big city ways coming in and raising the hopes of a girl like that. You'd better not be fucking around, is all I can say.'

'Severus, honestly, my intentions are entirely honourable,' replies Nasica genuinely.

'That's exactly what worries me, Nasica, all this "my intentions are entirely honourable" crap,' says Severus, mimicking a milksop upper-class accent; then, more seriously, 'Your answer doesn't exactly fill me with confidence.'

Holding his gaze, and looking deep into Nasica's eyes, Severus, who is about as intimidating as they come even without armour, grabs him by the shoulders and says under his breath so that only these two can hear: 'What I want to know is that if anything happens to me out there in that fucking circus tomorrow, are you going to look after her and keep her in the manner to which she has become accustomed for the rest of her natural days?'

Without hesitation, Nasica responds immediately, without thinking: 'You mean you would have nothing against our union? Of course! Thank you, Severus. Yes. I love her. I will take care of her. You have my word as a man of honour.' And then: 'Have you ever been in love, Severus?'

Severus ignores the question. He doesn't know whether to be relieved or annoyed, however, and wonders to himself what kind of further assurance he could reasonably ask for. He's also thrown by Nasica's piercing question. Of course, Severus's ability to love had been broken the moment his sword snapped off in his friend Lefty. He'd have to take Nasica's word under the assumption that the word of a patrician was much more reliable than that of a cutpurse. They both take a cup and a draught of Oceanus's unusually fine *malvasia*.

'*Sanitas bona*!' says Severus, a smile coming to his face.

'*Salutaria*!' is the swift retort, and with the clinking of goblets they sink the wine in one.

'And that's just if I don't make it tomorrow. If I do, that's a whole other story,' concludes Severus, giving Nasica a large wink and a theatrical dig in the ribs, knocking him sideways. 'Just kidding. You're all right, Nasica. You're all right.'

The matter resolved, Severus tucks in to his dinner with the healthy appetite of a very peckish and notorious *murmillo*.

The banquet was now just getting up a head of steam, with more and more lavish dishes being brought to the table. This *cena libera* had broken with tradition for once and been continued indoors for reasons only known to Oceanus. The requisite amount of time had been spent in the public forum, where much drinking had taken place and the public had had their pound of flesh. The gladiators were a little livelier than usual and were enjoying gorging out on a meal that went above and beyond their regular fare. They started off with baked goats' cheese with fresh salad as a starter – or *scilicet primum* as it was known locally – with endless loaves of bread. Then they moved on to large meat platters for the main course; this time it was a mix of deer, rabbit, and goat, with various bits of poultry thrown in, all prepared in a variety of ways – roasts and stews. This was followed by a choice selection of fish and seafood. And wine. Lots of it.

Oceanus was out-doing himself, that was for sure. But still there were the suspicious ones around the table, never sure of the motivation of a character like old Pretty Boy; and then there were others who simply abandoned themselves to the gluttony, as they would throw caution to the wind when they put themselves into the hands of the gods in the lottery that was tomorrow's gladiator show. These big fighters were nicknamed 'barley men' because their normal diet was mostly vegetarian: wheat, barley, and beans. A big heavy meal like tonight's did nothing for their chances of survival.

Then there were those like Nasica, strategists who resisted the temptations of the table and held their appetites back. They hoped to give themselves an extra edge in the arena by being more awake and vital, more fit and quick-witted than their hung-over opponents. Nasica was one of a new tribe of professionals who were educated and had the chance to study the science. The most haunted were old-school, those like Severus, of whom there seemed to be only a few. For the first time ever, and most uncharacteristically, Severus was giving a great deal of thought to making his last will and testament. He would never show it. But some vague superstition had put this in the forefront of his mind. And he didn't trust Oceanus. Not as far as he could throw him. Which was quite far.

'Tonight, we drink,' started in Oceanus once more, and Severus hoped it wouldn't be another of his motivational orations. 'Tonight, we drink the *vinum Pucinum* from the north of our *colonia*. This is the preferred wine of Livia Drusilla, the esteemed wife of Augustus Caesar, founder of the original amphitheatre, and who, like her great husband, was so important in the building of this city. Livia Drusilla lived to be eighty-two years old, and for sure this excellent beverage played a role in her longevity. Tonight, I drink to your health, gentlemen, and I wish you long life!'

'To a long life,' echoed the *familia gladiatoria*.

'Gentlemen, fighters, friends,' he went on, 'I will be brief. As you know, like you I am a former gladiator, a successful fighter who knows this business inside out. I've taken the best of you on from some of the most excellent schools in Rome and the empire. I've brought in the best *doctores*, expert fighter/trainers, and a medical team that has no equal. We have the crowds; we have the public on our side. There's a reason why I have organised this private dinner this evening. The gods have smiled on us. Tomorrow we will have the games. We will all acquit ourselves honourably as men before the emperor. Whichever way the day goes – I give you my word – the future of this *familia* is secured. From tomorrow, we enter a period of stability. Tomorrow, noble Domitian will confirm that I, Oceanus, will be appointed the procurator of the games and of the amphitheatre of Pola in Colonia Pietas Iulia. Together we will build the future of the gladiator shows not only here but also in the whole *colonia* – and eventually in the sacred city of Rome.'

Seneschal, Oceanus's right-hand man, leaps to his feet and declares: 'Let's hear it for Oceanus!'

'Ooh, ooh, ooh!' shout the *familia*.

'Oceanus!'

'Ooh, ooh ooh!'

'Oceanus!'

'Ooh, ooh ooh!'

'And to express my appreciation to you, noble fighters of the arena, and my gratitude for your support,' continues Oceanus, 'I offer you a special dish – the most precious delicacy of this peninsula. A rarity among rarities – we have scallops from the Laime Channel. And we all know what they will do to you! And that is not all. To celebrate this evening we have brought you the prized *terrae tufer* from deep in the ancient oak forests of Histria. Many of you have never had the chance to taste this rarity. The shards of this precious black devil, grated over the scallop, will not only increase the gustatory pleasure but will also add to its potency in other ways, according to the esteemed old fart and eminent naturalist, Pliny!'

Oceanus makes a vulgar sign, placing the palm of his left hand in the hook of his right arm and flexing it at the elbow; this being their cue, the servers who have been bringing the food all evening come back in carrying the platters of *capesante* with black truffles.

This is a rare delicacy, and the usually docile appetites of the 'barley men' are heaved back into action after the prior gluttony of the heavy meat dishes.

Severus and Nasica pour a little dash of deep green olive oil from Attinaenum and tuck in sharpish before the black truffles all disappear.

It's not just delicious; it's other worldly: words can't describe the ecstasy they are trying in vain to express. They look at each other and immediately dive into the rapidly diminishing platter of scallops with truffles.

They feel like they have, indeed, died and gone to heaven.

Bread and circuses, for the men from the circus.

★★★★★

There was no official gladiator school in Pietas, so the gladiators, the *lanistae* and their support team were all given quarters at the local garrison. Compared to some, the one in Colonia Pietas Iulia wasn't a bad billet. Whilst it was no Misenum, Ostia or Ravenna, the town was one of the most important naval bases on the Adriatic and because of this the quarters were well kitted-out.

As the first crack of a grey-fingered dawn appeared in the sky, the two gladiators both stirred in their sleep, troubled by what was essentially the same thing. Or, rather, the same person: Lucia.

For Severus, she was really the only love he had ever known. Of the unconditional kind, that is. And not just because he killed Lefty, her father, in the arena. They went way back to when he and Lefty were fighting in the legions in Britannia. What a godforsaken, uncivilised place it was, he thought as he lay in his bunk, surrounded by dozens of snoring giants sleeping off what was left of Oceanus's largesse and new-found generosity. Always a matter for suspicion, Oceanus's generosity. There had to be something behind it.

It was because of Severus that Lucia had first become close to dogs, when he and Lefty were off campaigning in Britannia Superior. He wasn't happy that Lefty was prepared to leave Lucia, her sister and their mother back in their village near the garrison without any protection, so he acquired a couple of ex-legion mastiffs to look after them. No one would dare mess with any of those. They were a couple of old lags, obedient to a fault and who specialised in attack. The handlers in the Romans' fighting dog company loved their animals so much that they dressed them for battle in spiked coats and trained them to run under the bellies of enemy horses to disembowel them. Disembowel the guilty was exactly what Lefty did when he came back to the village and found the dogs poisoned, his wife, his eldest daughter raped and murdered, and Lucia beaten, bleeding, mute, and Jove knows what else. He and Severus gathered all the men in the village. Twenty of them. For each citizen of Rome killed, ten locals had to suffer the same fate. And they set the legion's dogs on them, giving extra nuance to the phrase 'a dog's dinner'. Rough justice, indeed.

It was the welfare of Lucia that Severus had in mind as he slipped out of his bed and into his tunic and headed down to the harbour. Before turning in last night he had words with one of his chums from the *collegia*, the guild that looked after gladiators' affairs, and made sure that in the event of death they would be buried and honoured with dignity. He found out the name of an honest lawyer with whom he could make a will and ensure that Lucia was taken care of.

He also put in caveats so that his estate on his death wouldn't be eaten up by the emperor should he die intestate.

★★★★★

About ten minutes earlier Nasica has stolen out of the barracks and headed in the opposite direction, down to the amphitheatre. He surreptitiously slips into the underground chambers where the animals are held, and within seconds finds the dog pen where Lucia is rousing herself and beginning her morning ablutions. A low deep growl comes from the back of the dog pen, pulling Nasica up short.

'Britannica, quiet! It's Nasica. Shut up, you animal!'

They look at each other and smile at what she has just said. Lucia holds out her hand and pulls him to her. Another deep protective growl from Brutus.

'Et tu Brute?' she says wearily to Brutus, and just as Nasica is about to speak she puts her finger to his lips. 'Shhh, you too. I want to kiss you before you say anything.'

They kiss. Long. Loving. With the hunger of youth, passion and first love.

'That was nice,' says Lucia, clearly in charge. 'Shall we do it again?'

The growl, this time from Britannica, is more distinct and has an edge of disgust. They kiss again.

'Britannica, cut it out. Can't a girl have some fun? It's worse than having Severus chaperoning me all the time. What is it with you animals?' And then to Nasica, 'This is a surprise. What brings you here at the cock crow on the day of a fight, when you should be at home polishing your armour?'

Nasica, nervous: 'I couldn't wait to tell you. I spoke with Severus last night. Or rather, he spoke with me. It's fine. He's okay about it! About us,' says Nasica with growing excitement in his voice. 'We talked, and we talked, and he said that if anything happens to him in the arena today, he wants me to look after you and wants us to be together. Isn't it brilliant? I couldn't wait to tell you, my love.'

Silence. Nasica looks around. Lucia takes a deep breath, looks at the floor, and shakes her head slowly from side to side. 'Nasica. Look at me. No, look at me properly. Are you serious? Is *he* serious? Do you both really know me so little that you think this can make me happy?'

'But I thought it…'

'Well then, Mr fucking gladiator Nasica, you have got it wrong. Do you really think I should be doing a little jig of happiness because in the event that my guardian – no, actually my father in all but blood (the only man I have ever truly loved and respected in my life, by the way) – is skewered on a large pole and eaten by wild animals and buried in an unmarked grave? Do you really think that? Does he really think that? But let that go for now – I'll deal with that old sad-sack later. It's you I am concerned about. You.'

'We were only thinking of your…'

'What is it with you men that you think we are all poor-little-girls-lost, that we need your protection and can't do anything without you? Did you ever think that I might be able to survive on my own? Do you think I haven't got a good business going here with the dogs? I'm the best dog handler in this part of the *colonia* – and everyone knows it. So don't come in here giving me all the "I'll take care of you darling" blather. And don't think I won't tell Severus that I really don't need the charitable donation of a bodyguard for the rest of my life.'

Nasica: 'But…'

'I think this conversation is over now, Nasica. Don't you? Thank you. Yes, thanks for that. Goodbye! Brutus! Britannica! Heel!'

The deep growl from the bowels of the amphitheatre starts up again as the beasts rouse themselves. Nasica, perceiving discretion to be the better part of valour beats a hasty retreat in favour of the barracks.

As he emerges from the subterranean chambers of the animals, he runs the gauntlet of the early morning smells and sounds of wild beasts in the urban world. He turns a corner and comes face to face with a huge black panther having his breakfast, a young live deer. Fortunately, he is chained to the wall by a set of mighty links and watched over by a two-man armed guard, just in case. Nasica edges down the wall into the early morning light and breathes in a deep lungful of pure Mediterranean air untainted by the odour of methane.

*****

As he heads back up the hill to the garrison Nasica concentrates on the day ahead and whether he will be fighting. As a tyro he is the eternal understudy, waiting for his chance to prove himself in the blood and guts of the arena when the chance comes. He should be thinking of this. But he isn't. In the first place, he is thinking of Lucia. How, once again, he has failed to understand her, how she feels deep in her heart about things. The mind of a woman, he considers, is so different from how men think; however much, over and over again, he had tried to put himself in her place and anticipate and understand her needs and her feelings, nine times out of ten he tended to fuck it up. He doubts, as he trudges back to the barracks, that he will ever understand the secret of what these other creatures were about.

Nasica also has problems of his own. Having signed up to be a gladiator in order to pay for own father's funeral rites, he is a novice of two years' standing and he is still waiting for his first fight. It isn't that Nasica is a poor fighter – in fact he is one of the best. It's just that the wily Oceanus, whose complex stratagems and limited worldview often override his understanding of how the arena works as a fight club, is waiting for the right opponent at the right time so as to gain a popular victory: put the good-looking son of a bankrupted patrician family up against the muscle of a boy-next-door plebeian and he'd be made. Nasica is an honourable young man. He comes from a good family – but a family which fell into poverty after the death of his father. To save the family home and pay the death duties Nasica has volunteered to be a gladiator in a last-ditched effort to save the dignity of his mother and four sisters, now living in very reduced circumstances in Rome.

If Nasica doesn't get his first fight and a juicy purse soon they won't even be able to afford their current bare-bones existence. If only he could marry off his sisters, he could at least save his mother. But they, to their credit, and Nasica's burden, would rather choose destitution than a marriage that was not a love match. Such were the principles instilled by his forward-looking father.

As he turns off from the *Corso* into the barracks, he spies a weary figure walking towards him. It's Severus, back from the notary, sealed papers in hand. He hands them to Nasica.

'Here you go, lad. You keep these safe for me. Remember what we said last night.'

'I do, sir,' replies Nasica. 'But hadn't you rather give these to Lucia?'

'Oh, please stop it with all the "sir" stuff. You make me nervous.'

'Yes, sir,' comes the retort, which makes them both laugh.

'Well, look, that's all the paperwork. If anything happens, Lucia gets it all. And your job, young fella-me-lad, is to make sure she's safe, sound, healthy and happy for the rest of her days,' says Severus. 'No pressure, lad, no pressure.'

They laugh. Nasica more nervously than Severus, who adds, 'And have you seen the line-up for today?'

'No, I haven't, I've been…'

'Well, if I were you, I'd better bring a spare pair of pants down to the arena. I think you're going to need them.'

*****

Romans were superstitious. They believed that the souls of the dead were appeased by human blood; and so at funerals they sacrificed prisoners of war or slaves of poor quality specifically bought for the purpose. This was the morbid origin of the games – a funeral rite for the wealthy. The wealthier you were, the more slaves you sacrificed. One rich Roman even stipulated in his will that there should only be beautiful girls as gladiatrixes at his obsequies. Another Roman of more specific tastes was purported to have requested that young boys with whom he had engaged in pederastic relationships should be pitted against each other at his funeral games. Over the years this very real form of slaughter had become ritualised into what was by Lucia's, Severus's and Nasica's time known as the *ludi*, the games which took place the length and breadth of the empire. The scale was almost unthinkable.

Just over a hundred years previously Julius Caesar held gladiator fights for his deceased father; 320 pairs of slaves were planned to be brought in to fight. But these extravagant plans were deemed to be too 'showy' and were revised. From imperial times Augustus, at once the destroyer and builder of a new, improved Colonia Pietas Iulia, and his successors used gladiator games as propaganda in order to shore up their own positions of power: to demonstrate their ultimate authority and to consolidate the unity of the empire. Shows – like the one today offered by the emperor – were always free to the public. And today's performance, being the first in the newly completed arena, was planned by the Emperor Domitian to be an extravaganza to begin all extravaganzas in this not-so-remote outpost of the empire. Domitian intended it to be an event that would remain in the minds of the citizens of Pola and resonate throughout the region and back to Rome for some time to come. Domitian was, however, a tough one to please. His tastes in the arena were as wide and varied as they were in the bedroom. He was notorious for having staged a gladiatorial show at night in which female gladiators fought dwarves by torchlight. Death as comic relief was about as eclectic as it got in Rome – and was not unusual. It was another chance to show the emperor's ultimate and unlimited control over people, animals, and nature.

As the day began to rise towards its spring zenith, the town gradually came to life. More than 20,000 spectators could fit into the amphitheatre, and their numbers were swollen by all the concessionaires, merchants, hawkers, scalpers, and ne'er-do-wells who frequented the *ludi*. Games *aficionados* from all over the region had made their way to the tip of the peninsula, travelling down the Via Flavia from Aquileia and Tergest in the north and west, and Nesactium, Alvona, Lovriana and Tarsatica in the east.

All the bustle and preparations for the event meant little to Lucia and her team as she got her dogs ready for the trials and tribulations of what she knew would be a very long day. And Lucia would stop at nothing to give her animals the best possible chances of survival. At Pompeii a couple of years previously her dogs of war were pitted against a lion; however, she had procured, via a member of the notorious Marsi tribe, a potion strong enough to slow down the lion but not quite enough to knock it out. So her dogs, fierce creatures that they were in the arena, won the day. Lucia always made sure she kept up with someone from the Marsi or 'travelling people' wherever she was, for she prized their legendary magical powers as snake hunters, charmers, and druggists.

The original Roman fighting dogs were large, heavy, muscular animals. Lucia's dogs were different – they were the descendants of the original pair that she and Lefty brought with them from Britain, replacements for the original poisoned dogs. They were large, low and heavy, with a powerful build, a strongly developed head and a giant mouth. This type had a unique combination of dignity and courage, calmness with its master, and a keenness, too – the ideal fighter and guard dog.

She had also been breeding Molossian hounds, dogs like Irish wolfhounds, whose courage in battle was second to none and whose survival strategy and viciousness was highly prized. Her latest plan was to breed the Molossians with the mastiff, and thus create a dog of great speed with the ultimate strength of the mastiff. But for now, this was the last thing on her mind.

It was pandemonium down there below with many of the animals. The wild beasts were confused, ill-nourished and sick from their journeys across continents and climates they were unfamiliar with. Their handlers weren't as expert and as committed as Lucia. It was Lucia's task to make sure her dogs got into the arena to do their job and not become back-stage casualties in a run-in with a leopard. It was also up to her to make sure that her dogs were ravenously hungry so they would perform well in the arena – ergo the 'no breakfast' rule.

Her dogs were performers, after all; and they had their costumes, mainly made up of large, leather-bound, razor-sharp, spiked-neck armour. This had the dual effect of protecting the soft part of the throat and therefore the major arteries, as well as providing a nasty weapon for any other beast, human or animal, with which it came into contact as the dog charged at high speed towards its prey. Though some dogs fought with gladiators, that wasn't the case today. They were due take part in the *venationes*, or animal hunts, that made up the early part of the day's programme at the games. She was under pressure not just to prepare the dogs but to get ready for the aftermath – the injuries, some fatal. It was sometimes kinder if the dog was helped into the next world, and for that she needed supplies from Metella.

'Thelos, come here,' she called to her young assistant, handing him a small purse. 'Run down to the shop of Metella at the port where we were yesterday. Give her this purse and this note. She will give you everything you need and take what money it costs. Also stop at the market on the way back and buy a *congius* of acid vinegar as well as a *libra* of unwashed wool, short linen and silk strips of material. You know the ones I use. On your way, young man. Do not tarry. We're on soon.'

The silk bandages, she learned from Lefty, were the best because they also killed the infection. However, it was from a very wise woman she had met in Rome a few years back that she had learned of the powers of powdered opium as anaesthetic as well as painkiller. The mandrake root worked less well and was difficult to extract, but it was cheaper and grown locally. She knew corn poppy could be a good sedative – if she could get the dogs to eat it, as it had a pungent flavour, and their noses and palates were sensitive. The best and the most effective was a mixture that they say had been passed down to Metella by the famous poisoner Locusta who had shared with her the secret that was memphitic stone and henbane seeds ground together and smeared on the area to be operated on. It was a local anaesthetic without equal.

Metella, an inveterate gossip and impossible to stop once she got going, claimed that she had been apprenticed to the famous poisoner Locusta when a girl, and though her mentor had been convicted of many crimes during the reign of Emperor Claudius she was not executed immediately. It was suspected that Claudius's wife, Agrippina, hired her to do away with the club-footed old stammerer – the rest, said Metella, was history, as Locusta was kept on by Agrippina's son who had been Nero's special adviser on poisons. Indeed, it was at the bespoke school of poisoning he founded where she could educate specialists in her art that Metella learned her trade. She had left the school, Lucia was glad to hear, when she was obliged to test her poisons on dogs; but not before she had learned as many tricks of the trade as she would need to get by as a freelancer.

The thunder of marching men echoed through the subterranean area underneath the amphitheatre as the entire troupe of gladiators tramped into the arena, followed by servants, armourers, doctors, and trainers of the entourage needed to support a team of provincial gladiators of this size.

Lucia, more interested in brains than brawn, was unimpressed by the gladiators' martial strength. She looked out from her vantage point in the bestiary and caught Severus's eye as he went past.

'Hey!' she shouted. 'I want a word with you.'

*****

The mood in the gladiator preparation rooms is one of concentration, driven by the same thought they all have: who will survive the day? There's also a smell. Not just the odour that's there when a large group of big men with dubious hygiene gather in a confined space. But the sour odour of fear. The fear that comes from knowing that these last hours of preparation could be the last that are spent on earth.

They fix their equipment, get a once-over from the *medicus,* and have minor ailments treated.

'Severus – fancy a warm-up?' calls Verus the *secutor.*

Severus stands there as an armourer adjusts the leg plates – greaves – on his legs. 'Not ready, yet.'

'Is that OK?' asks the armourer, a little Galician who joined the tour for the excellent wages Oceanus paid.

'Yes. Check the *manica.* They've got to meet at the elbow. They don't.'

'Loosen his belt, too,' laughs Verus. 'I reckon he needs another notch put in it after last night's *cena libera.*'

A number will want last-minute adjustments to their kit, and for that the armourers and leather workers are on hand to bash out the metal in the forge and stitch the leather on their awls. Some can get a rub-down from the *lorarius* – the same man who will whip reluctant fighters into the arena if they have a last-minute change of heart. Then there is a work-out area, a kind of gladiator's green room, where they can warm-up, sing barrack-room favourites, or just sit around and chat – anything to pass the hours till it is their turn to be on. *Oldest Cock in the Shop* is by far their favourite ditty.

As he goes through the motions of trying out his kit, Severus thinks about his conversation with Nasica the night before. He's not a bad lad. And a left-hander as well. A *scaeva.* Just like Severus's best friend. For the life of him he tried but he couldn't remember Lefty's real name. He made a mental note to ask Lucia.

Nasica had been well-advertised throughout the town as a left-hander. Good for him, Severus says to himself. There was a natural advantage in being a left-hander, and their training focussed on fighting right-handers who were trained to fight other right-handers. It was only old lags like Severus who knew that they could far more easily be thrown off-balance by a left-handed attack. How many times had he seen it happen? And when it did it wasn't pretty. This was the reason the *editor/lanista* types like Oceanus took so much care to advertise the fact that the left-hander would fight today. It was only a matter of time before the truth would out.

The atmosphere is picking up in the dressing room. The *bestiarii*, or beast fighters, are limbering up for round one in the animal hunt. A mock fight is being played out with rehearsed moves by a lightly armed but nimble *Thraex*, or Thracian, armed with a small circular shield, and an evenly matched *hoplomachus* with his Greek equipment. These two were usually pitted against the *murmillo*, armed like a legionary, ironically mimicking the opposition between Roman soldiers and their various enemies.

Over in the far corner is the troupe's gladiatrix. Her stage name is Amazonia. Oceanus always had a nose for the crowd-pullers and Amazonia pulled in the punters. Standing a head above most of the common people in her bare feet, her shaved cranium gives her a martial demeanour. Few of the men cherish the idea of being pitted against her in the arena. No-one knows her real name or where she comes from. But she is one of the best *retiarii* in the business and can knock down a man at 30 paces with her barbless trident without even having to get her net out. She'd be bare-chested by the time she gets out in the arena, but for now her modesty is intact.

Severus, as the *murmillo*, has a lot of equipment to prepare. The *murmillones* took their name from a sea fish caught in nets. In the early days *murmillos* were often pitted against the *retiarii* with their trident and their net. Once he was fully armed, he was going nowhere except into the arena. He sees his chance and slips out, down into the further reaches of the underground passages to seek out Lucia. He finds her back in the bestiary with her dogs, and speaking with Oceanus who begins to beat a hasty retreat on seeing his *murmillo* half-dressed lumbering towards him

'Morning, Severus! Don't be long here. We need to have a little talk about today.'

'OK, boss, shan't be long. Just a bit of family business.'

Oceanus disappears down the subterranean corridor.

'What did Mr. Slippery want, slumming it down with the dog people?'

'We know what he's always after and he sure as hell isn't getting it from me. Do I look like a 14-year-old boy? It's Thelos I worry about. Thank the gods I sent him to do a bit of shopping.'

'I think he's looking to make himself respectable,' says Severus, 'what with becoming procurator, *editor* and Zeus knows what else that we don't know about yet. He needs an honest woman to make an honest man of him. He needs to keep up appearances in front of the emperor. Fat chance of that ever happening.'

'Nasica came to see me this morning,' says Lucia changing the subject.

'That's nice,' says Severus, not knowing quite what to say or where this is going.

'Well, it would have been,' replies Lucia, 'except the news he brought didn't exactly fill my life with light.'

'What's he been saying now?' says Severus, 'I thought you and he were…'

She cuts him off, but calmly: 'What did you think, Severus? That I'm just some piece of booty that can be passed on from one owner to another? I'll have you know, Severus, I am a free woman. The same way as you are a free man. And if you are worried about the fight and whether you will see out the day you should come and talk to me about it. I've been in the games for as long as you have. I know the score. One thing that I am not is some stupid *meretrix* who doesn't have a mind of her own. Passing me on like some chattel from one man to another. Come on, you know better than that.'

'I'm sorry, Lucia, forgive me. I wasn't thinking. I just want you to be safe.'

'But I am safe, Severus – look at me, look around at my family,' pointing to her dogs. 'And I've got my hands full looking after Philumena and Thelos as well – they are my children, too. But don't go looking to expiate your guilt by taking control of my future. If I want Nasica I will take him. But it's not for you to tell him. And it's certainly not for you to tell him without speaking with me first.'

A silence rests between them, tempered only by the sounds of the dogs getting restless.

'I know, Severus.'

'You know what?'

'I know what happened to Lefty. I know what happened to my dad.'

Silence.

'Have you always known?'

'Couple of years.'

'Why didn't you say anything?'

'I thought you would tell me when you were good and ready. It was your choice, Severus. It wasn't an easy choice. But you see what I am getting at here.'

'Enlighten me.'

'You are a free man, just like I am a free woman. I happen to think that facing up to the truth of things is better done sooner rather than later. But that's just me. I respect your free will, Severus.'

Another longer silence.

'And you need to respect mine. I love Nasica. I really do. But I will be the one to decide who is looking after whom. The gods only know what you two would do if I wasn't here to look after both of you.'

They both crack a smile.

'And I know what happened to Lefty – my first dad, and your best friend – wasn't your fault. You had no choice. That is the game. These are the *ludi*. This is the world we live in. You know whatever happens today, next month, or next year, this will still be the arena and you will still be my father. Children are the product of love, and not of biology. You showed me that. That's why I can show it to Philumena and Thelos. It's a chain. We're all connected. But by love. Nothing else. Only love.'

Before Severus has time to react, Nasica comes clattering down the steps into the alcove beyond the bestiary. He's finally found them. He's out of breath, red in the face, and looking scared.

'Have you seen the line-up for today?' he blurts.

'Why would anyone want to give a girly like me such important information,' says Lucia, not without sardonicism.

'This is no laughing matter, Lucia.'

'Did you know about this, Severus?'

'Lucia. You like a good dose of the truth, don't you?' says Severus, straight-faced. 'Well, that's what I came here to tell you. Me and him. *Murmillo versus Secutor*. Main event. At the tenth hour. Barring any accidents, that is.'

Lucia looks at Severus, who looks back at her and walks away.

Chapter III

The Partisan

Democratic Federative Yugoslavia, 1943

The bells from the tower next to the Church of the Holy Cross rang out with a crisp clarity through the night, cutting the profound silence of the deep Istrian countryside. The church was above Stancija Mihailić, family home of brothers Pino and Nino Mihailić. The pealing of the hour could be heard not only throughout the village of Draguć, but down through the valley to the outlying towns of Oslići, Juradi and Paladini, joining the chorus of distant chimes from Vrh and Grimalda in a nocturnal reminder not only of the hour but also of the all-pervasive presence of God and the Church of Rome and, depending on conviction, offering protection, or issuing a warning.

For 17-year-old Pino Mihailić the bells represented the latter. It had been half a year now since the Italians had capitulated and their army of occupation had broken camp and retreated. They took with them innumerable members of the Italian-speaking community of Istria back into the Veneto and beyond, fearful of whatever would follow in the country. Would it be the Communist Partisans? The German Nazis? Or the good old home-grown fascists, the *Ustaša*? Nobody knew and they weren't about to take the risk and find out with which one they would have to make a Faustian pact.

'Come on, Nino. We need to get moving. We'll be late.'

Rolling over in bed, Nino groaned: 'What time is it now?'

'Didn't you hear the bells? It's just after four. Come on. We need to get out before the old man gets wind of what we are doing.'

At the bottom of the bed, just about visible, was a small, yellowish-brown tiger-striped tail which hung down beneath the mattress. At the sound of Nino's voice the tail started waving manically from side to side.

'Come on, Vito, let's go,' said Nino, using the familiar trigger words that always activated his best buddy and soul mate, Vito, until then fast asleep under the covers between his masters. Technically, Vito belonged to them both, but it was Nino who did the dog caring. In truth, however, Vito was his own master.

'What are you doing?' whispered Pino. 'Don't get him over-excited. He can't come with us. It's too far.'

'But if we leave him here he'll just bark, and dad will know there's something wrong and come after us.'

Nino looked at Pino, out-manoeuvred again. 'OK, then, but you keep him under control. This is going to be a long day.'

Pino opened the cupboard beside the bed. Inside the door was a battered newspaper article on Stjepan 'Stevo' Filipović, the young Yugoslav Communist hero who led the Kolubara Company of the Valjevo Partisan Detachment during the 1941 Partisan uprising. He was captured and executed over a year ago in 1942 in Valjevo. The article gave an explicit description, recording the last moments of Pino's hero right up to his execution. Ever since he found the article Pino had been in awe of the 26-year-old Partisan and imagined him standing proud, hangman's noose around his neck, defiant to the very end – even to the act of death itself.

This was who Pino had wanted to be for the last 12 months. And the time was coming when he would get his chance. When he first tore out and stole the article from the library in nearby Pazin, he guarded it in a safe place. He read over and over again about how during his execution Stevo urged the Yugoslav people to resist and begged them to never cease resisting. As the rope was put around his neck, Filipović defiantly thrust his hands out and shouted, 'Death to fascism, freedom to the people!' And that's what Pino, after what seemed like a lifetime of knowing nothing but war, knew deep in his heart that he wanted as well.

As they slipped out of their sturdy stone-built house on the edge of the village in the grim early hours of the morning, the full moon gave the lie to the idea that the darkest hour is just before dawn. They crept through the farmyard, and when they left the village they took the old gateway to Draguć down into the valley. As they passed the Church of Saint Rocco, which in the sixteenth century the inhabitants believed saved the village from the plague, Pino, like the Communist he aspired to be, spat on the floor in what was more an act of disgust than superstition. Nino said nothing because he didn't relish another fight on the subject – suffice it to say he loved the frescoes inside the chapel by Antun of Padua. In perfect accord with comrade Tito, Pino rejected religion because he viewed it as a way the ruling classes gave false hope to the working classes – the ruling class in Europe at that time being generally backed by the church and there being no separation between church and state.

As the moon gave away its light to the morning star, the hill they were standing on was entirely enveloped in cloud. It was one of the great meteorological beauties of Istria that occasionally, when the conditions were right, the hills would sit perched on top of marshmallow clouds, as in a fairy tale.

'It's like we've died and gone to heaven,' said Nino.

'Shut up, you idiot. There's no such thing.'

The three then plunged downwards into the fog, and it enveloped them in its familiar morning wetness.

They made their way, more or less as the crow flies, across the unmetalled roads that had existed for centuries for farmers to get to their fields and down to the local towns to sell their produce. This was solid Istrian agricultural land, and to prove it they even had enough food – unlike many of the people in the urban areas.

For the most part, the centre of the peninsula had been untouched by the previous Italian occupation. The Germans as occupiers, however, were more aggressive. They didn't restrict themselves to activities along the coast as the Italians had. They weren't stupid, they knew that among the Slavs of the inland areas there were pockets of resistance. They also knew that it was in the areas away from the major conurbations that there was good chance of some decent wine and meat to be had, which in 1943 were in pretty short supply. A lot of the ordinary soldiers knew there was a willing black market for the finer things in life at the officer's mess at the Kriegsmarine's U-Boot station in Pula.

Pino and Nino, led by their ever-energetic four-legged friend, Vito, reached Grimalda in no time. As he skipped up over the crest of the hill Nino looked at his dog and thought that while he wasn't the prettiest of animals – indeed, he had the face of a hyena and the colouring of a curried tiger – but he had the heart of a lion and he was the most precious thing in his world. Growing up in the harsh countryside with no mother and a father whose bottomless pit of anger seemed to be driven by a primal need for revenge for all the pain in his life, he needed a companion. And his instincts told him that Pino wouldn't be around for him much longer.

The trio headed down the meandering slope from Grimalda to Cesari, past grapevines on the one side and olives on the other. From there they made their way to Bašići, keeping to the back roads and away from any passing German patrols. These 'white roads' were impassable to the German's lumbering equipment and motor bikes. The night before Pino had got the news via the underground message network that the Partisan warrior and leader, Pino Budicin, had been captured and was to be executed the next day at noon in the centre of Rovigno d'Istria, down on the coast. The Germans had widely publicised the event, defying the Partisans to come out of the woods, and at the same time making a very public spectacle of the death of the highest-ranking Partisan in the area.

Pino Budicin had been born in Rovigno d'Istria, a small town on the Istrian coast also known by its Slavic name of Rovinj. At the age of 21 Pino was seconded to the Italian Royal Navy at the naval base of La Spezia. When he completed his military service he made his way back to his home town and became a leading Communist agitator – arrested many times for his activities in the Italian Communist Party. On 8 September 1943, after he heard on Italian radio of the expiration of the armistice between Italy and the Allies, he quickly organised a revolt in Rovinj. When the German army retook the town a few weeks later he moved out of the city, along with his comrades, and became an active member of the Partisans. His Partisan life was short-lived, though. Slightly wounded after a small skirmish in Santa Brigida he was captured with another Partisan, Augusto Ferri, a former Italian Army Commissioned Officer, also known as the 'Bolognese'. They were scheduled to meet their end together and be executed by firing squad the day after the skirmish at Valdibora harbour in Rovigno.

They headed down the winding road to the coast, which Nino had wanted to visit for some time. The priest in Draguć had told him about a painting in the Basilica of Saint Euphemia. It wasn't the nineteenth-century depiction of her being fed to the wild beasts in Diocletian's arena that fired his imagination; or the myth that while she was praying to God to receive her soul one of the animals took just one bite from her holy body and the others licked her feet. No, what he wanted to see were the frescoes that told the story of how her remains had ended up in Rovinj.

Two fishermen caught in a storm were about to abandon ship. Instead, they fell to their knees in earnest prayer. While asleep, their prayers were answered, and they woke safely near Rovinj just in time to see a large object sinking into the sea. The object was too big to retrieve alone, and they rushed off to tell the townspeople of the miracle. One of the inhabitants, a pious widow, planned to retrieve the gift with oxen. When the oxen pulled the sarcophagus from the water and carried it up the mountain a sceptic was struck unconscious in the presence of the sarcophagus; he later revealed that he'd received a vision from Saint Euphemia that the sarcophagus contained her remains.

By the time the bus reached Rovinjsko Selo it was packed to the gills with day-trippers gathering for the execution: supporters, fellow travellers, ghouls, and voyeurs. A puncture and changed wheel meant that it had taken more than three hours to reach Rovinj, dashing Nino's chances of checking out the frescoes or, indeed, seeing a relic. Given Pino's views of the church, clergy and anything with a religious connection, it was a long shot. The bus delay made it an even longer, if not impossible, one.

Finding the Valdibora harbour was their next problem. It was solved fairly easily: they just followed the crowd. Despite the occasion, the crowd had a festive feel. The Nazis knew how to put on a show. Not just the décor of their festive, red and black over-sized swastika flags: already in place was a small section of ten members of the *einsatzkommando* stood at attention. The flags looked as if they had been made for a city with the proportions of a London or a Berlin, not the tiny confines of an Adriatic fishing village. Perhaps they had been sent in error from the *Vaterland*. Four Hanomag 250 armoured half-tracks were lined up, engines throbbing threateningly. This was the same model, noted Pino (for he followed such things in the newspapers), as the 15 that had just been gifted by the Nazis to the Army of the Independent State of Croatia and the dozen given to the *Ustaša* Militia in Zagreb, the over-zealous local version of the Nazis.

For the moment, in a weird kind of way, Istria was lucky; the vile *Ustaša* regime only started on the other side of the Učka mountain in Rijeka and Zadar, so they had so far been spared its excesses. Whilst the Hanomags effectively demonstrated the might of the Reich, they took up an awful lot of space – especially with the growing crowd, a number of whom Pino recognised from informal meetings in Buzet and Pazin. Just as the crowd started to become restless a roar of engines and the screeching of wheels was heard, and a massive German army truck appeared from the direction of the garrison. It was led by a Mercedes staff car with four heavily armed BMW R75 motor-cycle outriders and two armoured *kuebelwagen*. They came to a halt just at the entrance to the Valdibora harbour.

Holding Nino close, Pino edged his way to the front of the crowd. Nino had Vito, spooked by so many people, secured using his belt as a makeshift leash. From there they had a grandstand view of the dozen or so Nazi storm-troopers who marched the two Partisans, Budicin and Ferri, from the truck to their place of execution at the edge of the Adriatic Sea wall. They were followed by the *Generalmajor* who commanded the Rovigno German garrison, and his bodyguard and adjutants. The crowd, as if by magic, became still.

★★★★★

'These two men are saboteurs,' bellows the *Generalmajor*, through his translator, 'and as such they are enemies of the Reich. They have been sentenced to death by a military tribunal and will now be executed.'

The firing squad of twelve German soldiers moves into position.

'You should all consider yourselves lucky, for at this skirmish in Santa Brigida no German soldiers were killed. So it is only the prisoners who will be executed. It is hereby decreed that in the territory of Istria for every German soldier killed there will be 16 local men executed as punishment. Do I make myself clear?'

At exactly this moment, Vito slips his leash and runs up to Budicin and the 'Bolognese' and licks their hands as they stand blindfolded.

Budicin gets down on one knee and allows Vito to lick his face.

A cheer goes up from the crowd.

'Whose dog is that?' shouts the NCO in charge of the firing squad. 'Get rid of the dog or we will shoot it as well.'

A smile comes to the lips of the captain in one of the *kuebelwagen*.

Nino rushes forward to save his dog from the same fate as the condemned men. As he grabs Vito, he touches Budicin's hand for a second. He stops. And looks into the eyes of Budicin but sees only the rough cloth of the blindfold. As Nino sweeps Vito into his arms, Budicin touches Vito's face and with tenderness in his voice whispers, 'I had a dog.'

Budicin then draws himself up to his full height and shouts to the crowd: 'Out of every drop of my blood, one hundred Partisans! Death to fascism, freedom to the people!'

'Take aim!' shouts the NCO, and then 'Fire!' comes the order.

The storm-troopers let fly a volley of bullets, and the two Partisans slump to their knees, and then to the ground, their chests disappearing in the volley while their heads flop into the hole in their chests.

Pino looks on in disbelief. He has never seen a dead man before, let alone an execution. His tears for his namesake quickly turn to anger, and he turns as if alone and walks back to the bus station.

*****

The day was much longer than any of them anticipated, especially as every bus back to Pazin was full. They figured they would take their chances on the road. They reached Zminj after an exhausting six-hour trek. Even Vito was on his last legs, and he was designed to walk forever. But it was Nino that Pino was really worried about as he just couldn't be coaxed to take another step. They were about to give up when they saw a vehicle with its lights on in the distance. Pino jumped up and down beside the road, thumbing as if his life depended on it.

As the car drew close, they saw it for what it was: a Wehrmacht *kuebelwagen* being driven by a soldier of the lower orders with an officer sitting in the back. Their hearts were struck with fear when they saw it was the officer who gave the order for Budicin and the Bolognese to be shot.

'Where are you going?' asked the officer from the back seat of the *kuebelwagen*, whose air-cooled engine ticked away loudly in the rear.

'Draguccio,' Pino shouted back, nervously.

The officer said something in German to his driver. The driver gave a thumbs up to Pino. They had a ride.

The officer gestured to the two boys to sit in the front with the driver, and in doing so took Vito's makeshift leash and encouraged him to jump up onto the rear seat. The officer gave the order to go on.

The driver smiled at the boys and pointed to himself, 'Hallo! Hans!' He then pointed to the boys.

'Pino,' said Pino pointing to himself, and then 'Nino,' pointing to his brother. Both stared ahead, fearing that they would be implicated in something that they had no knowledge of.

Vito curled up happily on the back seat of the noisy vehicle, his head in the officer's lap and enjoying having his ears and tummy caressed by the dog-loving German.

Pino and Nino stared ahead at the road as it unfolded before them. It was the longest hour of their life so far, covering the thirty-odd kilometres from Zminj to Draguccio, and yet the fastest they had ever managed to cover it. Their exhaustion managed to adequately cover their fear.

The vehicle pulled up at the road above the graveyard. Looking down towards their village the officer tipped his cap in salute and said, 'Beautiful place. I must come back and look at it one of these days.'

'Thanks for the lift,' said the boys, not knowing if they were being understood.

'And this one, in his own unique way, is a beautiful dog. I shall not forget him. Or you. The friends of Budicin and the Bolognese!'

He laughed. The driver joined in. They both had a laugh.

Hardly able to believe their luck at getting a ride for the last leg of their journey, the boys were speechless at the fact that it was the German officer, the one that gave the order, who it seemed had befriended them.

Nervously laughing at their good fortune, they took the main road into the village. The elegant gravestones shimmered in the moonlight as they walked past the row of cypresses and alongside the wall of the Church of Saint Elisha. Pino was so tired he forgot to spit. Nino thought about the walls inside, where last summer he had rubbed on the white paint decorating the interior; it had miraculously started to flake to reveal the brightest vermillion colour beneath. He hadn't told anybody, but he knew that one day he would return to that dark corner of the church and find out what really lay beneath the veneer of white.

Any stray cats fled at the approach of Vito and only the occasional bark of a dog was heard deep in the recesses of the courtyards and cellars of this ancient Venetian village. It had survived the Ottomans, the Aquileia Patriarchs, the Counts of Gorica, the Habsburgs, the Italians, and now, thought Pino, with the help of the Communists would survive the Nazis.

Nino went first to check. It was rare that their father, Tomislav, beat Nino. It was his sole, strange, soft spot. One would have thought that as it was in giving birth to Nino his beloved wife Marija had died in blood and agony, he would have saved his most vicious anger for him. But somehow their father's anger didn't work like that. It had a logic. But a logic known only to him

Up in the bedroom they flopped lifelessly into their cosy pit with Vito between them and were drawn into a vast deep sleep within minutes. Nine hours of walking, three hours in the bus, the execution, then the ride home in the *kuebelwagen*. Pino almost prayed that no-one had seen them, before realising he didn't do that anymore.

*****

The next thing they know the room has flooded with light. The dog leaps up protectively and is rewarded with a belt across the head which sends him whimpering under the bed. Tomislav grabs Pino by the throat.

He throws Pino to the floor shouting, 'Did you not think I'd find out? Do you think I am stupid? Do you not know what a dangerous stupid thing you have done here today? I don't give a shit what you do to yourself – you are already lost to me. But what about Nino? He's only a child!'

Unable to control himself Tomislav starts to kick Pino as if possessed, as the naked boy lies on the floor trying to protect himself.

Tomislav rips the article about Stevo Filipovic from the cupboard next to the bed: 'Is this who you want to be?' and rubs it into Pino's bloodied face; 'Is it? Playing the big fella for your little brother? Is it? You think it's clever to be hanging from a German noose and shouting: "Death to fascism" do you? Well, you're not looking so clever now are you, you little bastard!'

He turns to Nino, offering a slap as a first course: 'You are old enough to know better.'

Before he gets a chance to strike Nino again, Pino moves to protect his brother by grabbling Tomislav by the ankles and pulling him down. As Tomislav falls he smashes his head on the iron bedstead and hits the ground. There is a moment of relief. A look between Pino and Nino doesn't have time to complete before up Tomislav comes again with a menacing roar: his face streaming blood, looking like some crazed mythical beast, he grabs the pair of them and throws them down the stairs towards the cellar, slamming the bedroom door on the growling Vito.

He pushes Pino into the cellar with a kick and locks the door. Turning to Nino he belts the other cheek with a slap for good measure. 'Get down to the church now. Kneel at the altar and pray for forgiveness. For all your sins. Not just this one. Pray for your brother because, I swear to God, by the time I've finished with him it'll be a long time until he wants to pray – but he might just get a glimpse of his maker along the way. Go.' And he throws him out into the street.

*****

Nino obediently went to the church and got down on his knees. He was supposed to be praying, and in a way he was. But not using words. With the light from the full moon and the few candles he managed to spark some life into, he looked deep into the eyes of the Christ of Sorrows that Antun had painted above the church entrance all those years ago. Christ, naked to his waist, in a wide tomb, with crossed arms and closed eyes. The longer Nino looked on it, the face of Jesus changed as if taking part in a hallucinatory dream. The face morphed into Pino's face. He told Nino everything was all right. On the opposite wall other fresco images depicted in gruesome detail a wide variety of dead people: plague victims and people skewered by arrows. Nino began to feel what it had been like. For people like him, from the beginning of time. And this memory gave him to realise, as if he needed any more convincing, why it was that Pino had to leave.

*****

Three days later, when he could just about walk again, Pino found his way out of the cellar. Nino could barely recognise him, so badly was he disfigured. Through the garble that came through his brother's broken teeth he could just make out what Pino was saying.

'I'm sorry. I have to leave you, my brother. But this is the time.'

He packed a small bundle with his few possessions. A razor he had barely started to use. He found the bloodied and battered picture of Stevo Filipovic on his bedroom floor, folded what was left of it carefully, and put it in his wallet. He kissed his brother on both cheeks and gave Vito a pat, saying: 'Vito, you're the most responsible one here. You need to look after Nino now that I won't be here.'

They exchanged sad smiles.

'Nino, be good; do your lessons, look after Vito. If you need anything, if it's serious – if he starts on you the way he finished with me – ask uncle Armando at the *konoba* in Buzet. But only if it's serious.'

With that, he turned on his heels, went out of the door and into the hills to find the Partisans. He knew where they were.

*****

With spring on the doorstep the days soon passed. The memory of Pino's beating became a milestone in his mind that he knew was there but did not quite remember, a kind of defence mechanism. Nino made an uneasy peace with his father and settled back down to life in the country village, driven by traditions and seasons. They were barely interrupted by the war, except when the Germans came in to the village looking for escapees, or Partisans, or more likely for something decent to eat or drink. Fortunately for the Mihailić family their wine was poor, their olive oil not much better, and the food in winter, after the pig slaughter, was meagre. Nino and Vito made their way every day from Draguć to Buzet to go to school, picking up a lift part way with neighbours and friends and walking the rest of the way.

Spring came and the work in the fields meant that school took second place for Nino: pruning the vines, cutting back the olive trees, and planting vegetables. By the end of summer they would have a classic Istrian crop of tomatoes, cucumbers, eggplants, peppers, zucchini, beet, spinach, onions, garlic, cabbage, beans, fennel. More than enough for two, and plenty to trade with the neighbours.

Summer arrived and still no word from Pino. Nino, however, was as good as his word to Pino; in the new Michelmas term he returned to walking every day to the school in Buzet. He took to dropping in to see his uncle Armando, his mother's brother, and leaving Vito there all day while at his lessons. Armando loved Vito and was the ultimate dog sitter, spoiling him endlessly despite the food shortages. His favourite thing was to give Vito little treats of bread soaked in truffle oil. His motives were ulterior: it was a shrewd investment in the future.

'This is one smart dog,' said the burly Armando, who had fought for the Italians in La Grande Guerra at the four battles of Isonzo. 'With the right training he could really start to earn his keep. You mark my words and keep an eye on him, Nino. Now he has the taste for the good stuff and he knows the aroma of ambrosia I wouldn't be surprised if he found something sooner or later. Every day you are walking through four or five kilometres of prime truffle forest on the way to and from school. Don't waste it!'

Armando was referring to the short cut Nino always took down from Marinci to the Mirna and along the riverbank, crossing the river at Juričići. Unbeknown to Nino, Armando had been giving Vito secret lessons – nothing short of a crash course in the art of finding truffles.

'He may be an ugly little bastard,' said Armando, 'but he's as sharp as a tack when it comes to recognising smells. If Vito picks up the scent, then he will go alternately left and right in the shape of a cone. That means he is on the track of a truffle, and it will be somewhere under the canopy of a tree – an oak, most likely.'

Armando gave Nino a small bag. Inside it were *cvarci* – a kind of Istrian deep-fried pork scratchings.

'These are not for you, my boy. I know they are tempting – but they are for Vito. If he ever finds a truffle or starts to act like there's the smell around, this is the treat you give him, OK? We don't want him eating the truffle.'

Nino's birthday, the first of October, passed without mention, a taboo subject in the house of his father. It had been a few weeks since Armando had started the truffle training with Vito, and they were on the way down the hill from Marinci in the forest that bordered the Mirna. The dog started to a walk erratically, moving from left to right; he was homing in on something, moving in the unmistakable cone shape Armando had spoken of. Vito became very excited and began to dig. Following his uncle's instructions, Nino held the dog back, giving him the pork *cvarci* treat and telling him to sit. Confused at first, as it was under a hazelnut tree, Nino got down on his knees, almost as excited as Vito, and started to gently pull at the earth. He needed a trowel or spoon, but he didn't have one. Using a small piece of wood he scraped away at the earth. Very soon the prize appeared.

The size of a small crab apple, it was a classic example of the *tuber melanosporum vitt*. It was globe-shaped, brownish black in colour, with a strange verruca-like texture at the top. Nino held it to his nose and inhaled deeply the intoxicating aroma of this, the simple black truffle; rich and earthy, as well as dirty and musky at the same time.

For Nino it was a Damascene moment. This was his first truffle, his first find, and he was hooked for life. Holding the black winter truffle in his hand, the gem from the moist earth gave him the same feeling that looking at the frescoes in the church did. A sense of freedom. A sense of life beyond Draguccio. Finally, he could see into the future, beyond the suffering, to a life of possibilities and independence. It was the best possible birthday present he could possibly have had.

In Buzet in his small restaurant on the main square Armando had laid on a big feast to celebrate Nino's birthday – and, coincidentally, the great success of Nino and Vito finding their first truffle; a moment, according to Armando, to be cherished.

'It was the hazelnut tree that confused me,' said Nino, taking a sip of the wine specially opened for the occasion. 'I didn't know that they grew on the roots of hazels.'

'And not only hazelnuts and oak,' said Armando. 'You can find them under beech, fir, hickory, birch, and pines. Although hickory is rare around here.'

'Thank you, uncle Armando,' says Nino from the bottom of his heart. 'Thank you for looking after us. Me and Vito. I wish Pino could be here with us.'

'Cheers to you, Vito – the keeper of the keys! And to you Nino, wishing you a very happy birthday!' said Armando, changing the subject and winking at his wife, Nino's aunt Dušica, to do the same. 'This changes everything: now you can make your fortunes!'

'Sweet fifteen and never been kissed,' piped in Dušica saucily from behind the bar.

'And here's to Marija, my sister. Never a better woman than your mother walked this earth. God rest her soul.'

That night when he and Vito arrived back in Draguć they went to Marija's grave just as the light was failing. Nino laid flowers and lit a candle. Cleaning up the little plot, he could tell that no one else had been there that day.

'Mum,' he said, 'I love you. And don't worry. It's going to be all right. I know it's going to be all right.'

★★★★★

Two days later, early on a dewy autumn morning, Nino and Vito are awoken by the sound of a commotion up in the village square. They clatter down the stairs of the farmhouse, eager to be first to find out what's happening.

'It's probably just another *festa* celebrating some new pagan ritual they've managed to remember,' says Tomislav cynically as he drinks what passes for his morning coffee.

'We'll go and have a look,' says Nino.

'And if it's Germans, come back straight away, bolt the door, and stay in, the pair of you. I'm off down to the olives. It's nearly the time.'

In the main square there's a big truck and a group of 20 or so Partisans, setting up as if for some kind of ceremony. The men look quite fierce, so Nino decides to ask one of the women in uniform, of which there are a number, what's going on; unusually for the day and the hour very few locals are about. He picks the woman who doesn't look as tough as the others.

'Excuse me, ma'am. Excuse me…'

The Partisan woman jumps down from the tailgate of the truck where she has been eating an apple. She passes over Nino for a moment in favour of Vito: 'Hey, you. Little tiger. Little jackal of a dog. How are you, sweet thing?'

Vito dutifully performs his rolling-on-his-back trick; at the same time his tongue is lolling out of the side of his mouth and the whites of his normally big brown eyes are showing. It never fails to impress the ladies.

'Look at this one. It's always the ugly ones who must try a bit harder. Actually, this one looks more like a hyena than a jackal. I used to have a little bastard like this back home.'

'Where are you from?' asks Nino.

'Bosnia,' says the woman, who, in reality, is little more than a girl herself and probably not much older than Nino.

'Wow! That's a long way away,' says Nino.

'It's closer than you think, young fellow! And, come the day, we are all going to be even closer than you think!' she says with a cheeky wink. 'Come the revolution!'

Nino blushes and looks the other way.

'Oh-oh, watch out girls – we've got a "blusher",' she shouts to her friends in her bawdy Bosnian lilt.

Nino starts to move away.

'Come on, I'm just joking with you,' she says quickly, smiling kindly at him. 'What's his name? The dog?'

'Vito.'

'And your name?'

'Nino.'

'Nino what?'

'Mihailić.'

'Mihailić? Hey, we've got a Mihailić in our unit. One of our bosses. He's from round here. Is he called Pino?'

'Yes, Pino! That's my brother. Pino Mihailić. He went off to join the Partisans nearly a year ago. Is he coming here? Today?'

'Should be here in a couple of hours for the ceremony. I'm Faida – from Tuzla.'

The young Partisan girl told him that the village of Draguć had been chosen to host a big *festa* today to celebrate the foundation of a new battalion. It was to be made up mostly of Italian-speaking Istrians, as well as people from the coast and karst. It would be called the First Partisan Battalion Pino Budicin of the Vladimir Gortan Brigade, 43rd Division of the 4th Army Corps of the Yugoslav National Liberation Army.

'It's a bit of a mouthful,' says Faida, laughing.

'Pino Budicin,' says Nino with solemnity. 'I was there in Rovinj the day they shot him. I went with my my brother, Pino. And Vito. Bastards.'

'Your Pino told me,' says Faida. 'But you know what? You know what the truth of it is? You didn't actually see him get shot. This is what they tell me. He was dead already. He was so badly beaten up that his face wasn't recognisable. And then there was the blindfold. No-one could tell whom the Germans were shooting. He had been killed the day before. By the traitor Steno di Pola, a terrorist. Steno killed Budicin and Ferri. The Germans, however, wanted to have a show and a public execution as an example to the people. Don't worry – one of our boys took care of Steno. God knows what happened to the poor bastard before he was executed. But you can be sure Steno took one in the guts from us.'

'Thank you for telling me this,' says Nino. 'My dad's down in the olive grove getting ready for the harvest. I'd better go and tell him that Pino is coming home.'

As Nino and Vito run away to tell Tomislav the news the improvised loudspeaker system crackles into life, and preparations got into full swing for the celebration of the foundation of the new battalion.

*****

Tomislav had spread his net out on the ground under one of the trees and was gently dislodging the more mature fruits with a wooden rake. By the time Nino and Vito ran towards him Tomislav had taken his ladder and started to hand pick the green olives so as not to bruise them; damage increased the possibility of bitterness in the oil. These olives he sold at a premium to his brother-in law Armando for his restaurant in Buzet. Armando liked his oil to taste young, fresh and peppery, and to have a good shelf life.

Vito's excited barks from the woods announce their arrival in the grove.

'Dad! Dad! You'll never guess!'

'What is it? Where's the fire? Hold on, calm down.'

'The Partisans have come. They're all up in the square. A whole battalion is coming.'

'What? They must be mad! If the Germans hear about this we'll all be in trouble,' says Tomislav.

'And guess what else!' Nino interjects excitedly. 'One of the Partisans says that Pino will be there. He's one of the leaders now.'

'He's what?' yells Tomislav. 'You go back there. When he gets there, tell him to never darken my doorstep ever again. He's no son of mine. And then you come straight back home. You hear me?'

Tomislav takes the ladder down from the tree, gathers up the olives into his net which he throws over his shoulder.

'I'm taking Vito with me. C'mon Vito,' Tomislav added. 'At least that way I know you will come home and not go running off into the woods.'

★★★★★

Nino makes his way back up into the hill and into the square just as the battalion begin their march into the village, down the slope from the church and the graveyard. Benches are laid out in the square. Under the hackberry trees, next to the old fountain, caskets of *rakija* are laid out on the table of the ancient County Prefect – the Župan – ready for the celebration. The tradition was a throwback to Venetian times and served the same function as the *loggia*: the table was a place for the elders of a village to debate and rule on important questions of local government. Faida and the Partisans are standing in a line smartly to attention in the middle of the square with their weapons shouldered.

Band music plays through the loudspeakers, martial music from all over the socialist world. One of them, Nino notices, is a jolly marching song about a man who had made his machine gun his girlfriend, best friend, and closest companion. The villagers are largely supporters of the Partisans which was why Draguć had been chosen over Cerovlje (too big, too near the main road) and Grimalda (the priest too friendly with the enemy). Food is laid out and a typical village *festa* prepared; it could have been for any saint's day, baptism, or confirmation day, but this *festa* is to mark the foundation of the First Partisan Battalion Pino Budicin.

Leading the twin columns of Partisans that march down into the square is his namesake, Pino Mihailić, now not only one of their number but one of their leaders. He marches proudly alongside Giuseppe Romano, 'the Neapolitan', the battalion commander. Around 120 men march into the town from their hiding place in the woods, making a show of strength to the people of central Istria that, in the small square, looks very impressive. The message will resonate far and wide.

Pino is shouting the orders. 'Battalion, halt!' The men and women come to a standstill alongside their colleagues.

Nino moves in closer, trying to catch Pino's eye.

Pino screams the order, 'Battalion, attention! Present arms!'

Along with the Neapolitan, Pino goes along the lines of men and women in open order and inspects them. They are a motley bunch, with a variety of uniforms and weapons, but they have done their best and Pino and the Neapolitan are proud of them. It is difficult to have polished shoes, perfect uniforms, faces shaved and everything in perfect vertical and horizontal lines when your billet is a cave in the forest beyond the karst. The battalion passes muster because of the looks in their eyes: they want to be soldiers, they act like soldiers, and despite their ragged equipment and arms they are a real fighting force.

Romano climbs up on the back of the truck on which the microphone has been placed. Pino clambers up beside him.

'Partisans, at ease,' says the Neapolitan. 'We are here today to show our support, our solidarity, and to hold out the hand of Communist friendship: first of all, to our brothers and sisters from Draguć, from Draguccio. We thank you for your support, both moral and alimentary, that helps us to be able to keep on fighting the Nazi scum that are raping our beloved Istria, our future Yugoslavia. But today we are here to commemorate and celebrate the foundation of the latest addition to the 43rd Division Gortan brigade. And to do that I will ask my comrade and colleague, a brave son and fighter from this very town, Pino Mihailić, to say a few words.'

Pino comes to the microphone.

'Friends, comrades, neighbours, family,' with this he at last looks over at Nino, who brims full of pride. 'Less than one year ago I left this village, along with my brother there, to go to Rovigno d'Istria to witness the murder by the Germans of our Partisan comrade in arms, Pino Budicin. That day, as he was about to die, he shouted to us in the crowd, "Out of every drop of my blood, one hundred Partisans!" Dear comrades, here in Draguccio today we have enough new recruits to avenge one drop of Pino's blood. Across Yugoslavia other groups like us are forming every day to avenge every single drop of his blood!'

Cheers from the crowd; flags are waved, and applause comes thick and fast from throughout the square.

'Today we are proud to officially found a new unit of the Yugoslav National Liberation Army: the First Partisan Battalion Pino Budicin of the 43rd Division of the 4th Army Corps here in Draguć!'

The gathered soldiers take their caps and throw them into the air with a huge cheer, embracing and shaking hands. The party can now begin.

'Death to fascism, freedom to the people!' shouts Pino into the microphone, stopping just short of raising his arms in a 'V' sign like Stevo, as described in the article he kept. 'And now, let us eat and drink and dance!'

Music plays over the speakers: popular dance tunes, country music and popular songs as a change from the previous military-style choirs.

Faida runs over to Pino and kisses him on the lips: 'You were wonderful.'

Nino, breathless, dashes over to them: 'Pino, I didn't recognise you!'

Embracing him, Pino replies, 'Nor I you. You've grown up so much in a year. You're a man. A real man. Let me look at you! What do you think, Faida? My brother, Nino.'

'Ah, Nino,' says Faida, casually walking away, adding, with another cheeky wink, 'Nino and I are old pals. I'll leave you two to catch up.'

They all laugh, and the two young men walk over to the Župan's table.

'Where's Vito? I thought he would be here to celebrate with us. I even brought a red neckerchief for him,' says Pino, producing a piece of red material with a five-point star at the centre.

'The old man took him. He said at least that would make sure I came home and didn't go running off into the woods with the Partisans.'

'So. The old bastard is still up to his old tricks. Still the same,' says Pino, smiling and waving over to some of his soldiers.

'Except he speaks less. I must tell you something. He asked me to tell you that you were no son of his. I'm sorry, Pino, but I had to tell you.'

Silence.

Pino turns to Nino and looks him in the eye. 'You have no idea what it feels like to have confirmation of what I knew already. That he's dead inside, and since I left here he is dead to me, too. So, we are evens. Now let's get a drink.'

Nino stops him, holds his arm, and looks at Pino hard in the eye. 'Pino, you are still my brother.'

Pino breaks the look, puts his arm around Nino's shoulder and says, 'C'mon little bro, let me introduce you to some girls.'

At the table one of the young Partisan girls serves them a generous glass of *rakija*.

'Cheers, brother,' says Pino, 'You and mother are always in my heart.'

They down the drink in one and fill up again.

'We can go up to the churchyard and see her grave if you want,' says Nino.

'I don't think that would be a good idea right now. Later, OK? I need to go and see my boss.'

Nino wanders through the crowd and sees various villagers engaging with the Partisans. Others, through parted curtains from the sanctuary of their houses, secretly watch what's happening – who is talking to whom. Coming out of the square Nino catches Faida sitting alone under a hackberry tree, looking out over the valley towards Grimalda.

In the distance he sees a man on a bicycle – his father, freewheeling down the hill from Grimalda before pedalling up again to the village.

'Oh! You gave me a fright,' says Faida, slightly tipsy. 'I was just having a quiet moment. Join me. That's quite a brother you have there. You should take more care of him!'

'He was the one who took care of me, until he left. Now it's just me and Vito,' says Nino.

'Do you miss him?'

'We have quite a lot to do on the farm now there's only two of us,' says Nino. 'We have to bring the olives in, take them to the mill, bottle the oil and store the jars and bottles. And then we get into the vine pruning season. Far too exciting for big city girls like you.'

'Hmmm. Kulak stuff,' says Faida with a smile. 'Sounds dreary. What does a boy do for excitement round here?'

'Do you want to see the church?'

'Not really. I'm a lapsed Muslim. Are you trying to convert me?'

'No. Don't be silly. You're a pagan. You're going to hell anyway. Let me show you something.'

He leads her down through the village to the Church of Saint Rocco, the one he knelt in all night after Budicin's execution. They slip inside.

'Look from over here.'

He makes her lie down on her back on the wooden pew in the centre of the church. Nino does the same on another pew.

'The Church is named after Saint Rocco,' says Nino in a hushed tone. 'He was a Frenchman who took care of the sick and cured many plague victims but was killed by the plague himself. Like an animal he went to wait for death in a remote and abandoned forest hut. He was found there by a hunting dog who became his friend and brought him food every day and licked his wounds.'

'Ewwwww!' exclaims Faida. 'Fancy licking the sores of someone with the Black Death. Not my idea of glamour, Nino. Sorry.'

'It's how he came to be the patron saint of dogs as well,' says Nino. 'I know people say that a dog is a man's best friend; well, there's a reason for that: because he is. Do you like the chapel?'

'It's a bit more colourful than the mosque in Tuzla,' she giggles. 'Not that they were keen on having women in there, bleeding everywhere, in the first place.'

'That's just it. It's the colours,' says Nino, passion in his voice. 'It's not the story. It's the colours. It could be anything – it doesn't have to be the Adoration of the Magi, or the Flight from Egypt, or the Annunciation. It could be the inauguration of the Pino Budicin Battalion. See the way the light refracts from the windows and makes the skin look real? Like you could touch it.'

Faida reaches her hand upwards. 'You're right; it's the way the light plays on the faces.'

'I guess if you were living here 500 years ago there wasn't a lot else on. You'd sit in your dark hovel from dusk till dawn with just a sooty fire for light and the odd candle on high days, holidays, and deaths. But up here you had all this colour. A little bit of glamour.'

They lie in the pews at peace, a little tipsy, enjoying the work of the artist.

'I'd like to go back to Rovigno one day,' says Nino, quietly, 'but not to see someone executed. I'd like to see something beautiful. September 16th. That's the day. Saint Euphemia's day. The town looks so pretty. A big celebration for a young girl from the third century. They eat mutton with sauerkraut on that day and *fritul*e. Have you ever had *fritule*? Did you have it in Tuzla?'

Suddenly all hell breaks loose. The roar and clatter of motor bikes and armoured vehicles break the silence of the church.

They rouse themselves and rush up towards the square where an ambush is taking place. German patrols have entered the village from either end of the access road and cornered the Partisans in the square. Pino runs across the square under fire and jumps into the driving seat of the Partisan truck, starting it up and swinging it around towards the main entrance to the square, facing the enemy head on. Suddenly he hammers the gear into reverse and swings the truck back around in a two-point turn that puts half a dozen German soldiers in the direct firing line of the 'Neapolitan' who has manned the German's very own MG 34 machine gun – its firepower blows their patrol away in seconds.

Seeing their comrades spattered into pieces at the other end of the square, the second patrol beats a hasty retreat down the rear exit road and over to Jurada, Cerje and Grimalda.

Faida and Nino run into the square.

'Where the fuck have you two been?' shouts Pino. 'I looked for you everywhere.'

'We went to look at the dog,' says Faida. Nino wasn't sure why she lied. 'Then we heard the commotion.'

'OK, we're packing up everything and getting out of here now. You stay with the truck and the Neapolitan. I will go with the men. We rendezvous at Peničići in an hour. After this there will be Krauts on their way from Buzet and Pazin. I don't know how this happened. The town was sealed from this morning. We must have been betrayed. We were lucky to lose no-one. Even the lookouts just made it back with their lives. Thanks to them they raised the alarm.'

With one last 'Death to fascism, freedom to the people!' the newly founded Pino Budicin Battalion forms up and heads out of the village towards Penićići.

Once the truck is loaded, Faida runs over to Nino.

'Why did you lie about where we had been?' he asks her.

'We don't do church. Especially where Pino is concerned. You should know that. God is dead.'

They smile at each other.

'You take care of yourself, young man,' she says, and kisses him on the cheeks three times. 'Keep safe, till we meet again.'

*****

Nino waited till late that night before going home. He didn't want to risk it with his father, however desperate he was to be reunited with Vito. At least he had the small comfort that if his father was a bastard to other humans, he wasn't cruel to animals. Nino stole back to the church of Saint Rocco. In the early evening gloom he lit the candles he kept hidden near the sacristy. He lay down again on the pew and stared at the painting of the Adoration of the Magi. He wondered what it would be like to be in such a family surrounded by so much love. The harder and harder he stared, the more the images blended together into a kind of movie from the sixteenth century about Roman-occupied Palestine seen through an Italian prism. Across the northern wall he saw extended before him the powerful images of the Three Kings: the gathering together of Gaspar, Melchior, and Balthazar; the departure from Herod's court; their long journey; and their ultimate homage before the Holy Family. As Nino looked even more closely at Mary her lips became redder and her face started to resemble that of Faida, the Partisan girl. He reached up, like Faida had done, as if to touch her. Then nothing.

Later, when he woke, he left the church and made his way home. His father's light was off in the house; Nino crept up to his room. Vito was waiting there, patiently curled up on the bed, confused as to what was going on but delighted to see his young master. He turned around and around in circles on the bed before settling to lick the hand Nino offered in welcome. Vito fell asleep in seconds. Images from the brutality of the German attack came flooding into his mind and it was all he could do to suppress them. He continued to look up at the cracked and yellowing ceiling of his room, his mind racing with images – but none of them as dazzling as the ceiling of the Church of Saint Rocco.

When they awoke the next morning, late even by Nino's adolescent standards, the house was silent and empty. Breakfast for Vito was yesterday's leftovers and some bread soaked in milk; Nino just had the bread and milk fresh from the cow. The pair left the house. They picked up the big canvas sheets and nets and headed down to the olive grove to carry on with the olive harvest. Nino didn't give it a second thought that his father wasn't there, as very often the old man went off to do various errands and odd jobs in the area as he was much in demand as a handyman and jobbing labourer.

Spreading out the net beneath the next olive tree, he started shaking the branches with a rake and making the loose and riper olives fall onto the sheet; for centuries olives had been harvested this way. Then Nino climbed into the tree with his basket to carefully remove by hand those that had not fallen, so as not to bruise any of the precious fruit.

Nino enjoyed the modesty of the olive trees. There was nothing showy about them, just an absolute sturdiness and dependability. Come rain or shine, drought or flood, the olive would be there every October, passing on its fruit for the harvest and oil making. In Greek mythology Zeus made Athena the victor in a competition because it was she who had bestowed upon mankind the most useful plant of all: the olive tree. He'd learned that from his teacher, Mr Valli, at the school in Buzet, and now the whole process made so much more sense to him.

Nino picked the higher-up olives and placed them in the basket carefully, saving them from damage, sliding the olives gently down the branch as if sliding the pearls off a woman's necklace. When he got lower down, he could speed up and allow the olives to drop onto the net below. For now, he concentrated on the greenest of the olives, although it didn't matter if a few black ones dropped in. The tree felt very pliable, very human in a way, thought Nino, offering very little resistance in the picking; there were no spikes or thorns to cut the skin, and the leaves were gentle and smooth to the touch with the lightest of aromas.

Coming off his ladder, Nino was careful not to step on any of the harvest as he started to gather together the net and bring all the olives together for placing into the large wicker baskets that his father had already prepared for the first part of the crop pressing. If they kept it unprocessed for more than a day before pressing the oil would turn out bitter and acid, and high acidity was to be avoided at all costs. Nothing could be simpler. The olives were washed, pressed, decanted, then bottled in a process that has been the same, more or less, for millennia – at least the last 6,000 years. Mr Valli had told him that the oldest living tree, the Olive Tree of Vouves on the island of Crete, might be the oldest alive, estimated at over 3,000 years old. This gave Nino food for thought.

As he walked up the hill to the farmhouse, the basket of olives on his back, Vito running alongside him, Nino mused that he was lucky to have these trees in his life: the olives, which gave him everyday food and a means of subsistence; and the oak trees, amongst which Vito was becoming better and better every autumn day at finding the truffles his uncle Armando had promised he would find. The wealth that these could bring might be the hope of the better life he dreamed of.

So far, he and Vito had found the black-spored truffle that uncle Armando called the 'Mediterranean diamond'. There were another couple of months to go before they had the chance of the precious white truffle. Then the black winter truffle would arrive in January along the Mirna, followed by the summer black; and then Borch's white as the autumn arrived to start the cycle all over again. As far as Nino could tell it was the gift that would keep on giving, and it held him in its thrall.

These bucolic reveries were short-lived, however, as the single bell rang out from Grimalda over on the opposite hill. It was never good news, especially after the Italian occupation and even more so with the Germans. A single bell tolling from the odd-looking Romanesque tower of the Church of Saint George had signified, for the last six centuries, that someone in the neighbourhood had died. The habit was discontinued during the plague years for obvious reasons. Whatever the cause was, Nino had rarely heard the bell rung for as long as this. It certainly wasn't announcing a single death – rather a major emergency.

Firmly shutting the door to the olive cellar behind him, he knew the olives would be good to take to the *frantoio*, the olive mill, tomorrow. He would get the cart out and wheel it down the main road to Pagubice. If he booked it in today, he could get Mario, who ran the mill, to do it overnight and beat the queues in the morning. It was the busiest season for the mill, and tension was running high as to whether it would be a good crop

*****

It is approaching three o'clock when he walks into Mario's yard. Saint George's bell has stopped ringing and Branka, Mario's wife, rushes out of the kitchen in tears.

'Thank God you are safe, Nino.'

'What's wrong, what happened?' he asks looking around, realising that the courtyard is deserted.

'The Germans came, they took everyone. There were more than 20 men waiting here for the pressing – you know what it's like at this time of the year with the harvest. Two big trucks with armoured cars and motor bikes. They rounded the men up and drove off up towards Grimalda.'

'Did they say why?'

'No, nothing, just, '*Raus*, *raus*, everyone in the truck' and off they went,' explains Branka with growing hysteria.

'I'll go and find out what's happened,' says Nino. 'I'm sure there's a simple solution. It's probably a work party,' he shouts back, taking control with a maturity beyond his tender years. He follows the low road out of the village that runs under the main track to Grimalda. He and Vito know the landscape as they know the back of Tomislav's hand. Then they carve a way through the fields, unseen, and come up through Pepe's smallholding to a gap in the fence behind the village shop. Seeing that the place is empty, Vito and Nino make their way into the living area where the owners, Marco and Marina, live. Both are absent.

As he peers out from behind the shutter on the upper floor of the *butiga*, Nino sees men being unloaded from the trucks, all of them local from the villages around, including a few from Draguć. They are being lined up in the square in two long columns. It doesn't look good. Then above the square on the small terrace of the priest's house he sees his father. Tomislav is with the priest and a German officer – it's the officer from the *kuebelwagen* – and they are in discussion. His father and the priest point to various men in the line-up and the soldiers pull them out.

The truth begins to dawn on Nino. It was his father who informed the Germans about the Partisans in Draguccio – he remembered seeing him head off on his bicycle. And here he is today with the priest, Father Frane, sharing the power of life over death.

On the opposite side of the square a group of women and children who have come to see what has happened to their fathers and brothers are being held back by storm-troopers armed with K98 assault rifles. A sense of panic pervades. The men are surrounded. Nino sees Mate, the cheesemaker from down in the valley at Cerje, suddenly make a break for the gap in the square by the old Church of Saint George. He almost makes it but at the last minute is mown down by a sniper hidden in the graveyard for that very purpose. The men understand that escape is impossible and a strange quiet comes over them, broken by the women and children wailing on the margins.

The priest, Father Frane, has put on his purple vestments for what appears to be a church-sponsored occasion. Tomislav, Nino's father, is still pointing out various men to the German officer and they are being removed from the line-up. When the men are counted and the number is correctly agreed, Father Frane calls for silence.

'*Hauptmann* Schiffer will speak. I will translate for him.'

The officer steps forward with the priest, leaving Tomislav at the back of the terrace. He speaks into Father Frane's ear, who translates:

'Yesterday there was a skirmish in this area, over there,' he points, 'in the village of Draguć. Partisans shot and killed four of my men, who bravely died in the line of duty – fighting for Germany, for the Fuehrer, and for the Reich.'

He pauses and looks around at each and every man in the square.

'You know the rules. You know the law. For every single German soldier whose life is lost to bandits we will take the lives of sixteen Istrian men. This is the reason all sixty-four of you have been brought here today, to pay for the stupidities of your friends the Communists.'

He takes a short pause. Father Frane gives the blessing.

'Deus, Pater misericordiárum, qui per mortem et resurrectiónem Fílii sui mundum sibi reconciliávit et Spíritum Sanctum effúdit in remissionem peccatórum, per ministérium Ecclésiæ indulgéntiam tibi tríbuat et pacem. Et ego te absolvo a peccatis tuis in nomine Patris, et Filii, et Spiritus Sancti.'

Then the *Hauptmann* shouts: 'Open fire!'

And with that the machine-gunners who had been posted on three open corners of the square begin firing with a vengeance and mowing down the Istrians in a tumult of blood, screams and terror.

Nino watches his father slip back into the priest's house. With Vito he slips down the stairs of the shop and hurries out of the village. He takes the long way around to Pagubice, down into the valley and up the steep hill back to Draguć. Running as fast as his young legs will carry him, and with the great pacemaker that is Vito, he gets home minutes before his father, whom he sees labouring up the last couple of hundred metres of the slope on his bicycle.

Nino knows without hesitation what he has to do. Going down to the cellar he rummages around in the dark and eventually finds what he is looking for. Emerging from the darkness, he locks Vito in the cellar and goes out into the courtyard of Stancija Mihailić, carrying a basket of olives on his back. His father comes in the gate, sweating, breathing heavily and leans his bicycle against the wall of the outhouse.

'I wondered where you were,' says Nino. 'I've just finished bringing in the rest of the olives. Or as many green ones that were left. We should get them up to Mario's for pressing tomorrow.'

'I had business with the priest,' says Tomislav, catching his breath.

Nino swings the basket of olives down to the floor and feels inside the crop. He takes two handfuls and says, 'These are the best we have had in years. They're full of oil and smell as fresh as the morning dew.'

'As long as that idiot Armando gives us our money, I don't care,' says Tomislav.

'I've got something for you from Armando,' says Nino feeling deeper into the olives.

Nino drops the olives and holds, with both hands shaking, Tomislav's own army service Beretta.

'I saw what happened. You told the Germans yesterday. You tried to kill your own son. You were choosing the people to die today in Grimalda. I saw you.'

The gun goes off. Tomislav holds his ear from which flow copious amounts of blood.

He walks towards Nino.

'I knew you weren't man enough,' says Tomislav falteringly. 'Just like your brother. Why could I not have had real men instead of *biscotti*?'

Nino pulls the trigger again. At close range Tomislav's head is blown off and plastered on the outhouse wall just above his bicycle.

In the house Nino collects a few things, wraps the Beretta in a towel and puts it at the bottom of his bag. Carefully he removes the wooden box above his bed. He opens it, plunges his face in and takes a deep draught of air. The scent of truffles after the smell of death is a welcome one and momentarily takes him to another place. He puts the box in his shoulder bag, as well as a picture of his mother and a heel of bread from the larder. He goes out onto the courtyard, takes a piece of rag from the rag box, and wipes the blood and brains off the seat and handlebars of the old man's bicycle.

He jumps on the bike, its tyres leaving the tracks of his father's blood in the dust of the courtyard, and with Vito running at speed alongside him they freewheel their way down the hill to Buzet into the dusk and the great wide unknown.

Part Two

Chapter IV

Stancija Mihailić

Istria: December 24th, 2019

Marco makes his way quietly through the family restaurant out onto the fabulously situated terrace of Stancija Mihailić. His grandfather and grandmother had re-built the old stone house themselves on their retirement 20 years previously and had turned it into a culinary hot-spot and treasure trove for truffle lovers. The pair are enjoying a late afternoon *aperitivo* of locally made prosecco and enjoying the magic hour as the fuzzy, blood-red winter sun drops down behind the hills beyond the Butoniga lake and into the Adriatic.

'Surprise!' shouts Marco as he rushes up to them, kissing and hugging both simultaneously, and in doing so bringing the rest of the family out to greet him.

'Jesus, you nearly gave me a heart attack,' says Grandma Faida as Zvonko's two kids, Marijana and Dado, dive-bomb him from the stairway of the upstairs apartment, crashing noisily down on him.

'Uncle Marco, what did you get me for Christmas?' shouts a clearly over-excited Dado.

'Do I get a kiss first?' says Marco.

'I'm too old for that now, big boy,' says eleven-year-old Dado, not without an element of his father's cheeky charm. 'But you can have a manly hug.'

They embrace, after which Marijana, a cool fifteen and smart with it, offers her cheek. 'You may kiss me now,' she says, and whispers to him as he does so, 'You don't need to get me a present. Your presence is enough.'

Marco steps back and looks at her, holding her shoulders. They exchange a smile.

Zvonko bustles in, all business-like and hoping to cover up for his absence the previous night when he had left his surrogate grandparents and Emina to look after his children. 'C'mon kids, we've got time to walk the dogs before the light goes,' he says. 'Leave uncle Marco to catch up with Nino and Nona.'

'I'll get our coats,' says Marijana.

'See you later,' says Dado. 'And I haven't forgotten about the present.'

'And I know I won't get away with it,' says Marco with an avuncular grin, adding as an afterthought, 'Big boy.'

Stancija Mihailić looks down on the valley and beyond to the lake-reservoir that serves as the main freshwater resource for the whole of the Istrian peninsula. In many ways it was Nino who was responsible for shepherding the political football that the lake had become in his time, as he was one of the key regional politicians pushing it through. In the end it was Nino's influential army comrades in Belgrade who greenlit the project at the highest level, and no-one said a word against it ever again. The loss of one village under water was the gain of the whole of Istria. That was, at least, the way things were perceived during the era of the Socialist Federal Republic. With the advantage of hindsight some viewed it as the halcyon days of the Istrian way of life.

Nino was connected. After his distinguished and highly decorated war service as a Partisan he stayed on as a career soldier, eventually moving to Belgrade to work in a top position at the Foreign Office. His job was to vet each and every military attaché at every Yugoslav embassy in the world. The Non-Aligned Movement founded by Tito, Nehru and Nasser was in its heyday. Indeed, both he and Faida had been junior officers present at the time of the famed Brijuni Declaration of 1956. This was when luxuries and foreign currency, not to mention coffee and medication, were scare in the fledgling socialist state. The job also gave him something else, something that couldn't be bought: it trained him to be an impeccable judge of a man's character.

It was during the seventies, hankering after the countryside and the quiet life, away from the smog and the bustle of Belgrade, that he was telephoned by the Minister of Tourism – one of the top men in a country that was relying more and more on foreign currency from international guests. He asked Nino to go home to his native Istria and kick-start a new wave in cheap package holidays for the factory workers from Italy, Austria, and Germany. It was a position of trust, and Nino was known in the higher echelons of Tito's civil service to be 'a safe pair of hands', which counted for more than knowing absolutely nothing at all about the tourist business.

This boost in foreign visitors was also intended to cater for a smattering of trusties from the Eastern Bloc countries who were hard core enough not to be seduced by the ideological and social depravity and decadence of Tito's own particular brand of socialist self-management; not quite a 'running dog of capitalism', rather the gambolling puppy of socialism.

The old ex-Partisan's connections were more than very good; he was a regular visitor to the Brijuni Islands, the private playground of Marshal Tito and his court. Mr Broz's passion for the archipelago-fiefdom in the Fažana straits that the ancient Greeks called Pollariae opened doors for Nino that would otherwise have been difficult to prise open.

Returning from the bar with a bottle and three glasses, Nino – short, stocky but powerful despite his advanced years – places them on the table.

'What are you doing, you stupid old fool?' says Faida. 'You've been drinking all day – if you have any more, you'll fall over. Speak to him, Marco. He doesn't listen to me.'

'We need to celebrate the boy's return. This is the son of my son. We need to drink,' Nino says sparking up, a well-practised twinkle in his watery blue eyes.

The drinks, however, are interrupted by Nino's cell phone. Without a word he goes indoors and answers it.

'I don't like it, Marco,' says Faida quietly. 'Something is wrong. People keep ringing all times of night and day. They even ring the landline, and when I pick up whoever is on the other end puts it down if it isn't him. I don't know what to do about it.'

'Have you asked him what's going on?' says Marco.

'He just does the usual and brushes me off, saying it's something to do with the export of the truffles and I shouldn't worry my "dear little girly head about it".'

'Sounds like business as usual.'

'On the one hand, yes; but on the other, it's strange. I've barely spent a day apart from him for more than 75 years, and there's not much you can get past me. He's frightened of something, Marco. I know Nino and I know when he's frightened. I wouldn't worry so much, but he also keeps forgetting things. Something's not right.'

'Here I am. Forgot the corkscrew,' blusters Nino as he comes back.

'Who was that on the phone?' asks Faida.

'No-one. Gino. He says some of the tree huggers are going to try some protest with the dogs over the holidays.'

'Don't worry about it, Nino. C'mon. Let's have a drink,' says Marco, changing the subject. 'The restaurant is closed through New Year, and we can all enjoy a little peace. I certainly need it. I'm sure you two also do.'

Nino pops the cork, sniffs it, and pours. 'This is what you are missing when you are off on your underground missions,' says Nino. 'Old wines stay more or less the same, and new ones come along like this one.'

Marco inhales the rich yellow of the sample Nino has poured him. 'Wow! That's a grown up. What is it?'

Nino had taught Marco everything he knew about wine. Which was a lot. Even without Istria's new generation of winemakers to educate him Nino had, even under communism, been able to drink excellent foreign wines regularly during his time in Belgrade and when travelling for the Ministry of Foreign Affairs; so he had some context by which to judge the contemporary local classics. And the blended white they have in front of them is certainly one of the latter.

'It's local. They've been growing over on their land near Grimalda, vineyard Brdo,' says Faida. 'And they call it "Grimalda", after our very own "Belvedere d'Istria", the most beautiful view on the peninsula.'

'I'm getting *malvasia*, for sure; that colour and depth couldn't be anything else. But there's something more here: chardonnay?' suggested Marco.

'And sauvignon blanc,' added Nino. 'Half chardonnay, and the other two a quarter each. Not bad. Not bad at all. They give it a year in oak barrels, which you can taste, and stir the sediment. It's perfect with the truffles. Whichever way you want. I sometimes think I can taste the truffles in there.'

'Classic terroir: heavy vanilla on top from the chardonnay, and the light fruity bits around the edge.'

'Enough bullshitting,' says Faida. 'Welcome home, son. Grandson. We missed you. Let us drink to your return.'

'Cheers, Nona. Cheers, Nino. It's good to be home.'

★★★★★

Stancija Mihailić had been inherited from his father after Nino returned from the war. For years the building lay empty. It was only after the death of Ivo, Marco's father, early in the so-called Croatian 'Homeland War', that Nino and Faida really threw themselves into Stancija Mihailić, making it one of the great culinary landmarks in central Istria.

Unlike many of their contemporary countrymen they both had first-hand experience of war as Partisans in World War Two. After the Italians' capitulation in 1943 Istria was under direct German rule. Most of the rest of Croatia was under the iron fist of arch-genocidal maniac Ante Pavelić, whose *Ustaša* movement in the Independent State of Croatia (NDH – *Nezavisna Država Hrvatska*) was more Nazi than the Nazis.

Nino and Faida didn't buy into the new post-Homeland War regime of the 1990s. They had the feeling that the fledgling country had still not really ever come to terms with its past. This was a throwback partly to Tito and his balancing of the nationalities in the newly founded Yugoslavia. Such things, however, were still discussed in a whisper, and veterans from this most recent war and their associations continued to be the most influential part of Croatian civil society. They had an interest to make sure the war never ended. They saw themselves as the creators of the state and therefore on the side of right and sovereign. Between them, the newly composed veterans were totally bound up with past wars and the duty to defend an unthreatened Croatia. Manipulated both by political parties and the Catholic church, they perpetually trumpeted that the need to defend the homeland was more than the need to maintain pensions and prescription drugs. They believed they had the right to dictate the moral code to the rest of the nation via the church and state.

Still, ever since he had returned from life in Belgrade and out in the wide world, Nino often wondered to himself if Istria had ever really come to terms with its own moral conscience, its Italian legacy and the schisms that naturally arise when a country or region is divided.

Now the old Mihailić residence that Nino and his dead brother Pino grew up in was all that remained, the sum total of a life spent in service to the former Yugoslavia and to the ideals of the self-management system of communism that Nino believed in. Still, anachronistically, does believe in. That, and the truffle business. In short, Stancija Mihailić was Nino's pride and Faida's joy.

It was retirement gift to himself and Faida. The restaurant that he always had a hankering to run in the congenial, convivial style of his old uncle Armando, who used to have a *konoba* in Buzet. Not that Nino was retired or would ever retire. He still had his finger in a number of pies. Most of the pies had truffles in them. The onset of capitalism in Croatia brought further advantages for a man as connected as Nino – a share in a winery, part-ownership of an olive mill, and his abiding obsession with the lure of the truffle.

The restaurant was something that really gave Nino a reason to get up in the morning, but truffles were where his heart lay. He had been active all his life – he was lucky to have so much to occupy himself with in his retirement otherwise he just would have faded away. The same was true of so many of the true warriors of World War Two.

★★★★★

Later, Marco leaves Nino on the terrace, answering his constantly ringing cell phone. Christmas greetings from his hunting buddies. For people who see each other all the time they certainly spent a lot of time on the phone in between meetings and celebrations. Such was the intimacy of country life.

He finds Faida down in the kitchen – she has carried on preparing the Christmas Eve feast. The restaurant chef is off for the holidays, so it is down to her and her ever-willing sous-chef, Marco. From childhood on he has been fascinated by how Faida worked magic in the kitchen, magic in the way that his own mother had never had the time (or inclination) to devote herself to during their life together in London.

'I've prepared the *sarma* in advance,' says Faida, 'I do that because one year we just didn't have time to do it and it got left off the menu. None of you Istrians gave a damn.'

A Bosnian by birth, Faida had left her hometown of Tuzla as a teenager to join Tito's Partisans in 1943. Her whole family was wiped out in the war, murdered before her eyes. She left for the Partisans in the woods. There was nowhere else to go. Completely unsentimental about it, Faida had never once been back to the town where she was born.

Food nostalgia, however, was a completely different form of sentimentality, far deeper than mere family. It was the basis of any real culture. No Bosnian Christmas table was complete without the rolls in which minced meat is wrapped inside pickled cabbage leaves. But every year she insisted on the *sarma*. The longer it was cooked the better – two days better than one – but in real life a bare minimum of three hours would do.

'What about the *bakalar*?' asks Marco.

'The salt cod has been soaking for three days,' says Faida, 'and it could do with a final rinse. It's there in the pantry. Could you do that? The old pot is getting a bit heavy for me. Thanks, son.'

Dried Atlantic cod had been a tradition for centuries. It was an extraordinary invention and perfect for developing countries prior to refrigeration – and, in economic terms, the making of countries like Iceland and Norway in the nineteenth century. They had been salting fish in this way for over 500 years, but the idea had never been exported. The salt preserves the cod and allows it to be transported thousands of miles to its eventual consumer. A staple of Istrian Christmas, *sarma* was one of the dishes Marco learned from Faida during the time spent in her kitchen in his holidays. Experience told him that his next job would be to take the fish into the scullery and give it a good beating with a wooden mallet.

As if reading his thoughts, Faida says, 'While you are beating it, I'll prepare the potatoes and chop the garlic. Then I think you should have a little siesta.'

'I could do with a rest. We'll boil it for about two hours, right?' says Marco.

'We'll see how it goes. Depends on the texture. We may need to go a bit longer.'

Marco gets to work on the cod. As he concentrates, he forgets about his dismissal, and about Janey – he finds himself immersed in the traditional way of preparing fish that went back to the times when the fish was landed from Norway in the early nineteenth century. As soon as the cod was cooked to perfection the potatoes would be added and boiled in the juices till soft but not disintegrating. The pot is drained, and the potatoes and fish separated; then the hard work begins, removing the fish bones and skin till just bite-sized pieces of the flesh and their glutinous fat remain. These are then beaten together with the potatoes until creamy, adding all the while extra liquid from the pot where necessary as well as chopped garlic, seasoning and parsley to taste. A few hunks of toasted sourdough bread and some oil from Nino's olives down the hill extracted from trees that had been in the family for over a century, and Christmas would be complete.

'What will we have to go with the *bakalar*, Nona?' asks Marco, sipping the last of the Grimalda white from his glass.

'First of all, I want you to promise me something,' she says looking him directly in the eye. 'If Nino does his usual and wants to have truffles on the *bakalar*, please ask him if we can do it individually. I'm sick of truffles with absolutely everything. Sometimes I just want to eat normal food.'

'No problem, Nona,' he replies with a laugh. 'I think what we have here is what we call a first-world problem.'

'He insists on spreading it around like it is ketchup, playing the big fellow. The truth of it is that the season has been very bad so far this year. So I don't know what he is playing at.'

'I'm sure he knows what he's doing. He's been in the truffle game for over 70 years. He practically invented the Istrian truffle business single-handed!' says Marco.

'It's not like it was before, Marco. A few local lads taking their dogs for a walk on a Sunday morning. The truffle woods aren't very pleasant places to be these days. It used to be a gentleman's game. Honour amongst hunters. And at his age, I'm not sure he's safe anymore.'

'I'll see if I can have a word with him and find out what's going on. And now, I'd like to have a shower, a shave, and a siesta. If that's OK. Before Zvonko and the kids come back from their walk, and it gets crazy.'

Faida leads him down by the side of the restaurant to a beautiful small cottage in the garden. It has a magnificent view stretching across half of Istria.

'I've put you in the Rose House. I had a feeling something like this might happen – that you might come home,' she confides. 'It's all made up for you. This can be your home for as long as you need it. Now that Maja is gone. I hope you're done with England. There's nothing there for you there. This is where you belong.'

*****

It was one of those dreams where you can just about see the end of it and you think you are about to find your goal, and then at the very minute when everything looks like it will be resolved it starts all over again. Marco called it the Dream of Sisyphus. This one was particularly deep and repetitive. It involved him running all over the Oxfordshire countryside trying to find Janey. No matter which of the usual haunts he goes to, having promised she will be there, he always just misses her. His quest is driven by a deadened erotic desire. Finally, when he gets back to their squat, he can hear her in her room. He bursts through the door. He sees her sitting in front of the mirror, her back to him. She holds up a piece of celluloid. He takes it. 'We're going to have twins,' he shouts in delight. Slowly she turns to him. As he looks up from the scan, he sees that it is his mother sitting there in her hospital gown.

He sits up in the bed. Outside the thick walls of the Rose House he can hear someone on the phone. He goes to the window. He sees the back of Nino's head.

'No, no. I cannot do this,' says Nino, exasperated, 'I do not have the money. What do you know about this? This is crazy. Stop this now.'

By the time Marco gets to the door of the cottage Nino is gone, and nothing is left but the upturned brick that he uses as an ashtray when he makes his secretive calls.

Marco returns to his room and makes straight for the shower to prepare himself for the evening's Christmas festivities. It had been a long 24 hours and it was just what he needed. As usual, Istria had not failed him and had delivered the escape that he needed into the bosom of his natural family, as opposed to the fake one he and Janey had tried to fabricate in the heart of the anti-globalist movement.

As he stands underneath the scalding shower, it feels as if all his woes are being washed away down into the red earth of Istria. Here at least he has the chance of a fresh start, a new beginning and, in a modest way, he can start to rebuild himself after the years of deceit, collusion, and delusion.

Looking in the mirror for the first time that day, he really looked like a different person: somehow cleaner, fresher, and more wholesome. He wondered as he gazed at his new face whether he would ever be able to feel like that inside.

Wrapping a towel around himself, Marco returned to his bedroom via the small sitting room.

'I brought you a drink,' comes a voice from the sofa.

'Jesus, Emina, you scared the shit out of me. Doesn't anyone knock any more around here?'

Emina had changed for dinner. She had got rid of her biker gear and was wearing a very simple black dress; her long, thick dark hair, freshly washed, fell down on her shoulders. She looked almost Asian; her dark eyes set off by a discreet pearl necklace around her slender neck.

'Faida lent them to me. The pearls. She thinks they make me look like her when she was young. I love your grandmother.'

'Faida loves you very much,' says Marco. 'Perpetually surrounded by malodorous machos like me, Nino and Zvonko, she thinks of you as the daughter she never had but always wanted. I think of you more as an additional fragrance to the community in general. But, then again, I know that you are far too pretty to be patronised.'

They look at each other and burst into laughter.

'I'm sorry I was a bit shitty with you when you arrived.'

'Shitty? You Emina? How could you ever be shitty?'

They laugh again.

'Anyway, I'm sorry. Zvonko pisses me off sometimes. Cheers.'

She offers him his glass and stands to give it to him.

'It's *viljamovka* from my uncle. Pears from Srebrenica never tasted so good.'

'I remember it from Grožnjan. Bosnian speciality liquor. Headache in a bottle.'

'Cheers.'

'Cheers,' says Marco. 'It has been far too long.'

They look at each other in silence, checking the familiarity of their faces for changes, signs of age, excess or pain.

'You've not changed,' says Marco. 'Still the same bolshy Emina, kicking ass and taking names. Trying to get naïve guys drunk with her uncle's hooch.'

'Unlike your good self, Mr Love Rat,' digs Emina, smiling. 'In the British newspapers yesterday you looked like somebody had dragged you through a hedge backwards and used your head for metalwork practice. Oh, and you looked like a sex offender.'

He grins back at her and says, 'Well, it's a dirty job, but somebody has to do it.'

'I'm glad to see that at least they didn't make you get too many stupid tattoos.'

She looks over his bare torso, checking for ink, and appraising him at the same time.

'That was one thing that I was careful about, which is why I went the piercings route,' he says. 'But I did have one tattoo. I had a 'W' inked on each butt cheek so when I bent over it spells 'WOW'. Would you like to see it? I can't work out whether it's better with an exclamation mark or without.'

Emina throws a cushion at him, laughing, 'No, I wouldn't! Now go and get dressed. We need to go up for drinks. The other guests will be arriving soon.'

Marco heads off to the bedroom to dress. Emina, already a little tipsy, mooches around the sitting room, checking out his stuff. She puts some music on his mini-system and studies the large metal object he has left out on the table – the Roman arm protector he has carried with him from London. It's quite big for a human to wear. The gladiator that wore it must have been an amazing specimen. She looks closer on the inside and tries to make out the small inscriptions that look like hieroglyphics.

She comes to a halt outside his bedroom door. It's slightly ajar. 'Marco? Can you hear me?'

'Yes. Nearly ready, just drying my hair.'

'Good, because I need to tell you something.' Silence, apart from the hair dryer. 'I fucked Zvonko.' The sound of the hair dryer continues.

'I SAID I FUCKED ZVONKO!' she shouts through the door.

He pulls it open and shouts: 'I HEARD YOU THE FIRST TIME!'

He comes back into the room and picks up the bottle of *viljamovka* and pours himself a good one. Drinks it. Pours her one. Raises his re-filled glass to her. 'I believe congratulations are in order. Cheers!'

He drinks again, strolls around the sofa, and, dripping comedy sarcasm, says: 'Fed up with being an outsider? Feeling lonely? Need to feel extra-special? Well, why not fuck Zvonko and join the hundreds of other unique and beautiful individuals who have fallen for his pathetic charms.'

Emina is furious. She throws the Roman *manica* at his head and it flies through the air, missing him by inches as he dives to catch it.

'Fuck you, Marco, and the holier-than-thou horse you rode in on. It was a fucking accident for Christ's sake.'

'This is a fucking one-of-a-kind antique, Emina. What the fuck are you playing at?'

Emina storms out, slamming the door.

Ten seconds later, the door opens again. It's Emina. She walks over to Marco at the sofa. 'Forgot my scarf.' And, as a throwaway afterthought, 'Bastard!'

Marco stares into the bathroom mirror as he makes last-minute adjustments to his apparel. As he does so a wry smile comes to his lips. 'Business as usual at Chateau Mihailić,' he thinks to himself.

*****

'Grandad!' shouts Marco as he makes his way from the Rose Cottage to the main gate of the property, where he can see the old man under the lights of the restaurant sign. As Marco approaches Nino hangs up and walks towards him.

'I just came down to open the gates for the guests. You know what Svetlana is like if she has to do it herself.'

'I just wanted to say, 'thank you', Nono, for taking me in like this. I really need somewhere to recover, rest up and start again.'

'You have come to the right place. The family is always the best place to be. We are happy to have you for as long as you want,' says Nino. 'And neither me nor your grandmother are interested in that British business. Any country that is stupid enough to want to leave the European Union and foolish enough not to want you on their police force can go and fuck itself in the ass.'

'Thanks, Nono,' says Marco, who had forgotten his grandfather's occasional use of colourful language, 'I really appreciate it. And one day I will tell you what happened. I want you both to know the truth. There's good and bad in every story, and I haven't been perfect in this. You need to know that.'

'Whatever you say, my boy,' says Nino. 'You'll tell us in your own time. In the meanwhile, if you need any money, you only have to ask.'

'Money is no problem, Nono,' says Marco. 'But what about you? Is everything OK? You seem a bit stressed out. Your phone never stops ringing, even though it's Christmas Eve. Is everything all right with the truffles?'

'The business never stops. Truffles are very much in demand over Christmas,' says Nino. 'Don't worry, my boy, everything's fine. We have a few problems with the animal rights people – that's nothing new. The season isn't great, so far. But we will manage. We always have.'

Marco holds his gaze, and begins to open the large gates to the property and as he does so a few very rare flakes of snow begin to appear out of the dark,

'Let's get these open,' says Nino, 'and hope it stops snowing before too long so Svetlana and that idiot new boyfriend of hers don't have to sleep over.'

'Oh-oh; that bad, is it?' asks Marco.

'Put it like this,' says Nino. 'Imagine how irritating Zvonko is and multiply times a thousand.'

'That's pretty bad. Thanks for the heads-up.'

Back up at the house a festive mood prevails. Both kids are washed and brushed and awaiting the arrival of their mother, Svetlana, and the hope of vast bribery in gifts from both her and her new rich boyfriend, Hrvoje. Even with only a dozen or so people coming for the Christmas Eve dinner the restaurant feels cosy. A big log fire is crackling in the corner, and as most of the restaurant tables are outside on the terrace indoors close to the kitchen feels more than intimate.

On his afternoon walk through the woods Zvonko had cut a log from a fallen oak with an axe. This was the *badnjak*, an essential part of Christmas Eve celebrations. Zvonko is now building the fire around it in the same way that people had prepared for the *badnjak* for centuries in this village and all over Istria.

As Zvonko is busying himself with the fire his ex-wife Svetlana makes a grand entrance with Hrvoje, her new beau. The kids rush to greet them, eager to find out what the Christmas gift situation is. Emina appears, looking slightly more sober. Marija and Ema, two old friends of Faida, widows with nowhere else to go in the holidays, come in quietly. After the festive introductions, in traditional Croatian style, they head for the kitchen to help Faida; she is looking resplendent in an appropriately seasonal and floral dress, hair done and extra make-up for the occasion. Kisses, hugs, and greetings are exchanged.

While Zvonko handles the pyrotechnics, Marco has managed to put his hands on a primo bottle of *biska*, the grappa infused with the flavour of mistletoe berries. Having made up with Emina by getting her to wear a hat as silly as the one he is wearing, he persuades her to carry a tray of glasses while he carries the mistletoe and offers kisses in exchange for drinks. Such is the ancient and mystical power of the mistletoe.

'This year, to celebrate my return to Istria,' announces Marco, already feeling the effects of the *viljamovka* from earlier, 'we will begin the celebrations by combining British tradition and Istrian tradition. First, if I may, grandmother, you get the kiss under the mistletoe and then you get the glass of *biska*. OK, who's first?'

Bang on cue, Zvonko jumps up and says, 'I have another suggestion. I think it would be better if Emina was doing the kissing and you were doing the waitressing.'

'Brilliant idea,' says Emina perking up, handing the tray to Marco. She takes the mistletoe and walks over to Zvonko who crouches down for his peck on the cheek.

'Happy Christmas, everyone!' says Emina as she kisses Zvonko full on the lips, just long enough to be mildly indecent, but not quite offensive.

Slightly taken aback at this turn of events, Zvonko returns to the fire to get it burning as fast as possible. It looks like it is going to be an interesting Christmas.

The log is lit. It was kept lit through the night to keep the baby Jesus warm in his first hours on earth. But at first it was a pagan, and then an ancient Slav tradition, a symbol throughout the ages of fertility, rebirth, resurrection, and family around the hearth.

The children, Dado and Marijana, are given the job of distributing the rest of the kisses and *biskas*. Nino watches them as he quietly slices the haunch of Istrian ham, the *pršut*, over at a side table.

Marco joins Zvonko at the huge hearth in the corner of the room. He offers him another *biska*.

'Cheers, brother, good to have you back,' says Zvonko, adding bigger branches to the fire as it starts to pick up.

'Cheers. It's good to be here,' says Marco. 'Need some help with the fire?'

'No thanks, looks like it's catching. We'll be ready to add the *badnjak* soon.'

'I'm assuming you've done everything by the book here?'

'What do you mean?'

'Up before dawn. Chop the tree down. Choose the branch. Recite the Lord's Prayer three times, ask for forgiveness. You know, bro, everything according to tradition.'

'Well,' says Zvonko wryly, 'I think you know that I'm not really a big stickler for tradition. We Istrian Catholics tend to have unorthodox interpretations of the scriptures and canon law. Or anything else for that matter.' He gives one of his winningly wide grins.

'You mean like the unorthodox (or even un-Catholic) tradition that it's really bad form to fuck your best friend's ex-girlfriend?'

Silence.

Whoops of joy from the other side of the room as Dado is allowed to open his present prior to Christmas morning as his mother won't be there.

'What can I say? It was an accident.'

'That's what she said.'

'It was, it really was. I'll explain. I can't now – it will take too long, and I need to go and pretend to be impressed by the presents that bitch and her idiot boyfriend have brought for my kids.'

'I just wanted to say it's OK,' says Marco. 'I'm over it. I'm over any relationship with any woman for some time to come.'

He smiles at his friend, who shouts: 'Look at that – what a present! Fantastic. Did you say, "Thank you", Dado? Wow! That's the best bike I've seen for a long time. And blue, your favourite colour!'

Faida and Emina come in from the kitchen with another tray of *biska* and a bowl full of what looks like grain.

'As the only two Muslims here,' announces Faida, 'Emina and I had better get the local customs going so we can get on and eat. You papists are useless at keeping up your own traditions – you need us heathen infidels to do it for you. Everybody! Come over here, around the fire. Including you, Nino, hiding over there behind the *pršut*. Emina, give them their drinks and then begin. Dado, Marijana – you take the grain.'

Taking the bowl of roasted buckwheat groats, the *kasha*, the children wait patiently while Emina hands out the *biska*. Coming over to the fire, Emina begins: 'May Jesus be praised! I wish you a good Christmas Eve and feast day of Adam and Eve!'

To which the rest of the group responds: 'Today and always!'

They then all throw their *biska* over the log on the fire, creating a flash and a puff of smoke. The kids then throw a couple of handfuls of wheat grains and rice on the *badnjak*, which has started to smoulder. Glasses are refilled. Nino steps forward and throws a glass of wine on the fire and says: 'I drink to your health!'

'Cheers, everyone,' says Faida, 'and now, finally, we can have dinner.'

Technically speaking, Christmas Eve in Istria is a time for fasting. However, where there's a will there's a way, and Catholic precepts were invented to be circumvented, hence the existence of the confessional. The rule was that major meaty things should probably not be eaten. This meant that the exquisite *pršut* that Nino had been carving was allowed, and a large platter of it is placed in the centre of the table, flanked by two bunches of *psenica*, wheat grass planted on Saint Lucy's Day which sprouts in perfect time for Christmas.

'Tonight, we are drinking wine from our own vineyard,' announces Nino proudly, 'an honest *teran* and a very straightforward *malvazia*. I'm saving the best stuff for New Year. I just want it to be clear: I threw a good glass of wine onto the fire as a good pagan, and nothing to do with this Baby Jesus Catholic shit.'

As he pours, Marija and Ema come through from the kitchen with the *bakalar* and toast, swiftly followed by Faida and Emina with the large pots of beans and chickpea stews. The table, set for twelve but seating eleven, groans with food on this eve of fasting.

'I'll make one toast this year and I'll keep it short,' says Nino. 'In keeping with tradition, I'd like us to raise a glass to the memory of my brother, Pino: brave soldier, Partisan, and good Communist.

We keep a place at our Christmas table to keep him in our hearts for another year. But this year is a special for another reason. Our son – our grandson, Marco – is back with us. And, God willing, he is back with us to stay. To the memory of Pino and the return of the prodigal.'

Without warning, Nino falls back into his chair and bursts into floods of tears, his head in his hands. Nothing can be done to stop it. Faida comes to him and holds him in her arms. He sobs even more. Marco stands and replies to the toast, at which point Nino begins to recover, wiping his eyes with his napkin.

'Bless all of our mothers and fathers. May they be happy and healthy, and if they're not with us any more may they rest in peace and their memories live on!'

'Cheers!' comes the reply.

Zvonko and Marco exchange a look.

'And now, let's have no more tears and be happy and grateful for what we have – and not mourn what we don't have,' says Faida, wiping Nino's cheeks. To Marco's eyes, his grandparents suddenly look very old. And vulnerable.

The whole family dive into the food with gusto; even the children take delight in the creamy flavour of the codfish. Recovering, Nino returns with his grater and a large white truffle.

'I know Faida says we always have too much truffle. But this one is a beauty. Vito found it this morning, just after Marco called me. It was an auspicious sign. Look. As full as a tick. Smell it. Feel it, Marco. Squeeze it. It's heavy with aroma and moisture. Almost perfect. May I?'

He takes back the truffle and goes around the table grating it on to each person's portion of *bakalar*. He comes to Emina.

'No thanks, Nino,' she says. 'And by the way, what's Vito having for dinner this evening?'

Faida kicks her under the table, signalling her not to sermonise about animal rights.

'He'll get a special treat this evening. Remember, Saint Nikola is the patron saint of animals as well.'

'That's a rich one, coming from you, you old commie. What about the poor bastards the rest of the year? You let them starve. That's not very Christian, is it? Not very Saint Francis of Assisi.'

A silence comes over the table.

'Well neither are we, Emina,' says Faida. 'Come on, it's Christmas – let's have some fun. Cheers, everyone! Happy Christmas. And cheer up; it will be Muhammad's birthday in a few days.'

Nino, conciliatory, turns to Emina: 'Play something for us, Emina, please; before midnight, play something. I want us to be happy when we see Christmas in, so we can stop this fasting and start eating properly!'

A smile comes to Emina's lips, which is not so often these days; it feels like a gift.

'Of course, of course,' she replies, and under her breath says to Marco and Zvonko, 'Old bastard; could charm the knickers off a nun.'

Before she can get the piano, Marco has beaten her to it and has begun his party piece, the opening of the Rachmaninov Piano Concerto Number Three, as it always gets the party going. 'And now, ladies and gentlemen of Buzet – and, indeed Grimalda, and what's more Cerovlje – I give you the one, the only princess of the piano, the queen of the keys, the…'

Zvonko throws bread at him, 'Shut up, you fool, and let's see some real talent…'

Marco continues, unstoppable: '…the exceptional, the elemental, the exciting, the euphoria-inducing… wait for it, wait for it… Emina from Srebrenica…'

He goes into a tango, and she dances in a sultry way across the floor. This is a routine they have done many times and the audience enjoy its familiarity. Marco sings:

'*Senorita Emina, from Srebrenica,*
Knew all the answers,
And though her relatives and friends were perfect dancers,
She swore she's never danced a step until she died.'

She takes over the tango from Zvonko on the keyboard and speeds it up a notch. Marco ties a napkin around his head like a headscarf, to demonstrate his femininity; and Zvonko places a rose from the vase on the table between his teeth as a mark of his romantic masculinity. Marco and Zvonko tango. Expertly, dramatically, and to the wild applause of the family who look on laughing ready to join in at any minute, especially the children.

Emina marks a change in tempo which is the men's cue to take a bow and settle back down.

'Ladies and gentlemen, welcome to Christmas Eve in Dragué!' announces Emina over her piano interlude. 'This was the comedy act of the evening. Please show your appreciation for the artistes!'

The children throw bread; the adults throw coins and applaud.

'Next up. This one is for Faida and Nino, who picked me up and looked after me when things weren't looking so good. And to whom I wish long life. And in their honour, I give you the first song they sang together, here in Buzet, back in the war.'

She strikes up a martial tune. Takes it back down to a romantic ballad, which she and Marco sing couplet by couplet:

'*Avanti o popolo, alla riscossa*,' sings Emina. '*Bandiera rossa, bandiera rossa*.'

Then Marco, super romantic:

'*Avanti o popolo, alla riscossa*
Bandiera rossa trionferà.'

Then in unison:

'*Bandiera rossa la trionferà*
Bandiera rossa la trionferà
Bandiera rossa la trionferà
Evviva il socialismo e la libertà!'

Nino solos, holding his fist to his temple in the Partisan salute: '*Evviva il Communismo e la libertà*!'

Then loud barking and even more celebration as Vito the truffle hound joins them in the celebration. Zvonko is dancing. The children are throwing bread and *kasha* like it's a wedding. Svetlana and Hrvoje are trying to get them to behave. Marija and Ana are waltzing together, and Nino is drunkenly saluting and singing. Only Faida is alert.

'Why is the dog here? How did it get out of its box?'

Chapter V

Once More Unto the Breach

Colonia Pietas Iulia, 81 AD

Watching the animal hunt in the arena was always the last thing that Lucia wanted to do. However, as the chief dog handler for the games it was expected of her. The human slaughter she had come to terms with – there was some choice in the matter, in most cases. But the animals? 'Free will' was not part of their job description. Today, however, she just didn't have the stomach for it and remained down in her lair in the bestiary. For once she let Philumena and Thelos and some other slaves take the dogs from the kennels and lead them to the upper levels of the arena to prepare for their entrance with the other specimens from the animal kingdom. The bellowing of bulls and the roar of lions, tigers and sometimes other exotic wild beasts, which came from the various sections on the ground floor of the Pola amphitheatre, were terrifying. These noble, wild beasts were about to be killed as symbols of the great Roman conquests of untamed and distant lands, proof that the Romans put nature itself under their yoke.

It took special nerves to handle animals in these conditions and Philumena and Thelos were more than up to the task with the dogs. The real question was, under how much control were the other animals? There were always casualties even before they went on. Lucia's main concern was to do damage control and make sure as many of her pack survived the day. The night before she had made a clear inventory of all her dogs and chosen which would fight and when. With the bellowing of the elephants Lucia knew that at that very moment the first team of her dogs had just been let into the arena for the opening section of the games, the *venationes* – the animal hunt.

It was held in the Pietas Iulia Arena. The magnificent edifice was finally completed under Titus, who was a great lover of the games. After his Jewish campaign in the year of the Four Emperors, he took almost 100,000 prisoners – most of whom found their way into the killing machine of the arena.

However, Titus never got to see it in use because he died of a fever earlier in the year. The diagnosis of 'fever' was probably code for being poisoned by Domitian, who had just succeeded Titus and acceded to the position of emperor of the Roman Empire.

The atmosphere in the arena at Colonia Pietas Iulia on this bright, early spring morning was unprecedented. Never had there been such a crowd fighting for seats: there was something about the day that had inspired the imagination of the public of the *colonia*. Oceanus had widely publicised the programme of fights, and as he looked down on the scene from his vantage point up in the gods, he counted his blessings. His elevation to procurator gave him complete control of the gladiatorial events in the arena, as well as a big say in the animal and sea battle re-enactments. If he played his cards right it would afford him access to wealth and power that would set him up for the rest of his days.

But now all he could see was the last of a full house coming in, and the first of the not-so-wild animals emerging into the arena. A full house meant at least 24,000 people. Officially there were 23,000 seats, but the soldiers guarding the entrances always let in a few of their friends. The amphitheatre faced the sea, and as its back was built into the hillside it was hard to stop particularly young and athletic kids from sneaking in without a ticket; many of the security guards turned a blind eye to the practice, having been kids once themselves.

The seating areas were packed with a festive crowd who had brought their food and drink for the day, as well as cushions and other paraphernalia ranging from sunshades to whistles. In high summer the arena's own sunshades would have been rigged by the sailors from the fleet to stop the crowd from burning up. Today they would not be needed, but the sailors were beneath the arena operating the winches and capstans that allowed teams of slaves to pull in unison and hoist heavy animals from the basement to the main arena. Oceanus was lucky to have such skilled labour at his disposal to make the games as spectacular as possible.

Their work was now in evidence as the huntsmen began the big chase of animals to get the *ludi* going. Some huntsmen were on horseback herding the beasts, whilst other lightly armed crew on foot kept them under control with their spears and swords. Once they were all herded into the arena they began whipping the animals into a frenzy. The earliest casualties in the arena were the more domestic kind – donkeys, dogs, deer and cows; they were consumed mainly by their fellow animals. Lucia had trained her dogs to fight on the side of the huntsmen, so they had a chance to be spared as the noble canine friend of the hunter. Sometimes it didn't end that happily.

As the antelope and gazelle danced elegantly around the arena as part of the warm-up act, the horsemen and dogs rounded them up and began the first part of the systematic killing for the day with the baiting and tormenting of the dumb, defenceless beasts. Then they slowly began to excite the animals and the crowd into a whirlpool of bloodlust; this would be continued with the fighting of the wild beasts before moving on to the lunchtime executions, and finally the apotheosis: the pitting of man against man, gladiator against gladiator.

Philumena and Thelos watched from the side-lines. Their dogs were doing well, savaging ostriches, gutting donkeys, and working in a pack to bring down a magnificent stag with fine antlers that were capable of doing major damage. The dogs were very efficient killing machines, and no wonder the Roman legions were happy to have them fighting alongside them in the real world, in real wars. The huntsmen were pleased with their work, and it was beginning to look as if there would be few casualties. For now. Meanwhile, the baying public barely had time to catch its breath before the next phase of slaughter began. It was the turn of the more dangerous wild animals, and so the stakes were raised.

Deep in the lower depths of the arena the rumble of the ecstatic spectators calling for more and more blood could still be heard, and above them the occasional screeching of a slaughtered beast raised its voice.

Down in the gladiator boot room Severus was not only considering his fate, but he was also trying to come up with a strategy to bring both himself and Nasica out of this alive.

Severus didn't mind fighting. Once he was in the ring he went into the zone and his instincts took over his body and mind. It was the waiting beforehand. So much waiting. Naturally, he had no appetite at all to kill Nasica, the left-handed tyro. In many ways it was more logical if Severus took the *gladius* himself. For that was certainly what the crowd and the emperor would prefer him to do. The luck of the draw. Or was it the other way around? Or was his number up? It was suspicious that, after the draw, Urbicus had broken his arm after falling down the stairs to the armoury. Nasica, being the only other *hoplomachus* available, had to step in. Self-inflicted injury more like, thought Severus. Every permutation ran through his mind as to the whys and wherefores of the situation. 'Pretty Boy' Oceanus had decided that the old lag Severus at the fag-end of his career would, in fact, become known as the great gladiator who snuffed out the 20 candles of poor little rich kid Nasica. What a way to go. Severus comforted himself that he only had two more games to do in his contract with Oceanus – then he was as free as a bird.

As he had these thoughts, above him further proof that the highly civilised customs of Rome had tamed the unruliness of uncivilised nature was just about to be demonstrated, with the entry into the amphitheatre of a bewildering variety of savage beasts. Various *vomitoria* were opened and trap doors released a wide range of animal victims to be dispatched by the huntsmen and *bestiarii* – or beast fighters as they were known. Half-blinded by the bright morning light, bears, lions, tigers, leopards, hyenas and wolves stumbled, confused, enraged and disorientated into the open space of the arena, relieved to be out of their prison, yet further confused by the ugly noise of the bloodthirsty baying throng.

Often the *bestiarii* were, in fact, terrified individuals (at least as terrified as many of the animals): criminals on death row or prisoners of war, poor creatures with no chance against the animals they fought, with no real training and often no means by which they could defend themselves. Thrown to the beasts as punishment and diversion, many chose suicide rather than take their chances with the bears, lions, tigers and leopards, as well as exotics like crocodiles and giraffe, hyenas and cheetahs, jaguars and rhinoceri that would feature in the quotidian slaughter of the *ludi*.

As Severus considered his options, the first canine casualties were brought down to Lucia's makeshift hospital in between her lair and the kennels. Up above in the arena the carcasses from the first part of the day's carnage had been removed by the slaves. Between the various killing sprees that would take place during the day the bloodied sand was sieved and filtered to remove animal limbs and blood and give the appearance of a pristine fighting space. Some of the meat would be used to feed the surviving animals. A portion of it would reach some of the kitchens of Pietas Iulia, and bear stew, leopard *fricassee* and other rare offerings would be on the menu somewhere in town that night.

Meanwhile, in the dog kennels Lucia and Philumena had their work cut out for them.

'Bring him over here. Put him down on the bench,' said Lucia to the two slaves who had brought in a large mastiff on a stretcher under Philumena's instructions. 'He's lost a lot of blood.'

The dog, a Cane Corso, a descendant of the light Molossian fighting dogs so popular in ancient Greece, looked beyond repair as far as Thelos could see from his vantage point outside the room.

'Come in here, Thelos,' she shouted to the young boy. 'I need you and Philumena to hold him while I stitch up his eye. I can't use anaesthetic there, it's too corrosive. We'll just have to hold him down and restrain him the best way possible.'

Putting on a muzzle made for this very purpose, Philumena skilfully tied the dog's legs to the bench. She and her brother immobilised his head as Lucia began to stitch the massive wound across his eyelids. There was blood everywhere, and despite Philumena's efforts to staunch it with the clean linen it kept on flowing. Slowly the dog stopped struggling and the blood flow ebbed. Philumena looked up at her mistress in panic.

'Don't worry, Philumena, the morphium from the poppy seeds is beginning to work. I gave it to him on some ostrich meat when he came in.'

They exchanged a smile.

'He should be OK now but keep a watch on him. And clean up the wounds on his back. He's been gored or bitten by something there. Probably a wild pig. Use the antiseptic and the silk bandages. Thelos knows which ones. And keep the muzzle on for now.'

As Lucia walked out of her makeshift field hospital, she thought to herself once more what a senseless waste of life this whole thing was, and she wished she were out of it for good. Lucia was the polar opposite of most ancient Romans, for whom it was not a matter of regret to kill the vast swathes of wild animals that were sacrificed in the name of bloodlust in the arena. The truth of it was that for the Romans these were proud and great achievements.

They especially believed that in liberating the areas in which the wild predators had previously lived the land could be used for livestock breeding and agriculture. It was their religion. The liberation of entire regions from wild animals was regarded as a good achievement and the animals' slaughter a pleasurable and entertaining by-product. As Lucia moved down towards the gladiator's boot room the meaninglessness of it all hit her like a blow from a *gladius*.

★★★★★

'Look at these poor bastards: they haven't got a chance,' said Severus to Nasica as they looked out at the lunchtime entertainment of death sentences. 'The executions of citizens have just started over there. The emperor has stayed on for these.'

'At least they get the citizens over with quickly,' said Nasica. 'That's how my father died, you know. A falling out with Vespasian one day, chopped liver in the arena the next. Only he wasn't given such an easy ride. He was somehow mixed with the *damnatio ad bestia* group by accident. He was tied to the tail of a stampeding bison and dragged to his death. Makes our situation look pretty good by comparison.'

As they brought out the non-citizens for 'assisted' crucifixion (real crucifixion took too long) and others to be burned alive or eaten by wild beasts, the crowd roared; they were almost getting out of control to such an extent that the soldiers guarding the arena had to prod them back to their places with their spears. The reason for the hysteria was extraordinary. The lunchtime spectators tended to be the members of the poorer classes who didn't have a slave to keep their seats or who brought their lunch with them for the purpose. But it was more than that – it was the 'there but for the grace of the gods' factor. It could have been them and because they were grateful to be alive they wanted to celebrate it.

As a form of social control it was in its own way a brilliant technique to solidify the social code of conduct. Crossing the line between criminal and good citizen only took a second and could be punished by summary death. This was the tightrope that most ordinary Romans walked every day.

Nasica and Severus looked on as the procession of the slaves, a large group this time strung together by metal rings around their necks, was brought into the centre of the amphitheatre. The lowest in social status were given a bargain-basement group discount even in death. The trap doors opened – but nothing. No animals, no wild beasts. Silence.

A series of boos started up from the crowds. The slaves didn't know what to do and started to try to run in different directions to escape; however, unable to separate themselves from each other they fell into a pile. At that point the guards released the animals from the cages, and four fully-grown tigers approached the struggling slaves to a huge cheer from the crowd. This quartet were a particularly aggressive ambush of Caspian tigers, native to eastern Turkey; they had once roamed the forests of northern Iran, Mesopotamia, and the Caucasus around the Caspian Sea through central Asia to northern Afghanistan. The tigers leapt forward as one, mauled, and began to eviscerate the twenty or so men all roped together. Then they settled down to the feast; the sound of the crunching of human bone and the sluicing of human flesh echoed through the amphitheatre's perfect acoustics. Another wave of cheering came from the spectators, concurrently filling their own stomachs with their own lunches.

The feast proved too much for the tigers who lay around sated and in need of a siesta. This was when the jackals and hyenas were released to finish the job and clear the arena in time for the great procession preceding the main event: the gladiator show.

'I thought I might find you two here,' said Lucia, joining Nasica and Severus in the fighters' gallery watching the spectacle.

'Discussing tactics?'

'Well, not exactly. We were just getting to that,' said Nasica.

'The procession starts in about half an hour,' said Lucia, 'and you two need to get into your armour and out into the arena. So, I suggest you work out a plan of what to do. Because I swear if anything happens to either of you out there today, I will kill both of you.'

With that, perfectly aware of the irony in her comment, she turned on her heels and walked back down into her lair, the canine bestiary below the arena, to join her beloved *canes pugnaces* and clean up after the day.

★★★★★

The lunchtime performances over, the show must go on. For 'Pretty Boy' Oceanus this was his first in the newly-completed arena and in the presence of the mighty Domitian, so it had better be good – otherwise his new job as procurator, *editor* and *lanista* was on the line barely before it had begun. He knew he had to make a spectacle of it, and the fact that the emperor even stayed for the executions at lunchtime meant that things were going well. The *ludi* could make or break the reputation of their procurator and so he had planned every last detail meticulously, however grandiose, however small.

He was well aware that he had to make the games more extreme, more fantastic, and more spectacular, and in turn this would make him more and more popular with the general public; the more popular the games, the more this would increase the influence he could have on the emperor. Indeed, such was Pretty Boy's ambition that he had already made fantastic plans to connect the amphitheatre to the sea so that it could be filled with water, and vessels could sail directly into the arena from the port.

The spectators were returning to their seats as they heard the first notes of the trumpets that proclaimed the start of the *pompa*, the solemn procession that announced the beginning of the gladiator programme, the main event of the day.

Out in front were the two *lictors*, servants of Oceanus. The procession began, led by slaves dressed in fabulous golden armour and blowing long trumpets. The musicians followed, blasting out martial melodies on flutes, whistles and horns, made more piercing by the excellent soundscape provided by the arena. After them came Pretty Boy Oceanus himself, riding in a chariot drawn by two zebras. His masterstroke was to be accompanied by a semi-domesticated ostrich in the chariot, proving to the emperor that he wasn't taking himself too seriously.

The dog team had climbed the many steps up to the top gallery of the amphitheatre. Their favourite place was beneath the water cisterns. Each of the four towers of the arena had two cisterns filled with perfumed water that fed a fountain or could be sprinkled on the spectators. Lucia preferred the fragrance of this position. From their vantage point next to one of the sail turrets Lucia, Philumena and Thelos watched as the spectators cheered, barracked, and threw food in true, typical Roman style at the arena. Acrobats, dancers in exotic costumes, and the hunters and beast fighters who had survived the morning entered the arena. They then formed up in a semi-circle in front of the podium containing Domitian, his wife Domitia Longina, and their babe in arms, Titus Flavius.

Finally, the sound of marching feet and heavy armour – and the gladiators entered the arena, dressed in the armour that they would be wearing later in their fights. Lucia caught her breath as she saw Nasica in his *hoplomachus* equipment looking so handsome and so young. He was wearing a gold embroidered cloak that she hadn't seen before, and which made him look more noble than ever, so much so that her heart skipped a beat. Then a huge cheer went up as Severus, in full *murmillo* garb, entered the arena in his giant fish-helmet, shaking himself vigorously and bowing in response to his popularity.

For the main event Oceanus had come down from the gallery and joined the emperor on his podium. The gladiators paraded around the arena in formation and came to a halt in front of the emperor's podium, forming ranks in front of Domitian, his family and their guards.

The music came to an abrupt halt and the gladiators fell down on one knee. They greeted the emperor with a bellowing out of the ritual chant in homage to Claudius: *Ave imperato morituri te salutant!* 'We who are about to die salute you!'

The procession retreated into the subterranean passages of the amphitheatre and the 'warm-up' fights began, the men engaging in mock battles randomly with each other using the wooden swords similar to those used in training in the gladiator school. They had been stuck down in the dressing room since early morning and took pleasure in stretching their limbs and warming up.

Lucia had been scrutinising the whole event in great detail to see if there were any clues as to which way the day would go. She passed a note to Thelos, saying: 'Take this message down to the umpire and ask him to give it to Nasica. Run!'

Meanwhile Severus was warming up with Nasica. He tried to get the feel of the young man, as it had been a long time since he had fought a left-hander and didn't think in a million years he would be fighting one today.

'Remember what I told you, son,' said Severus. 'Our best way out of this is to trust in the gods and fight to the death as if we were sworn enemies and mean to finish each other. You have youth on your side, I have experience. We're well matched. But if it looks like you need to finish me, make a clean job of it. And, whatever she says, make sure you take good care of Lucia.'

'I promise you sir – ah, Severus – I will do as you say. And in the event of the opposite result occurring, I assume that you will, on your honour, do the same.'

'On my honour, I will do the very same,' promised Severus and added, 'Nasica, do people actually still talk like that? You know "on your honour, you humble servant, my liege, etcetera"?'

Nasica looked at Severus directly in the eye. His face softened into a smile of recognition.

The two men grasped each other by the left forearm. Their right arms were holding the sword and protected by the two-piece *manica* armour on the fore and upper arms. They stared hard into each other's eyes for a second or two, holding each other's gaze, looking for an answer to what the big question of the day would bring.

The chief umpire signalled to the gladiators to leave the ring. As Nasica passed the umpire he was handed the note.

'Someone's got an admirer,' joked the umpire. 'Don't worry, Nasica, I didn't peek. I hope for your sake it's not Domitia Longina. She's a notorious man-eater. Would have you for breakfast, lad.'

Back in the gladiator holding area he opened the note:

Nasica. I will see you after the fight. I know you and Severus can survive this as you are both the finest men I have ever known. I love you. Tell my father Severus I love him. And when this is over we need to start to find a way out of this. This is no life for humans. Or animals. Your Lucia.

★★★★★

The crowd is becoming restless. The umpires are being slow in changing from the fake fights to the real combats and are now completing the installation of the 'well-honed metal,' *the ferra actua*, just outside the fight boundaries that had now been accurately adjusted by the assistant umpires. The crowd starts a slow hand clap and is in danger of becoming out of control if the delay continues, so the chief umpire hurries on the *praegenarii*; these are the 'opening act' gladiators, fighting with a whip, club and shield. The first few engagements happen to be a couple of clowns and they soon have the audience in the palm of their hands with their hilariously slapstick routines. Even the emperor and his wife are laughing. So is Oceanus.

'He seems to be in a good mood,' says Nasica to Severus. 'Perhaps the day will go well.'

'Don't count on it,' replies Severus, his usual cheerful self. 'It's these bastards you've got to worry about,' indicating the frenzied mob. 'He will do whatever they tell him, and no mistake.'

'Lucia sent down a note. She said, "Tell my father I love him".'

'Right. Good,' says Severus. 'If you see her before I do, tell her I love her too.'

Nasica nods.

'And now, let us prepare. We're on after the *Thraex versus Retiarius* bout. Pity the *Thraex*. Domitian hates Thracians. Any kind of Greeks, for that matter. Good news for me. Not so good for you. Sorry, mate.'

By this time the crowd is roaring with laughter. Two more *praegenarii* have come on, dressed as *provocatores*, complicating the joke even further. They make things even more amusing for the crowd because one of them is a dwarf and the other has only one arm. Turning the role of the *provocator* on its head the *praegenarii* can easily outwit and keep the mock *provocatores* at bay.

The crowd is lapping it up. Oceanus has them well pleased from the get-go. To round it off he has a pair of *laquerarii*, or lasso fighters, walk into the middle of the fighting area spinning their ropes, unseen by the dwarf and the one-armed clown who are then caught, roped up, and carried off as part of the novelty act. For Oceanus, at least, the day is going well. He knows how to put on a show and what the audience likes. He tempers the bloodshed with a few good laughs.

Before the chief umpire can make the sign, the *retiarius* for the next bout strides into the arena. Much to the spectators' delight it is the gladiatrix Amazonia. A loud cheer goes up as all six and a half feet of her raises herself up to her full height and strips off her tunic. She reveals her muscled, naked torso from the waist up and roars to the crowd doing an African tribal war dance, her huge firm breasts quivering in time to the beat that she sets with her trident.

The crowd roars back in response to her war cry, and in an almost foregone conclusion (one never knows with the mob) the crowd is won over. Whatever entrance the *Thraex* makes now he can never follow the roar of Amazonia nor the magnificence of her upper torso. The umpires call them to the centre of the fighting area and the game is on.

Meanwhile, in the armoury, Severus is having some adjustments made to his *manica*, while Nasica takes the opportunity to visit the latrines. Strange, he thought, facing death, that only the smallest details of the here and now seem to be important at this very moment. Hooking up with Severus they march in step together down the main corridor towards the roar of the crowd, helmets under arms, swords in hand.

Nasica has the advantage in that as well as being younger and lighter on his feet than Severus he is also more lightly armoured, with quilted protection leggings, metal shin guards, shield, and *gladius*, but with the added bonus of a spear; whilst not so useful in hand-to-hand combat, it could give him a one-off advantage to wound and disarm his opponent. Like the *murmillo*, he has a two-piece *manica* arm guard and a large helmet with a brim and a dashing plume of white to set off the brilliance of his white loincloth.

Severus as *murmillo,* on the other hand, is heavily armed with equipment that certainly slowed him, but with his extra strength and power he can turn it to his advantage. He also has the added bonus of a good-sized *gladius* almost a metre long and the legionnaire-style shield, which were exactly the ones he used in his military service across the empire for the best part of two decades, and they fit him like gloves. He is topped off by his great bronze helmet, a fish on the crest finished with a horse-hair plume for style, and has a forbidding-looking, ornately sculpted, 'grill' face visor.

Halfway down the tunnel they hear the roar of the crowd. And start to run as best they can to the holding area at the side of the arena as the previous bout reaches its climax. And over, indeed it was. It had lasted all of five minutes. Amazonia, having already rattled the *Thraex* beyond belief in the warm-up, had stalked him around the arena for a few minutes putting the fear of Jove into him with her mighty roars, until, fully in command of her stagecraft, she forced the *Thraex* to end up directly in front of the podium and the emperor's entourage.

Amazonia threw aside her net, took aim and as she did so the *Thraex*, not feeling himself in danger, turned and bowed to the emperor and his retinue. As he turned back, he didn't even hear the rush of air as Amazonia's trident, which she had launched like a javelin thrower only with twice as much skill and accuracy, plunged through his throat, pinning him to the floor like a butterfly on a collector's spreading board. Slowly the life began to ebb out of the *Thraex*, who didn't even have the strength to stick out his left index finger to ask for mercy. He was too far gone. And the crowd in turn were even further gone.

'*Iugula! Iugula! Iugula!*' they chanted as one, demanding his throat be cut. The *Thraex*'s last act was to look up to the crowd and see them giving the *police verso*, the turned thumb. Domitian nodded his assent and Amazonia took her *gladius* and delivered the *coup de grâce* to the throat, in line with the mob's demands.

★★★★★

'*Habet! Hoc Habet! Habet! Hoc Habet! Habet! Hoc Habet!!*' chant the chillingly thrilled spectators, delighted that the *Thraex* had received the iron.

Amazonia is the heroine of the day. Severus and Nasica have retreated to different sides of the holding area to make their peace and pay their respects to the goddess Nemesis. They catch each other's eye simultaneously and exchange a 'tough act to follow' look. But follow it they must.

Amazonia deservedly takes her bow as the crowd salutes her. The slaves run on to clean up the fighting area, remove the corpse and leave the sand looking as if there had been no slaughter.

Up on the podium Domitian looks through a basket of balls that has been handed to him by Oceanus. He casually makes his selection and throws it to Amazonia, who catches it first time. She calls one of the umpires over to have him read what it says.

'A horse!' shouts the umpire. 'A horse!'

The crowds cheer and Amazonia walks proudly and triumphantly back down the corridor and into the dressing room without looking left or right.

Not wanting to lose the momentum the chief umpire double-checks with his assistant umpires that the sand has been cleaned up properly and immediately moves on to the next combat: Severus the *murmillo* versus Nasica the *hoplomachus*.

Already the favourite, the crowd has already started to chant Severus's name, breaking it into its component syllables and providing a warm welcome into the arena. Pretty Boy Oceanus had advertised the *murmillo* as a home-town hero when in fact Severus had nothing to do with the *colonia*. As the *hoplomachus*, Nasica was already marked out as a 'Greek': the main justification for this type of gladiator class was to represent the enemy in the amphitheatre by replicating the Greek warriors of the time. He was the ancient equivalent of the 'baddie'. He was also left-handed. As far back as the earliest of Roman times the left side had a positive sense given that the *Augures*, the divinations, came from the eastern side. The negative, or sinister, meaning came later from the Greek and henceforth in all romance languages.

The chief umpire brings the pair together for the pre-match pep-talk and sends them to either side of the fighting area. Nasica, the more lightly armoured, leaps nimbly over to the perimeter, while Severus clunks heavily over to face his opponent. The chief umpire gives the signal that the combat may start.

While Nasica is still adjusting his greave, Severus, who until that moment has been exaggeratedly lumbering around like a juggernaut, suddenly leaps into action and quick as a flash has rushed Nasica with lightning speed in an attempt to knock him immediately to the ground. At the very last minute Nasica realises what is going on and leaps backwards and in the process drops his spear, forfeiting in an instant one of the main advantages he has over the *murmillo*.

Stepping back, Severus raises his arms to the crowd and shakes his fish-shaped helmet, causing them to break into cheers and further cries of 'Se-ver-us, Se-ver-us Se-ver-us!' Nasica is rooted to the ground – stunned by the noise of the arena and blinded to danger by a sense of primal fear deep down in his being. It's the first time he has faced naked iron for real, and every veteran says that it is a feeling that you remember for the rest of your natural days.

Coming to his senses, Nasica pulls himself together and rounds on Severus, his ego bruised by this first opening gambit. He baits him, dancing into the centre of the fighting area, and uses the advantage of his light armour to move the *murmillo* around and in doing so tire him and hopefully lure him into a vulnerable place. At a certain point Nasica sees his chance and comes in under and aims for the flesh on Severus's sword arm at the elbow, which is only protected by rough cotton wadding in between the plates of the *manica*. He catches the material, but it doesn't pierce; however, he delivers a strong blow that nearly makes Severus drop his sword and he goes down on one knee to maintain his grip on it. If he drops it, he is lost. He struggles to his feet and faces the *hoplomachus* down. For that is what he has become. A type of gladiator. Nasica, his future son-in-law, is a mere memory.

And then he's back in his face, up close and personal, slashing desperately, trying to find some purchase with his feet and a way through the armour and the shield. The clash of iron-on-iron echoes through the amphitheatre as they cross swords back and forth over the arena – thrust, parry, thrust, parry, then a massive whack to the body of Nasica with his legionnaire's heavy shield sends the young nobleman flying across the sand where he flails like a gutted fish on the quayside.

The gloves are now off, and Nasica is seriously angry. A mouth full of sand further fires his fury. What also doesn't help is that he has dropped his sword, which in the mêlée he hasn't noticed. In a second Severus is on it; he discards his shield and retrieves Nasica's sword with the nimbleness of a ballet dancer. Now he has two and Nasica has none.

The crowd roars. They can smell blood and they want it to be Nasica's.

'Se-ver-us, Se-ver-us! Se-ver-us, Se-ver-us!' they cry, howling for Nasica's guts to be spilled.

The *murmillo*, however, is far from being buoyed by his success, as he now realises. He finds himself completely out of breath, out of adrenalin, and a searing pain in his chest tells him he needs to fill his lungs, calm down, re-charge and find a way out. In a flashing blur he hauls his two swords around to face Nasica, who has miraculously recovered, taken possession of the *murmillo*'s hefty shield, and recovered possession of his spear.

Severus looks to the umpire for support. Surely this was illegal? Apparently not. As Nasica launches his spear at Severus there is a silence, and as if in slow motion the trajectory of the object takes it directly into the soft tissue of Severus's left flank between his belt and body armour, causing him to scream out in pain – and rage at having left himself wide open.

'You fucking left-hander,' shouts Severus, and moves towards the *hoplomachus* with a vengeance, the spear still stuck in his side.

'I thought you liked to fight left-handers,' says Nasica through gritted teeth, spitting out sand from his mouth. 'You didn't do too badly against Lefty Urbanus, your old mate from the legion.'

This is a low blow, but Nasica was learning. You have to use every method at your disposal to catch your enemy off guard. Nasica is calling on his training and channelling all his energy into hating the man behind the *murmillo* helmet. At that very moment Nasica slams the ex-legionnaire's shield into his face, crushing his helmet against the flesh of his skull and causing untold pain.

Severus hits the floor.

Boos from the crowd, and shouts of derision follow.

'Come on Severus, you fat bastard, you can beat a poncey nobleman easy.'

'Get up, old timer, or he might stop the clock on you!' quips one wag from the cheap seats.

Severus is face down in the sand and Nasica approaches with the *gladius* Severus dropped as he fell. Severus rolls over like a beached whale, breaks the spear in half, pulls it through out of his side and fires it at the approaching *hoplomachus*, spearing him in his right shoulder and immediately disarming him. Nasica is at the mercy of Severus who heaves himself to his feet and, sword in hand, begins to move towards Nasica, who by now is completely unarmed and losing a lot of blood. Severus has the sword, but he has also been haemorrhaging blood at a serious rate for the last ten minutes.

At the same time they both fall to their knees, exhausted, totally wasted, and several litres of blood the lighter. It is all they can do to remain upright. Two grown men wearing helmets that look like the heads of very ugly fish kneel before each other and fall on to their hands and knees unable to make another move, the sweat pouring off their bodies only superseded by the blood which flows freely from their wounds.

Raising both his arms in the air in the air and holding two wooden sticks in his hands, the chief umpire declares the fight over to the massive approval of the crowd which is now acting as a single unit and up on its feet, cheering and bellowing and generally have a great afternoon at the games.

This is what it is all about, thinks Pretty Boy to himself in self-congratulation at having paired the two, however stealthily.

Then the crowd begin their chant. Slowly at first, and then building to a massive roar, made great by the acoustics of the amphitheatre which amplify everything into another dimension.

'*Mit-te! Mit-te! Mit-te! Mit-te! Mit-te! Mit-te!*' over and over again they chant, demanding that both men be allowed to live.

Picking up on the cue from the crowd and having had his bloodlust satisfied with the perfectly agreeable slaying of the Thracian in the previous bout, the Emperor Domitian steps forwards.

Silence reigns in the arena. You can hear a pin drop.

'People of Pietas Iulia,' he begins, 'these tokens that I hold here can never recompense Severus and Nasica for their bravery in the arena today. The amphitheatre of Colonia Pietas Iulia deserves to be one of the finest in the empire. Look at the edifice. It is truly a jewel in the crown of our empire.'

He looks over to Oceanus and continues, 'Oceanus, our new procurator, *editor* of the games, and *lanista* of the gladiators that you have seen fighting here today, has been charged to make the games in Pietas Iulia the leading games of all the colonies. To that end I have asked him to form a school of gladiators which will be attached to the arena.'

The audience cheer and applaud politely. Oceanus beams, smug, thinking of the money. And the fun he can have with it.

'But after this performance today by the tyro Nasica, whose father I knew and who was a good and noble man from the line of Scipio Africanus, defeater of Hannibal; and Severus, whose career I have followed since I was a boy, we have found the perfect team to lead the gladiator training in our newly founded school. We therefore free them from their further contracts as fighters in the arena and appoint them to the position of doctor and assistant doctor of the new gladiator school of Colonia Pietas Iulia!'

Oceanus is not looking so smug now, as he wasn't expecting this one, but there's nothing he can do about it. He'll fix the 'doctors' later, he thinks to himself.

As the crowds show their appreciation and applaud, the next pair of gladiators, a Samnite and a *secutor*, enter the arena. Stretcher bearers rush on to carry off Severus and Nasica to have their wounds tended to.

Lucia is waiting ringside.

'Take them to my quarters,' she says, indicating the waiting official surgeons from the saniarium; 'I wouldn't let those two butchers near my dogs, let alone two valuable ex-gladiators.'

Chapter VI
The Killing Fields
Democratic Federative Yugoslavia, 1943

As he freewheeled on the old sit-up-and-beg bike down the winding roads to Oslići, followed at speed by Vito who enjoyed nothing more than a good run, Nino was still high on the adrenalin of dispatching his father into the next world, and also at the sheer thrill of the prospect of being able to leave a life that had shown him nothing but misery in his 15 short years. His brother would be proud of him, and he would go to the Partisans, join Pino, win the war, and play his part in the building of the Socialist Federal Republic of Yugoslavia. The fear of capture and retribution had yet to kick in. The remorse would come later. But, so far, so good; the full moral force of his pre-meditated patricide had yet to kick in.

It was only when he got to the outskirts of the village of Oslići that he started to get his wits about him and realise that he could not allow himself to be seen racing away from Draguć. Even more incriminating would be that he was on his dad's bike, a vehicle that Tomislav prized above all his other possessions and would never allow anyone else to ride, let alone his least-favourite son. Also, in the wake of yesterday's reprisals, there would be patrols and Nino was immediately and easily identifiable by having Vito in tow.

Pulling down an unpaved road to the right, he and Vito diverted off in the direction of Hum, a strategic move designed to throw anyone in pursuit off the scent. He hid the bike deep in the undergrowth a short distance from a *kazun*, a traditional, dry-stone circular building used as a shepherd's shelter; he would have a solid landmark that he would be able to use should he by any chance need to retrieve the bike in the future.

The *kazun* was as Istrian as the goat or *manestre* or *malvasia*. It was synonymous with Istria. These simple little huts provided shelter from the storm, the winds that drove men mad, and the burning heat of summer. They also protected against pilfering during harvest time. Protecting people, shepherds and sheep, the *kazun* symbolised a safe haven to Nino and his ancestors. Now it would hide his father's treasured bicycle for posterity.

Taking the bag with all his worldly possessions, his truffles and his father's pistol, he headed swiftly across the countryside, more or less as the crow would have flown, following ancient paths and deer tracks which from years scouting the area as a young boy and hunting with his father had become second nature to him.

This was rich and largely unexplored truffle country, and it was hard to keep Vito, in his new-found incarnation of truffle-dog, moving swiftly through the forest, as the dog felt there were a myriad of opportunities to earn treats of extraordinarily high value. Nino, whose own covetousness for the black diamond had grown, made a note for future reference to return.

He reached the outskirts of Hum, a tiny municipality, in an hour and skirted the village. It contained a café which, proportionally speaking, contained the biggest number of gossip mongers in the universe. It also, by virtue of being a municipality, had a policeman – and news travelled fast in Istria. Taking the track to Brnobići and then on up in the direction of Roč, Nino and Vito had taken one of the most ancient paths in Istria: a route marked, literally, by its history.

Nino's history teacher had told him that the area was one of the cradles of the local Glagolitic script, the oldest-known Slavic alphabet created in the ninth century by Saint Cyril, and examples of which included, most famously, the Hum graffito. They had been on a school trip one day with Mr Valli, their teacher, and he had shown them the painted walls of the small church of Saint Jerome at Hum cemetery, where there are about 40 inscribed examples of Glagolitic graffiti. So he was very familiar with the highways and byways of the area.

The class could hardly believe it when Valli, an Italian from the Veneto, and who seemed to have come from the twelfth century himself or even could have personally known the monks Cyril and Methodus, bent over an ancient inscription said to be from the 1100s on the right side of the apse and read aloud, translating and transliterating: 'For Martin the Blacksmith has had 30; yet one more is for him.' The teacher's words rang out in his memory.

This is how history had become real for Nino: the fact that an unknown Glagolitic-using priest from Hum could register the number of offered masses for Martin the Blacksmith. His desire to go in and look at it again was overridden by the thought that he needed to get to his uncle's in Buzet by nightfall and the dawning realisation that he might never see the frescoes on the Church of Saint Rocco in Draguć again, let alone discover what was under the whitewash on the walls and ceiling of Saint Eliseus.

He made a vow to himself there and then as he passed the Church of Saint Jerome that he would reveal what he believed to have been painted over by someone in Saint Eliseus's. He then cursed his stupidity. He was a Partisan now; and as Faida had told him, God was well and truly dead.

Caught in a reverie, he was nuzzled by Vito as a signal to move on. He had to keep going forwards for at least another three hours to Buzet, via Kotli. Nino, the weight of the whole world on his shoulders, hoisted his duffle bag onto his back, broke into a trot and left another story from his past behind him.

He ran, as hard as he possibly could, with Vito trotting ahead of him as a pacemaker. As he ran, Nino could think of nothing else but his mental snapshot of the face of his dead father. Somehow at peace. A serenity on his face that Nino had never seen in life. Like one of the frescoes. But more than anything else he felt a huge sense of relief. Like the lifting of a heavy burden. No longer would he have to see daily the look of grief and disappointment on his father's face, and the hate in his eyes that he never lost for Nino for killing the only person he had ever been able to love in his whole life.

*****

Since beating a rapid retreat across country in the wake of their inauguration in Draguć, the newly formed Pino Budicin battalion hadn't had much luck in getting very far from the enemy. The marching unit made it across country in a few hours to the safe village of Vrh, the highest town in the area. From a strategic point of view it dominated the landscape, looking down on the one side to Buzet and the Mirna, and on the other to Brtonigla, Draguć and Grimalda. With every man woman and child in Vrh loyal to the Partisan cause – including the local priest, Father Marino – the truck and the troops find refuge in the capacious barn of a Communist Partisan sympathiser.

'Our scouts have been out, and there is a lot of activity on the roads. Looks like the Germans are still searching for us and don't think we can have got very far,' Giuseppe, the 'Neapolitan', tells Pino as they feed themselves on a welcome *manestra* in the farmer's kitchen, the farmer and his family keeping a respectful distance.

'I've also been talking to the priest, Father Marino,' says Pino. 'We can trust him. There were reprisals in Grimalda today. Sixteen of ours for one of theirs. Sixty-four men. It will be hard to bring the harvest in this year around Grimalda.'

'I'm sorry, Pino.'

'Don't be sorry, Giuseppe,' Pino comes back quickly. 'I'm just hoping the bastards got my old man. That would be a real cause for celebration.'

'How are the men doing?'

'We have three injured quite badly, stretcher cases who have to ride in the truck, and a couple of walking wounded. Faida and the girls are taking good care of them, and everyone has been happy for the rest. But we can't stay here for much longer.'

'No, we need to be on the move tonight. We'll head out at nightfall. I'll give you the details later.'

'OK. I'll go and tell the men,' says Pino, picking up his rifle and cap and heading out into the farmyard. He shouts back to the farmer's wife, 'Best *manestre* this side of Učka! Thank you!' And as an afterthought, he adds, 'What's the secret?'

The farmer's wife, suspicious eyes framed by thick wrinkles carved by years of outdoor labour, looks at him as if checking whether he can be trusted to be told where the family jewels are kept. Eventually, grudgingly, she speaks. 'There are many secrets. But this one I will tell you. It's in the thickening. Chop very small the uncooked bacon, garlic and parsley and mash it to a paste. Boil it and add to the soup. Cook four hours. At the end add two spoons of olive oil in a pot this size. Then leave it. Cook and soup must both rest a little.'

Lighting up a cigarette, Pino walks over to barn to warn the men of their imminent departure this evening. As he enters, he hears Faida's voice. She has been teaching some of the men how to read and write, the Partisan thinking being that if you didn't have actual literacy, you could never have political literacy. In any case, Pino is curious to see what she is doing. He stands back, near her makeshift infirmary, where the patients are all eagerly listening in as well.

The six o'clock Angelus bell rings out across the hillside between Vrh and Motovun with the great bell tower of Motovun, known as Veli Jože, as the main landmark visible in the distance between the two towns. Through the west window of the barn the early evening light falls on Faida's face, and to Pino she is simply the most beautiful woman he has ever met.

'Can you hear the bell?' says Faida. 'It's coming from the bell tower you can see in the distance. The tower is called Big Joe. It's called Big Joe because it is named after a giant. Yes, a real giant who lived in Motovun around 500 years ago.'

Faida looks around at all the men. They are aged from 16 to 60, hardened by battle, ill-equipped, a rag-tag bunch of mostly ethnic Italians, but this 18-year-old girl from central Bosnia is confident that she can command their full attention. Not only is she a born storyteller, but she also knows that the story she tells was written by of one of the Partisan's own home-grown storytellers and authors, and this adds to her confidence.

'Veli Jože, Big Joe, lived in the lands around the Motovun Venetian hill village. One day he was taken by ship to Venice across the bay, the Gulf of Trieste, by his landlord. On the voyage he shared a bunk with another giant called Ilija, for there were many larger-than-life people in Istria, just like today. Ilija gave Jože one piece of important advice: that he should live his life as a free man and not let anyone be his master. Before they reached Venezia their ship sank in a storm, but Big Joe, who had learned to swim in the fast-flowing Mirna, the river below Motovun, was able to save himself. That river had earlier been furrowed by another giant. The greatest Istrian giant, Dragonja, who according to ancient legend ploughed the channel that was to become the river Mirna. But that is another story. Before long he came into contact with other giants in the Veneto and they worked in the hills around Aquileia. After a while they discovered gold, finding the nuggets easily accessible everywhere. Soon the landlords came to join them and even acted as servants for their former slaves, and they too became rich.'

The Partisans are not happy with the turn that the tale is taking and there are some boos and whistles from the audience.

'Soon it became time for the giants to divide up their treasure. It was at this point that a big fight started, and the greed of his fellow giants drove Big Joe so far to distraction that he set fire to the shed of grain they had been keeping for winter. And so the other giants chased Big Joe away and he took refuge with Civetta, who took him in and because he became leader of the serfs he was able to look after Big Joe, who had lost his faith in everything.'

'And they all lived happily ever after,' says a cynical old Partisan, spitting out a load of tobacco juice onto the floor of the barn.

'Well, they did. But not in the way that you think,' replies Faida. 'The story ends like this. Although Jože had everything he needed, he burned with a desire to return to his hometown. He travelled through the Veneto and down through the mountains to Istria with hope in his heart and ready to make a new start. But just before he entered the town, he remembered the words of Ilija: that he should live his life as a free man and not let anyone be his master. And so he left Civetta and Motovun and was never to be seen again. Except in spirit. Every day that the bell rings out the hour we remember the giant Big Joe, who freed his own mind and body from serfdom and who lived in freedom for the rest of his life. He gave his name to the great tower we can just see now in the mist, over there in Motovun.'

Pino starts the applause, and the Partisans pick it up, especially the younger ones who more than anything else need to have some kind of break from their war.

'Thanks to comrade Faida for the story,' says Pino. 'One thing she didn't tell you is that this story was written by one of us. Another Partisan, fighting to free our brothers and form the Socialist Federal Republic of Yugoslavia. He is one of our greatest poets. Like you, he is fighting the good fight. And it tells us the importance of so many things, not least the learning of our letters. Because if we can't read or write it's very hard for us to share our dreams.'

'Thank you, comrade Pino,' says Faida. 'Perhaps in our next lesson in literacy we will ask you to tell some of your stories.'

'I would like to do that,' replies one of the young Partisans in the makeshift field hospital. 'We have many more stories of giants in Istria. Vrh had its own giant, as did Buzet and Grožnjan. Each giant lived on the hilltops and founded villages there in which small people also lived. They lived there all together and ate truffles and drank *malvasia* and everyone was happy. Then one day the evil dwarves came and put the black poison on the truffles. The giants loved the truffles so much they were unable to resist them and so they ate the poisoned truffles.'

'What happened after that?' asks Faida.

'I don't know. I didn't hear the end of the story.'

The room erupts in friendly laughter mingled with a few crude barrack-room farting noises. It has been a couple of hours' respite from the misery of war and the soldiers are grateful.

'I'm sorry to rain on everyone's parade,' says Pino, 'but tonight we are pulling out. As soon as we have the all-clear we'll be leaving. You have two hours to gather your kit together and be ready for the road.'

The men gradually start to move and gather their belongings for the long march through the night.

'What about the injured?' asks Faida. 'We have a couple who are still in a critical condition.'

'They have to come with us,' says Pino. 'They can ride in the truck. I know it's not ideal, but we can't leave them here. The good people of Vrh have already put themselves in enough danger by giving us shelter. The Neapolitan will give us our orders on departure.' In a lower voice, so only she can hear him: 'And you were fabulous. The Nazor story of Veli Jože is one of my favourites.'

Walking away, Faida turns and mouths 'I love you!' to Pino and goes out to get her supper in the farmyard.

★★★★★

The storm came out of nowhere. It was a classic *bora*. The wind came from the north quickly and brought with it a huge drop in temperature, which even had the ever-hardy Vito shivering up against his master's legs. Nino had spotted the gathering of the gun-metal grey clouds over the Učka mountains and feared the worst. He had just cut around the village of Kotli and was heading down to the flat flood lands of the Mirna riverbank. This had long since been straightened by Josef Ressel of the Austro-Hungarian Forestry Commission, inventor of the propeller, who diverted the once-winding river around Motovun in order to take the mosquitoes and the concomitant threat of malaria away from its inhabitants.

This had created a flood plain with a new forest that was also humid enough to be of interest to people like Nino and Vito because it also accidentally increased its fertility in truffles.

The wind whipped up a terrible mess. It was known to be one of the most powerful winds in the Mediterranean, reaching up to 300 kilometres per hour in the Kvarner region. Nino was currently huddling under a bridge trying to get shelter, as it was almost impossible to walk without getting blown over or, indeed, scooped into the river. It was on such a night as this that the *bora* blew a hurricane-force gale and caused Veli Jože's boat to wreck on the Veneto coast, where he met Civetta, who later saved him. 'Civetta' was also the name of the boat on which Josef Ressel's propeller was first tested in 1829 in the Trieste harbour, making around six knots without the *bora* before the steam conduits exploded. All further tests were banned by the police. What goes around, comes around.

For Nino, sitting in the wet under the bridge, his moral trials and tribulations were the furthest thing from his mind. But he did see a break in the storm clouds coming, and as the storm abated he quickly changed his clothes using the few pieces he had thrown in his duffle bag. He smartened himself up and wearing one of Pino's cast-off jackets he cut quite the figure as he crossed the bridge into Buzet and headed up the steep hill to the old town towards his uncle Armando's restaurant.

★★★★★

He is slightly out of breath as he makes it to the central square in Buzet which is busier than normal, it being a Saturday, and with several off-duty German soldiers out for a night on the town, in so far as that is possible in the town of truffles. The irony of there being a delicious surfeit of culinary aphrodisiacs being offset by the paucity of female companionship is not lost on the German officers sent to this outpost of the Reich. Still, it could be worse: they could have a posting on the Eastern Front.

As Nino walks into the bar of Armando's restaurant he sees that a few German NCOs and officers have chosen the terrace to entertain a few of the local ladies.

Armando spots Nino on his way in and nods for him to sit out on the terrace. There is an immediate complicity between them.

'What'll it be, sir? Your usual beer?'

Nino, man of the world, nods his assent and pulls Vito close under his legs. Germans make the dog nervous. Not so for uncle Armando, who appears to revel in the special relationship he has with his German guests, conversing easily with them in their native tongue and showing no signs of resentment that a couple of them happen to be out with local girls having a good time.

The bell from the clock tower rings out eleven chimes. Armando goes to each table and settles up every bill. Finally, when the last guests have gone, he reaches Nino's table.

'Right, you, indoors now,' says Armando. 'I don't know what's happened, but you coming down here with luggage doesn't look good.'

Coming out from behind the bar, Dušica reaches out to embrace him. Before she gets to him, he bursts into tears and is sobbing uncontrollably into her breast. Armando locks and bolts the door, goes behind the bar and re-appears with three *loza* in double-quick time.

'Here, have this,' he says to both. All three drink. Nerves steadied; Armando starts. 'Here's what I know. The Pino Budicin battalion was formally inaugurated in Draguć two days ago. Correct?'

Nino nods.

'It was ambushed by two German patrols, and the next day there were reprisals for the four German soldiers killed. Sixty-four men executed in the square in Grimalda. Half the battalion made it back to the caves in the mountains. The other half is still missing.'

'I don't know about the battalion,' says Nino, recovering from his emotional outburst, and blowing his nose with the handkerchief that Dušica has given him. 'But I saw everything in Grimalda. It's worse than you think. Father Frane and my father were there. Helping the Germans. Choosing the men to execute. There wasn't much choice; they had rounded up pretty much everyone in the area. Then they machine-gunned them. With their families watching.'

Dušica and Armando exchange a look.

'And that's why when I got home,' continues Nino, hardening, 'I shot him.'

As Dušica moves towards Nino to embrace him again, there's a harsh rapping at the front door.

'We're closed, go away!' shouts Armando.

The knocking continues, accompanied by a gruff German voice, 'Open up, immediately!'

Armando unbolts and opens the doors to the café. Standing in the half-light of the entrance is the *Hauptmann* from the *kuebelwagen* who gave Nino and Pino a lift that night from Rovinj. The night that everything changed.

'Good evening, Armando,' says the *Hauptmann*, and with a nod and a gallant heel-click to Dušica, 'Madame!'

Vito comes out from under the table and walks up to Schiffer and licks his hand.

'Ah, my friend from Rovinj. Such an ugly little specimen. But smart, very smart. Like his young master, I am sure.'

'And to what do I owe the honour of a visit at this late hour?' asks Armando.

'I am going on leave for a week back to Munich tomorrow, and I wanted to drop by to see if you have any of your wonderful fruits of the forest floor in stock. White, preferably, but any will do. Beggars can't be choosers back in Bavaria these days. They have barely a *wurstchen* between them, poor things.'

'I'm afraid we had a complete run on them for the weekend, *Hauptmann*,' says Armando. 'It looks like many of your comrades with the same furlough had the identical idea. It's a pity; if you had told me in advance, I would have spared you the best of them.'

'Not to worry, Armando,' says Schiffer, 'we will survive. Give me a couple of bottles instead of your excellent walnut brandy, the *orahovica*.'

'Coming right up!'

'Sir,' ventures Nino, 'thank you for the lift home that night. I have some truffles for you, sir.'

Reaching into his duffle bag he pulls out his softwood box of truffles. He opens it for the *Hauptmann*. Inside are half a dozen pieces, wrapped in old newspaper and as fragrant as an autumn morning. Schiffer breathes in the scent: two little Istrian white truffles, the *magnatum pico*; a couple of fine summer truffles in good condition, if a bit dry and light; and finally a few excellent-sized pieces of black winter truffle, the *aestivum*. All make a welcome package for the captain, who turns to Vito.

'You are lucky, young man, to have such a dog,' says Schiffer. 'That he can find such riches in these soggy old woods is nothing beyond a miracle. Almost as miraculous as the wonderful frescoes I saw in your village yesterday.'

'In the Church of Saint Rocco?' says Nino.

'Yes, the least impressive of churches and the most impressive of frescoes,' says the captain. 'I had some business to do there yesterday. No doubt you heard: the Partisans killed four of my men who caught them while out on patrol. Apparently, the Communists were having a big party in your village in broad daylight. Idiots.'

'You only found them because you had an informer,' blurts out Nino.

'Let me weigh these for you, sir,' butts in Armando, changing the subject. 'Then I can give you a price. Special discount for regular customers.'

'Well, someone seems to be well informed,' says the *Hauptmann*, walking deliberately towards the door.

'And what would your name be?' asks the *Hauptmann*.

'Nino. Nino Mihailić.'

The officer turns sharply back to Nino, and as he does so he moves to unbutton his service revolver. But he's too late – Nino already has the Beretta in his hand which he fires and at such short range it cuts the officer down with a single bullet to the forehead, blowing his brains over the mirror immediately behind him. He falls dead at their feet.

Armando and Dušica look at each other in disbelief and then at Nino, who holds the gun in hand as if in a trance.

Rushing to the door, Armando bolts and secures it, and telling Dušica, 'Come on. We'd better move this one and get cleaned up before the breakfast rush starts.'

As they drag the body past Nino to the cold storage at the back of the restaurant, Armando looks at him, a cross between disbelief and awe: 'My son, my son, what have you done?'

Part Three

Chapter VII

Swimming with Dinosaurs

Istria: December 26th, 2019

A row of cypress trees marked the perimeter of the garden at Stancija Mihailić, and in the clear morning light they stood as proud and beautiful as any in Tuscany; far wilder, occasionally bent by the wind, and significantly less manicured than their Provençal counterparts, but things of beauty just the same. The theme of curated wilderness was one which permeated the whole of the extensive gardens of the property; a taste of what the countryside could look like if worked just a little, maintaining a narrow variety of indigenous native plants that, given the altitude of Draguć, would be able to survive some vigorous weathering, summer and winter. In the general disarray of the countryside in this part of the world a little attention to aesthetics went a long way.

Leading down to the cypresses, which were all of 10 metres high, were an ancient olive grove on one side and a more recently planted lavender field on the other, interspersed by a vast carpet of prostrate spider rosemary which lapped down the slope arriving at the pool; this was surrounded by a thick windbreak hedge of regular rosemary a metre and a half high. These were the sights and smells that had lit up Marco's senses as he ventured out onto the rear terrace of the Rose House and gazed in wonder at the expansive Mediterranean grounds of Stancija Mihailić. Indeed, the Rose House also did what it said on the tin, and with the onset of spring its walls and roof would become ablaze with rambling roses. After his three-year sojourn in the squats of Oxford and Hackney – and through the haze of his emerging hangover – it all unfolded before him as if in a surreal dream.

Walking down the gravel path to the main house, Marco revels in the thought that the sun is on the back of his neck, and he can sit and have his breakfast in little more than a T-shirt on the terrace on Boxing Day or, as the Istrians call it, Sveti Stjepan after the first martyr of Christianity. It's winter but the sun is out. The sky is a piercing clear azure. The view towards the coast to Trieste gives off, real or imagined, vague outlines of its factory chimneys, barely visible across the horizon in the shadow of the snow-capped Julian Alps.

In the 24 hours since his arrival in Istria he had celebrated Christmas with the best part of his natural (and un-natural family); been told that his best friend had accidentally seduced his ex-girlfriend (apparently the accidental nature of it made it OK); and been witness to an intrusion that had caused all his grandfather's precious truffle dogs to be released from their cages down on the edge of the property and either stolen, poisoned or let to run free through Istria, freelancing in the hunting spree that takes place between Christmas and New Year in the area. Never a dull moment, thinks Marco as he contemplates the countryside before him.

Faida silently appears beside Marco on the terrace. She comes bearing caffeine and, equally important, *baklava*.

'I think you are in need of these,' says his grandmother, joining him at the table in the sun.

'Where would we be without the Turks,' says Marco. 'The Ottomans have a lot to answer for.'

'You're telling me. Now you enjoy your breakfast,' says Faida. 'Zvonko and the kids have left. He's dropping them back to Svetlana for the rest of the holidays. Emina took her motor bike and rode home. Crazy girl, riding that thing in winter. She told me to lend you my car.'

'She's an expert biker, grandma,' says Marco, 'and she wouldn't ride in unsafe conditions, believe me. In this weather nothing could be finer than being on two wheels and enjoying the open road and open countryside. And thanks for lending me the car; are you sure you don't need it?'

'No thanks, my dear,' says Faida. 'The more I see of the world, the less I like it.'

They share a comfortable silence.

'I don't blame you, Nona,' says Marco, with a sweeping gesture of the hand. 'When you get up every morning and are blessed with this view, why would you want to go anywhere else? I will never get used to it. It is spectacular. Almost too beautiful for human contemplation.'

'It counts for nothing if your soul is troubled,' says Faida. 'And after what happened on Christmas Eve, we know now we have something to be worried about.'

'The police thought it might be kids just drunk on Christmas playing a practical joke.'

'Are you aware of the value of those dogs, Marco?' says Faida. 'In this day and age some of them are worth an absolute fortune. That is why they have gone missing. None of them have been killed, otherwise there would have been blood. No sign of poison anywhere, so it's not an angry neighbour. It must be the competition. Or criminals. The police have no idea what they are doing, and they like to think everything can be sorted out amongst village people like in the old days. Anything to avoid real police work or paperwork.'

'Emina is convinced it's not the animal liberation people,' says Marco. 'She says she would know about it, but her people don't operate like that: they go for maximum publicity.'

'This is still not clear,' says Faida. 'For sure it is nothing to do with Emina. But it could have been others. Who believe in more direct action.'

Emina was the leader of a local green organisation called the Istria Environmental Defence League, a grassroots ecological movement representing a wide range of interest groups whose principal goals were the protection of the environment, its natural resources, and the defence of social justice on the peninsula. Whilst it acted strictly within the law, there were occasional rogue elements who let their enthusiasm to make the world a greener, more nature-friendly place get the better of them. Hence the suggestion that the league could have been involved in the attack.

'Where is Nino now?'

'He's out with the lads and with Vito trying to see if they can pick up a scent on any of the dogs. Of the eight that have gone missing, three have been recovered and there have been further sightings. I told him to leave it to the boys, but he's so stubborn. Honestly, Marco, he'll be the death of me – and of himself, as he tries to run around the countryside like men half his age. He won't admit that he's slowing the others down. He says his knowledge of the woods is better than anyone's.'

'There's some truth in that,' says Marco.

'I know. But it's little comfort,' says Faida. 'When we came here, he promised we would be able to live in peace after a lifetime of running around. I'm sick of it. And it has become dangerous. Out in the woods. The poor harvest this year makes them more desperate. The criminals, I mean. They lay poison to kill the dogs of their neighbours. And the Italians are here all over the forests now that Alba is drying up as well. They used to do it for pocket money. It was a bit of fun with the neighbours. But it's all too serious now. The dogs are worth thousands, and the stakes are high. Someone's going to get killed one of these days, you mark my words.'

'I'll keep an eye on him, Nona,' says Marco. 'I'll also have a word with the Pazin police. Maybe they'll talk more freely to one of their own if I go down and see them. In the meantime, you need to take it easy and get some rest. We've got a big new year coming up, and you need to conserve your strength.'

'Heavens above, I'd almost forgotten,' says Faida. 'His ninetieth. The celebration at least. His real birthday was in October, but as he was in hospital for his heart surgery, he agreed we would postpone it till new year and do both together. Ninety years old and still acting like a nineteen-year-old. Honestly, he's worse than Zvonko. I hope that he survives until new year.'

'He will, Nona, he will,' says Marco, 'with you leading from the front. Because without you he would fall apart.'

Faida lets the thought linger in silence.

'And you'd better move quickly if you don't want to lose Emina,' says Faida out of nowhere. 'She has no shortage of suitors, you know. You two remind me of me and Nino when we were your age, or even younger. I was 17 and he was 15 when we met. Just like you and Emina in Grožnjan. And we've been fighting ever since.'

'Just like me and Emina,' says Marco with a growing smile.

'The best ones are worth all the fighting, and worth fighting for,' says Faida. 'What else are you going to do – stay home and tell each other how much you love each other? That's just pathetic.'

'Grandma, I told you,' says Marco, 'I don't think I'm ready for another relationship. At least not in the immediate future.'

'Talk with your grandfather,' says Faida definitively. 'You know it's never too late for me to leave him either. He needs to stop. It's greed. God knows we have enough of everything. But he can't stop.

He's driven, he's mad. He thinks everything will be taken away from him. And I can see the fear in his eyes. He's scared. And he won't talk. This truffle business. It's a bad business and the bad company he keeps.'

*****

It was late afternoon by the time Marco left Stancija Mihailić. Nino still hadn't returned, and his phone was still switched off. Thanking Faida once more for the use of her car, he kissed her on the cheek and headed off down the road to Cerovlje and Pazin. The more things changed, the more they stayed the same, thought Marco to himself. And he wasn't just referring to Faida and Nino's marriage. He also considered his on-again off-again relationship with Emina, his friendship with Zvonko, and indeed the very road he was driving on. Freewheeling down the hill to the Grimalda intersection he took the hairpin left, carrying straight on to Cerovlje. He wound down the windows and let the chill of the breeze cancel out the competing voices in his head.

He drove past the car junkyard/wood merchant in Stancija Previš, then the green shuttered Austro-Hungarian railway station in Cerovlje. He took a hard right on the road to Pazin, by what used to be his favourite restaurant. Where his dad used to take him for over-salted soggy pizza and Coca-Cola as a special treat when on leave from fighting at the front. They called the restaurant Franz Josef because of the faded picture of the old Kaiser in the low-lit gloom of the grubby pizzeria.

But to Marco having lunch at Franz Josef was like having lunch at the Ritz. He would have eaten any kind of wilted pizza as a kid just to have another hour with his father, feel the roughness of his uniform and his manly smell before the terrifying goodbyes at Pazin bus station; there he regularly threw shame to the wind and refused to let go of his father's leg, bawling his eyes out. Maja almost had to surgically detach her son from his departing father.

The old Franz Josef had been given a post-modern makeover and become an altogether fancier *konoba*, with a column of Mercedes, BMWs and Range Rovers lined up in front to bear witness to its success. *Plus ça change*, indeed.

The rolling countryside between Novaki and Pazin had changed little in the last one hundred years. Cut through by the gently meandering and still operational Buzet to Pula railway, its unassuming beauty endured and provided homes and livings to local farmers who still did things the traditional way and on a traditional scale, only these days with slightly shinier equipment.

*****

Marco pulls into the drab outskirts of the county capital of Pazin; it shared that honour with his onward destination, Pula, further down on the coast. The familiar sights and smells of Marco's childhood come to life. The sleepy train station, the old waterworks, the municipal veterinarian office, and by the petrol station the trio of public housing high-rises that could only be the result of the Communist 'fuck you' Brutalist excesses of the sixties.

These buildings couldn't be further from the Bauhaus utopia of Gropius, and when added to the local concrete works and sileage tower they dwarfed every and any historical building in the old town, blotting out their capitalist memories and, in a way, making them redundant in a kind of a historical no-go area. Beneath them the local bus station was a torrid exercise in municipal distress, whose only redeeming factor was the heritage graffiti that sprang from its concrete walls – *PUNK'S NOT DEAD* being the familiar graffito, still there all these years later and in all its vicious glory.

On the one hand, unlike Punk, it was a dead town. On the other, it was a place where people lived, loved, procreated, and died. As the administrative centre of the region it also had a political function. Given the dire state of the bus station, the lack of facilities and basic amenities, there didn't seem to have been much local government administration going on for a number of years. But it was there, apparently.

Nonetheless, this was where Marco's happy formative years were spent. Each individual has a different relationship with their own hometown. Never leaving is one problem; not being able to wait to get out poses another. The safe bubble and familiar routine versus facing the fears and challenges of failing at a new venture. Hometowns are tricky subjects, especially when they are one-horse towns, but Marco's forced departure at the age of ten allowed him to retain a lack of guilt at having left, as well as a small sense of nostalgia for the place even though it probably didn't deserve it.

He drives slowly towards the town centre, taking it in with new eyes now that he is officially back. He nears the Austrian-owned bank; in common with most of Croatia's major institutions key assets it had been sold off by local political carpetbaggers to foreign interests at cut-down prices after the war. Such was the price of freedom. He makes a left past the butcher's and the travel agent, and another left to the post office. As he swings Faida's compact around the corner he almost runs over an elderly gentleman, who yells loudly at the car: 'Howzat!' He whacks the bonnet with his walking stick and shouts, without fully taking in the driver, 'Watch where you are going, boy racer! Watch it!'

The gentleman cuts an eccentric figure, dressed in tweed jacket, corduroy trousers, brown suede shoes and a knitted tie. He wears a small trilby hat in the style of Jeremy Thorpe perched raffishly atop his extravagant ash-grey locks. He walks defiantly on without looking back. Marco immediately recognises him as old Mr Dalrymple, the English teacher from the Gymnasium around the corner. A former colleague of his father's, a polymath and amateur archaeologist who taught classics and music at the same Gymnasium, he was one of the rare, unique figures in the town. After his studies in England he moved to Yugoslavia forty-odd years earlier as an idealistic young socialist and never left. There was not much inspiration to return to England during the depressed years of Callaghan and the Winter of Discontent; then came Thatcher, the Falklands; then New Labour. Even with the departure of his revered Tito and the subsequent wars he still decided he was better off where he was.

Marco shouts out to him: 'Watch where you are going, you old codger!'

Outraged, Dalrymple stops in his tracks. Pauses dramatically. Slowly turns on his heels, sees Marco, and bursts into a roar of laughter. 'Marco! Dear Marco! Hello there, old boy – back for the hols? How the bloody hell are you!' he shouts expansively. 'Nino didn't tell me.'

'I'm back for good,' says Marco. 'Well, let's see how it goes. Bit of an experiment, really. I had to leave in a hurry. Kicked out of the force. Starting over. Nino and Nona have taken me in.'

'Not to worry, old chap, you're far better off here than in Blighty – they're making a terrible mess of things over there,' says Dalrymple. 'I'm glad you've come home. Let me look at you. Goodness, you're the very spit of your father. He was a good man, Marco. Very good man. And from what I know of the Metropolitan Police these days I understand they are a bunch of cunts, if you'll pardon my French.'

'So it turns out, Mr Dalrymple,' replies Marco, 'so it turns out.'

'Remember, Marco, the words of the prophets are written on the post office walls,' says Dalrymple, pointing to the graffitied side of the post office where is written in giant letters half a metre high the long-forgotten acronym, ACAB.

'All Coppers Are Bastards!' says Marco smiling.

'Tell you a secret old boy,' says Dalrymple. 'I did that myself back in '79. And the *PUNK'S NOT DEAD* at the back of the bus station near the pharmacy. Don't tell anyone: got my reputation to keep after all these years. But there was a time...'

'How's the cricket team going?' asks Marco.

'Speaking of other offences against Croatian culture!' quips Dalrymple. 'It died a death Marco, about four years ago. Usual reasons: the internet, cell phones, philistinism, and health and safety. Mainly mollycoddling parents frightened that little Hrvoje or Zvonko would get a bonko on the head from a cricket ball. Warrior nation and all that! Great defenders of the homeland. Frightened by the game that conquered the world.'

'It's a pity; Dad and I used to love playing. Crazy game. Although Dad always thought it was the expression of a colonially dominant ideology!' says Marco.

'Well, that's where he was wrong, and I told him as much,' replied Dalrymple. 'He failed to realise that, to the colonised, cricket had a different meaning than for the colonisers. In the pink parts of the globe cricket provided – and still provides – a way of asserting equality. The new countries developed the game and took it to the next level. The game has been changed forever by the intervention of the ex-colonies where it thrives independent of the coloniser. Today,

Indian cricketers are not playing the colonisers' game because they have made the game their own.'

'Dad said that cricket had always been used for the purpose of ideological control by the colonial oppressor and in return exploited as a means of resistance by the socially and colonially oppressed.'

As he says this, Marco also muses that he and Mr D. were the only two people in Croatia at this moment in time having a conversation about cricket.

'We have choir practice for the New Year's concert at your grandfather's place on Friday – Nino at ninety, indeed. Will you come? In fact, I need you to come. Will you join us? You won't have another chance till Nino's century, and I certainly won't be around for that at this rate.'

Back in the day Dalrymple had been Marco's musical champion. He had encouraged him, less so Zvonko, to go to the *Jeunesses Musicales Internationales* to improve his vocal training.

'I'll do my best. Maybe I'll try to bring Emina.'

'That would be capital,' says Dalrymple. 'The older boys will be over the moon. Me too!' he adds with a cheeky wink. 'And give my best to Nino. I haven't seen him since he got me to translate for his Chinese business associates last month. I hope his deal came off. It was a biggie!'

'Sure, of course I will. See you Friday, all being well,' says Marco, tucking the privileged information about Nino's Chinese business associates away for future reference.

★★★★★

Marco pointed the little Japanese car in the direction of Pazin's political and administrative counterpart, Pula, and the home of his oldest friend, Zvonko. This night was to be their boys' night out, when they could catch up about what really had been going on in their worlds without interruption by pesky family and loved ones and before the ritual and rounds of family duty started again on New Year's Eve.

Accelerating the engine to maximum revs Marco decided that he needed to blow some of the cobwebs out of Faida's little run-around. The underpowered vehicle felt as if it hadn't been over 40 kph for years and he knew that deep inside its little Nippon heart it really wanted to be a big car. Entering the toll barrier to the Istarski Ipsilon road at the top of the town, Marco took his ticket and blasted his way down the four-lane arterial highway whose 'Y' shape connected Trieste, Fiume, and Pola, as they were known back in the days of Italian rule.

Pulling past the turn-off to Žminj, and over the brow of a hill down the road towards Kanfanar, an elegant modern chrome and glass building appeared – the Rovinj tobacco factory. Its appearance gave Marco the urge to smoke, even though he had given up years ago, but it also reminded him that tobacco had been a major industry in the region for years. Tobacco had been processed on an industrial scale for over a century and a half, employing many from the job-poor parts of central Istria so the avid tobacco consumers of the Balkans could be well stocked with fine Istrian, Virginia-style cigarettes

Marco and Zvonko had had summer jobs at the tobacco factory the same year they went up to the music summer school in Grisignana. Basically, they stood around a lot, smoking (naturally), and sweeping up. They arrived in Grisignana directly from their last shift, a day late, stinking of tobacco and smoke, their bags jangling with home-made booze. They also brought with them vast sums of cash, comparatively speaking, for a summer job, and thousands (literally) of cigarettes, many of them rejects that they exploited to good effect, making them easily the most popular and certainly the wealthiest double-act in the summer school.

Ironically, Marco had just read an article on the plane over that said the tobacco factory of Rovinj had been sold off a couple of years ago by its Croatian owners in order to diversify into the cleaner businesses of hotels, fish farms and mixed industries, anticipating a downturn in smoking across the region. The upshot of the article was that British American Tobacco, the new owners, were pumping out 10 billion cigarettes a year to a Balkan market that was still puffing away, despite overburdened healthcare facilities that were barely able to cope with tobacco-related illnesses. Smoking in these stressful times had never been more popular, and Marco was amazed to find out from the article that whereas only just over 20 per cent of adult Britons smoked tobacco, the respective figures for Serbia, Croatia and Bosnia were close to 30 per cent for women and 40 per cent for men.

On the final stretch of the road into Pula, the straight line on the two-lane blacktop that was the old Roman road, or Via Flavia, allowed him to cast his mind back to the last time he had been in the city. He drew a blank. Without going into forensic mental detail, he guessed that it must have had something to do with the fact that it was probably when he broke up with Emina for the last and final time; and so he had drawn a curtain over the affair in both his conscious and subconscious.

Love it or hate it, Pula was the happening place in Istria and he loved the town for the sheer feeling of freedom it gave off. James Joyce hated the place. He called it his 'naval Siberia on the Mediterranean', having suffered six months there teaching English to officers of the Austro-Hungarian navy at the Berlitz language school. Indeed, his fellow writer Chekhov had much the same feeling for the region; Antosha described nearby Opatija as 'a filthy little Slav town with only one stinking street.' The school's most illustrious alumnus was Georg von Trapp, scion of the musical dynasty. On the plus side, Pula had a proud anti-fascist tradition and Mussolini's one and only visit to this Italian outpost ended with him being physically assaulted by members of the crowd. Legend had it that he later wrote about the incident in his diary and noted the lack of enthusiasm the citizens of Pula had for his fascist ideology.

Marco had ditched his cell phone the moment he arrived back in Croatia. There was nothing he needed from the UK and very little from the life that he had left behind that wouldn't be either abusive or painful. Equally, with both Anonymous and the Metropolitan Police in his past, the chances of surveillance were more than high. He was just enjoying this new-found freedom when he realised he needed to call Zvonko and tell him he was arriving. But then he caught himself in the act and wondered at this twenty-first century reflex. He had an appointment to meet his friend at a bar in town at eight and so he would simply turn up at the bar at eight. No earlier, no later. Or if he was late, then so what? It wasn't as if either of them was about to find the cure for cancer or perform a life-saving operation on a child. Constant online-ness fed an unhealthy sense of the individual's centrality to the universe.

Pulling into town on the old road from Vodnjan, the massive and looming spectre of the Roman amphitheatre dwarfed everything else.

When it came to the games, the *ludi*, the Romans thought big, even in colonial outposts like Pula. By standards both ancient and modern the elegance and sheer scale of the arena was impressive, and it made a far deeper impact on Marco every time he saw it again after a long break. The memory of it could never do justice to its reality. It had the same effect on Michelangelo when he came in the fifteenth century, and even more so Palladio in the sixteenth; yet both were influenced more in their later work by two other classical edifices in the town: the Arch of the Sergii and the Temple of Augustus.

Even the Brutalist architects of Socialism didn't try to compete with this masterpiece. Memories came flooding back in waves as soon as Marco saw it, and he pulled over in its shadow to wonder at the scope of its grandeur as well as the fond thoughts of his father, Ivo, who could communicate his passion for the ancient world to his son better than anyone he had ever known.

Childhood visits were a treasure to experience. He savoured each individual excursion they had made over the years, reliving them in his mind in meticulous detail, keeping them completely intact. No aspect was ever forgotten, so his bond with his father remained unbroken in his memory. It wasn't necessarily the facts about the amphitheatre and life during the Roman Empire that stuck with him from his conversations with his father but his sense of what the Roman psyche was all about. That the gladiator and the activities in the arena were a kind of microcosm of the casual cruelty of Rome and the sense that life was cheap. This was ritualised violence in the midst of a highly organised society, a society that had little to do with what we now recognise as the Judeo-Christian moral sphere. It was something else entirely. It did take a certain moral flexibility of conscience to find the random fighting and killing of men entertaining.

Parking up with an hour to spare he decided to pay a quick visit to the arena for old times' sake. The amphitheatre was always a place of love for Marco. He did a lot of his dating here with Emina. She lived in Pula, he in Pazin. One of the reasons she fell for him, she told him later, was how he could make the arena come alive for her with his detailed knowledge of the games. This was something he knew and ruthlessly exploited as he showed off his knowledge to the impressionable young Bosnian refugee, the same details his father had passed on to him at an early age and which had become second nature to him.

His mother also loved the arena but, unlike his father, rather than stick to the historical facts she told him some of the old myths of the city of Jason and the Golden Fleece. She told him of how legend had it that the stone amphitheatre was built by Vespasian as a love offering to his mistress, concubine and former *contubernia* Antonia Caenis, or Cenide as she was occasionally known. According to Maja, she was his mistress before his marriage to Flavia Domitilla. She came from hereabouts, working in Rome first as a slave and then as a freed woman as the secretary of Antonia Minor, the mother of Claudius. It was after the death of Flavia that Antonia and Vespasian became *contubernales*, the name given to two people connected by ties of intimate friendship and living under the same roof. To Maja she represented the lifelong love of a slave/freedwoman to a man who could not marry for love, and she had always told Marco that if he must marry then it could only be for love.

Thinking these thoughts of years gone by, and life lessons learned, Marco fell in with a group being guided around the arena by a blonde woman with a Slavonian accent. He was fascinated by a small American family of five involved in the process of learning their own life lessons. The three young boys barely looked at the place, refusing to listen to either their parents or the guide and constantly squabbling among themselves. Eventually the squabbles turned into an argument – a nasty one. The last thing Marco heard as he descended the main the steps to leave, beating a hasty retreat before it got ugly, was the father screaming at his unruly offspring: 'I can't believe you kids. We come halfway round the world to see this amphitheatre and all you do is fight. THIS IS NOT THE PLACE FOR FIGHTING!!!'

With that, he wandered off to find his old sparring partner, who apparently was hiding out these days in a watering hole dubiously named The Orient Express.

★★★★★

Finding the hostelry in question, however, is more complicated. Everyone he asks knows where it is, but few are able to provide directions. Having lived so long in the teeming London metropolis he is surprised at how people from relatively small towns can provide accurate local orientation. In the end he wanders about and stumbles into it by accident. No wonder. It is an unprepossessing little place and packed to the gills with smokers who look as if they had invented the vice in all its forms. He finds Zvonko in a corner talking to one of the waitresses, puffing away like a steam train.

'Aye aye, captain!' says Marco.

'Welcome to the Chattanooga choo-choo as I call it,' says Zvonko. 'But if you ask Martina here, she probably has a different name for it. Martina, say hello to my old school friend Marco. "Old" being the operative word.'

'Yes, I can see that. Welcome, Marco, good to meet you,' says Martina. 'And keep an eye on this one; to keep up the nautical theme, he's already several sheets to the wind.'

'Aye, aye, captain!' says Marco again.

'What's with all the "aye, aye, captain" bullshit?' asks Zvonko, not unreasonably.

'I don't know. It just came to me. Maybe because this feels like a transatlantic steamship. The *Titanic* without the band. And you know our old company motto!'

They recite in unison, their two voices as one: 'REPEAT UNTIL FUNNY!' which they both find really funny, having repeated it so often.

'OK, you're as bad as he is,' says Martina. 'What'll it be? More beer?'

'Aye, aye, captain!' says Marco, now giggling.

'And if this is the fucking Orient Express, send over Hercule fucking Poirot, I want a word with him.'

'This place is like a metaphor for your life,' sighs Marco.

'Oh, yeah,' says Zvonko, anticipating the inevitable lecture and careers advice from his oldest mate. 'Do you think I might be gay?' he says, desperately trying to change the subject.

'With your appetites it's possible you could be omnivorous,' says Marco. 'However, I will not be diverted. It's this train. In the middle of Pula and going nowhere. Just like you, my old friend. Just like you.'

Martina arrives with the two beers.

'Martina, your sense of timing was always impeccable. It's

what I love about you. Cheers. To the only woman I ever loved. If you hang around long enough even you will finally find out what a loser I am.'

'Aye, aye, captain,' she repeats, not without irony, and slipping a sly wink to Marco as she does so.

'You just can't help yourself, can you?'

'No, I can't. Which brings me to my theme.'

'Which theme?' asks Zvonko, scratching his head inquisitively.

'Joyce. No, not Lord Haw-Haw, clever dick,' says Marco. 'Jimmy. Brother of Stanislaus. Reluctant resident in this shithole from October 1914 to March 1915.'

'What's with the history lesson? I'm not going to be taught anything by the man who was more interested in writing about his wife's farts than assimilating into this pan-Slavic Habsburg paradise.'

'It's just that I had a thought,' says Marco, serious. 'Maybe it's time you got the fuck out of here. You've done your time. You can afford to. Pula is like this version of the Orient Express. A very large, outmoded piece of machinery going nowhere fast.'

Zvonko looks at Marco, gets his synapses straight, and comes back at him: 'What? And leave at the very moment when the great prodigal returns garlanded with laurels and on a victory parade direct from his glorious global triumph in London. What? And miss the grand reunion. 'With whom?' I hear you ask. Why, with the beauty from Bosnia! The sister from Srebrenica! The songbird from the sultanate!'

'What about her?' says Marco, annoyed that Zvonko has managed to turn the conversation 180 degrees back to him. 'Really, Zvonko, I've thought about it and I really don't have a problem with it. I don't know why you two are so hung up about it. It happened. It was an accident. End of story.'

They drink their beer.

'OK, OK. Let's have a line! To celebrate. That it's not a problem!' Zvonko dangles a little plastic bag with white powder in front of Marco's nose.

Whipping the bag out of Zvonko's hand Marco says, 'I'll take that, son, as evidence. As an officer of the law (retired, defrocked), anything you say will be taken down and used in evidence against you.'

'I'm sorry, officer, but the long arm of the Metropolitan Police isn't long enough to reach this godforsaken hole. You are out of your jurisdiction. And you were fired for being a love rat, anyway! We don't have love rats round here.'

'It's a fair cop!' says Marco, handing back the bag and raising his hands in the air. 'OK,' he continues, indicating the toilets. 'Do you want to go first, or shall I?'

'In there?' says Zvonko, offended. 'Have you been in there? Those fucking toilets are a total disgrace. I wouldn't take a piss in there, let along snort something off the theoretical filthiness of its non-existent lid. Basically, they've taken the lid off the shitter, no flat surfaces. The door is an invitation for limbo dancing practice and there are security cameras linked up to the Pentagon. No, no, laddie. In plain view we are more invisible.'

With that he masterfully racks out four generous lines, one for each of their four experienced nostrils, vacuums up two and hands the straw to Marco who makes light work of the rest.

'Jesus Christ, what the hell is in that?'

'Ah, the old tooting on Beelzebub's Bugle can be a risky business these days,' says Zvonko. 'Probably a cross between speed, the cider of drugs, Ajax, and Fentanyl.'

Marco considers the consequences of the concoction, shrugs, and continues: 'So, are you doing any painting these days?'

'Oh, oh. A hit, a palpable hit,' says Zvonko. 'You bastard. Why go and spoil a perfectly good night out? You are determined to get me on some charge or other aren't you, officer?'

Silence. Assorted sniffing and grating of the soft palate.

'No, I'm not painting,' confesses Zvonko. 'I haven't painted for a year. I'm far too busy making shedloads of money selling out to the Man. Or maybe not. I can't remember any more.'

Zvonko, seeing that Marco is struggling to speak, helps him out and changes the subject completely: 'You can have my other car. I don't need it. Don't drive that Japanese piece of shit round here. Faida told me she'd lent it to you. You'll look like a dick. And you make me look bad. My other car is a ragtop Mercedes. Maybe you might get laid.'

'Fuck you,' says Marco. 'And thank you.'

'May a dog fuck your mother.'

'My mother's dead.'

'So is mine.'

'Quits. Pax?'

'Pax vobiscum.'

'Et cum spiritu tuo!'

'Very good, Oscar,' says Zvonko. 'I see you've lost none of your native wit. And, speaking of which, let us further moisten our wits so that we may utter yet more bright and clever things!'

He calls over to the bar, 'Martina! Two more beers, please. Two shots. Two for yourself, whatever Hercule Poirot is having, and a crocodile sandwich. And make it snappy.'

'Repeat until funny!' Marco and Zvonko chant in unison.

The next thing Marco remembers is waking up fully clothed on Zvonko's sofa with a thermo-nuclear, rock-star-style hangover, and the doorbell jangling like it was lockdown time in the maximum-security wing.

*****

'Alright, alright,' groans Marco to himself. 'Give me a break. What time is it, anyway?'

Marco is alone in Zvonko's luxurious bachelor fuckpad. To add insult to injury the landline rings. Marco stumbles about the apartment trying to find the handset. He follows the ring down the corridor to the toilet. He reaches out to pick it up and it stops. As he's in the bathroom he considers throwing up, but at the last minute he changes his mind, opting for urination. He's just about to start when the doorbell rings again. He zips himself up, retraces his steps down the corridor to what he thinks is the main door, and picks up the interphone.

'Jesus, you look like shit!' says Emina, fresh and fabulous and ready for the morning swim date she had talked him into the previous afternoon. 'You have precisely ten minutes to get your sorry copper ass down here or... you know what will happen!'

He scrambles around Zvonko's understated post-modernist living quarters whose walls are tastefully adorned with muted colours and a few abstract pieces. The place had been fitted with blinds which, whilst terribly elegant, don't keep out the light. Marco gathers his few possessions, resumes the unfinished business of the urinary matter, splashes some cold water on his face, rubs some toothpaste on his teeth for form's sake, and adds a dash of Zvonko's high-end cologne over his unshaven chops for good measure. He looks at himself in the mirror.

'Should just about pass muster,' he says to himself, gulping down a half litre of water directly from the tap.

Exiting out the front door, Marco clocks exactly where he is. It becomes apparent that Zvonko's newly completed apartment is not only in a rather wonderful art deco building, but is also situated in what is probably the most expensive, if not the most fashionable, part of town. It dawns on him that perhaps the olive oil business isn't a bad one to be in. Olives as the new truffles.

'Jesus, you stink like a New Orleans whorehouse,' says Emina as Marco leans in to greet her.

'Sorry,' says Marco. 'I had a bit of a late night.'

'You are one lucky brother from a different mother,' ventures Emina, sitting in the driver's seat of her clapped-out Renault 4. She checks her phone, sassily chewing gum. 'I was just about to leave.'

Seeing her, fit, healthy, athletic (and sexy), Marco has second thoughts about being able to pass muster, preferring to swerve rather than riposte. 'I don't know what's wrong with me. It must have been the seafood I ate last night because I think I've picked up terrible food poisoning from something.'

'Get in, you lying English toad,' says Emina. 'And eat this,' she orders, throwing him some *burek* and a pot of yogurt. 'This is the best *burek* in Pula,' she continues, eulogising the iconic cheese pastry pie that is ubiquitous in south-east Europe but cooked best in the southern Balkans. 'There's a Bosnian baker downtown, and he looks after his people. Now be grateful, eat up and shut up.'

'This is a far and away the nicest thing anyone has done for me in –' he searches for the amount of time, '– in at least the last decade. Thank you, Emina.'

'I spoke to Zvonko first thing. He was on his way to the olive processing plant,' says Emina. 'He told me what happened. Do you want to know?'

'Go on, enlighten me,' says Marco wearily, and then, 'No. On second thoughts I don't want to know.'

'OK, just highlights. Eight beers, half bottle of tequila, two grams of white, and innumerable piña coladas at Pula's one and only notorious after-hours gay nightspot. Where you were last spotted bare-chested, waving your t-shirt over your head, in a conga with a number of gentlemen of similar persuasion to a generic Pet Shop Boys number. Pick a track, any track, to be the soundtrack to your shame.'

Marco mock holds his head in his hands, though deep down he's quite impressed with his performance.

'Actually, I made that last bit up. About the Pet Shop Boys. But everything else is true.'

'A boy's night out with Zvonko,' says Marco.

'*Plus ça change, plus c'est la même chose*,' they chant in unison.

Being a morning person, Emina has been up since the crack of dawn working, though technically a holiday, alongside planning their picnic. She'd already hit the Kumparička goat farm to get a fresh goat's cheese infused with saffron. The bread she got from the Bosnian. And she'd hit on a good local winery in Šišan not only to get some decent wine, but she also wanted to show Marco the novelty of the 'Che' red they made; a real gem, named after the Argentine revolutionary Ernesto 'Che' Guevara.

Almost going up on two wheels, for that was how the old Renault rolled, she points her Katrca – as the car was known in the former Yugoslavia, a play on the French word *quatre* – down the right-hand turn to the Premantura road. She puts pedal to metal along the *piste* that leads down to the very tip of the peninsula at Cape Kamenjak.

Arriving in the vicinity and ignoring the neatly signposted parking and toll suggestions, Emina braves the stony bumps of the white roads as if she were driving a Land Rover Defender and not a saloon made for the asphalt road in Slovenia 45 years ago. In terms of sustainability, it was definitely a status car for an eco-warrior to drive; however, in terms of emissions she was way out of the ballpark. But never mind, this sturdy little beast takes them across country with ease, coming to rest at the southernmost tip, the apex of Istria, in the Kamenjak National Park.

Emina wastes no time as she makes her way through the mothballed summer-only Safari Bar, climbing down the steep cliffside in the manner of the goat that produced her luncheon cheese on the Kumparička farm. Marco toddles unsteadily behind her, in a vain attempt to show willing, carrying beach towels and water.

The sun breaks through the clouds of an otherwise grey winter's day, flooding the Mala Kolombarica Cove in a golden glow.

As she pulls off her slender-fitting – and not unflattering, thinks Marco – sportswear, he diplomatically looks the other way, not wanting to remind himself of Emina's powerful olive-skinned physique. As she removes the remainder of her clothing she shouts over her shoulder, intent on skinny-dipping: 'Last one in is a sissy!'

'Oh,' shivers Marco. 'I think I know who that one might be. Can we just conclude that I am a big sissy and go and get some lunch?'

'It doesn't work like that, Ke-mo sah-bee,' yells Emina, about to dive into the water.

Running down the rocks barefoot and bare-assed Marco overtakes her with the cry, 'High-ho, Emina, and away,' diving in ahead of her and soaking her in the process. Emina dives in after him and disappears under the waves. She stays under for a minute. The sea is as grey as a battleship and it's impossible to see underneath.

'Emina, stop fucking around, I'm serious,' shouts Marco, becoming concerned as she has now been under for about two minutes.

A second later she whooshes up in front of him and grabs him around the neck, playing: 'Oh, Marco, you do care, after all,' mocking, laughing. 'There was I thinking you didn't like me.'

Marco pulls away through the rough ebb and flow of the waters; not so much a tide as the eddying pull of the waves against the cape. He yells, 'Whose fucking idea was this, anyway? I'm freezing my balls off here.'

They swim out into the open sea in silence, enjoying the moment and the exercise.

'By the way. Emina. Did you know that in Spanish,' Marco continues, shouting to Emina, again changing the subject, 'the character of Tonto is renamed "Toro" – the Spanish for "bull" or "Ponto" in Spanish-speaking countries? Interesting fact, no?'

'Everyone knows that, Ke-mo sah-bee,' says Emina, who amongst other things was known to be a bit of a smart arse. 'What I bet you didn't know was that during World War Two kids in America could support the war effort and at the same time confirm themselves as fans of the Lone Ranger with the simple purchase of the "Lone Ranger Atom Bomb Ring".'

'Fucking Americans,' says Marco, as they emerge from the sea. He throws Emina a towel and rubs himself down. 'They can find a retail excuse for anything.'

'Don't you just love capitalism,' shivers Emina, moving closer to get some of Marco's body heat.

'Come on, be fair, Emina,' replies Marco. 'Whilst I find your use of irony becoming, if there is one thing that sums up more than anything else the concept of a grizzly masked cowboy saving the Old West it's the threat of a nuclear holocaust. What else could it be?'

They look at each other for a second, burst out laughing, get back into their clothes and rush back to the relative warmth of the old Renault.

'Let me drive,' says Marco.

'Why?'

'Dunno,' he replies. 'Well, maybe I do. I want to feel what the motoring experience was like in the middle of the last century. This beast is a relic. An archaeological find. Where did you get it?'

'It was in an old shed up in Draguć. There were chickens living in it. It used to be one of Nino's truffle smugglers!'

'Ah, of course. I remember it now. We used to drive to Italy in this one. He had an old Fiat 500 as well,' says Marco, enjoying the memory.

'I fixed it up and here we are. I have something to get about in when I can't use my motor bike,' replies Emina. 'By the way, talking of antediluvian, pull over there. I'll show you antediluvian.'

Marco pulls over to what amounts to nothing more than a wide spot in the road. Emina jumps out and runs in front of the car.

'Look here,' she says, pointing to what looks like a crack in a rock with a circle around it. 'We've just been swimming with dinosaurs.'

'How do you mean?' asks Marco.

'This is the thing about Kamenjak that I love,' she says. 'These are dinosaur footprints. Real dinosaur footprints. I don't mean the children amusement park kind, but the real trace fossil footprints. These are genuine behavioural marks left by ancient organisms in the rock record. Isn't that just amazing? I love your Roman archaeological finds, don't get me wrong, but these are just mind-blowing. This is real history.'

Marco is genuinely amazed.

'I've been reading up about it,' continues Emina. 'There used to be an Austrian here in the thirties called Adolf Bachofen-Echt. He was not only a noted brewer back home; he was also an enthusiastic palaeontologist and he found dinosaur footprints in the area of Cape Ploče on Veli Brijun. This was the first discovery related to dinosaurs in Istria and was followed a few years later with more footprints being found on Fenoliga Island, as well as in this small bay here in Premantura. Best of all they found a place with bones on the sea bottom near Bale, which is the only site with the remains of dinosaur bones in the entire Mediterranean. So today, Ke-mo sah-bee, this is why we have been swimming with dinosaurs.'

Marco nods in the affirmative. 'Could dinosaurs actually swim?'

'Good question,' says Emina, adopting her much practised know-it-all voice. 'And the answer is "maybe". There were *brachiosauri* round here. Long giraffe-like neck, nostrils at top of an egg-like head, and probably pouches in the body that inflated and made them buoyant. If that is tantamount to swimming, then I rest my case.'

'Lunch?' ventures Marco. 'It's something that humans have been doing for millennia. Even longer. I reckon in the Pula region for sure, since the presence of *homo erectus* one million years ago has been confirmed in the cave of Šandalja.'

'Absolutely. Onwards to Fažana. It's a complete coincidence you mentioning the pre-Cro-Magnon, pre-Neanderthal *homo semi-erectus*. We're having lunch with Zvonko in Fažana. He has something for us. Something special, apparently. What can it be?'

*****

Half an hour later the trio have seated themselves on a blanket in the park between the beach and the town in pretty little Fažana, gateway to the Brijuni islands and ancient centre for the production of olive oil and the amphorae that carried the oleaginous treasure back to Rome. Now it was just the oil that was produced, and this was what Zvonko, having abandoned his former ambitions, spent his life doing.

Five years previously Zvonko finally gave up the idea of being a full-time visual artist and gave himself over to the production, processing and marketing of one of Istria's most marketable and traditional products: olive oil. Using a small plantation that he had inherited from a relative, a little money that his family invested, a lot of chutzpah and commercial nous, Zvonko had built up a business that made him one of the leading producers in the region. Now he was on the cusp of having to make the first-world decision of whether to remain boutique or expand into the kind of exponential growth demanded by a volume business.

He was torn, and his indecision was infuriating everyone around him.

'We are gathered here today in the sight of God,' begins Zvonko, his usual expansive self, 'under the spiritual aegis of Comrade Tito and his island kingdom of Brioni. Let the ceremony begin. The oldest olive trees in the world are in Crete and estimated to be around 2,500 years old and here we sit almost in the shade of one of the oldest olive trees in the world, not half a kilometre away on the erstwhile Insulae Pullariae.'

'Come on, maestro, get on with it,' says Marco. 'We came here to have lunch and a glass of wine, not to buy a fucking carpet. And your point is?'

'My point, oh non-creative garbage,' says Zvonko, 'is that I have been in my little laboratory with all my modern equipment perfecting the olive-processing procedure to create tastes that the public find easy and anodyne, and which don't involve any commitment on anyone's part except to get fat and rich. So, I've been thinking. About going primitive. What if you turn the process on its head and use the original techniques of the Greeks and Romans – and get the original flavour and experience that the Greeks and the Romans and the Phoenicians tasted? What would happen then? That is the purpose of my quest.'

'You mean stop making the stuff that people want to consume and pay good money for, and make something more difficult and possibly less profitable? That was what you did with your painting. And people stopped buying. I see history repeating itself and you turning a perfectly good business into a vanity project that just pleases yourself. It's like so-called natural wines. Have you ever tasted any? How can you be so stupid?'

Marco knows that his role is to be devil's advocate here, and he plays the part to perfection.

'No, wait, Marco,' says Zvonko, rising to his bait, 'wait. You need to taste this. Hold your horses. And don't ruin your palates by drinking any of the red that Emina has just dispensed.'

Zvonko hands a shot glass each to Emina and Marco, a twinkle in his eye as he reaches into his bag and brings out a terracotta container holding his latest concoction. He pours the fluid into their shot glasses; it's a cloudy yellow and looks nothing like the olive oil they know.

'Don't say it, Marco,' says Zvonko, anticipating his friend's lewd sense of humour. 'Taste it first.'

Emina sips hers hesitantly at first and then greedily. Marco does the same.

'I've never tasted anything quite like it,' says Marco.

'Extraordinary,' says Emina. 'Acidity that errs on the side of caution and as smooth as a baby's bottom. Let me try it with some bread.'

'This is what Homer meant when he spoke of "liquid gold",' says Zvonko, warming finally to his theme, and handing Emina the bread, 'and this is what I want to make. No chemical processing, no centrifuges, no hammer mills or metal tooth-grinders, no use of inert gasses; just the natural process itself of the curating of the olive from seed to bottle. And native Istrian varieties: *belica*, *buza* and *karbonaca* – and my favourite, the *rosinola*. It can be the elixir that Apicus first talked about when he wrote about Istrian oil in *De Re Coquinaria*.' Zvonko concludes by referring to what is considered to be one of the first-ever cookbooks, written in the time of Tiberius.

'It's sort of at the crossroads of where the wilderness ends and cultivation and civilisation begins,' says Marco, 'without going too far; neither completely wild nor totally cultivated and refined. It's. Very. Real. I don't know what else to say.'

'This is a relief to hear you say this, Zvonko,' says Emina, kissing him on the cheek. 'I'm proud of you. I was worried you were going to go the industrial route. This is far better for the ecology of Istria and for your sanity.'

The fact was that with any of the delicacies of Istria, whether they be oil, wine or, indeed truffles, they had the age-old problem of never being able to produce at volume. Zvonko in his oil business was discovering what the vintners and the trufflers had already discovered. Croatia had some world-beating olive oils but produced only 0.2 per cent of the global market, which meant that it was handicapped from the start. Hence Zvonko's less-is-more approach. People would be expected, naturally, to pay a premium.

'Before the war, and I mean the Second World War,' continues Zvonko, 'there were over 40 million trees along the Adriatic coast here on our side – now there's a fraction of that. It's like the truffles in France. So natural forces and market forces are trying to tell us something.'

'I agree with Emina,' says Marco. 'I thought you wanted us to come here to demonstrate your new line of oil paints made from olive oil. The artist eats then excretes Jackson Pollock-like on the canvas, and bingo! Well done, sir – have a Turner Prize!'

'Hmmm?' muses Zvonko, 'not a bad idea. Marco: you have no idea how happy I am that you have returned to the fold. I can see you are going to be a great ideas guy to have around. Blue sky spatter-thinking. I'll drink to that.'

They take their glasses of Che and toast.

'Cheers: to revolutionary ideas and a bright new future,' says Marco.

'What about you two, then?' says Zvonko. 'Any developments? Emina: when was the last time you played the piano properly? Not just fucking around with Liberace's less talented, camper younger brother here.'

'Sorry, maestro,' says Emina, 'I'm too busy changing the world.'

'And as for you,' says Zvonko, addressing himself to Marco, 'after your performance last night it would seem that your vaudeville career is back on track again.'

They pack up their picnic of bread, cheese and wine, and, feeling a little woozy-siesta-like, stuff everything into the little car and head via the port of Fažana to Pula. Just as they drive past the National Park Office, Marco shouts, 'Stop. It's Nino. Or at least someone who looks like him.'

'I can't, there's a pack of cars behind me.'

'Never mind. It probably wasn't him. Nino has become a bit generic-looking in his old age,' says Marco. 'I guess we all do.'

'You speak for yourself, love rat,' says Emina with a smirk. 'We're all one-offs round here. Leave uniforms to the Americans.'

'She's right, you know,' chips in Zvonko. 'Have you noticed how the best-dressed people now are the Russians, while the Americans all look as if they shop at the very same thrift emporium?'

'Sort of GDR civil service surplus shop couture,' says Emina. 'Très chic, indeed.'

'Whoever it was back there had just been into the ferry office for Brioni and headed in that direction. It's years since I've been,' says Marco. 'Shall we go one day?'

'Try phoning him if you are worried,' says Emina, handing him her phone.

Marco tries. Nino doesn't pick up. Must be out of range.

After dropping Zvonko back at the mill, it takes them more than half an hour to get back through the rush-hour traffic to Pula.

'I'll drop you back at your car. But first I just want to stop by the office and get some stuff to prepare for a meeting with the prefect's people tomorrow. Is that OK?'

'Fine by me. I've been wanting to see where the eco-warriors hang out when they're at home.'

'Do you remember when I first moved here and I had that Greenpeace poster with the babe on the catwalk dragging a fur coat with blood pouring out of it? The slogan was, "It takes one hundred dumb animals to wear a fur coat. And only one to wear it".'

'Vaguely, yes.'

'Well, all the girls who came over to my apartment used to point to the fur coat and say, "That's exactly the fur coat I want". And all the guys went, "Phwoar, look at the legs on that babe". Sometimes I think times will never change here quite as fast or as far as they have in the rest of the world.'

'Don't be so sure of that,' says Marco. 'You are doing an amazing job and things are changing faster than you think.'

'Oh, yeah?' says Emina, with an edge of cynicism.

As they turn the corner into the cul-de-sac that houses the Istria Environmental Defence League, she brings the car to an abrupt halt.

In graffiti two-foot-high is written: FUCK YOU DOG LOVING BITCHES. Worse still, they notice that smoke is pouring out of an upstairs window. In that moment a scooter blasts out from behind the bins and tries to make its escape. Marco opens the door and makes chase.

With superhuman effort he manages to catch the back of the Vespa and pull the rider up, who, falling to the ground, takes a swing at Marco. Marco's reflexes respond by hitting the driver in the face. The driver is still wearing his motor-bike helmet and Marco doubles over in pain, having smashed his hand unnecessarily. A knee in the face and a kick in the balls as he goes down is followed by multiple kickings in the ribs, and the biker runs off into the side streets of the city.

The last thing Marco remembers before passing out is Emina screaming down the phone to the emergency services.

Chapter VIII

Old Dogs, New Tricks

Colonia Pietas Iulia, 81 AD

Colonia Pietas Iulia Pola Pollentia Herculanea woke up the morning after the games with a massive hangover. Celebrations had gone on long into the night and finished as the dawn broke over the amphitheatre, still clogged with the debris of the previous day's carnage despite the Herculean labours of the cleaning gangs of slaves who had worked through the night to bring everything back, as far as possible, to its regular state of ordered cleanliness.

The drunks sleeping in the various arches and hideaways in the amphitheatre's structure had been evicted and moved on, the rubbish gathered up and the sand cleaned back to its original blood-orange colour ready for Oceanus's next gladiator line-up of savagery. The main problem the cleaners and public hygiene team had now was what to do with all the dead animals that remained after the terrible slaughter of the previous day's inaugural games.

The one thing all species of mammal had in common was that they would start rotting as soon as death occurred, and along with this came maggots, flies, and concomitant health risks. The queues had already started around the back of the amphitheatre to give handouts to the poor of the meat from those animals which were edible from both a cultural and a hygienic perspective. Food shortages in the Roman Empire were not unusual and for the poor, who largely lived off a grain diet, meat was a rare treat, as was any kind of protein. It mattered little if it was hippopotamus, leopard, or elk. Protein was protein. Though for Romans there were few beasts which couldn't be eaten for cultural reasons alone, or any other taboo. They would be given that which the remaining living animals, to be kept for future games, could not eat, and would not eat in the coming days as the flesh putrefied in the storerooms and menageries under the arena. Sometimes animals could be a bit pickier than humans about their diet.

While the plebs and the artisans were happy to have any protein, the handouts wouldn't last long and then the rotting remains of the beasts would be taken to garbage sites, dumped in the many ravines in the region. This was easier said than done; it took a small cohort of men to dissect and load a rhinoceros or a hippopotamus onto carts and transport it for safe disposal; anything else up to 80 kilos was easily handled.

On a less industrial scale, there were a few black marketeers who were in the business of gathering the blood of slain gladiators and selling it as a quack cure for epilepsy and other ailments. As an aphrodisiac it was well known, but the trade in plasma – and occasionally in major organs, like the liver or kidneys – was one of the shadier by-products of a nice day out at the games. This having been said, an antelope's blood looks very much the same as pig's blood, which to the naked eye bears a remarkable resemblance to human blood.

Cannibalism, however, was the last thing on Severus's mind as he made his way with Nasica and Lucia down the Via Flavia under the Arch of the Sergeii to the port at which were moored the ferry boats that were to take them to a celebratory lunch at the Villa of the Laecanii, hosted on behalf of the emperor by Oceanus.

Domitian had left earlier in the morning to attend to urgent business in Rome. He had lent his spectacular villa set in the bay of Verige, or Val Catena, on the Insulare Pullariae for a lunch to celebrate the founding of the Imperial Ludus Gladitorius for Colonia Pietas Iulia. The villa, which was about an hour away by boat, was rumoured to be a sight to behold.

As they boarded the swift, felucca-like vessel, Severus greeted the boatman, Apion, like a long-lost friend. The three sat in the prow just as Apion cast off, the midday sun taking the chill off the early spring breeze. Apion skilfully manoeuvred the boat out of the busy harbour and into the channel that separated the island from the mainland, while discreetly taking a slug of something from a gourd cached beneath his seat.

'Of course, it's a blessing,' said Severus to Lucia and Nasica, 'but it's also a poisoned chalice.'

'This is the first step to getting out of this shitty business altogether,' said Lucia. 'If we play our cards right we could be out of it completely within the year.'

'That is very easy for you to say, Lucia,' says Nasica, explaining his situation, 'and you know I agree with you in all these matters. But it still doesn't solve the problem of getting money back to my family in Rome. My sisters and my mother are in dire need.'

'We will be able to help you with that in the short term, Nasica,' said Severus. 'You are a part of the family now. Your problems are our problems, and we will deal with them as a family. Especially after the performance you put on in the arena. That was some fight. In fact, if you carry on fighting and do the school I think you could be big. Very big. Good left-handers are hard to come by.'

'Severus,' said Lucia, with growing impatience, 'that's the whole point. We want out. We want an end to the killing. So, let's hear what Oceanus's proposal is over lunch and then we'll decide what we are going to do. I, for one, am not going to allow my dogs back into the arena again. As of yesterday, they are in honourable retirement, and we should celebrate that fact above all else. You two can do what you like. But count me out.'

With that final statement from Lucia the three remained silent as Apion guided his swift-moving vessel with some dexterity towards their destination which, after just under 60 minutes of brisk sailing, was coming into sight. And what a sight it was.

Originally the edifice had been built by the senatorial Laecanii family. It came under imperial ownership on the death of the scion of the family, Caius Laecanius Bassus, the olive oil and *amphorae* magnate and politician. It was said to be among the three most luxurious villas in the Roman Empire, alongside a villa in Pompeii and another on the island of Capri.

A family of the Senate with distinct Etruscan origins, Bassus (who had the same name as his father), was also a consul but died without an heir, and thus his *amphorae* and oil workshops and mills became the property of the empire, which was good news for Vespasian as the house fell to the state as well.

The *amphorae* produced in the workshops of Vasanium, all marked with the stamp of Laecanius Bassus, were used to transport the highly prized Istrian olive oil around the empire. Mainly it went to the greater Danube region and the Roman territories along the Padus river to Augusta Taurinorum.

Approaching the emperor's villa across the Verige Bay allowed the invited guests to enjoy the building in all its splendour: set like a jewel in the corner of the inlet, it shone brighter than any other of the luxurious so-called 'rustic villas' in the area. If Severus and his gang had been silent for the last part of the journey because of a family argument, they were only silent now because of shock and awe that a simple country house could be so fabulous.

'It must stretch over about a dozen *heredia*,' said Lucia.

The sumptuous gardens and the three terraces that rolled down from the main residential building were indeed a sight to behold.

A more than gracious Oceanus was waiting at the port to welcome his new team, drinks at the ready served by handy catamites. He was in his element representing the emperor, and Severus commented quietly to Lucia as they jumped out of Apion's boat that he hoped Oceanus wasn't getting ideas above his station – as that could mean trouble for them.

'We took our own transport,' joked Severus, 'instead of your oarsmen from Vasanium. Just in case we needed to make a quick getaway!'

'No need for that, Severus,' said Pretty Boy, with uncharacteristic grace. 'You and your most charming family are my family. Part of the *famiglia*. And, for today, the home of our great Emperor Domitian will be our shared home.'

'Thanks for the hospitality,' said Nasica, ever the good-mannered patrician.

'Oh, don't thank me,' said Oceanus, 'thank the emperor. This is all on him, so eat, drink, make merry for tomorrow – you know the rest.' He swept off with his boys down to the Temple of Venus, from where he was being called by Seneschal, his chief acolyte.

'Lunch in an hour,' he shouted back.

★★★★★

Severus went off with a number of his old gladiator buddies in the direction of the kitchens, where Caecilius swore he had seen some of the best-looking housekeeping staff he had ever clapped eyes on. This gave Nasica and Lucia a chance to explore the house and gardens undisturbed.

Though the gladiators were dazed by the opulence of the estate, they chose alcoholic oblivion rather than take in the reality of where they were and the wealth it took to possess a place such as the villa.

It was easy enough for Nero. He just took it. And as for Domitian, he just allowed his brother to die of a 'fever'.

The luxurious property had whole sections divided up for use in summer and winter and was designed in an integrated fashion for both simultaneously. Summers were cool, spacious and at one with nature. Winters were warm and cosy, with indoor and outdoor pools. The garden had wide lawns, slopes, and promenades, with plane trees for shade and box hedges for structure, as well as high walls for security. Although the island itself was safe enough, the wealth that was known widely to be contained here would prove temptation enough for idle hands, especially when left uninhabited.

Nowhere else in Histria was such a villa to be found. It stretched leisurely over six *acnuae*, and aside from the living accommodation there was an amazing summer house which Lucia declared she would be perfectly happy to spend the rest of her days in, as long as they could build an extra room for the dogs and spare bedrooms for Philumena and Thelos. For Nasica, his favourite space was the *palaestra*, or *gymnasium*. Laecenius had clearly been a man of fitness and health; this was a huge indoor area which opened out onto a great open-air garden that operated as a space for exercise. The swimming pool edged down to the sea, with a broad colonnade outlining the entire perimeter of the *palaestra*.

The whole territory around the bay had been built, literally, into the landscape. Nowhere was this better seen than in the baths where the privileged guests could bathe and spa at leisure with a spectacular view of the sea, while enjoying one of the most beautiful climates of the Mediterranean. Superb promenades, laurel groves and landscaped *arbutus* dingles, edged by wonderful magnolia that filled the air with an intoxicating perfume that exuded not only beauty and luxury but also an absolute peace.

Lucia and Nasica had been sitting in the grounds of the *palaestra*, admiring the excessive luxury of everything, when a servant came out onto the top terrace of the main building of the house dressed as the god Pan; he blew into a golden trumpet, signifying that the banquet was about to begin. All the guests slowly began to move from the various parts of the gardens. It would take a while for everyone to gather, as they moved towards the house from all parts of the vast property; all these edifices were linked by a series of open and closed walkways rolling in and out of the coastline for about a mile, as one and in complete harmony with the natural order of things.

*****

By the time everyone has settled in the opulent dining room Oceanus is just getting into his stride in his role as host. Lucia knows she should be listening to what he is saying, but in her own mind she has heard it all before; and in any case she is too intent on taking in her surroundings, figuring it will be a long while before she will be invited to anywhere like this again – with its huge and extensive library, its rooms for healthy exercising, extensive bathing, and peaceful meditation, as well as the statues, the frescoes, the paintings, mosaics and the cultivated greenery, pools and fountains. It is a place, almost, of perfection – intended to stimulate everything the Roman élite aspires to. What amazes her most, though, is the fact that nobody lives here.

They are all present and seated now, drinks have been served, and Oceanus's key crew of around thirty members of the *familia gladitoria* are all waiting to hear what Oceanus's plans are after the emperor's shock announcement that he would invest in the building of an Imperial Gladiator School with Oceanus as procurator, *editor* and *lanista* at its head, backed by Nasica and Severus as *doctores*. Nothing else apart from that is known, not least to the crucial members of the team, the *doctores*. For Severus and Nasica the most important things are their contractual obligations and how to manage both their former and future relationship, given that both know they aren't in it for the long haul.

The dining hall is a sight to behold, with Oceanus sat at the head of the table and his chief trainers, Severus and Nasica, on his left and right. Around them are other seasoned, veteran gladiators as well as trainers of the *secutores*, *murmillones* and *retiarii*. Severus has insisted that Amazonia is to be the *Doctor Retiarii* – specifically for the training of the *retiarius*. She is, with Lucia, the only other woman at the table, although they sit at the far end away from the important action. Oceanus looks down to his trusty major domo, Seneschal, seated strategically at the opposite end of the banquet, then leans over to Severus, whispers a few words, and declares to the table: 'And now, a speech from the new Chief of the *Doctores* of the Imperial Gladiator School of Colonia Pietas Iulia: all hail our very own Severus!'

Cheers and stamping of feet echo around the dining chamber which has rarely seen such a rowdy (or happy) crowd.

As Severus stands to speak, he looks around and sees his old comrades from the ring: veterans, first swords, *tirones*, second swords, *doctores secutorum*, *provocatores* and the whole gamut of professions that make up the travelling show of a *familia gladitoria*. Now they would make up the bulk of what it took to put together Domitian's new *ludus gladiatorius* in Pola.

'Gentlemen! Oh, and ladies!' begins Severus, in his naturally unassuming manner. 'Firstly, I must thank the Emperor Domitian for the honour of being invited to be the Chief Trainer, as well as Oceanus for getting fully behind this decision, along with my colleague Nasica of the newly formed *ludus gladiatorius* in Colonia Pietas Iulia. I'll try and keep this short because I know you want your dinner.'

More cheers and stamping of feet. Severus has just made himself even more popular.

'One door closes and another opens,' he continues. 'And for many reasons I will be sad to say goodbye to the fighting game, a game that has served me so well over the years – and my opponents slightly less well. I've been fighting all my life. And now is the time to pass on that knowledge to the next generation.'

Severus takes a moment as he is visibly moved. 'But I am happy that Lucia will retire from the arena and her soon-to-be-husband, Nasica, my son-in-law, will be at our side as my assistant and right hand. Never an abler or nobler opponent fought with me in the arena, and for that I pass on to him my treasured *murmillo* armour and I appoint him to be, in addition to his daily work, the *Doctor Murmillones*.'

Applause for Nasica rings out around the room with the chant:

'*Vivat Nasica! Vivat Nasica! Vivat Nasica!*'

'And, finally,' says Severus, 'I want us to raise our glasses to the men who died yesterday in the arena. We will bury them in Pietas Iulia tomorrow with the honours that are due to them as warriors and as gladiators. We will have five days of mourning and rest and reflection before we start our work in the new school of Pola.

To those we lost yesterday, *ave atque vale* – hail and farewell! We salute your spirits!'

'Hail and farewell!' comes the response from the table, along with a rowdy raising of goblets.

*****

Two days later and the obsequies of the fallen gladiators have been completed with the Guild of Gladiators having done what it could to reasonably help the families and loved ones of the deceased. Lucia, Nasica and Severus found themselves once more down at the port of Pietas Iulia and ready for yet another departure. They were always suspicious of the motives of Pretty Boy Oceanus who had, on leaving the Insulae, handed a larger-than-usual bonus to Severus and Nasica as a down payment on their future success. Nasica chose to take advantage of this opportunity for a trip to Rome to pass the money to his family and visit his ailing mother and sisters.

Severus and Lucia were also packed for a short trip. They planned to use the break before the formal establishment of the school to visit Severus's brother, Festus, and his wife, Vita, who lived halfway up the peninsula on the road to Aquileia on the long narrow inlet called Laime. Lucia had brought her dogs Britannica and Brutus with her, and they were sitting well-behaved at the gangplank of Apion's small but speedy vessel. Having sailed with Apion to the islands for the banquet Severus decided that, with the spring winds in their favour, the trip by boat would be faster and more comfortable, so he had booked him on the spot. Severus broke away from Lucia and Nasica to give them time to say goodbye in private.

Seafaring was generally safe on the route between Pietas Iulia and Rome, but the *mare clausum*, the four-month hiatus in sea travel imposed by law in Rome, had just come to an end; however, it could still be dangerous, especially in this area as it was the season when the Boreas wind was most likely. This north-westerly could reach 300 kilometres per hour and had a power that had been known to throw fish out of the sea.

'Travel safely, my love,' said Lucia to Nasica, 'and please pay my respects to your mother and to your sisters. I hope one day to be able to meet them.'

'Of course I will,' said Nasica. 'And you know I will miss you. Every day.'

'It's not for long,' said Lucia. 'You will be back soon, and what's more important is that you – that is, we – are out of the gladiator game. Somehow, we managed to survive. I feel like we are on the home stretch.'

Apion shouted out to the couple, 'If we don't leave now we'll miss our chances with the winds and we'll be tacking up the coast for days; and by the time we get there it'll be time to come home.'

'*Bonum cursum!*' shouted Severus to Nasica as he went up Apion's shaky gangplank, laden with gifts for his brother and his wife. 'Come on you two love birds, get it over with!'

Brutus and Britannica began their barking as soon as the young lovers started kissing, to the general mirth of all concerned.

'I love you,' said Lucia, stretching out her hand as she walked on board the good ship *Fides*.

*****

Brutus and Britannica loved the life on the ocean wave; they stood up at the front of the *Fides*, Apion's pride and joy, looking like a silent but furious double-headed Cerberus figurehead. They enjoyed the wind on their faces, the sun on their backs and the relative peace of the journey as an antidote to the racket and row in the animal quarters in the amphitheatre. The same went for Lucia, who sat towards the back of the boat with Apion and Severus as they sailed at a fairly rapid five or six knots in the felucca-like ketch up the coast of Istria.

'We're making good time,' said Severus as they sailed by the bustling port of Vasanium. 'We should make it by nightfall.'

'I'm not so sure of that,' said Apion, who, now sober, was reliable, honest, and realistic. 'There's the channel to negotiate, and that can be slow going. Let's see how we fare, and as a last resort we can row for the final few miles. You can see I brought the oars for that very purpose. Coming back isn't a problem. The winds will be more favourable.'

'You could use a bit of exercise,' said Lucia good-humouredly, patting Severus's stomach. 'You look like you've been eating for two.'

'Steady on, you,' said Severus. 'I was building myself up for the big fight. But now I'm free I can eat as much or as little as I want and, hopefully, drink more than I need. Why do you think I wanted to go to see Festus and Vita? They are a couple who really know how to live.'

By live, Severus meant eat and drink.

Festus was also a former legionnaire who, like his brother, signed up for the standard 25 years. Once he had served his time he got out of the army at the first possible opportunity, having seen some atrocities when on active service in Judea. He had been there at the Mount Gerizim massacre in the first Jewish-Roman War when 12,000 Samaritans and Jews were butchered. Decanus Festus, a private soldier who had been the leader of a group of ten recruits, was among the infantry contingent led by Cerialis, commander of the Fifth Legion, who had been sent by Vespasian to besiege the enemy with 3,000 infantrymen and 600 cavalry horses. It was a bloodbath. To add insult to injury the Romans proceeded to erect a shrine to Zeus Hypsistos on the top of Mount Gerizim and then place the bronze gates from the Temple in Jerusalem there for good measure.

On his return from Judea he was posted to the central Istrian town of Pinguentum. It had been old Augustus who had moved the border of the Roman Empire from the Formio to the Arsia River at the turn of the century. In annexing a large part of the Istrian peninsula to the northern Italic region that Venice called 'Venetia et Histria', the territory thus made up the Italic region. Eastern Istria, or Liburnia, remained a part of the Roman province of Dalmatia. It was there, just coming to the end of his 25-year service, that Festus had met local girl Vita, and he decided to settle down with her, having been honourably discharged with an *honesta missio* at the end of his distinguished service.

Pinguentum in this era was a bit in the back of beyond, and if Vita and Festus were to survive in these rapidly changing times they would have to adapt. And that meant moving away. Vita's family owned some land over by Laime and it was here that she and Festus set up an inn for travellers, located not far from the Via Flavia and beside the picturesque inlet of the Laime Channel. By the time they moved there the predominantly Romanised population was inhabiting these southern and western parts of the peninsula. The land was more fertile, the towns more developed, and the need to travel by road to Tergeste, Tarsatica and Nesactium had increased. Thus there was traffic for the inn that could produce a better living than anything on offer in the strategic military stronghold that was Pinguentum.

Severus had been right. They'd made the journey in about 12 hours, which was something of a miracle and much easier than walking. Privately he swore to Lucia that it was only because he had hidden Apion's family-size flask of posca white wine in his outsize kit bag, and so the boatman was more than usually desperate to get to their destination in order to have a drink. Severus also knew that Festus's generosity was legendary, and he kept a solid and dependable cellar. Carrot and stick.

The light was fading as they came into the harbour where 'The House of Festus and Vita' – 'festus' meaning 'joyful' and 'vita' meaning 'life' – was nestled in the crook of a small bay, just below the Via Flavia and in a very fertile river valley which made contact with the open sea about 10 miles up the road. A cross between a *hospitia* and a *stabula* their kind of inn was not uncommon on major routes like the Flavia where both humans and animals needed to stop, refresh themselves and prepare for their onward journey.

In the twilight Apion, who had remained both involuntarily and therefore uncharacteristically stone cold sober for the whole of their epic voyage, took out an ancient kind of foghorn from a box beneath the rudder, put it to his lips and blew three deep blasts, shaking the countryside with its noise. The hounds, Britannica and Brutus, still in their position at the prow of the boat, decided to join in and add some infernal howling to the racket announcing their arrival.

The ensuing clamour roused the household of Festus and Vita, and as the two hosts appeared at the door of their cosy inn they too joined in the festive howling with their own animals as they ran down to the jetty to greet their guests, weary from their travels yet happy to see their dear family.

★★★★★

Lucia wakes early the next morning and steps out onto the terrace in front of the inn. She breathes deep the scent of fresh sea air mingled with the forests of pineta that grow wild on the banks of the Laime Channel, which is like a fjord and continues inland for around thirty miles, all dense woods and limestone karst caves. The ideal hideout for anyone on the run.

Britannica and Brutus rouse themselves from their heavy, sea-air-induced sleep and join their mistress on the terrace. They open their light-brown eyes with some difficulty in the morning sun and shake the sleep out of their short muzzles and loose-skinned brows. They stretch their great broad backs and muscular legs. Lucia looks at them and considers the beauty of their comparative ugliness and snaps them into action.

'Come on, you two,' she orders, 'let's go explore.' Together the trio head down the lush slopes to the water, along the bank of the channel and up into the woods on the opposite side.

Indoors, Vita has just put the finishing touches to the breakfast table. It is more of a *prandium*, or brunch, than an *ientaculum*, which would have been more appropriate for the early morning. Vita puts wheat pancakes, *tiganites*, on the table, having made them from wheat flour, olive oil and curdled milk, fried in a pan and served with lashings of honey and berries. Fresh goat and a selection of sheep's cheeses, bread, and wine as well as some cured meats make for an excellent table in the dining room.

'Come and sit down, you two,' says Vita in as gentle a voice as possible as Festus and Severus emerge from their respective bedrooms. 'You don't seem as smart this morning as you were last night. I'll be surprised if you can remember anything that was said. Shall I do a summary?'

'I knew we should have had those swallows' beaks before we started on the red lora wine,' says Festus, invoking an old Roman panacea against hangovers.

'Prevention is better than cure,' replies Severus. 'As old campaigners we should know better. It is a far greater thing to prevent the whole nasty hangover situation in the first place. You should have remembered, Festus, you old soak. Just like our dad. Could never get enough.'

'Look at the pot calling the kettle black,' replies his brother.

'The apple falls not far from the tree!' replies Severus, jesting.

'Pack it in, you two,' says Vita, 'or I'll bang your heads together. Here, take this. Boiled pig's liver, fried with onions. You'll be as good as new in a quarter of an hour. Take it.'

Severus and Festus fall greedily on the liver as if it were their last meal on earth. They wash it down with large goblets of breakfast white wine, light yellow; a delicious thing to ward off the early spring chills.

'OK. To continue our discussion from last night,' says Severus pointedly to Vita, proving he doesn't have alcohol amnesia, 'we only really got as far as the subject that I know that is dear to all our hearts – me. What about you, big brother, what about you? What's been going on here – how is it going?'

Festus, a little worse for wear, takes another draught of white and scrapes the last of the liver out of the earthenware bowl. Vita comes to join them at table, bearing soft cheese and some warm goats' milk with her wheat pancakes.

'Well, frater minor,' says Festus, ever jovial. 'The inn and the stabling business isn't bad. We're more or less well situated, a day's travel from Caprea in the north and Pola in the south, and there are very few places on the road like this that have the aspect of the sea, so for that we are grateful. But in winter it's dead. Even with the *mare clausum* you would have thought that there would be more people taking the roads, but no. The trade more or less stops. So, we've had to make do in the best way we can.'

'What about the restaurant?' asks Severus. 'Are there at least some people around who want to come and eat?'

'There are a few locals who eat out, but nothing to write home about. Aside from the occasional traveller, there's a little community over at the marble quarry. There's a small garrison at Duo Castri, but it's five miles away, and on a soldier's *salarium*, even if he does want to impress his girlfriend, he doesn't want to walk a ten-mile round trip – and neither does she.'

'Last autumn we decided to try and cultivate oysters,' says Vita, taking up the story. 'This place has the perfect conditions: brackish waters, constant temperatures, not too cold in winter, and so our first harvest was amazing. We had to get rid of it locally because of the *mare clausum*, but Tergeste and Pola are easy to reach in a day. With the odd traveller or two and old big guts over here, we managed.'

Oysters were highly prized in Rome above all other shellfish because of their rarity, for the southern Mediterranean tides – or rather, the lack of them – do not provide ideal conditions. So merchants looked to colonial outposts to supply the insatiable demand of the Imperial City. When Gaul was conquered Romans were amazed at the seafood treasure of western Armorica, and they were able to gather vast quantities of oysters from the massive open tidal flats of the Mare Tenebrosum during low tide. Armorica was the producer of huge quantities of oysters that were transported to Roman cities and garrison towns throughout Gaul. Other shipments were insulated in snow and sent as quickly as possible across the Alps to Rome. By the time they got to table the likelihood would be that the oysters would be a health hazard and not very palatable.

'It was in early spring that we hit the jackpot,' continues Festus. 'The boats started running again, and with insulated boxes and packed ice from the Mons Maior we managed to get a couple of lucrative shipments to Rome before the hot weather set in. I took them myself, with Apion and a mate of his who shared the sailing. I've made contacts in the markets and so in winter we think we can survive on that. But all you need is a bad crop or a cold winter and you're stuffed. By the end of March to mid-April the ice from Mons Maior is gone and it's bye-bye Roman market,'

'I see what you mean,' says Severus. 'Is there any other way of preserving them for transport? Or actually transporting them alive?'

'We're looking at a few things,' says Festus. 'The point is, we have the capacity, we have the contacts, we have the means of transport: all we need now is the idea – the product. What can we find here that doesn't rot easily and can be transported quickly to Rome? Because Rome is where the money is.'

'And with the 64,000 *sestertii* question having been asked,' says Vita, 'I'll leave you two philosophers to solve that eternal puzzle and go and see if I can find Lucia.'

'I would join you,' says Festus, reaching for the stoup of white, and indicating his nether regions with his head, 'but I don't want to ruin my chances. I still have some hope of being a father.'

Vita, hands on hips, a formidable woman, stands in the doorway with the noonday light silhouetting her as the fine figure of a woman that she is.

'You're all talk and toga,' she says with her ribald barmaid's laugh. 'I think you're better off doing your usual shaking hands with the unemployed, more like.'

*****

Vita walks down the verdant slopes of the Laime Channel towards the calm limpid blue waters of the river valley. She makes her way through the mature maquis of the canyon formed by millennia of water erosion. She thinks to herself that there is no more beautiful vista on the planet; the Alpe Iulia to the north and the wide-open expanses of the *Mare Adriaticum* to the west. And in between, on the water, she looks at the small outcrops of oyster beds that Festus laid down the year before and which now provide an almost permanent supply of seafood delicacies, which also include wild mussels and scallops. These continue to grow while supply outstrips demand.

As she looks up from the water she sees Lucia on the opposite bank, descending the southern slopes through the oak and ash forest that flourishes on the south side of the canyon. By her side are the ever-present British bodyguards who gambol through the brush woods like it was their natural habitat.

'It's so beautiful, Vita,' shouts Lucia from her side. 'I want to come and live here, too.'

'Why don't you come and join us here?' Vita shouts in response.

At that, Brutus, Britannica and Lucia come running down the hill and all three dive into the brisk waters of the channel, swimming across to Vita on the other side. They arrive in double-quick time and Vita envelops Lucia in a large linen sheet to dry her off. She shivers in the arms of Vita as the two short-haired, water-loving hounds shake off every drop of water and head up to greet Festus and Severus who have moved out on to the front terrace of the inn to continue their philosophising.

'It gets warmer – the water,' says Vita to Lucia. 'If you're thinking of staying, that is.'

'It's very tempting,' says Lucia. 'It's so great to feel so close to nature. We've just been in the woods walking endlessly – and nothing but nature. You can smell everything just growing and growing. The woods are alive, and it's a great thing to feel.'

'I used to think it was a lonely old place,' says Vita, 'you know, just me and Festus in the winter. It would be a great place to bring up kids, but that hasn't happened.'

'Never say never,' says Lucia, 'and, anyway, I'm sure that with all these oysters – you know. That won't be a problem.'

'Oh, no, that's not a problem at all,' says Vita. 'The winter nights pass very quickly in that respect. It's just. Nothing ever happens. Maybe we're too old.'

As the pair sit in a companionable silence it is eventually broken by a pheasant scuttling clumsily through the maquis. As if shocked by its waiting public it flaps back into the undergrowth again. A rustling comes from the bushes. The dogs stir up on the terrace but can't quite be bothered.

'What about you?' says Vita. 'Severus says there's someone.'

'Nasica. Over a year together now,' says Lucia. 'I thought he was way out of my league. But it seems not. I used to think that being loved-up was for fools and idiots. Until it happened to me. Now that he's not with me I think about him every hour. He's each and every point of my compass. Whichever way I turn. He's gone to visit his family in Rome. He'll be back next week when we start the new school back in Pietas Iulia.'

'Sounds like you've got it bad,' says Vita, grinning.

'You know how it is,' answers Lucia with a coy smile.

Changing the subject, Vita says, 'What are we going to do about Severus? He's alone. All alone. Always has been. Is there anything we can do?'

'I think he was married to the legion,' says Lucia, 'then the arena. And he always felt he had to look after me. After he killed my father. He finally told me. I know Lefty was a good friend of Festus's, too. From the Britannia campaign.'

'I don't think he has ever forgiven himself,' says Vita.

'Maybe he will be able to now, as soon as I am married to Nasica and off his hands,' says Lucia.

'Come on, don't be so miserable about it,' says Vita, pinching

Lucia under the damp linen. 'Shall we go and have a drink? Then you can help me to prepare the dinner. We've got some amazing stuff. I can't wait to show you. We live from nature's bounty.'

*****

The dinner table as prepared by Vita and her two kitchen maids is a sight for hungry eyes. In honour of it being a big family occasion, exceptionally, they eat reclining around a banquet fit for an emperor. The table is laden at the beginning with a number of cold dishes, to whet the appetite. Vita takes them through the choices: 'Over here on the left are field mice stuffed with pork and sunflower seeds. Here on the round plate is boiled tree fungi with peppered fish-fat sauce; and here is boiled ostrich with sweet sauce – thank you, Lucia, for being so thoughtful as to bring the fresh ostrich from the games. Better we eat it than those nasty old lions.'

'And this white has seen better days,' says Festus, slightly underwhelmed. 'Where did you get it?'

'This is the white wine that I hid from Apion so that he wouldn't get drunk before delivering us safely here. Old habits die hard.'

'I was wondering whether it was some kind of a joke. Well, the joke's on Apion, God speed his barque. He should be back in Pola by now.'

'If he didn't stop off in Arupinium on the way. It would have been about lunch time, and you know what he gets like.'

'This is the wine I brought you from Pola,' says Severus, producing a large wicker flask he has kept hidden under the table. 'You're going to like it. Falernum – from the actual slopes of Mount Falernus. Ten years old and as tasty as the morning dew.'

One of the serving girls takes the flask and, on Festus's instructions, pours it into fresh goblets, having dispensed with Apion's slightly less palatable *cru*.

'This will go perfectly with the next course,' says Festus, quaffing liberally of the Falernian. 'And from whomever you picked up this busy little number, they have excellent taste. For sure you didn't choose it!'

'Absolutely spot on,' says Severus. 'I picked it out of the emperor's reserve cellars when I was at the Villa of the Laecanii on the Insulae Pullariae, as one does.'

'He may know nothing about women,' quips Festus, 'but he knows where the good stuff is hidden. Congratulations, Severus. Good man yourself.'

The servant girls bring in the warm dishes from the kitchen, making space on the table for a big platter of oysters, a vast dish of scrambled eggs with wild asparagus, and a plateful of boletus mushrooms.

'Everything you see here,' says Festus, 'is taken from nature: the oysters from the sea, the fungi from the tree, and the eggs from the chicken's ass. You see, take this stuff – this wild asparagus. I tried to make a business out of it. But it only grows under certain trees and it's impossible to cultivate and get the same taste. It's also a bugger to find. Everyone knows it's delicious, everyone loves it. But first of all, to pick it – it's quite labour intensive. That's not the problem – we have the people for that. It's just that it only lasts for a couple of months and when you preserve it, say in salt water, it just doesn't taste the same. Impossible to cultivate and get the same flavour. Drying it and adding it to the eggs afterwards doesn't work. Too bitter.'

'But these are fresh,' says Vita, 'picked this very morning from under the oaks on the south side of the canyon. Just come into season. They taste like you've died and gone to heaven. Same with these boletus mushrooms. Fry them gently in butter with freshly picked wild garlic. You can't beat it with a stick.'

'Ladies and gentlemen, dearly beloved family,' Severus begins the toast, 'let us raise our glasses to our hosts, Vita and Festus; this banquet is a gift from the gods – and also thank them that I brought this Falernian to go with it. And let us not forget the ladies. Women are responsible for the best and worst moments in men's lives. But to live means to go through good and bad times. So, let us drink to women who bring us joy and trouble, making us alive! To Vita and Lucia.'

'And before you toast any further, my dear brother, we have one further delicacy for you, with which this excellent Falernian will be perfect.'

On a signal from the kitchen eight perfectly formed scallop shells are brought in, with the centre of each containing a bivalve of extraordinary proportions.

'These are straight from the channel,' says Vita. 'I picked them from the water myself not one hour ago. They have been cooked gently in butter and garlic and are perfection itself.'

'Only they can be made more perfect with this,' says Festus, upon which, with a magician's prestidigitation, he pulls out a small white-ish lump from a pouch in his belt, along with a small razor-like instrument. 'This is the magic mushroom of desire!'

With that, Festus begins to scrape at what appears to be a white truffle, the *tuber magnatum pico*, flaking it over the king scallops thinly enough for the essence to almost melt over the seemingly still throbbing flesh.

'This little delicacy is what happens when the god Jupiter throws a lightning bolt at an oak tree,' says Festus, waving the truffle under his nose and everyone else's around the table. 'Taste it and know how it feels to be on the stairway to heaven.'

They eat in silence and in reverence to the dish.

Lucia gets up and leaves the table.

The remaining three look at each other and don't know what to say.

Severus breaks the silence first: 'These scallops with this aromatic flavour are just out of this world,' he says. 'It is just spectacular. Funnily enough, I had something like this the night before the last fight. Pretty Boy brought it out. Used it in the same way. But it was black. Same thing as yours, but black. The *tuber terrae* he called it.'

Lucia comes back into the room carrying a large handkerchief.

'And this is the future I was talking about,' says Festus, 'when I said that we have the capacity, we have the contacts, we have the means of transport, and all we need now is the idea – the product. This is the product, brother, this is the product. If only we can find the way to cultivate it. Or even find enough of them to make it work. In Rome, this is the latest thing and people are willing to pay a small fortune for it. And it doesn't perish. Or you can keep it in oil. It keeps the taste and aromatises the oil.'

'Uncle Festus,' says Lucia, a smile growing on her ruby red lips. 'Uncle Festus, I think we have solved your problem.'

She carefully places the kerchief on the table and opens it up. Inside are a half a dozen perfect examples of *tuber magnatum pico*.

'I wondered what these were. This morning on my walk through the forest I sat down to rest in the glade of a hazelnut wood. No sooner had I done so than Brutus and Britannica started to become slightly agitated and go round in circles, as if they caught a scent but the scent wasn't travelling, it was staying in one place.

'Then in one moment, Britannica started to dig, swiftly followed by Brutus, not far from here. Then she stuck her muzzle into the earth and started to eat with a passion and a frenzy like she had found a pieces of raw beef down in the hole. And then I saw Brutus do the same. I let them do it a few times. Because I didn't know what it was, I took these specimens they dug up to give them as treats later if there were no ill-effects.'

'Do you think they can do it again?' asks Festus.

'I am sure of it. In fact, I made them do it several times before we came home.'

'Ladies and gentlemen, please stand for a toast,' announces Severus, a little worse for wear but as merry as could be. 'I give you the dogs of war, Brutus and Britannica. Along with solving their current unemployment issue, I think they have managed to answer our little conundrum.'

They drink long and deep of the emperor's Falernian.

'To the future,' says Festus.

'To our future,' say the others joining their voices together as one.

Chapter IX

Brotherhood and Unity

Democratic Federative Yugoslavia, 1944

Two hours before dawn, in the dead of a cool Istrian night, Armando, Nino and Vito slipped silently out of Buzet with the utmost discretion. If anyone had been awake to witness their departure, they would have seen a bizarre sight: two men on a motor bike and a dog sitting in a sidecar, the hound looking more like Rommel entering victorious into Tobruk after the Battle of Gazala than a mongrel with his masters. All Vito was missing was the Desert Fox's trademark goggles. Armando allowed the bike to freewheel down the steep cobbles of Buzet old town, springing the engine to life as they turned a sharp left at the base of the hill and headed north, lights blazing along the asphalt road to Učka.

Nino held his uncle's expansive girth tight as they blasted full speed ahead through the village of Roč towards Lupoglav, making a hard left onto a white unmetalled road at Ročko Polje, almost sending Vito over the edge of the sidecar and into the ditch.

'Sorry, Vito,' shouted Armando. 'Don't worry, boy, we'll be there soon.'

Now that they were on the open road Vito thought twice about perching himself on the seat like a soldier. He wisely chose to curl up on the floor of the sidecar for the rest of the journey. It was just as well, because he thus avoided witnessing Armando switching off the lights of his ancient Zundapp motor bike and driving almost blind through the darkness, illuminated only by the sparse winter light of a crescent moon.

From where Nino was sitting the crescent shape hanging in the heavens appeared to slowly shift toward the south and began to stand on its end. They were entering sheep country, and it was an old Istrian shepherd's tradition that this represented the moon assuming a pouring position in which it would lose its water and result in great summer rains. So much for ancient superstitions.

It was still pitch black when they hit the asphalt again, swung left towards Lanišće and climbed upwards into the portentous shadow of Mount Učka; its snowline was clear now from Nino's vantage point, for when he looked down to the right he could just make out the spindly finger of the Island of Cres and the sheer cliffs of its western coast.

Nino looked at the silhouettes of Cres and Lošinj and imagined the rest of the Apsyrtides archipelago of Unije, Ilovik, Susak, Vele Srakane and Male Srakane, as taught to him by his schoolteacher, Professor Valli. As he did so he fell easily into one of his favourite reveries of the story of the mythical Argonauts. Legend tells that here in the northern Adriatic they succeeded in fleeing their persistent pursuers as they were carrying on their ship, the *Argo*, the golden fleece that Jason stole from Colchis. When Aspyrt, Medea's brother, was tricked into negotiations by his treacherous sister and stabbed by Jason, Medea chopped Apsyrt's body into pieces and threw them into the sea. His limbs were transformed into islands, and the archipelago was named Apsyrtides in his memory. The route that delivered the Argonauts was, according to Mr Valli, the ancient amber route, the oldest of European sea routes that connected the north and the south of the continent of Europe; its origins were in the trade in amber that was transported from the Baltic across the continent down to the Mediterranean.

'Don't worry, don't be nervous,' shouted Armando back to Nino, somewhat belatedly, 'I know this road like the back of my hand. I could do it blindfolded.'

At 600 metres above sea level the temperature had dropped significantly, and the wind chill from the velocity of the bike wasn't helping either, although the steep ascent had caused Armando, thankfully to Nino's mind, to slow down significantly.

Just when Nino thought he probably couldn't take any more of this cold, Armando pulled over to the side of the road and parked up into a culvert that neatly, almost too perfectly, camouflaged his bike. With the application of a few strategically placed branches, left there from a previous visit specifically for the purpose, it was hidden entirely.

'Are we nearly there yet?' shivered Nino, reverting to nephew-uncle family relationship. 'I'm freezing.'

'I'll pretend I didn't hear that,' said Armando, stiffening a little. 'You're in the Partisans now. You've killed a man. You've killed two men. So, man up. Partisans don't feel the cold. And don't let me hear nonsense like that from you again. Especially up there.'

Vito had recovered from the trepidation and noise of the motor bike ride and was ready for adventure. The prospect of a hike made him even more excited.

'We can't approach the Rašpor ravines the direct way as we don't want to arouse suspicion. We have to take the back way, by foot: up to the top of Orljak and down to Gomila, and back to the abyss at Rašpor. That's where Pino's detachment is, awaiting further instructions from high command.'

The first slivers of dawn were breaking over Učka and the Kvarner as they began their ascent to Orljak on the small mountain path, still below the treeline and far enough from the snow line. Armando walked swiftly through the beech woods which gave way to chestnut forest as they broke the treeline towards the summit of Orljak, a kilometre above sea level. This was nature at its most majestic.

Vito was running on ahead.

'Look at him,' said Armando. 'He's a beauty. He will bring you many years of good fortune. He's young and he loves you. You take good care of him up here.'

'Yes, uncle, I'll do my best. I love him too. But I'll need to take care of myself as well.'

'Don't worry. War is not like they say it is. It's mostly waiting around for something to happen. It will be a good time for you to share with Vito. You know, a good truffle hunter is a dog's best friend and vice versa. If you stay close, study each other; try to understand each other's movements in the hunt. You will have an unspoken comprehension of each other and together you can discover great things. And I don't just mean truffles. But mainly.'

Just as they came to a clearing in the chestnut wood there was a huge flapping of wings as they witnessed an eagle owl caught in the act of eviscerating a good-sized pine marten which had given up the ghost not long before. In the chiaroscuro of the forest glade Nino just had time to restrain Vito as the owl, cool as a cucumber, looked around, the guts of its prey still in its mouth. The owl looked back, blinked unsurprised, with its huge saucer-like orange and black eyes, and gave a little hoot of disgust. It picked up the remnants of the pine marten and flew off with a great flapping of wings to a safer place to finish its breakfast.

'Jesus Christ, that scared the living shit out of me,' said Armando. 'But don't tell anyone,' he added with a cheeky wink. 'You're a Partisan now, and Partisans aren't afraid of anything.'

Vito growled in agreement, moderately peeved at not being allowed to take on the owl.

'And as for you, Vito,' said Armando, 'the only thing we want you to hunt is the Istrian gold. The little nuggets from down by the Mirna. Up here will be a bit of a holiday for you – no treasures to dig at this altitude.'

But Armando was genuinely frightened. It wasn't the first time he'd encountered an example of the wilderness that was pre-eminent on the Učka mountain, for it was the home of wild bears and wolves. He had met a goatherd up here who had told him that on his nocturnal missions he'd occasionally been up close and personal with a lynx. In spring, when the new-born kids were still fresh out of their mother's womb, he had to be on 24-hour watch because the eagles could swoop at any time of day or night.

'Nature is amazing,' said Armando, almost to himself. 'You know, I once saw a flock of sheep hanging about underneath a clump of hazelnut trees. You'll never guess. They were pawing at the ground as if intoxicated. When I started to scrape the surface, I found some amazing little black pearls. And I don't mean sheep shit!'

Turning back down the hill the home run was a little easier. After a kilometre or so Armando told Nino to stop and wait. He went into the forest where the treeline began again. 'Wait here with Vito,' said Armando. 'I'll go and get the all-clear. I'll be five or ten minutes.'

While he waited, Nino looked around. The morning star was growing in the east. The dawn never failed him; it always took his breath away whenever he watched it. There was something in the first crack of light that inspired a profound sense of well-being in humans. This moment was not an exception for Nino. As dawn revealed itself over Učka and down over the islands of the Kvarner, he was reminded of the line from the hymn he'd always loved: 'and glory shone around'. This dawn was glorious, made more important for Nino in that it was the first day of the rest of his life. A genuinely new day was dawning for him, literally and metaphorically.

'Daydreaming again, brother,' came a voice from the bushes. 'No time for daydreaming up here!'

Pino had come down alone to fetch him to the camp, since Armando thought it best for them to have a private moment after the action of the last few days.

'I'm proud of you,' said Pino, holding his brother in a close embrace. 'I always hoped that you would come and join us.'

'Did uncle Armando tell you?' asked Nino.

'The fascist scum had it coming,' spat Pino through a haze of tobacco smoke.

'No, I mean about dad.'

'That's who I am talking about. The bastard. The other one was just doing his job. The German. But the old man: there's nothing worse than a stool pigeon. Finally, we know who the informer is. It looks bad for us, but you did your duty for us both. The priest won't be much longer for this world, either.'

They looked at each other in silence. Finally, Nino stepped forward for another hug. Pino turned on his heels.

'None of that softy stuff now, Nino,' said Pino, using his army voice. 'You're a Partisan and we don't have time for that shit. Come on, it's another ten minutes' hike to the camp. Watch closely how to get there. You may be coming back on your own next time after a mission, and you will need to be able to find your way.'

*****

The karst caves of the region had long been places of sanctuary and retreat, not just because of their relative isolation in the extreme landscape but also for the cover and shelter that they provided. This particular one, above the town of Rašpor, lying between Orljić and Gomila, was part of the Ćićarija cave complex, its centrepiece being the Rašpor abyss.

Nino had no idea of the existence of such places so close to home and yet so far from everything. As Pino led him down the mountain path, they passed a makeshift sentry box where Pino received the Communist clenched fist salute from the Partisan guarding the small entrance.

Inside was another world away from the forest. Fires burned and lamps lit the busy underground encampment which made the 75 or so fighters that were in Pino's detachment completely invisible to the outside world; and yet it was a perfectly functional base within striking distance of any targets they wished to attack.

Partisan life in the woods that covered nearly three-quarters of the nascent state of Yugoslavia was tough. Harsh climates meant five months of snow and only three summer months, and the Partisans were constantly moving on with no guarantee of cover, shelter or clean water. But the woods provided the perfect base from which to launch hit-and-run attacks on the enemy, which was their stock-in-trade as guerrillas whoever was the target – German, Italian, Ljotićev, Četnik or *Ustaša*.

As Nino walked into the cave it seemed to open up beneath him, like Aladdin's grotto, and there was a whole community of soldiers at work. Pino told him that the cave actually went on for several kilometres, so far that they had never found the end of it. Some light came in from sink holes in the roof, but for the most part it was a shadowy place with braziers and naked flames on the walls providing extra illumination, along with some battery-powered lamps for security in an emergency.

Faida came running up, excited. 'Nino, how great to see you again,' she said, 'and you, too, Vito. I didn't think I'd see you both again so soon. It's great to have you here. Pino told me what happened. Forget it. They had it coming. You did the right thing. And now you are with us you are on the right path. We'll make a good Partisan of you – and, who knows, maybe a good Communist.'

'Comrade Faida will show you round,' said Pino. 'I need to go for a meeting with the regional commanders. I'll be back this evening. And keep Vito under control: this is an army camp, not a playground for dogs. Let's see if you both can do something useful.'

'Yes, sir, Comrade Pino, sir,' says Faida, half-saluting, and muttering as he walked away, 'What's eating soldier-boy today?'

Faida took Pino in hand and introduced him to the various parts of the unit. She showed him the sleeping area where the

Partisans simply slept on the floor on leaves and whatever else they could find to make themselves comfortable, using their packs as pillows. A number of Partisans were sleeping in the sitting position; Faida explained that this was how they got used to sleeping out in the woods and so they didn't want to change the routine.

'This is where we eat,' she said, pointing to a line-up of three cauldrons, one of which was bubbling away. 'Everyone has their plate and spoon which they can wash in the tub over there. Sometimes it's tough to eat, especially when we are out in the woods and come under attack. Say hello to Dino, the cook – he's the most important person here.'

'Ciao, Dino, I'm Nino – very pleased to meet you.' He paused and added as an afterthought, 'Comrade.'

'It's OK, mate, you don't have to "comrade" me, I'm a petit bourgeois deviationist,' he said, his army hat on his head at a jaunty angle. 'I just don't like fascists.'

Vito sidled up to Dino and nudged his leg with his muzzle.

'This one knows which side his bread is buttered on,' said Dino, good naturedly, slipping Vito a treat.

'You've got a friend for life, there,' said Nino. 'And by the way, if you need any truffles for that stew you're making, Vito's your man. My uncle Armando says there are two kinds of truffle hounds: the ones who do it instinctively and the ones that do it to please their master. This little beauty just wants to please his master.'

'Speaking as an unreconstructed anti-social element,' said Dino, 'I thank you for this intelligence.'

'Don't take any notice of him, Nino – or you, Vito,' said Faida. 'He's an anarcho-syndicalist with royalist leanings, and not fit for construction, salvage or reconstruction. But he's a damn good cook and plays a mean squeeze box.'

Faida took Nino by the hand and led him over to the field hospital that she had set up after the attack on Draguć. She had five casualties, four of whom were stable and on the mend; but the fifth was not looking too good and needed to be transferred.

'This one here,' she said, indicating a sleeping Partisan who seemed to be about 15 years old and was attached to an intravenous drip. 'He has a bullet in the leg which has shattered.

It needs to come out. I'm also afraid that there may be gangrene, which is why we need to ship him out to the hospital right away.'

'Hospital?' said Nino. 'What do you mean – the hospital in Buzet? The town is packed with Germans.'

'No, we have another place for urgent cases,' she said. 'It's over at Zalesje in the Brkini area. I need to take him there today. It's the best place for him. It's near Boršt, a 12-hour hike. We'll take two stretcher crews and alternate every half hour. Do you think you can handle it?'

'I've not got a whole lot else on,' said Nino, with a grin.

'Right, then. Let's get moving. And no. Vito can't come. Dino will look after him. It's a match made in heaven.'

*****

The journey to Zalesje turned out to be one of the most demanding physical efforts Nino had ever put his young man's body through. A 24-hour round-trip forced march, with a short sleep in the middle, across some of the most difficult terrain on the Istrian peninsular. Faida accompanied the men on their long trip to take care of Božidar, the patient who had been heavily sedated for the arduous journey. Just for good measure came the rain and followed by sleet; then for parts of the journey some snow when they ventured above the treeline and out in the open countryside, where most danger lay.

Nino was impressed by the organisation of the Partisan units, and even more by the size, scale, and level of professional competence at the hospital, which had been relocated to the north-east of the region on the Šmagurje farm in the vicinity of Ostrožno Brdo. Faida explained that it used to be in Padež, but an informer had betrayed the location and it had to be moved.

This time the clinic was newly built. Supplies for the patients and staff were provided by the villagers of Ostrožno Brdo, an act which put the whole community in grave danger. Security was of the utmost importance. If the Germans discovered them then every man, woman and child in the municipality would be put to death. And after that there would be reprisals. Faida told Nino that urgent cases were treated in the hospital unit which had 20 beds and constant care; there was an operating theatre and a small storehouse for the limited amount of medical supplies and the fairly primitive equipment they had access to. Elsewhere in the vicinity were hideouts with beds for recovering soldiers.

It was to the kitchen that Nino first repaired when they returned to the cave in the Rašpor ravine. He was not only famished with hunger, but he had also missed Vito. The dog, excited beyond sanity, came to greet him, turning little circles time after time and rolling on his back over and over again until he finally calmed down.

'Was he a good boy?' was Nino's first question for the cook.

'He was very good,' replied Dino. 'But when I took the little bastard out to try to find some truffles he was completely useless.'

'You have to know how to handle him, Dino. He only works for the party and Partisans. He knows that petit bourgeois deviationist elements will just exploit him for his labour.'

They laughed.

'He bloody well nearly did get his come-uppance,' confided Dino. 'We went deep into the forest on the Učka side, and he uncovered a bunch of charcoal burners who had just completed their *krbunica* and were on the verge of setting fire to it to make the charcoal. The dog scared the shit out of them, and they ran like hell.'

'That was dangerous; the Ćići usually don't take prisoners,' said Nino.

'No, it's OK, they work with us,' said Dino. 'Whenever there's any trouble or possible threat to our safety, we often hide out with them. Can't understand a word they say. And black as the ace of spades. Bloody Ćiribiris. Should fuck off back to Romania if you ask me.'

Nino decided not to start the discussion about all minorities and languages being welcomed in the new Yugoslavia and reached down to scratch his ugly little dog's ears. Vito dutifully rolled over on his back, maniacally lolling his tongue, and rolling his eyes with pleasure in time-honoured fashion. Nino then took him to the corner of the cave he had staked out as his personal space. He had made it comfortable with dry leaves and wood chippings from the forest floor, giving a semblance at least of some home comforts. Whilst he had had a house and a bed in Draguć, there was no camaraderie, comfort or, indeed, solidarity from his cold, cold father when he was still alive.

The stretcher-bearer team took their food tins back to their places and ate in silence. Nino finished up in record time and washed up his tin and fork ready for the next meal. He took out the Partisan manual that Pino had given him on one of his brief supervisory visits and returned to his studies. In fact, the trip to Zalesje had been useful. Whilst they had spent some of the journey across the mountain singing Partisan songs, his new comrades had helped Nino learn the Partisan oath of allegiance, which he would have to recite when he came before the officers' committee later that day. What helped to pass the time also helped him to appear to be a good Partisan.

The likelihood would be that after he was accepted as a fully-fledged Partisan that evening he would start off on courier duties. Whilst there was some radio contact, the reception in the Rašpor cave was poor so messages were sent by hand. Young teenage couriers like Nino would be expected to carry messages across enemy lines, whatever the weather and whatever the terrain. The golden rule was that if capture was looking likely, orders were that the messages should be chewed and swallowed to avoid them falling into the hands of the enemy.

★★★★★

'Comrade Mihailić, it's time to wake up.'

Faida is shaking Nino gently by the shoulder. 'It's time to meet the top brass.'

Pino appears by her side as he wipes the sleep from his eyes and pulls himself together.

'Are you sure you are up to this, Nino?' asks his brother sternly. 'We need strong, committed, and good Communists here if we are to win this war and if this brigade is ever to become a proletarian brigade, do you understand?'

'Yes, brother, of course I understand,' replies Nino. 'I killed the German captain, didn't I?'

'You're not going to be able to dine out on that for much longer!'

'Come on, the Neapolitan is waiting for us. We don't have much time.'

Pino leads the way out of the cave and down a grassy bank further into the ravine. About 50 metres downhill they come to another sentry and another cave opening; the landscape was like a Swiss cheese; the limestone having been eroded over the centuries into a warren of corridors and caverns created by underground rivers and the dripping of falling waterways.

Entering the main cave, Nino notices that the accommodation is slightly less primitive than in that of the other ranks. There are truckle beds and other items of furniture but, by and large, there is little comfort. As they enter, the commanders of the battalion are poring over a series of maps on three wide trestle tables. In the far corner, nearest to the entrance to the cave, a radio operator with headphones is twisting a dial trying to make contact with the outside world.

Pino marches Nino and Faida in and brings them to attention in front of the top brass.

It is the Neapolitan who turns first.

'Stand at ease,' says Romano; then, 'Stand easy.'

'Comrade Mihailić here, sir, for initiation,' says Pino.

The other three officers in the room join Romano behind the desk where four chairs are set up as a kind of tribunal. Seats are taken by the veteran Giusto Benvenuti, the political commissar Benito Gasparini, and Major Bruno Scavolini, the Neapolitan's deputy.

Faida and Pino step aside, leaving Nino alone in front of the officers.

'I understand from Comrade Armando in Buzet that this young man has already distinguished himself in our service,' says Romano.

'That's correct, sir. He shot a German captain in Buzet three days ago.'

The officers look at each other and mutter sounds of approval.

Faida speaks up next. 'And when we needed stretcher bearers to carry comrade Božidar to the field hospital at Zaselje, comrade Nino was the first to volunteer and he acquitted himself very well, sir.'

'That's not an easy trek, especially in this weather,' says Benvenuti, taking a sip from the coffee cup that has just been brought in by a young Partisan girl. 'Good man.'

'Well, what have you got to say for yourself, young man,' interjects Gasparini. 'Are you a good Communist?'

'I want to be, sir!' says Nino.

'Well, either you are, or you aren't. Which are you?'

'I am,' says Nino. 'But I'd still like to know a bit more about it.'

'Report here tomorrow morning at 06.00 for political education,' says Gasparini. 'I like a soldier who has a brain and can think for himself, and not someone who agrees and spouts the ideology.'

'Do you believe in the principles of brotherhood and unity?' continues the Neapolitan. 'That all people should be given equal status, regardless of ethnic identity, race or religion?'

'Yes, sir!' says Nino.

'Is there anything you'd like to tell us, Comrade?'

'Yes, sir,' says Nino, taking a deep breath. 'I also killed another man, sir. He was a Nazi informer.'

'What was the name of this man, Comrade?'

'Tomislav Mihailić, sir. My father.'

The officers look at each other as if to say this is enough evidence that they need to prove the young volunteer's loyalty and commitment. Romano steps forward, gives the Communist salute, and says, 'Welcome to the Partisans, Comrade Mihailić. We expect great things from you – just like your brother, here.'

They shake hands, and the other officers do the same, followed by Pino and Faida.

'Permission to speak, sir,' says Pino. 'We've forgotten to do the oath, sir.'

Major Scavolini, who had been silent until then, says, 'I think we can dispense with that. He did kill your father, after all. Good enough for me.'

Nino steps forward, with a small conspiratorial look to Faida. 'I can do it, sir,' he says, stepping back into the centre of the cavern. As the tribunal resume their places, Nino begins to recite, looking straight ahead, without hesitation:

We, the people's Partisans of Yugoslavia,
have taken up arms to wage a relentless struggle
against the bloodthirsty enemies
who have enslaved our country
and are exterminating our peoples.
In the name of liberty and justice for our people,
we swear that we shall be disciplined,
persevering and fearless,
that we shall spare neither blood nor life in fighting
the fascist invaders.

'Thank you, comrade,' says the Neapolitan, and with another salute, 'Dismissed. Not you, Pino – I need you here for the strategy meeting.'

*****

After Faida and Nino leave the cavern, the mood in the room lightens.

'Quite a character, your young brother, Pino,' says the major.

'He's still very young, sir. He'll learn, don't worry. I'm sure he will be a good Communist.'

'I'm sure, I'm sure. He's a very impressive lad,' says the major. 'I hear he has a very talented dog if Armando is to be believed.'

'Anyway, to business,' says the Neapolitan. 'We've had word from the high command that it looks like we're getting to the end of the road. The Germans are on the run and the Allies are stepping up their campaign in the Adriatic to finish them off. I have had a personal message from comrade Tito, via Dedijer, giving us a special mission.'

'While the campaign to finish off the Germans is going according to plan, the Marshal wants us to clear up some unfinished business,' says Gasparini.

'As I explained when we last discussed the domestic situation,' continues the Neapolitan, 'Damjanović has replaced General Mušicki of the Serbian Volunteer Corps – the SDK – and has become part of Mihajlović's so-called Yugoslav Army for the Homeland, basically, the Četniks. We think that this will change the relationship of the SDK with the Waffen-SS. We are reliably informed that in three days' time Hermann Neubacher, the Fuehrer's Special Envoy for the Balkans on political matters, will meet Dimitrije Ljotić, the chief of Zbor and the SDK, in Trieste. They will discuss German strategy about what happens when SDK and Četnik forces in Istria come into contact with British and American units who are expected to move in from Italy.'

Benvenuti, who has been silent until now, steps in and says, in his distinctive Rovignese accent, 'We think it's too dangerous to go after Ljotić in Trieste. However, a mole inside the Ljotićevci camp has confirmed that after this meeting with Neubacher, Ljotić will travel by car to the town of Postojna to meet General Damjanović in order to coordinate a Četnik-SDK withdrawal towards Italy.

'Our orders from Tito are, very simply, that this meeting should not take place and that Ljotić should disappear. This will be our mission over the next 48 hours. When Ljotić is dead we are to march on Trieste.'

Part Four

Chapter X

Dancing with Death

Istria: December 28th, 2019

It took 24 hours to get the all-clear from the city authorities for Emina and her team to return to the offices of the Istrian Environmental Defence League after the arson and graffiti attack on the building. The writing on the wall had already been cleaned off by their regular contractor (it happened a lot), and the attempts to set fire to the place by igniting the contents of the wastepaper basket weren't, as usual, being considered as serious by the municipality, the emergency services or the forces of law and order. Neither did the fact that Marco had incurred a couple of broken ribs for his trouble seem of much concern to the police, and in the event of there being no other witnesses, newspaper reports, or any way to track down the rider of the motor scooter, the local constabulary quietly filed the case in the 'hope it will go away' rotating file. In some ways this was a blessing in disguise, as the last thing Emina wanted was the police to start thinking that the Istrian Environmental Defence League was connected to the incident in Draguć two nights previously. Her confidence in their incompetence led her to immediately put this thought aside.

It was on a sunny morning three days after Christmas that the staff and crew of the IEDL began to slowly drift into their hipsterish offices in the former Communist government-owned warehouse. It was here in the nineties in the post-Homeland War period that the organisation was founded. They and a load of other 'creatively minded' companies and organisations occupied, squatted and then formally took possession of the building. These days there was still a lot of old former state-owned property lying around in Pula – and much of it ripe for development. The political scene had changed since the heady days when occupying and squatting actually worked. In today's current real estate market there was too much at stake, especially in a world where the dodgy end of the state-owned property business met the rapacious carpetbaggers of the free-market economy. Coastal real estate in Istria was big business, which meant unhealthy corruption at all levels of the game.

After Marco got out of hospital the previous evening, he could neither face the long drive back to Draguć nor another night anaesthetizing himself in a non-medical way with Zvonko. So he opted for the only offer available – the couch in Emina's bachelorette flat. She hadn't mentioned at the time that he would have to share it with an extraordinarily large feline. Fatso was its entirely apposite sobriquet and by the time he and Marco had installed themselves on the couch there wasn't much room for anything or anyone else. After the events of the day Marco just crashed into oblivion. He was grateful for the good night's sleep and for the fact that he felt better the next morning. He was even more grateful that while he limped around to her offices Emina had made an advance raid on her favourite bakery and had brought back *burek* and yogurt to the IEDL.

'The work we were doing over there,' says Marco, speaking with his mouth slightly full of the delicious cheese pie, 'was infiltrating the animal experiment laboratories. Finding out the names and addresses of management and employees, naming and shaming, as well as liberating groups of animals from facilities which experimented on live creatures. Other times we would just picket the research facilities so that when the workers arrived in the morning they would have to line up in order get past us. We didn't make it easy for anyone and we had loudhailers that would wake the dead. The louder and longer we could scream at them that they were puppy killers the better. Basic intimidation technique.'

'What still isn't clear to me, Marco,' inquires Emina, 'is just exactly whose side you were on. You are speaking as if you weren't a cop.'

'Essentially, come the end, Emina, I wasn't actually a cop. I just hadn't got round to telling the Met that,' says Marco emphatically.

'Well, with regard to the aforementioned, here it's not quite as simple as that,' says Emina. She is sitting at her desk under a sign which says, 'The greatness of a nation and its moral progress can be judged by the way its animals are treated – Mahatma Gandhi', and under it in big letters '*WELCOME TO CROATIA*'. 'Very often here it's a lot less anonymous. Everyone knows everybody else and, aside from the serious problems of physical revenge and comeback, people's livelihoods are important. So, we need to tread a fine line between disrupting but not alienating the people whose ultimate interests we have at heart.'

'I get it,' says Marco. 'There are different rules of engagement everywhere.'

'And of course,' says Emina, 'the real question in your case is, were you working in defence of the animals or on behalf of the forces of law and order?'

'Both, I guess,' says Marco. 'I suppose I justified it to myself as wanting there to be some kinds of checks and balances so that the ultimate beneficiary wouldn't be alienated.'

It is the first time that Emina and Marco have had a grown up political and ecological conversation for years. Separation, alienation, rebuilding of trust, and finding friendship again had been the arc of their relationship from the time Marco had joined the police. Emina is relieved to find that, in spite of the circumstances of his engagement in the animal liberation movement, he is actually a committed and dedicated activist and hasn't become institutionalised.

Taking up the subject of the local problems, Emina explains that the whole issue in the region with the truffle hunters and their animals is complicated because of the general low level of animal welfare. The truffle dogs have it easier than other animals, especially other canines like hunting dogs or strays. First of all, the dogs in the truffle season are consistently kept on the point of starvation so that their senses are sharpened, and they are more sensitive to and grateful for the high-value food treats they receive on success. Secondly, the dogs themselves are potential victims of sabotage from rival groups who go after the trained dogs of their competitors by leaving poisoned meat lying around in the forests. Thirdly, the issue of where the truffle dogs go when their noses don't work any more.

'One particularly callous truffle hunter told me that when the dog became past it he wouldn't want to waste a bullet, and made a sign to break the animal's neck with his bare hands,' says Emina. 'But I think he was just trying to impress me and pick me up. These Istrian guys really know how to charm the ladies.'

'Sensitive types, eh, those guys from the interior?' says Marco. 'I spoke with my colleague policeman the other night after Nino's dogs had been set loose. He told me that truffle prices have gone so high in recent years that all pretence at friendliness between truffle dog owners has disappeared. There are trufflers coming in from Italy, and even from further afield like Albania; they're causing trouble and intimidation working on the local patch. It's made things a lot worse, and many of them are now carrying guns.'

'That's right,' says Emina. 'And the fact that it hasn't been a good year after a bumper harvest last year just exacerbates the whole situation. It used to be that those smugglers like you and Nino supplied the Italian market; now they just come over and take what they can. They reckon that at least 15 per cent of all the white truffles sold in Asti come from Istria. Now the Turks and Ukrainians have started to muscle in on the market. It's all got that bit more competitive. It's the global problem in microcosm: belief in an ideology that has exponential growth as its central tenet in a world in which there are ultimately limited resources. It's an unrealistic ideology to hold – breaking point is always just around the corner. The fact remains that the best prices are still in Italy.'

Emina gets on a roll and goes on to explain to Marco that it is – and remains – a very democratic kind of activity. Anyone can do it as long as he or she has a trained dog and knows where the common land is. But proper training, which includes feeding a puppy bit of the fungus until it acquires a taste and then burying other bits ever deeper underground, takes three to four years. That makes a fully trained truffle dog's death a huge setback in terms of an investment of time in a single animal.

'Let's say you have 20 competing truffle hunters in Nino's part of the woods,' she explains. 'So, you hide poison in strategic places. Eventually, one or two of your competitor's dogs will find it and perish and all the other hunters will avoid the place. You know where you have buried the poison, you pick it up again, and then, bingo, the area is all yours to exploit. That's the way it is here, Marco, and I haven't even begun to tell you about the living conditions for the dogs.'

She explains she had one situation where there was a metal cage of no more than three metres by three metres in which five dogs were kept in lockdown during the height of summer and under the burning Istrian sunshine. Someone reported it and she camped out by the cages for two days to talk to the owner when he came to feed the dogs. His pathetic excuse was that it was true they were dogs for finding truffles but that during the months when there were no truffles he had no option but to cage his animals. Not much fun for the dogs.

'And, on top of that, dogs are the least of our worries. We have chemical companies polluting, we have filthy old coal-fired power stations, we have inadequate waste treatment, and a clean water delivery system in some towns that still has lead piping. The list is endless and there aren't enough hours in the day. Fortunately, though, unemployment is high so those who haven't escaped abroad are happy to volunteer with us.'

'You'd have a lot more luck with the dog issue in the UK,' says Marco. 'I used to think that the Brits preferred their dogs to people, and I know there's a strong tide of feeling that prefers them to immigrants. Look at that Nigel Farage.'

'True,' says Emina. 'But when you consider the lot who are in power here they make people like Farage look like well-meaning kindergarten teachers. You don't know the half of it. Now that the country has been well and truly looted by the post-Tudjman acolytes, they can get down to the business of tweaking the constitution so that their white-collar crimes can be perceived as legal. Brighter than bright, whiter than white. Bastards. Is there no end to the greed?'

'Of course, the solution to this conundrum is simple,' says Marco, with an impish grin. 'Fly truffling.'

'Fly truffling?'

'Yes. No dogs needed. The delicate art of fly-truffling is a subtle form of hunting the black pearls. I met a bloke in Provence once whose passion and obsession was the art of stalking flies that lay their eggs directly over the sunken truffle. It could catch on.'

'I think that's a bit of a subtle art for our people,' says Emina. 'It's too retail as opposed to wholesale.'

'Oh, well. It was worth a try,' says Marco, giving her a warm smile, and then changing the subject. 'So, who do we think tried to set fire to the offices and beat me up? Could it be a reprisal for whoever set free Nino's dogs? A lone wolf, so to speak?'

'Look, in reality, Nino is one of the good guys,' says Emina. 'He is one of the main truffle hunters in the region, and the restaurant at the Stancija, exclusive though it is, sells hundreds of kilos every year, whether in the restaurant or in the little shop. He's also buying from a lot of the locals at good prices. And do you think I would visit Faida and Nino if I though he mistreated his dogs? I get that they are working dogs and need discipline, but his dogs live at the Ritz compared to most of the others. He has always had to be above board and squeaky clean – because of his past. Those bastards at the local paper are always trying to bring down the tall poppies – and they'd love to scalp an ex-Partisan with keen relationships to his former Serb buddies in the old JNA and foreign ministry of Yugoslavia.'

'Look, Emina, there's only one thing for it here,' says Marco. 'I'm going to see Nino to find out if he knows anything. I have a feeling that he might be in danger. He's old, he's vulnerable, and the new kids on the block don't give a shit about his eminence in the forest. There was that story a few years ago in your old stomping ground in Italy about the old truffle hunter forced off the road by the Italian mafia on his way to sell his wares in Torino. Then there was the French guy who simply knifed and murdered someone who he thought might be on his truffle patch. It's no life at all for a 90-year-old gentleman to be fearful in his own back yard. I also think there's something fishy going on with the Chinese.'

Marco goes on to explain that there had been a lot of rumours in recent years that local sellers were adulterating their crop with the Chinese equivalent which looked exactly the same. And with local truffles going for around €500 per kilo and Chinese truffles, the *tuber indicum*, costing a mere €30 euros a kilo it made sense if you could get away with it. The difference was that while they looked the same, they didn't smell the same, and with the collusion of some local chefs the noble *melanosporum* and *aestivum* were being counterfeited. With a bit of truffle oil on a Chinese truffle the neophyte can hardly tell the difference.

'I've been reading up on this. Zvonko and I were discussing it the other night,' he continues. 'There is a shortage of truffles in the world at the moment. In countries like France, who are fiercely protective of their national treasures, they are only producing

50 tonnes of truffles per year as opposed to the 800 tonnes at the beginning of the twentieth century. You can thank the First World War for that. In reality, it is in France where this Chinese fashion took off. It spread to Alba and eventually to Istria. They reckon that about 25 tonnes of Chinese truffles reach Europe every year.'

Emina looks at Marco. For the first time we see a glimmer in her eyes of tenderness for him.

'Are you OK?' she says. 'I know you've been through a lot. Thanks for everything you've done these last days.'

She reaches out her hand. He holds it.

'I'm OK, I promise,' he says, getting used to the feel of her hand in his. 'I'm just glad to be back home.'

*****

Marco picked up the keys for Zvonko's Mercedes and reminded Emina that she was to bring Faida's run-around up to Draguć at New Year. By the time he got on the road towards Rijeka the sun had reached its winter apex and was bouncing off the blacktop as if it were water stretching like a long winding river before him. Fortunately, he hadn't forgotten his sunglasses. His exchange with Zvonko in Pula was brief and to the point. He explained to his best friend about Emina and the trouble down at the IEDL, that the place had been fire-bombed and that he had a pair of suspected broken ribs for his pains. Zvonko reiterated his belief that whoever had done this was an amateur, and maybe a threat from people close to Nino – but not Nino himself – to warn the ecologists off. The only thing to do was to speak with Nino and try to discover from him what was going on. There was far more to this than just some local row between animal rights activists and truffle hunters. Marco knew he had to get to the bottom of it or the family would know no peace.

Marco had also relented on the mobile phone front and accepted Zvonko's offer of his burner phone which went with the Mercedes. He had Nino on re-dial since he left Pula, but to no avail. Finally, he got a signal again as he passed Vodnjan and pressed the button one more time.

'What do you want this time?' shouted Nino.

'It's me, Nino, Marco,' he told his grandfather.

'Oh, I'm sorry, son. I didn't recognise the number. I thought it was one of those sales calls.'

'Grandad, where are you? I want to come and see you. We need to talk, grandad.'

'I'm at Beram, walking Vito and Strigo. There was a rumour that some of the dogs had been seen over here, but that turned out to be bullshit. Two are still missing.'

'I'll meet you there in half an hour.'

'Come to the chapel. I can pick up the key now.'

Marco was relieved that Nino had finally responded. As he came through to the periphery of Vodnjan, he turned on to the old road taking him through Kanfanar, Sveti Petar u Sumi and around Pazin on the back road towards Motovun.

Nino, meanwhile, had been to Mrs Sonja's house and picked up the key. In keeping with local tradition the key to treasures such as Saint Mary's Chapel at Škriljinah was held by a local and could be picked up at any time. Indeed, such keys are held for churches and monuments all over Istria. In this respect the region had a safe, trusting feel to it. It was also an economical, grassroots way of curating places off the beaten track away from the ugliness of the mass tourism of the coast. Nino was a regular visitor, a generous donor to the upkeep of the frescoes, and the keyholder knew him well. As no-one else was visiting on this sunny winter's day, out of season, she willingly handed him the key, reminding him to return it and switch off the lights when he had finished.

Sitting now in the gloom of the confraternity church of Saint Mary, looking up at the fine depiction of Saint Martin the Horseman, Nino sat in wonder at the beauty and simplicity of the painting. Ever since he was a little boy he had been passionate about the frescoes in his village church of Saint Rocco in Draguć. It had been here through his careful and diligent eye that the greatest of the frescoes in the village had been discovered at all. Having no interest in religion himself, Nino was beaten mercilessly by his father when a child and had often sought refuge in the chapel of Saint Eliseus. One time while hiding there he thought he saw shadows behind the whitewash on the thirteen-century walls. As he wiped this paint gently away with spit on a handkerchief a dazzling colour started to appear beneath. Realising he had found something important he kept the information to himself when he went off to join the Partisans in the forests below Učka. He swore to himself that if he survived the war he would restore the chapel of Saint Eliseus to its former glory.

Despite everything, Nino had no religion. Partly because of what he saw in the war, partly because of Communism. But mostly because he worshipped at the altar of the truffle. It was deeply infused in his DNA. The power of the memory of the flavour of the truffle got him at an early age and, not heeding his uncle Armando's warnings that the lust for the truffle was like a drug, it had taken him over. In a way it had become his religion. The black magic apple of love, as George Sand called it. Sitting in the church and considering his position, he felt more than ever the sinister nature of the business he was in and was reminded that in the Dark Ages the truffle was known as the devil's handiwork grown from the spit of witches.

Now, though, as he sat and waited for his grandson to join him, Nino turned his mind to more positive thoughts and enjoyed the simple story of Saint Martin. The experts believed the fresco was probably a joint effort by Vincent de Kastav and his team. Saint Martin was a well-to-do Roman cavalry officer trying to live his faith. When he came across a poor beggar, he had nothing to offer him but the clothes on his back. De Kastav showed Martin cutting his heavy officer's cloak in half and making a humble gift of it to the poor man. Nino admired above all the sense of movement within the frame; and the strength in Saint Martin's body and the power of the horse that he sat on when compared to the weakness and vulnerability of the beggar. As he sat looking at the piece, now over five centuries old, he thought to himself that he wished someone like Saint Martin existed today and would come to his aid.

*****

The sound of dogs barking followed by the calming sound of Marco's voice outside the chapel wakes Nino from his reverie. He heaves himself up from the pew and shuffles outside. He is finding it harder and harder to get around these days, but he doesn't want to let it show. Marco meets him at the door. They kiss on both cheeks and Marco turns to take in the splendour of the images on the ceilings and walls that team de Kastav had brought to life. Nino turns with him, and together they take in the late medieval pre-Renaissance razzle-dazzle concision of its pictorial maze.

'I used to take you here when you were a boy,' says Nino, 'Do you remember?'

'Oh, yes, I remember all right.'

'Your father didn't like me bringing you here, or to Saint Eliseus and Saint Rocco,' says Nino with a smile. 'He thought you were too impressionable and might find God.'

'I imagine back in those days it wasn't such a great idea. Church and all that,' says Marco. 'Ironic, really, when you think of how Catholicism has caught on, nowadays.'

'It was the dying days of Socialism. Tito had been dead almost a decade, and the country had started to fall apart. No-one really noticed those things any more,' says Nino. 'It's like sub-consciously everyone had started to prepare for war. And for an upsurge in Catholicism. Fucking Milošević and Tudjman. And religion. Fucked everything up between them. Each one as bad as the other.'

'To tell you the truth, grandad, I used to dread you bringing me here. It used to scare the shit out of me.'

Marco and Nino move as one towards the centrepiece of the frescoes, the Danse Macabre, or Dance of Death, which was a powerful piece to behold for children of any age. This motif had been an all-pervasive one throughout Europe from the thirteen and fourteenth centuries, largely driven by the equalising phenomenon of the plague or Black Death; it combined the essential ideas of the inevitability and the impartiality of death.

'I used to think that all these frescoes were like movies,' says Nino. 'When I was your age and first saw them, I hadn't even seen a movie, but I had read about them in the paper. This is what I imagined they were like. When I finally got to see one, it was very disappointing. They left very little to the imagination.'

'When you brought me here for the first time, I must have been about eight or nine,' says Marco. 'All I could see was that little boy in the fresco, and I wondered what it might be like for him, joining the jolly skeleton dance with the cardinal and the bishop, the king and the queen, and the innkeeper – all jigging along to the rhythm of the *surle*, those Istrian bagpipes, and the others playing those things that look like medieval oboes, bagpipes, and the double-whistle. Even that beautiful Istrian hound would go to its death. That is what touched me. It made me think that kids, too, were fair game for death. And that was pretty scary.'

'I'm sorry I traumatised you,' says Nino, with a little edge in his voice. 'Kids traumatise easy these days – well, compared to what we had as kids. I suppose in those days we were a bit primitive, wanting to know about art, music and history, instead of video games and disaster movies. There's a lot of traumata about, these days: PTSD and conditions that didn't exist in my day. I know they are real.'

'There's truth in what you say. But I can't help but think these conditions are created and exaggerated by the free-market economy, the political manipulation of and by the veterans and the widows, but most of all the collusion between little local medics and big pharma. But it would have taken a lot to traumatise me, Nono,' says Marco, 'growing up in the dying days of Yugoslavia with everything that was going on. We didn't know what the right answers were, what the right ideology was, how were we to answer at school. The macabre of the artistic fictional world was easy compared to the confusion of real life.'

'I used to run away down here during the war, over the hill from Grimalda, me and the first Vito. And only once with Pino. He was allergic to churches. I was drawn by the "movies",' says Nino. 'I told Pino to come because he would see how egalitarianism really worked. Especially in this one, where the order is broken. Even I saw that as a 14-year-old boy. Of course, the king comes first, bearing his sceptre and flowers, with the queen; but the innkeeper, the child and the mendicant come before the knight, which breaks the rule: usually the dance of death follows the social hierarchy. I told him it was a Communist Dance of Death. Especially because the clergy the bishop and cardinal went first and the merchant, who tries to bribe the devil with his riches, gets the same treatment as everyone else. Socialism in action, at least. He wasn't convinced.'

'It must have been hard to come to terms with Pino's death, so young, so full of life,' says Marco.

'It changed everything. And in its way is still changing everything,' says Nino, rather obtusely. 'Look, see the boy. There's a German *Totentanz* I remember in which a child asks, "Must I die when I can't yet walk?" Makes our version seem light-hearted. Nobody seems terribly troubled about dying. But maybe that's because de Kastav couldn't do faces.'

The grandfather and grandson swap a brief smile.

Then a silence that allows them to contemplate the other frescoes: the classic Adoration of the Magi and, as it was a confraternity church in honour of the Virgin, the Marys; the Last Supper; the Entry to Jerusalem. They were all there. Marco saw his chance in the lull in conversation.

'Grandad, you've helped me so much in my life,' says Marco. 'I – I mean we, Zvonko, Emina and me – we are worried about you. The thing with the dogs, the attack in Pula yesterday. Is everything all right?'

Nino is silent for a moment, and then turns to Marco and looks at him straight in the eye. 'I won't lie to you my boy,' he says. 'It has been a bad season. Whole areas of the forest have dried up. I'm starting even to believe in climate change. To be honest, I'm having trouble fulfilling some orders. But I'll make it, I know I can; I feel my luck is about to change. I owe a bit of money here and there but nothing I can't handle. It should be sorted by New Year. We're expecting some good news.'

'It doesn't sound that great, Nino,' says Marco. 'You know you can always ask me or Zvonko if you need money. We're in good shape. I have some savings I made while working underground, and Zvonko's olive business is a gold mine. You only have to ask.'

At this, Nino sits down in the nearest pew and looks up at the ceiling.

'Thank you, my boy, thank you,' he says, wearily. 'But I won't be needing anyone's help.'

Marco sits down next to him, and they remain there in silence for a good few minutes. Eventually, Nino reaches out and takes him by the hand.

'When you reach my age, these paintings start to speak to you in a different way. They speak to me differently every time I come to look at them. Have you noticed with this one, where the skeletons are walking more than dancing? Do you suppose that's a Croatian thing? And maybe I was wrong about the movies. There was one. Must be 50 years ago. Death was there. Playing chess with a crusader. The man with the eyes hanging on to the branch while Death saws away. The virgin in the rose garden leading the child. This was the movie that looked like a fresco from these times.'

'Come on, grandad,' says Marco, 'let's not dwell on this. Just proves that there's nothing new under the sun. Art imitates life imitates art. The film you're talking about is called *The Seventh Seal*, by a Swedish director called Ingmar Bergman. He has a lot to answer for. And obviously, he knew his medieval frescoes. Look, I need to make tracks. I promised to look in at the rehearsal for your New Year's birthday party.'

'I think I know how you felt,' says Nino, 'when you were nine and you looked at the little boy up there. The seven ages of man thing is true. Here I am, wading into my tenth decade and I'm no wiser than you were, and just as scared. Pick a character, any character. The merchant seems the most obvious now. God knows what my penance will be. And talking of the last dance as cold comfort, you need to get to your rehearsal.'

Outside the church, the dogs have become restless and are pulling on their leashes as they walk them back up to the village of Beram to return the key and pick up their cars.

Suddenly, back to reality, Nino starts again about the dog débâcle and becomes defensive about the community and the other trufflers: 'They aren't bad people, you know,' he says. 'Times around here have been tough for the regular hunters. It's true there are a few bad apples, but none would do something like attack Emina or let loose the dogs. Most of the people in our community round here know Emina and love her.'

'They've known her since Grožnjan. Nearly 20 years. A whole generation,' says Marco.

'It will be 25 years this year since your father died,' says Nino. 'He has been dead longer than he was alive. No father should have to live to see his children in their grave. Such a needless, unnecessary war.'

'I'm sorry, grandad, let's not go over this now,' says Marco. 'Stipe was right when he said that Milošević was responsible for the war and even more right when he said that bastard Tudjman was right behind him. Fuck them all. And Hans-Dietrich Genscher and his grubby yellow pullover. Old men without consciences sending young men to their deaths. May they all rot in hell.'

The dogs start to bark from inside the back of Nino's car.

'The only thing I can remember about that time was how when he came home on leave – when he wasn't with you, or while you were sleeping – he loved to come out with the dogs and then how Doggi, his old dog, died of grief when he didn't come back from the war. He's under the rambling rose tree next to your room.'

'I remember how the dog suffered from his absence. Every morning he trotted down to the gate to wait for him to come back. Then he just lost the will to live.'

'I gave him a gift when he went for basic training. The Roman gladiator arm guard. The *manica*, I think they were called. I wanted to give him the most precious thing I had.'

'He and I spent hours trying to work out the Latin letters carved into the back of it,' says Marco. 'But it didn't make any sense. He could read the names "Severus" and "Lucia". That was all.'

'Six months later he was back on leave after his first deployment,' says Nino. 'He was a different person. He didn't want to discuss anything. Just stayed in his room. The only thing he would talk about was the armour. He wanted to know how I got hold of the piece. I told him it was entrusted to me by a prisoner-of-war when I was in the Partisans. He went on and on about how he thought that the engravings on the inside were a code. He became obsessed with cracking the code. To encourage him, I told him if he could find out what it meant legend had it he'd never want for anything. I told him that the prisoner said there was a superstition that the code told of a hidden truffle forest richer than anything that had been ever found in Istria. He looked at me hard, deep in the eyes, and said, "Is that really the legend?" They were the last words he spoke to me. The next thing I know your grandmother and I were collecting his belongings from the barracks. Maja didn't want to go. There was no body, you see. Nothing left. Only the *manica*. And a note for to you. I'm glad that your mother decided to leave it to you in the end.'

'She didn't,' says Marco.

'She didn't what?'

'She didn't leave it to me. She didn't want me to have it. She thought it was cursed, that there was bad blood attached to it. I found it in a bag of rubbish that she didn't have time to throw away before she died. Along with his letter. I'll show it to you. I have the letter and the arm guard up at the Rose House.'

*****

The rehearsal is already well under way by the time Marco enters the main assembly hall at the Pazin Gymnasium. He can hear Mr Dalrymple's heavy-handed choir-master's thump on the piano, repeating a single chord over and over again as if to make the point.

'No, no, no!' shouts Dalrymple to the mildly amused gathering of 16- and 17-year-olds who make up the school choir. 'It's all very well to sing the note – anyone can do that. But you have to EEE – NUN – SEE – AYTE, otherwise I can't understand what you are singing. And if I can't understand what you are singing then you are disrespecting the song – and what is the point of doing something with disrespect?'

Dalrymple looks over to see Marco and waves. 'Come on over, Marco,' he says. 'God, sometimes I feel like a superannuated, undepilated Julie Andrews. Meet the "Murderers of Music", as I call them. No, they're not that bad. In fact, some of them are damn good – and the others could be if they just got their fingers out of their arses!'

The kids think this is uproariously funny.

'You see this big lad, here,' says Dalrymple, indicating Marco. 'I first met him when he was your age. We had a choir in Grožnjan, and he used to come for his summer holidays over from England. Every year for about four years we spent the summer singing, and smoking hundreds of contraband fags. Back in the day when tabs were good for you. Big Jack Charlton used to spark one up at half-time. They were fine old times, eh, Marco?'

Marco nods his agreement as the kids start to get bored, imagining the dark ages of Dalrymple's depraved, tobacco-addicted past.

'OK you lot, before I lose your gnat-like attention spans and you get back to more important stuff like your telephones, iPads and putting selfies of your genitalia on the worldwide interweb. We all meet here at six o'clock on New Year's Eve. We are playing at the restaurant of this gentleman's grandfather at Stancija Mihailić. You know the numbers. It's your first paid gig, so be on time or we will go without you and you won't get paid. Did you hear me, Juranić? What did I just say? Come on!'

'Uh. Sorry, sir?' says Juranić.

'You have to watch out for this one, Marco,' says Dalrymple, 'Rovignese, you see. You know what they're like. The great Victorian explorer Sir Richard Burton ended his days in Trieste as the British Consul-General. He said that of all the Istrians those from Rovinj were the most turbulent, and even their women were handy with a knife. Is that not so, Juranić?'

'Yes, sir,' says Juranić, not without a little pride. 'And Dante also said that we speak a dialect which he described as "barbaro, incongrue e crudele".'

'Correct, Juranić: go to the top of the class! I have taught you well!' exclaims Dalrymple.

'Sir, I have a question,' asks another of the boys. 'Do we have to wear our choir uniforms? I'm only asking because we want to go to the New Year disco straight after, and the uniforms are a bit square.'

'Square? Square?' shouts back Dalrymple. 'In my day it was hip to be square. Still is.'

He looks over to Marco for affirmation, who shakes his head.

'The oracle has spoken. Who said the age of Punk isn't dead? OK. White shirts it is. There's a reason. And if there are no further questions you can all fuck off back to your hovels. Thank you for giving up your valuable time for something as trivial as the muse that is Euterpe.'

To Marco: 'Not, you Mihailić, not you. You get to stay behind. Detention for being late. And I have a further punishment.'

He pulls out some sheet music from his battered leather briefcase.

'This is the number you will be singing at Nino's party, and Emina will be doing it with you. It's my surprise for the old bastard – it's his and Faida's "song". Faida asked me specially. She doesn't want him to know about it. It will break the soppy old sod's heart.'

Marco looks at the sheet music and reads, '*Oh Youth* by Arsen Dedić. I have a dim memory of Nono and Nona bill-ing and cooing to it. Do I have time to learn it properly?'

'With a talent like yours, my boy, not a problem. I've already emailed the music to Emina; she will rehearse with you separately. Very simple. Both in unison. If we have time we can do some fancy bits around the bridge, but for a song like this less is more in my view. Anyway, forget about that for now. The choir will come in on the choruses and the final verse. Shall we begin? Let's go straight in. It's got quite a long intro: G minor, C minor 7th, then D7. Ready? One, two, three, four.'

*****

Later in the bar Marco and Dalrymple have ordered their drinks and settled in at a quiet corner table.

'Thanks for that, Mr Dalrymple,' says Marco. 'It's a beautiful song. How have I missed out on it all these years?'

'Marco, I think it's time we dropped the "Mr Dalrymple" nonsense. We've known each other far too long. And look at you, mid-thirties; probably the age I was when I first got to know you.'

'What should I call you?'

'Just call me "Bonkers".'

'Bonkers?' says Marco, almost spitting out his beer.

'Yes, Bonkers. All my close friends call me Bonkers. It's a long story.'

'Bonkers Dalrymple,' says Marco, enunciating and trying it out for size. 'I like it. I like it.'

'I'll give you a clue. Have a read of John Irving's *The World According to Garp*. Or – as good as – check out the movie. George Roy Hill's masterpiece, and Robin Williams at his tragi-comic best. All will become clear. I was a bit of an old dog back in the day.'

They drink and relax into the evening.

'So, uh, Bonkers, what do you think of the song?'

'Look, you don't have to use it all the time. Just now and then.'

'Me and Zvonko we have this thing. We have this thing. Repeat until funny. Bonkers.'

This time they laugh.

'See – told you. It works,' says Marco.

'The thing about the song,' says Dalrymple, 'is that you don't find out about it until you are old enough to remember what youth was like. While you are still experiencing youth, you're not very interested in the running commentary. That's why it's good for Nino at Ninety and why it will be the penultimate number. The encore will be more upbeat. But that'll be a singalong, not the depressing old musing on the passing of youth.'

'The thing about this one, though,' says Marco, 'is that it starts out as a regular popular song and then becomes something else. It crosses the line where a catchy tune becomes poetry. It's like Auden: "Time that tires of everyone, has corroded all the locks and thrown away the key for fun." It's not as negative as the old adage that youth is wasted on the young. But close.'

'There was a young actor I knew from Belgrade who died very recently,' says Dalrymple. 'He said, "Time is our biggest enemy, not people. People are transient as everything else, but time will always be there to take away everything. Years, youth, love, memories, loved ones, and finally you. Time does not forgive anyone; no-one has escaped it yet." He knew he was dying. He hadn't told anyone else. He was a dear boy, taken far too soon. I got to know him translating at the Pula Film Festival. Liked a drink. I think Nino will like it.'

'Well, I've just been at Beram, looking at the Danse Macabre with him. Nothing like a good Dance of Death to get you in the festive spirit. It's a Croatian thing, I gather. Nothing like a good funeral.'

'Yes, it's rather chilling,' says Dalrymple. 'Concentrates the mind wonderfully.'

'While we are on the subject of Nino,' says Marco, 'tell me about Nino's Chinese buddies. What's the story there?'

'Well, between you and me, and breaking the confidence of the confessional,' says Dalrymple, 'they seemed like decent, straightforward chaps. They came in the summer and then turned up just before Christmas. They must have some clout because they are staying in one of the villas on Brioni, which is technically closed for the winter break. Somebody pulling strings, if you know what I mean.'

'What game are they in?'

'Same as Nino. Truffle business. High-end clients in Hong Kong, Macau and the mainland. Scarcity of supply, apparently, in Alba and Périgord. Someone tipped them off to Croatia and Istria. Turned up one day with bundles of cash and eventually the cash found Nino. Nino asked me to come along to translate – you know his English is shit even after a life in diplomacy and tourism. So, as far as I know, all they do is deal truffles. That's it. End of story. I have no head for business, but I do have a head for smelling out trouble. They just talked sizes and prices and it was all Greek to me. Well, no, it wasn't. In fact, if it had been it might have been a darn sight easier for me to understand. The ancient variety, of course.'

'What were they like? Dangerous? Did they threaten him?'

'No. They weren't like that. Utterly charming. Could charm the skin off a snake. But with the Chinese you can never tell. Inscrutable, you see.'

'They sound like regular businessmen doing a regular deal.'

'Nino was very keen to take their money up front. He's usually not so brazen. But this time he wasn't going to do business without a significant down-payment. I excused myself from the room while they talked numbers. Discretion and all that. But I understand it was a significant sum.'

'Bonkers, you are a saint; let me buy you another pint. This is really helpful.'

'If you insist. Never look a gift horse in the mouth and all that.'

The waitress brings over two more beers, on Marco's signal.

'Cheers, old chap, all that singing gives a man a thirst.'

'I thought it was mostly me doing the singing,' says Marco.

'You've not heard of passive singing, have you. It's the bane of every accompanist's life. We know too much, that's our trouble.'

'Here's to passive singing,' toasts Marco.

'Cheers! I don't know, Marco; what is it with you and your bloody family? I'm always involved in some complex issue or another – life can be simple, Marco. Look at me, nearly forty years here and not a worry on me! Cheers to that.'

'This year, Bonkers, I promise everything will be simpler. Starting on New Year's Day!' says Marco. 'But there's one last thing.

Grandad started talking about the gladiator relic again, the *manica*. You remember? Dad's treasure from his childhood that he bequeathed to me.'

'What? The gladiator's arm protector?' asks Dalrymple.

'Yes, that's the one.'

'What? You mean the code?'

'Yes. Did you ever solve it?'

'We struggled for fucking days over that when he was home on leave. On the one hand it's a kind of a map but seems incomplete. On the other hand, the lettering is a code.'

Marco takes out a piece of paper from his pocket and shows it to Dalrymple.

'I've copied it down for you. I've also taken a photo that I can forward to your smartphone, if indeed you have joined the twenty-first century. Do you want to have another go at cracking it?'

'Buy me another pint,' says Bonkers, seriously.

'OK,' says Marco.

Chapter XI

Striking Out

Colonia Pietas Iulia, 81 AD

Is there any news? shouted Lucia, barely catching her breath as she saw a grim-faced Severus coming down the gangplank of Apion's boat, which had just docked in Pietas Iulia after arriving from Vasanium.

'Nothing,' said Severus. 'Apion has spoken to all the transport ships going in and out of Vasanium to Rome and I've been checking all shipping going to and from Rome from here. So far there is no sign of him registered on any of the official barques. There have been no shipwrecks reported and there's been fair weather for the last three weeks. He must have been held up somehow.'

It had been a week since Nasica should have returned from Rome, but there was still no sign of him and Severus and Lucia were becoming seriously worried.

'His mother and sisters would have known,' said Lucia. 'As far as their messages tell us he left home ten days ago heading for Ostia Aterni to pick up a boat for Pietas Iulia or Vasanium.'

'I don't know what to say,' says Severus. 'Apion thinks he might have taken a boat that got into trouble, and they have either had to put in at Issa or are limping across and in need of repair. Come on, let's get back to the school. We can't do any more here today.'

Since returning from their jaunt to Festus and Vita at the Laime Channel a week previously, Severus had been thrown in the deep end at the newly founded gladiator school. He was working from their temporary accommodation at the barracks of the Legio II Adiutrix Pia Fidelis. Since Vespasian's time it had been based in Pietas Iulia and had overseen the first part of the building of the stone amphitheatre under the emperor's supervision.

Construction had already begun on a purpose-built school near to the arena, and both would be connected by an underground tunnel to allow easy access for the gladiatorial family. Oceanus was hoping to get approval from Domitian to use the opportunity of these major works to open up a channel from the sea to the amphitheatre so he could stage sea battles on an unprecedented scale. Until then,

Severus was comfortable to be under the protection of his old legion, whose standards, the Capricorn and the Pegasus, flew high and proud above the fortifications of the camp.

Oceanus was waiting for them at the entrance to the parade ground when Lucia and Severus returned.

'What news?' asked Oceanus, concerned.

'Nothing as yet,' replied Severus. 'If we don't hear from him in a few days we'll send to Rome to search further.

'Very wise,' said Oceanus. 'But let's wait and see. The *mare clausum* has only just finished and sometimes boats can get into difficulties during this season. Let's give it a few more days. Meanwhile, dear Lucia, you must be out of your mind with worry. Would you like to have a sedative, or some wine sent to your quarters?'

'Thanks, Oceanus, that won't be necessary,' answers Lucia and moves off in the direction of the officers' barracks where rooms had been allocated for her and Nasica. Until this morning she had taken delight in preparing and making things cosy for his eventual return, but with each passing day hope was running out and her spirits had been failing. Then this morning, ten days after he was due to return, she finally started to face the reality of the situation: that he might not be coming back.

*****

It had been a full week since Severus had been presented with his first set of raw recruits for the school. And what a terrible shambles they were. There were a few old lags who knew their stuff but were lazy and had run to fat. There were some ex-legionaries who had spent what was left from their 5,000 *denarii praemia* and were looking around for the kind of simple security they had known as soldiers. From his experience in the legions Severus knew exactly what to do with them for the first month; and it had very little to do with being in the arena and more to do with the rigours of being a soldier.

Fitness and discipline were the first things that Severus worked on with his new lads. He wanted his gladiator training at the Pietas Iulia School to become known for getting the raw recruit to an absolute peak of fitness. In the very first instance he deliberately forbade any gladiator or member of his team to come anywhere near using real weapons for the initial month or so of training. This was welcome news to the trainers and staff of the school, until they found out that they were expected by Chief Doctor Severus to take part in the training regime as well. In real life, the old lags could do with a bit of tuning up. At first this didn't go down too well, but later towards the end of the month everyone agreed that it was a morale-boosting idea and a co-operative spirit of collaboration, in the military style, prevailed.

Only after the first month would Severus and his team introduce the idea of weapons, albeit dummy ones. They would start off with the wooden training sword, the *rudus*. These held special symbolic value for a gladiator for it was the *rudus* that was also presented in the arena to a successful combatant. Thus it was important to impress on the *novicius*, or junior recruit as they were first referred to when joining the *familia*, the symbolism of the *rudus* as a totem of freedom. This would become even more important for them when they completed their initial training and were ready to fight in the arena; this was when they received the title *Tirones gladiatores* or *Tyro*.

Once he had become familiar with them, and they made an effort to live up to his standards, Severus grew to be happy with his first intake. There were 30 novitiates, about half of whom were ex-soldiers who had volunteered after spending their lives slicing up the enemies of Rome all over the empire for modest pay, but a damn good pension. By signing up with the school they figured they could become gladiators and slice up people on a voluntary basis, but with the chance of winning fight purses that could contain significant sums – enough to retire or buy freedom with. Severus had made it a condition of taking the job that he didn't want his group to be polluted by any men who had been committed to the gladiator school as a way of sentencing them to an entertaining (for the audience) death. Not with the first intake, anyway. Severus wanted his gladiators to be incentivised. Thus the real innovation he had made was avoiding the school being run as a quasi-prison. The gladiators themselves were their own wardens.

★★★★★

Lucia was beside herself with worry. Whichever way she went over it in her mind, there was no way of finding any mental peace. The thought of Nasica's potential fate and the reality of his absence haunted her every waking hour. She almost regretted not accepting Oceanus's offer of a sleeping draught, or even a flask of wine. As she walked around her empty quarters, she cursed herself for allowing Nasica to go to Rome in the first place; but on the other hand she couldn't wait to have him back with her there to tell him the good news that she and Severus had regarding the potential truffle business. They really did have a plan that worked, and which could secure everyone's future away from the trials and tribulations of the fight business.

But life had to go on. She had to think about the future – for the moment when Nasica returned. The best way to do that was to continue her master plan to get herself and her own as far away from the arena as possible. Step by step it was working, largely due to her own force of character. Prior to leaving Laime, Festus and Vita, along with Lucia and Severus, had confirmed that it wasn't just a fluke that Brutus and Britannica had the gift for finding the precious truffles. They had decided that, after Nasica's return to Pietas Iulia, Lucia would go back to Laime with the dogs, along with Philumena and Thelos. There she would thoroughly explore the area to find the prime sites that the tubers were growing in and try to establish some logic to their seasons. At the same time Festus wanted to work out if there was any way of cultivating the truffles so that they could actually secure supplies and set up a business that could survive the ups and downs of the seasons and the vicissitudes of Roman colonial life.

Lucia was in the process of deciding which of the dog troupe to take with her when she heard a gentle but firm knock at her door.

'Lucia, Lucia,' said the man's voice, 'are you there?'

'Who is it?' called out Lucia as she went to open the door. 'Just a minute!'

It was Oceanus with a flask and a covered plate of food.

'I hoped you'd still be here,' said Oceanus. 'Do you mind if I come in? I've brought you something. Perhaps it will help you take your mind off things.'

'That's very kind of you, Oceanus. I was just about to lie down and try to get some rest. Another time.'

'These are fresh oysters from your friends at the Laime Channel,' said Oceanus.

'How do you know about Festus and Vita?'

'Apion is a very good source of information – and treats. He was there yesterday and he brought these for me.'

'Is that right?' asked Lucia suspiciously.

'He also says there is no further news of Nasica at Vasanium.'

'Yes, he already informed us, thank you, Oceanus,' she said, stiffening. 'Now I'd better go and have that nap.'

'It's not looking very good. Is there any reason why Nasica wouldn't want to come back? Maybe his family disapproved of his relationship with a freed woman?'

'Even if they did, Nasica isn't bound, like some, by such snobberies.'

'Why not have a drink of this excellent wine I've brought before you sleep? It'll help you get some rest. I'll leave it here. And if you don't want the oysters, so much the better. More for me and Seneschal.'

'Thanks, Oceanus, that will be all,' she said, moving him towards the door.

'Look, Lucia, I know you and I haven't always seen eye to eye, but – well – if Nasica doesn't make it back... You know I am always here for you.'

Too shocked to speak, Lucia slammed the door in his face, and threw the flask after him. It hit the back of the closed door, shattering and spraying wine everywhere. Lucia immediately regretted wasting it. But her loathing for Oceanus and his devious ways had long ago driven a wedge between them.

*****

Another week passed of strict physical training and health checks by the *medicus* as the novices got used to their new situation. This being an army garrison camp their living conditions were cramped, and the 30 men all shared one big room in which they had various cots and mattresses spread out along with all their possessions, which in most cases were few. Oceanus promised their situation would be much improved when the new *ludus gladiatorius* was completed in the coming months. Still, these gladiators-in-waiting had the advantage over most gladiator schools in that they were allowed to come and go as they pleased when they weren't training and, like soldiers, all food was provided for them.

The menu wasn't exactly exotic or exciting; in fact, it was endlessly dull and boring and the tyros-to-be would have to supplement the dreariness of their diet with whatever they could pick up at the market. Every day endless amounts of what was called *sagina* was laid on by Oceanus's kitchens. *Sagina* was a sort of mush made from wheat, barley, and beans. It was tasteless, stodgy, and lay heavy in the stomach like lead. But it was at least nourishing, and it fed the huge appetites of big men who trained vigorously, often twelve hours a day. The *sagina* was where the barley men got their nickname from. While the food may have been dull and predictable it did its job and bulked up these athletes to give their frames some flesh and fat protection if assaulted by anything sharp and metallic.

It had been a long day of physical training and Severus, who had been working round the clock to make the school function properly, was feeling the absence of his assistant trainer, Nasica.

'Before we break and you go off with your individual gladiator trainers to see which particular style of fighting we think is best for you,' announced Severus on the parade ground, 'it's time we all started to think about dying. Because sooner or later, in or out of the arena, it catches up with you. We don't know anyone who has managed to avoid it yet, but the sooner you all get used to the idea, the sooner you can get on with the rest of your lives and I can make you into the best possible gladiator that I can.

'What we are doing here,' he continued, 'is not just about getting tough and well trained in order to fight in the arena. To fight and win is not enough. You have to know how to die. This will be the next part of your training. If any of you are too faint-hearted for this, I want you to see Oceanus, deal with your contract and leave now. For those of you who have no fear to die bravely, to offer yourselves to the sword in noble defeat and be finished off in cold blood by your opponent, you can stay. Before you learn how to fight in the arena you must master the art of how to die. So, before any weapons training begins, you will learn this art with some grace, some dignity and not a little honour. There's an adage in our business. It goes like this: "He who has learned to die has learned not to be a slave". Memorise it. It will come in handy for you some day.'

Just as he had finished speech and was dismissing his 'troops', Philumena came running across the parade ground to the central area that had been laid out for the sole use of the school. Before she reached him, she blurted out, 'Come quickly, Severus, something terrible has happened.'

'What is it, Philumena?' asked Severus. 'Is there something wrong with the dogs?'

'No, it's Lucia – she's had word from Rome.'

*****

Severus and Philumena rush over to the officers' quarters. As they enter the building, they can already hear Lucia's wails of grief and discover her weeping on the floor of her rooms with poor little Thelos trying to comfort her. In the next room the sounds of Brutus and Britannica whimpering at Lucia's distress can clearly be heard. Lucia is already bleeding; she had torn clumps of her own hair out and is pulling at the flesh on her arms, face and neck and is wringing her hands in grief. There is blood. Severus swoops picks her up in his powerful arms, preventing her from damaging herself further.

As he holds her, her wails continue unabated, and she tries to struggle free and to cause hurt to Severus himself. She is out of her mind with grief, and as her lamentations grow louder and louder Severus tries to calm her with soothing words of comfort. But nothing works and he realises that he will have to wait until she has exhausted herself before there can be any further reasonable discourse.

Thelos and Philumena have the same idea as Severus and when signals 'OK' they bring in the dogs from the next room. If there is anything that can comfort Lucia it is her mighty *canes pugnaces*, or dogs of war. They come to her with their tails tucked firmly between their back legs and their huge heads bowed as if trying to walk as close to the ground as possible, in an act of submission and empathy rarely seen in such fighting dogs. As Severus continues to hold Lucia on the low couch with cushions, the two canines curl up by her, one on either side, and nuzzle her gently. Slowly she stops wailing, starts breathing deeply, and comes to rest.

It takes a while for her to speak. 'Apion brought a message from the port,' she says.

'It's all right, it's all right,' says Severus, 'you don't have to say anything. It can wait.'

'No,' she says, recovering some of her habitual strength, 'you need to know this. The message from his family says that he was found murdered, down near the port in Ostia Aterni. He was joining a cargo ship that had agreed the previous day to take him to Vasanium. He had been strangled and his purse cut. Who would do such a thing, Severus, to my Nasica? To my beautiful Nasica?'

It was then that Oceanus arrived in the room. 'The guards told me that they had heard cries of great grief from up here,' he says. 'I came as quickly as I could.'

'It's OK, Oceanus,' says Severus. 'Give us a moment. We're just calming things down here.'

'I'm so sorry, Lucia. He shouldn't have had to die like that,' says Oceanus.

'Like what?' says Lucia, recovering. 'I guess your man Apion has told you everything, as seems to be his habit.'

'I don't know. I just assumed from all the caterwauling that Nasica won't be coming back.'

'That's right, Oceanus – you seem to be well informed, as usual. He's dead. Thanks for asking. Now please leave me to grieve with my family.'

'Of course,' says Oceanus, using his humble voice, 'of course. Take as much time as you need. As I told you before, I'm always here for you if you need anything.'

Oceanus leaves the room.

Lucia looks at Severus. Then around the room at Thelos and Philumena and the dogs. There was so much love there for her in that small space. And with Oceanus gone at least she felt as if she could breathe again.

'Severus. There's something not right about this,' says Lucia, recovering and picking up her strength after her *lapsus*. 'I want to leave here, and I want to leave here tonight. Thelos and Philumena are coming with me. And the dogs. We'll go on foot. Tonight.

We'll go to Festus and Vita; from there we will start our plans for the truffles. You can join me later when you are ready, and you can resolve the issues of your contract here.'

'Lucia, don't you think you are moving too quickly?' asks Severus, 'You're not thinking straight. Give it a few days. Just to let things rest and to settle down.'

'I'm sorry, Severus. But I have to get out of here. You can call me what you like. A hysterical little girl. Whatever. But tonight I am taking Philumena and Thelos and the dogs and we will walk through the night down the Via Flavia to Laime and no-one – not even you, my father – is going to stop me.'

Severus knows better than to argue with her when she is like this. But then again, she has never appeared just quite like this before. Versions of this. But never this. He is worried about what will happen if she leaves. And then there is the way she spoke to Oceanus; he is worried what she might do if she stays.

'All right, all right,' says Severus. 'You all know the road and you'll have the dogs. We must use the time well. Let's get moving. And Lucia, come here.'

He embraces her deep into his chest and holds his child close.

'I am so, so sorry,' he says, barely holding back his own tears. 'He was a good man. The finest there was.'

Lucia comforts Severus, strokes his head and says: 'You are both good men, and I'll never, never forget that. I'll never forget what you have done for me.'

The family all hold each other for a few minutes before Lucia kicks off again: 'Come on. We need to get ready. Severus, father, and dear friend, we need to make some good from this. And, as far as I see it, the tubers are our ticket out of here. I'm not going to let us miss this chance.'

Without taking a breath, she points to the bowl on the dining table and signals Philumena to bring it to her. Lucia turns and vomits into the bowl. 'Get me some water and a towel, Philumena,' she continues, and carries on as if nothing has happened. 'Our trick with the dogs gives us a monopoly for now. And that will get us ahead of any competition. But our dogs can be trained to find these things, and Vita has even heard rumours that there are tracts of them growing wild near to where she grew up around Pinguentum.

There's lots to do. Let's get going. We can turn this to our advantage. Nasica's death can have some meaning.'

'I'm with you, Lucia. We are all with you. Let's move.'

★★★★★

The weeks went by and the length of basic training and boot camp that Severus had insisted on before any weapons training was paying off. It took a while for him to shake off the loss of Nasica. His experiences from a life on the battlefield and in the arena had steeled him against absences of this kind but having seen how Nasica's death had so deeply affected Lucia he was moved in a way that he had never been before. He reminded himself that he was well out of the frontline, and he should not have to worry about that again. But as the days of training went on he saw some real talent in the young fighters who had signed up. The promise of a young potential *retiarius* called Montanus and a budding *murmillo*, Spiculus, inspired him to work harder with his recruits on a regime that would make the school something to be proud of.

As well as being a personal matter the loss of Nasica was also a professional one. Severus needed an assistant whom he could not only trust implicitly, but who also had to be at the top of their game physically, professionally and from the point of view of gladiatorial technique. In Nasica he had all this in one person. In the absence of a single gladiator to replace him he decided to open the position up to two assistants. It caused something of a stir, therefore, when he chose the young female gladiatrix Amazonia to be one of them and an old lag and recidivist criminal who had won his freedom three times called Tetraites to be the other.

'I can't believe that you are being serious with these suggestions,' said Oceanus when he was first informed of Severus's decision.

'They are the best, and they are the only two real fighters on the team that deep down I can fully trust,' said Severus.

'There are far more reliable people on the team you could have chosen. For example, Seneschal, here,' he said, indicating his own major domo standing next to him. 'His experience in managing gladiators is second to none.'

'But that's my point, Oceanus, I don't need management – I need people who know how to fight. With all due respect to you, Seneschal, your experience in the arena cannot match that of Tetraites's. He has appeared in the arena as a solo fighter 36 times, and while this isn't a record it's not a bad number when you think of the risks involved. Of his 34 contests he won 21 of them and only lost four. The remaining nine times the contest ended in a draw. You can't beat a record like that. And look at him, he's still the fittest man out there. And fittest of them all is Amazonia.'

'I don't like it Severus, and I don't like the fact that you have presented this decision to hire a criminal and a woman with big tits to me as a *fait accompli*,' says Oceanus, working himself up into a state.

'As the Doctor of this school it is my job to hire the best and deliver the best, otherwise I will be failing in my duty to the Emperor Domitian,' said Severus.

'I don't think it's wise to go down that particular line of argument,' said Oceanus. 'The emperor is back in Rome and your loyalty, and indeed your contract, is with me.'

'Will that be all, sir?' said Severus, abruptly ending the meeting. 'In that case, I have work to do.'

'Just a moment, Severus,' said Oceanus, stepping forward. 'How is dear Lucia? We haven't seen her or her little entourage for a while. I trust she has completed her mourning and will be re-joining our happy band of brothers very soon.'

★★★★★

Lucia's departure from the inn at Laime was almost as precipitous as her arrival. She had insisted on setting off on their reconnaissance mission to find the purported truffle fields almost as soon as they had settled at the Laime Channel. She had refused to talk about Nasica, even to Vita, and her obsessive determination to get on with something useful in the immediate aftermath of Nasica's death left no time for further mourning. She was a woman on a mission. Festus and Vita soon realised that if they weren't going along for the ride with her, she was going alone. In the end, Festus accompanied her, leaving Vita to take care of what meagre business there was at home, to tend to the oyster beds and to continue her research into the optimum solution for the preservation and transportation of the truffles.

The long walk across country to central Histria began well, but eventually the pace took its toll on Festus, who was a little out of condition. For Lucia and the dogs, it was a relatively easy day's walk along the Via Flavia to the bridge over the Ningus River at Porta Porton and the little harbour at Palada Bastija. Philumena had stayed behind with Vita at Laime to look after what remained of the dog pack, which now numbered around 15 working dogs, two of which were still recovering from their wounds after their battles in the Pola arena. Lucia, seeing that Festus and the minor problem of his supplementary poundage was causing him to struggle with the walk, suggested that the next day he should take the boat down the Ningus valley to the fortress at Pinguentum, the place where he had met Vita and fallen in love all those years ago while completing his 25-year stint as a legionary.

'Festus, I think we can make the best use of our resources,' said Lucia, taking command, 'if you go on from here by boat down to Pinguentum. If Vita is right, you should be able to pick up confidential information there or hearsay as to where the best forests might be for our dogs to do their work.'

'Good plan, Lucia,' said Festus. 'There are still a few old soldiers there, as well as Vita's family who can give us the inside knowledge.'

'Meanwhile, I can take the river valley down beneath Montona with Thelos and the dogs and explore the woods to see if the pickings are good. If Vita's memory serves her well, this was an area where the tubers were found on more than one occasion.'

'You know we used to pick them out of the ground when we were in Carthago,' said Festus, taking a long drink from a gourd of the Falernian that he had brought with him for comfort. 'Not a word of a lie. The locals called them *terfez*. They looked a lot like our tubers in shape and texture, but were a pale colour tinged with rose. The worst thing about them was that they didn't have any taste, so we used them as stomach fillers or as a carrier of flavour. Very one note. Unlike these little black diamonds of ours, Lucia, which have all the colours of the rainbow inside them – and which are finally going to make our fortune.'

Lucia smiled, happy that Festus was getting in the mood.

'If we unearth enough of these,' he continued, holding one of Brutus's recent finds up to the light, 'Rome will be our oyster – if that's not mixing my delicacies.'

'Hand over the gourd,' said Lucia. 'I want to have some of what you are having.'

*****

With the young gladiators' basic training complete and a general level of fitness, even in the larger gladiators, raised to an acceptable level, Severus was amazed at how fit even he had become as he worked on a daily basis with the fighters young and old.

The time had come to begin the training with weapons, and this was where Severus came to depend more on his two assistants, Amazonia and Tetraites. In this next phase of the gladiator training the *familia* focussed on the various styles of fighting and hardware used by the vast variety of fighters of the arena. Gladiators who fought in heavy armour were not so quick on their feet and the techniques and skills necessary for survival, and indeed victory in the amphitheatre, were very different to those in light armour who were quick and spry. So that was where Amazonia and Tetraites came in: eventually they would tailor the gladiator's regime using the appropriate hardware, whether it be armour, weapons or technical skills.

The novices had been divided into two groups, based on the rating of Amazonia and Tetraites as to which of them would have the best aptitude for light or heavy armour. Tetraites took the first group of potential *secutors*, *murmillones*, *Samnites*, *hoplomachi* and the other heavily armoured types, while Amazonia tried to knock some shape into potential *laquerarii*, the lasso fighters, *paegniarii* who fought with whips, clubs, and shields, as well as her very own *retiarii*, who fought with net and trident.

'This, you bunch of good-for-nothing slackers,' shouted the veteran Tetraites, pointing to a large post in the middle of their training ground, 'is what we call the *palus*. Who can tell us what the *palus* is for?'

'Yes, sir,' came the answer from the novice Spiculus. 'It's what we are going to use for target practice when we get issued with our swords, sir.'

'Correct! Well done, Spiculus, you will go far!' said Tetraites, who waved over the armourer to bring the weapons. 'You will now be issued with your wooden sword, called the *rudus*. You know what the *rudus* is for, so I won't go to the trouble of patronising even you Spiculus by explaining again.'

Laughter came from the group of novices.

The *palus* was the first object that potential gladiators used as a target to practise moves with a sword. The trick of the wooden sword was to make it twice as heavy as the heft of an actual weapon, thus making sure that the gladiators would train well and effectively, and work on their upper body strength as well as the musculature in their arms.

'Later, when you enter the arena for your first fight,' said Tetraites, 'and when, of course, you survive, you will become a veteran – like me, like Amazonia, and like Severus. Then you have the chance of something else. Something which in a new school is a big chance. Because you are all capable of doing it. So, the *palus* is not just a post to bash with your fake swords – it's far more than that. It's a symbol for the top combatants of the games. The top *veteranus* of the school – he or she who has won the most fights – will be known as the *primus palus*, and that is a noble position to hold. And it means cash. Lots of lovely cash.'

Tetraites was an expert with the post, and he began to demonstrate to the group various vicious strokes and manoeuvres, such as thrusting, cutting, and slicing. Had there been an opponent they would have been in pieces on the floor.

'OK, that's how you do it. Now your turn. Spiculus, you think you're so fucking smart, you have a go. Oh, and a word to the wise. It's not as easy as it looks.'

*****

Severus leaves the crew in the safe hands of his assistant doctors and, anxious for news of Lucia, takes his leave of the gladiator school for the day and takes the short walk down to the port of Pietas Iulia.

The early summer had brought wave upon wave of shipping back to the town, as well as the onward movement of troops who used Colonia Pietas Iulia as a disembarkation point for the legions that defended the Danubian Limes in Pannonia between Aquincum and Singidunum. Equally, the trading routes of the upper Adriatic crossed here. Aside from the sea routes, the roads like the Via Flavia provided excellent communications to the rest of the empire – which itself was criss-crossed with trade routes, by water across the Mediterranean and Black Sea and by land. Trade and moving the Roman army around were the two principal reasons for building roads.

Severus isn't thinking of trade as he spots Apion's boat moored on the central mole of the port; but there is no sign of the bibulous sea captain himself. It's not hard for Severus to track him down. The Popina of the Port is the place frequented by sailors, soldiers and many a ne'er-do-well and vagabond, and when he isn't sailing round the Histrian peninsula or out to Issa, Apion can be found spending his hard-earned cash on the *mulsum* that he is a little over-fond of. Honeyed wine is very popular among the sailing fraternity, a sweet and simple mixture of wine and honey whose sugary mixture heightens the alcoholic effects of the grape in an effective and economical way.

Finding him at his usual place, Severus sits down next to him.

'My dear friend Severus,' says Apion, happy to have some company, 'my friend, have a lovely, lovely drink.'

'How are you, Apion? How's business? The life on the ocean wave is treating you well, I can see that.'

'And doing well for your brother Festus. I've just dropped off another load of seashells to his contacts down here.'

'Excellent, my friend. How are they tasting? I bet you tried an oyster or two.'

'Oh, no, sir. Never touch the merchandise, that's my motto. And to tell you the truth, raw seafood doesn't agree with me,' says Apion, pouring Severus a large one.

'Cheers, friend.'

'Cheers!' says Apion. 'So how's it going up at the new school? Any sure-fire bets you can tip me off on for the next games?'

'There are a few potential talents there, Apion. And you mark my words, in a couple of years we'll have some of them at the games in Rome.'

'Not sure I'll be around in a couple of years, but thanks for the heads up,' says Apion with a wry laugh, 'Oh, and sir – I almost forgot. Lucia sent this down for you. She told me I was to put it into your hands and your hands alone.'

'Ah, a letter! And what is in here, a gift? Excellent, I have been waiting to hear from her.'

'Sorry it got a bit mangled. I hope you can still read it, and the seal got a bit broken.'

'Not to worry Apion, as long as I can read it. And I know I can always count on your discretion, anyway.'

'Thank you, sir. A top-up for you?'

'No, I need to be getting back for supper at the school. It's chaos if somebody sensible isn't there to keep an eye on them. And you can't trust Oceanus and Seneschal.'

'No, sir?'

'I mean they're always out and about entertaining, schmoozing, moving and shaking. You know, the entrepreneurial spirit and all that.'

'I'm sure I don't know what you mean, sir.'

'Good night, Apion,' says Severus. 'When are you headed back up?'

'Tomorrow, sir, first thing. I am bound for Parentium, so I could drop in on the way back. If you make it worth my while.'

'No fear for that, Apion. I'll make it worth your while. I'll be down first in the morning and give you a reply. I'll find you at the boat. Don't leave till I get here.'

'Right you are, sir. We're setting off at the fourth watch of night, just before dawn.'

Severus walks briskly back up the hill to the barracks and immediately heads for his quarters to read the letter.

My dear Father Severus.

Be of good cheer. Festus and I set out two days after our arrival with Thelos, two dogs and an extra servant to do the bearing. We walked the Via Flavia between the inn in Laime and the Aquilis river at Porta Porton and Palada Bastija. To say we slept like dogs would be an exaggeration. Festus is a bit out of practice in marching, but after the first five miles his military training returned, and in addition the dogs made good pacemakers. You know how they love to strike out. Twenty miles for an ex-legionnaire isn't bad in one day. But he was exhausted. The next day I sent him on by boat to Pinguentum to save his feet and save time so he could do some intelligence gathering while I caught up on foot coming across country with the dogs and Thelos. Brutus and Britannica were happy to get in some serious running on the open countryside. From there we headed east along the flood plain of the Aquilis towards Montona and further to Pinguentum. Here, as we go deep and around the south side of the Montona elevation, we have had the greatest success in finding the fungus. I have entrusted two pieces to Apion for you to test the quality. I have told him to give them to you immediately or I will set the dogs on him when I get back. You know what he is like as soon as he gets into harbour. He has a terrible thirst and one that must be slaked at all costs.

Severus breaks off from reading to open the small bag that Apion handed him along with the letter. He opens the bag, raises it to his nose and takes a long savouring intake of breath.

'Ambrosia,' whispers Severus aloud. And then to himself, 'By Jove, she has done it. She's found the source of the tubers.'

He reads on:

I have mapped the areas with Festus, whose old army friends along with Vita's family members have been invaluable help, in so far as it is possible. So we know where the rich pickings are for next season, which local folklore has it will be the late summer. Let's see. We have also found some of the white variety which are much more delicate, much more powerful – and Festus believes they are therefore more valuable and will achieve a better price at market. He is so funny, has already started to mentally spend the money that we haven't got yet, and Vita is already berating him for celebrating his success before any arrives. It's so nice to be with normal people in real life away from the stink of the amphitheatre and its intrigues and death cults. Festus has sent samples back to Rome with a merchant who was here for the shells. We should know in about a month what the situation is.

We miss you, all of us, and send love,
Your loving daughter,
Lucia

Unable to control his enthusiasm, Severus does a little jig around his room in celebration. The failing light forces him to spark up a couple of candles. He takes a wax tablet and begins to write a reply for Apion to get off in the morning.

My only Lucia:

The news you have sent me about the potential of the truffle business is marvellous. Both you and Festus (and the dogs) have managed to achieve so much in such a small space of time. I am very impressed. But you are a capable woman and will make a success out of whatever you turn your hand to.

Your letter brought me much comfort, although you were right. I had to go to the inn by the port and prise it out of Apion's hands. He wasn't completely drunk, but well on his way. You and Festus need to know that he really isn't trustworthy. Drunks rarely are. I am now convinced that your suspicions that he has been passing information about us to Oceanus are correct. Please refrain from using him for all but urgent message transfers. To avoid suspicion Festus should keep on using him for various jobs with the oysters locally, but not to involve him in anything that has information about our truffle business. And, yes, send me only urgent news via Apion. Remember to use the code I taught you, the one I use here.

Things at the school go well, but Oceanus and I have locked horns – not for the first time, but this time seriously on the matter of my new assistants. I was waiting for him to begin his power games; now he has started. It does not bode well, and you may be seeing me sooner rather than later. Of course, that might cause problems as I have signed a contract to train gladiators for the next two games at the arena, but we will cross that bridge when we come to it.

Meanwhile, I must finish this letter, as Apion will be leaving at first light for Laime.

With love, your loving father and friend,

Severus

Severus lights another candle and takes down papyrus, pen and ink and begins to transcribe his letter. Instead of writing in sentences that are immediately understandable, he writes in a code known only to him and Lucia. It is a version of the cypher that Julius Caesar invented to confuse his enemies over a hundred years before.

When Caesar needed a way of communicating his battle plans and tactics to everyone on his side without the enemy finding out he wrote to his generals in code. Instead of writing the letter 'A', he would write the letter that comes three places further on in the alphabet, the letter 'D'. Instead of a 'B', he would write an 'E'. When he got to the end of the alphabet, however, he would have to go right back to the beginning, so instead of an 'X', he would write an 'A' and so on. Lucia and Severus had long ago created their bespoke version of Caesar's code to communicate safely in the cut-throat world of the Roman arena. It was known only to them.

The treacherous Apion, and his masters Seneschal and Pretty Boy Oceanus, would have no idea of the contents.

Chapter XII

The Mission

German Occupied Istria, April 1945

The tide of the war had turned, and the Partisans had their enemies on the run: the Germans, the Croatian *Ustaša* and Serbian nationalist groups the Četniks under Mihailović and the Yugoslav National Movement under Dimitri Ljotić. They were driven towards the outer reaches of the territories that were to become the borders of the Socialist Federal Republic of Yugoslavia under Marshal Tito in just over a year.

Ever since the liberation of Belgrade back in October the confidence of the Partisans had grown. The feeling amongst those in the Rašpor cave complex was one of optimism and strength now that their battalion was part of the of the 'Vladimir Gortan' Brigade, 43rd Division of the 4th Army Corps of the Yugoslav National Liberation Army.

So when the direct orders came down from the High Command from Comrade Tito himself that the Neapolitan's brigade was to be entrusted with the elimination of Ljotić, it was a matter of some pride that they had been chosen to carry out the attack on the rabidly anti-Semitic Zbor leader and that it needed to be done quickly, ruthlessly, and efficiently. In return for this they had also been promised that success in this mission would earn the battalion a place in the army of liberation that would eventually enter Trieste.

After the announcement of the mission, whole units within the cave complex that Nino wasn't even aware of sprang into action in preparation for the attack which would take place in 48 hours. The actual ambush itself would be over the border in Slovenia in the small village of Ajdovščina. Of course, only the officers knew the objective and location, and it would remain like that until a couple of hours before the operation. Pino had been charged with leading the ambush and it was he who would reveal to the 15-man squad that they would be liquidating one of the most important targets of the Partisans – one of the bogeymen most hated by members of the Communist Party and its cadres in the Balkans.

Pino and his *bombaši* unit had been used to carrying out ambushes since he joined up two years previously. In Istria this was the main form of Partisan engagement with the enemy, first against the Italians and then the Germans. Ambushes were the most powerful means of attack that the Partisans had in their guerrilla arsenal, and they were renowned and feared for their skill and brutality in this area of warfare. Sometimes they would use a handful of soldiers and other times it could involve several brigades. They operated in all kinds of terrain and whatever the meteorological conditions. Surprise was the great strength of the Partisan ambush, and meticulous preparation and intelligence was imperative, along with security. Pino was well-known for his strategic abilities and would often take up position under camouflage well in advance of an operation; his Partisans could wait several hours sometimes, or even overnight, before receiving the order to attack.

More specifically this time, Pino would take his key *bombaši* with him on the mission. The *bombaši* were part of the vanguard; shock troops who carried out special and sabotage missions, and their experience and courage would be invaluable. They would be supported and covered by machine gunners, and that was Pino's biggest headache: getting the machine gun and ammunition safely and in one piece to the bridge location in Ajdovščina in the time allotted to him.

This would be the key to the success of the Ljotić ambush.

*****

Nino, as a raw recruit and the newest member of the brigade, would not be participating in the ambush itself. Instead, he would be part of the group that provided security and logistic support to the ambush teams up until they reached the borderlands, which they were confident of being able to reach without detection by daylight. From there the ambush team would proceed alone, carrying their own weapons, ammunition, and supplies on an eight-hour overnight forced march across some of the most difficult terrain in the region.

While the caves buzzed with activity in preparation for the departure of the ambush unit in the morning, Nino took Vito out on a long walk around the Gomila hillsides above Rašpor and into the forests of the Spinov Vrh. After about an hour walking due west on small deer paths through the thick woodlands, Vito started to become excited and pulled Nino deeper into the oak forest. After about 20 minutes of roaming around, in a seemingly random fashion, Vito started to home in on the odour of his prey. At one moment his tail went up, his nose went down, and he started to dig. Nino, who had no intention whatsoever of getting Vito to practise his hobby whilst on active duty with the Partisans, was very surprised to find any truffles at this altitude. In half an hour Vito's industrious little paws had pulled over a dozen little aromatic nuggets from the moist earth under the oak trees of the Spinov Vrh. Vito filled his pockets and walked on in the wood, a little disorientated but hopefully still able to find his way.

Coming out of the woods and over a spur he immediately knew where he was: overlooking the town of Dane, between Trstenik and Vodice. Or, rather, its ruins. It had been razed to the ground in a German reprisal less than a year previously. It reminded Nino of the Grimalda reprisals, only worse. Everyone and everything in the town had been the subject of a scorched earth policy in a frenzy of revenge waged by the local SS. Probably that bastard Schiffer. Nino took Vito and his trove of truffles filling the pockets of his Partisan uniform and returned to the woods to make his way back to camp.

★★★★★

Deep inside the caves, meanwhile, Pino is giving his final briefing to the detachment that will be responsible for dispatching Ljotić from this world.

'We leave at 05.00 tomorrow morning. It'll be a five-hour march across open country till we make our first stop. There we will rest up for eight hours, get some sleep, and do any necessary repairs. We'll move on under cover of darkness and dig in at the location of the proposed strike before dawn. The first part of the journey we will bring a six-man guard who will alternate in carrying the machine gun to keep the gunners as fresh as possible for the overnight trek when they will take over sole responsibility.

We will then remain in place until around noon, the day after tomorrow, when the target is due to cross the bridge. You will be informed of the identity of this high-level enemy individual when we reach the target location. Any questions?'

At that moment Nino and Vito appear in the cave and Vito rushes across to Pino to greet him. Pino slaps the dog away and makes for Nino.

'Good of you to turn up, soldier, and where the fuck do you think you have been?'

'Sorry, I didn't know. We went for a walk over to Dane.'

'Are you a complete fucking idiot, going out in broad daylight and so far, when we are preparing for the most important ambush this battalion has carried out during the war – and on the high orders of Comrade Tito?'

Nino looks in shame at the floor.

'Come here, soldier. Empty your pockets.'

Nino hesitates. Vito growls.

'Empty your pockets, that's an order.'

Slowly, Nino reaches into the various pouches on his rag-tag uniform, and also empties out his Partisan cap that he has been using to keep some of the truffles safe.

'What is this? Truffles? You've been out gathering truffles while you should have been here at the briefing. Get out of here now. Report to the officers' quarters at 18.00. Meanwhile, send in Comrade Siniša – he will be replacing you on the auxiliary guard. You are a disgrace. More like some *petit bourgeois* capitalist scum making money with these mushrooms. Get out.'

Nino and Vito leave, heads bowed in shame.

'Right, where were we?' says Pino. 'Ah, yes; any questions? No-one? Righto, reveille is at 04.00. See you in the morning.'

*****

'This is a very serious accusation that you are making against your brother, comrade Pino,' says Major Gabrielli, 'and one which, if found true, could result in a court martial for him.'

'There was a clear dereliction of duty, sir,' says Pino. 'There can be no exceptions in cases like this. We are on the eve of our most important mission, and he missed the briefing because he was out trying to find truffles in the forest in broad daylight. He was risking the safety of the whole unit, sir.'

Nino stands silently in front of the officers, exactly as he had a few days before when being welcomed into the Partisans as being a loyal killer of Germans and informers. Gabrielli, who oversees discipline, is trying to make sense of the accusation.

'I just took the dog for a walk. No-one told me there would be a briefing. And then we got lost in the forest and Vito found the truffles. I don't know what all the fuss is about. Sir.'

'Be silent,' shouts Pino, unrecognisable to his brother. 'You speak when spoken to. He put the operation in jeopardy because he was collecting materials in the forest that he wanted to sell for personal gain, going against the collective spirit. This is typical *kulak* behaviour, and the *kulaks* are in the pockets of the capitalists; therefore, they are the enemies of socialism.'

Gabrielli looks over to his political commissar, Benito Gasparini, for support.

'We have discussed this in our morning sessions,' says Gasparini. 'Comrade Nino proposed to me that he and his dog could search for truffles which could be sold to the Germans, and the money could be used to buy arms or food. I explained to him the moral dubiousness of this argument and I am sure that it sank in. Whilst this is a serious matter, Mihailić, the boy can hardly be at fault if his dog came across these precious gifts of the forest. Meanwhile, we are left with a dozen or so truffles. And I know what I would like to do with them, political commissar, or no political commissar.'

Benvenuti, the Neapolitan, Gabrielli and Gasparini all join in laughing.

The Neapolitan cuts in. 'OK, Pino, let's look at this. We know you are a good Partisan – this is the most important thing. And we know that you are a good Communist, which is fine by me, and by all of us. That is a matter of choice for you. Whilst the ideology is an important matter and will become more important after the war, now we are concerned with ending this terrible war. We need to use Communism, socialism – call it what you like – to unite all factions of our society; to reconcile differences and bring them together in a single direction.'

'And that single direction,' continues the political commissar, 'is the struggle against the occupier, his servants, and national traitors. Do I make myself clear?'

'Yes, sir,' says Pino, hesitantly, not sure in his revolutionary zeal why he is now deemed to be the one on trial.

'If we cannot show that people – whether they be men, women, *kulak* or capitalist – are of equal status,' says Benvenuti, 'regardless of race, identity, religion, social status, class, political beliefs, we will never be able to convince anyone to be part of the country that we want to build. Our movement has grown stronger, and we are near the end, and we must have a diversity of opinion across socialism.'

'And another thing,' says the Neapolitan. 'I have always supported you, Pino, because you are a good, loyal, and committed Partisan and have been a brave soldier under my command. But hypocrisy is something that goes against what we are doing here, and when I see it I don't like it.'

Pino looks confused and has no idea where this is going.

'I hadn't wanted to bring this up, but you leave me no choice. As you are well aware, the party discourages romantic relationships among our Partisans. Normally in a guerrilla army like ours I should separate couples and assign partners to different units once we discover a relationship has been carried on. In some units you both would have been shot by now. We cannot in any way encourage the engagement in promiscuity between Partisan and Partizanka. We have all turned a blind eye to your relationship with comrade Faida for some time. The party promotes self-discipline and sexual propriety as the values of all Partisans; why do you think you and comrade Faida are the exception?'

'But, sir,' Pino interjects, 'that was different…'

'Silence,' shouts back the Neapolitan. 'I am now going to give you a series of orders. At the end you will tell me if there is anything you don't like about them. First, you will withdraw the charges you have laid against you brother. Secondly, you will go out there, say goodbye to Faida, and start to make the final preparations for the ambush. Thirdly, and finally, you will go to the target tomorrow, you will complete the mission successfully, and you will come back here a hero. Have I made myself clear, Mihailić?'

'Yes, sir! Understood, sir.'

'You are dismissed!'

Pino salutes, turns on his heels, and marches out and back to his quarters.

Nino is left there with the officers.

'As for you,' says the Neapolitan, with the beginnings of a smile, 'you can leave those truffles here. We are confiscating them forthwith, and if you find any more you are to bring the immediately to Major Benvenuti here.'

'Yes, sir. Thank you, sir.'

'And just stay out of the way for the next few hours. We don't want any more trouble. By the time they come back all this will have blown over. Dismissed!'

*****

The 15-man unit with their security and porters sets out as planned at 05.00. Nino keeps a low profile and stays in his corner pretending to sleep. He has seen enough trouble for a while and wants to keep his head down as Benvenuti suggested. It is around 07.00 when he feels a gentle shake of his shoulder and he wakes to a close-up of Faida's face, who whispers gently to him, 'I've brought you some coffee. Well, it's coffee-coloured. Almost. I thought you might need it after yesterday.'

Nino doesn't quite know what to say. He had no idea that his brother and Faida were a couple, and if he had he would have warned his brother to be careful; he knew how ambitious Pino was and that the Partisan authorities frowned on fraternisation between the sexes, especially when out on the front line. There should be no distractions; everything should be focussed on the cause.

'Thanks. I'm sorry about what happened. I didn't know.'

'Didn't know what?'

'About you and Pino. I thought you were just good comrades.'

'There's a lot you don't know, young Nino,' says Faida, reaching out to caress Vito who is snuggled against Nino's legs. 'Whereas this one, he knows quite a bit. Especially about where to find the good stuff.'

'If I had known they were going to use that against Pino…'

'What would you have done?'

Silence.

'The point is, Pino was behaving like an idiot with his own brother, trying to make a point to prove himself a better Communist. What he doesn't understand is that there are Communists with a capital C and Communists with a small c.'

'You mean Socialists and Communists?'

'Sort of, yes,' says Faida. 'The officers, especially the Neapolitan, have been waiting to put him right on the double-standards for a while. And to be quite honest, one or two of them are more liberal than the others. They're missing a few luxuries in life, and they were happy to have the truffles. I suggest if you find any more in future you pass some on to Gasparini and Gabrielli – they're the worst.'

'I'll bear that in mind,' says Nino, sipping slowly at the scalding Turkish coffee and acorn blend, wondering if exotic coffees like this will ever catch on.

'The most annoying thing about the officer class is that they are perfectly happy to have all the boys go on the big ambushes and let off the bombs without giving a thought to the Partizankas, leaving us behind to clear up their shit. It's well known that me and a couple of the girls are far better with a rifle than some of these peasants, and also we're not half as clumsy and can move more stealthily close quarters.'

'Yes, but you aren't going to be able to carry the MG 42 machine gun on a twelve-hour hike across open country.'

'You'd be surprised, young man, what we can do. You mark my words. After the war. There's a big change coming to this country, you'll see. If any of us make it through.'

Faida is right. Women had been a key part of the Partisan force since 1942. Tito himself recognised that there was more and more demand from women to join the Partisans, and he understood that with them the units were stronger, more galvanised and better at fighting. Tito was clear that women shouldn't only be used as nurses and cooks but also as fighters. He considered it a national disgrace if women were to be prevented from actively participating in armed conflict, taking up arms alongside the men for national liberation. Sometimes it took time for the more liberal attitudes of High Command to filter down to the woods and the ever-fluctuating front lines.

'There was no reason why I couldn't have gone on that mission today,' says Faida, 'but because I am in this relationship with Pino, he couldn't be seen to favouring me by pushing to have me in the squad. I'm losing out both ways.'

Indeed, when the war started and Tito's forces became active all over the region, there was no formal plan for the entry of women into the Partisan units. Yet very soon after the beginning of the war, women's committees were organized at different levels – village, local and county. They were asked to assist the Partisan units and the new government, to organize ambulance training, and to participate in the political education of women. From there the first female fighters came, going into combat alongside men in many different roles. At the same time women were enabled politically through the founding and organisation of the Women's Antifascist Front of Yugoslavia.

'Let's see how it goes. There's no use thinking about that now. All we can hope is that they will get back safely.'

'Amen to that,' says Faida, and goes off to the infirmary to treat her remaining patients.

*****

Pino and his men make camp in the hills above Kozina at around midday after a 17-hour hike from Rašpor, which took them longer than expected because of bad weather. They had made their way across country via Dane and onwards up higher into the foothills of the Julian Alps at Vodice, Podgorje and Presnica. They kept to the back roads and went through the woods where possible, using ancient tracks and well-worn animal pathways. They made good time and settle in to some ready-made, open-roof caves that the limestone karst has carefully prepared for them over the millennia. They gather to eat some of their rations before being briefed by Pino.

'OK, listen up. We are acting on intelligence received from High Command, and on the direct orders of Comrade Tito, that the fascist leader Dimitrije Ljotić of the Yugoslav National Movement, those bastards at Zbor, is tonight in Trieste for meetings with the Germans.'

The men in the unit exchange glances with each other that acknowledge that this is a big kill, and a much more serious mission they have ever been entrusted with before.

'Intercepted messages supplied by British intelligence confirm that, just days ago, the forces of Ljotić and Mihajlović came together under the command of Četnik General Miodrag Damjanović. They are reaching out to our western Allies in Italy as a unified group, trying to get help from international forces for a proposed anti-Communist offensive to restore royalist Yugoslavia. Comrade Tito has ordered that this must not be allowed to happen.'

'When I was living in Belgrade,' says machine gunner, comrade David, 'these bastards at Zbor were the only group of Serbs that the Germans ever trusted. They were called the SDK and they rounded up us Jews with far greater enthusiasm that the real Nazis. It was Zbor who sent my whole family to the Banjica concentration camp. I never saw them again. That's why I am here. This Ljotić boy is handy with a Bible, too, so it seems. They call him "Devotionalist Mita". I swear to you, here and now, I will blow this Devotionalist Mita to eternity and back with my machine gun.'

With that, Pino lays out the plan. They would ambush Ljotić and his entourage, which they expect to include four outriders plus a truck of 20 guards. They would use the classic horseshoe approach, with a front ambush plus an assault in the rear to prevent withdrawal. Basically, the intention of the horseshoe is to seal Ljotić in a closed trap. Pino's men are well trained, and with the frontal attack coming from an MG 42 machine gun Ljotić and his people would have little chance of surviving.

'He will be on the road from Trieste to Postojna in the morning. We expect him to cross the Hubelj River at Ajdovščina. This is the dividing line between the two largest parts of Ajdovščina, locally known as Šturje and Ajdovščina. There's no other way through. They have to cross the bridge. That's where we will trap the bastards. Now, get some sleep.

We'll leave here at eight. That will get us there under cover of darkness to set up and dig in.'

*****

'You should have come and seen me first,' says Dino the cook to Nino, dropping a choice piece of pork on the floor of the cave for Vito to pounce on, and pounce he did. 'I can shift the truffles, black, white, winter, summer – whatever you've got. You certainly shouldn't go around handing them out the officers.'

'I didn't have much choice in the matter,' says Nino. 'For a start, I was shafted by my brother who didn't even tell me there was going to be a briefing. And second, I was doubly shafted by my brother who obviously wanted to prove the point that I am some kind of anti-social parasitical element of the bourgeois speculator class. I don't know what has got into him. He has changed.'

'There's a lot of it about, comrade,' says Dino. 'I try to keep my head down in the kitchen and do my job, but it doesn't take long for some *arriviste* to start whingeing about how I am skimming off food/money/privilege – pick whichever one you want – for myself. It's dog eat dog, to coin a phrase.'

'I understand what it is they are on about,' says Nino, 'but me and Vito could probably go out and get enough truffles for everybody.'

'Ah! Finally, a boy after my own heart – a fellow champagne socialist!'

The two fall about laughing so much so that Vito joins in barking.

'You know what happened to your truffles last night, don't you? While our brave boys were shitting their pants about to start off on today's big mission to kill Ljotić? The fascist bastard…'

'What's going on here, then?' says Faida, re-entering the cave having picked up the breakfast plates from her patients. 'Sounds like far too much fun. What happened to the discussion that we, the advocates of socialism in one country, have not abandoned the goal of ultimate world communism – but we consider it naive to think world revolution was imminent? Sound familiar?'

Faida joins in the general amusement until Dino, calming everyone down, says: 'You know the officers had your truffles for dinner last night?' The bastards didn't trust me with the truffles, they just asked me to cook some plain *fuzi* with butter if I had it and that would be enough. Their poor little stomachs needed something lighter after my wild boar stew from yesterday. That Gabrielli is the worst; he has his own little truffle grater, and I know where the truffles that got you into trouble last night went.'

'Luckily,' says Faida, 'you were saved by the scarlet woman herself. The Whore of Babylon who has seduced your brother into doing things entirely against his will. I haven't had so much fun without alcohol since the Germans broke up our party in your hometown, Nino!'

Erupting in laughter, Dino says, 'Your wish is my command. What the beautiful lady wants, the beautiful lady gets. I think this calls for a drink. Shhhh. Don't tell a soul,' he says, returning with a half-empty bottle of walnut liquor, *orahevac*. 'Get this across your throats and down your necks, Partisans.'

He pours out three generous helpings into the first cups he can put his hands on. 'Cheers, comrades,' he says. 'Here's to brotherhood, sisterhood and unity.'

★★★★★

Pino's detachment arrived on the outskirts of Ajdovščina, having passed through the hillside towns of Planina and Dolenje about an hour before dawn broke on the day of the ambush. They cut east across country to Ustje from where they could see the town on the flatlands of the valley. Then they moved under cover of darkness with nothing more than a half moon to guide them to the bridge over the Hubelj river. It was quiet. Almost too quiet. Pino, having set up the horseshoe ambush as planned, ran down from the side of the cover above the bridge to check in on the machine gunners.

They were exhausted but weren't complaining. Comrade David was chomping at the bit to give Ljotić – 'the Bible basher and his God squad' as he called them – what they had coming to them. The gun team consisted of three big lads: David, Brdjan and Janez; they had not only made good time but also kept up with the rest of the Partisans on the eight-hour march. The gun was heavy, unwieldly and could sometimes be temperamental. Everyone was depending on the machine gun to take out the car and the rest of the unit to finish them off, so the weapon had to be fully functional. Obviously, they had no chance of a rehearsal.

'How's it going, lads?' asked Pino, as he came in behind the bridge into the trees on the opposite bank. 'Are we all set?'

'We had a problem with the hinge on the tripod,' said David, 'but thanks to Brdjan's skill at metalwork and woodwork he's fixed something up that will get us through.'

'Great. And how are we doing for ammo?' asked Pino. 'Do you think we have enough?'

'Pino, you can never have enough. That's like asking me how long a piece of string is,' chipped in the normally taciturn Janez. 'But if we had to carry any more we wouldn't have made it across the mountain. And now I could eat a fucking horse.'

'Here, I still have some hard tack,' said Pino, handing it over with some dried sausage as a bonus to Janez, sympathizing with the big lad. 'I can never eat before these things. Go on, finish it off.'

Janez stopped cleaning the gun and drew himself up to his full and not inconsiderable height. He took a huge bite out of the sausage. As he did so, a crack rang out from a house opposite the bridge and in a split second Janez had taken a bullet in the head and his brains were all over the tree in front of him that was supposedly giving him cover.

Then all hell broke loose. Machine-gun fire from a truck that had backed out of a barn, along with more sniper fire from all sides. Pino looked at David and his eyes said it all. David put it into words: 'We've been set up!' he said as he shouldered the machine gun and turned it on the truck, taking out the machine gunner and spraying a fountain of death across the facades of the buildings in front of him.

'Either that or someone betrayed us,' said Pino grabbing his rifle.

'I think we're leaving this one behind. I'll just disable it and remove the recuperator. Best I can do. I'm not sure the Reich is doing spare parts right now for Hitler's Bone Saw.'

Pino shouted to the team on the other side of the bridge: 'Give us fire cover now!'

Shots rang out from both sides, neither enemy seeing the other. Pino and David ran like the wind across the short stone bridge, ducking for cover beneath its parapets and reaching the relative safely of the other side.

'OK, lads,' said Pino. 'I think we are only one man down. And he's not coming back. Let's get the fuck out of here.'

Part Five

Chapter XIII
277 Metres Above Reality
Istria: December 29th, 2019

A massive gunshot rings out in the night, creating a deafening blast and shaking the shutters of the Rose House. Marco jumps up in the bed in a cold sweat.

Another macabre scene from yet another nightmare. He had been dreaming he was back in the commune and there was another police raid. Just as the cops kicked the door down the eardrum shattering noise of the shotgun went off. Well-used to these nocturnal events since his arrival back in Istria, he rolls over and goes back to sleep.

Just as he reaches the threshold of consciousness and is about to fall once more into the welcome abyss, another blast jolts him immediately and utterly awake. His heart racing like the rat-tat-tat of an old telex machine, he jumps out of bed, pulls on some jogging pants and leaps through the latticed doors to the terrace to find Alen, one of Nino's neighbours, re-loading his treasured Fausti shotgun ready for another pop at something he may or may not have seen in the bushes.

'Marco! How the fuck are you?' says Alen, not standing on ceremony. 'I heard you were back, but I thought you were staying down in Pula with bad boy Zvonko?'

'Alen,' says Marco, slightly bemused that his neighbour is out hunting wearing high-visibility overalls, 'do you know what time it is? It's seven o'clock in the morning.'

'I know,' says Alen, with a chuckle. 'But Nino lets me come down and keep an eye on his vegetable plot in the night. The roe deer like to come and nibble at the veg just before dawn. If I'd known you were there I would have come earlier.'

The super-sized hunter pulls out a hefty chrome-plated flask from his inside pocket and offers Marco a pull. Marco is obliged to drink, even though it's before breakfast and he will probably throw up afterwards. There is the small issue of local machismo at stake.

'Cheers, Alen,' says Marco, returning the flask. 'Oh, it's a good one. *Loza*?'

'The best one, made with wild grapes from old vines in Grdo Selo where I was conceived. Every year I go and pick the grapes that grow there and no-one else wants. Make it myself.'

'Just one thing, Alen: I don't like to be a pain in the ass, but the roe deer season is only till the end of September.'

'Is that right, Marco? I know you were a policeman in England, but I didn't know you were one here,' says Alen, locking the barrel of his new Italian-made over-and-under shotgun and taking vague aim into the bushes at the end of the property. 'I heard you were even thrown out of the English police.'

Alen lets go with both barrels and a few birds scatter from the woodland.

'Because if I manage to hit a roe deer, I'm sure it would be because I mistook it for a red deer, and the season for red deer is till the middle of January.'

'Well, Alen, congratulations, you seem to have it all worked out,' says Marco, doing his best not to get into an argument with the locals on his first week back. He knew they were sensitive about their traditions and loath to move with the times; many of them were also just plain belligerent.

'Now you are back, maybe you'd like to take over the graveyard shift watch on Nino's veg – if you're up to it,' says Alen. 'If Nino was smart, he could kill two birds with one stone. Save his vegetables and get some venison. But he's too crazy for the truffles. See you later.'

Alen walks off into the woods, shouldering his rifle. It crosses Marco's mind that when it comes to most things – taxes, education, roads, municipal aesthetics – the locals would endlessly plead poverty, yet it wasn't unusual to see a simple road worker like Alen going around with a shotgun that cost between 5,000 and 10,000 euros and driving an SUV that cost about the same. It didn't add up. It had something to do with the black economy and everyone paying cash for everything; but in certain things the locals seemed to be very well off, and in others completely broke.

*****

He didn't bother Faida for coffee, as he could make it in the Rose House. While it brewed, he showered, got his heart rate back down to normal, and considered the difference in how things were in the UK with regard to hunting. How it was politically correct to sabotage hunting with dogs, not just because the way it was carried out was cruel to the foxes, but because it was a ruling class activity and, on that basis, it had become profoundly political. In Istria, mess with anyone's fundamental right to hunt in the countryside, whether boar, deer, or pheasant, and you'd have a revolution on your hands.

Still, there was something deep-seated and primal about the desire to hunt wild animals. In contrast to the hunt saboteur approach that might have been advocated by Emina, in defence of Alen and his ilk at least they were only shooting something they were going to eat themselves. There was also something in the argument that in a world of industrialised meat production and slaughter kids grew up not knowing where their food had come from or how it had reached the table. It was also super organic. But still the bold facts remained: more than a third of American kids think that cheese, bacon, hot dogs, chicken nuggets, shrimp and hamburgers come from plants.

As his coffee brewed and he shaved, Marco's mind flickered around his past life in London and his previous life and times here in Istria. When he arrived a few days ago he had no plan, but without intending to form one it seemed to be coalescing of its own accord. Maybe he should just go with the flow. What was wrong with the easy Istrian life? One of the few places in the world where the word 'lifestyle', even as separate words, still meant something.

As he came through the living room with his coffee, he looked at the gladiator's armour on the table. He wondered again why it was that his mother wanted to keep it from him. A highly-educated woman, keenly aware of the importance of ancient artefacts, there was something that she didn't like about it – otherwise she wouldn't have had it in the bins ready to be thrown out. If she hadn't been taken ill so suddenly, he would never have known about it.

He sat outside on the terrace, freshly showered, and enjoyed his coffee overlooking the extraordinarily verdant sweep of countryside that lay before him. Marco smiled to himself that even without Emina here he was having an ideological argument with her in his head. He thought about the events of the last few days. For sure, never a dull moment. Time to breathe. Time to think. And so full circle back to Emina. She looked great at the swim down in Premantura. She looked better when she held his hand in the office. And, if he was truthful with himself, his heart did a little jump when they sang the old songs. The old stirring came back. And then, just as he was getting to a warm place – the image of her coming out of the hospital in Trieste after the abortion 15 years ago. The slap and the dismissal. Gone from her life. Never to return. Or so he thought.

How swift the mind was to move from light to dark. There was only one thing that would clear it. A good run.

*****

At the same moment, Nino walks about manically on the terrace of the restaurant, trying without success to get a mobile phone signal and cursing loudly and colourfully as only an ex-soldier can. Faida sits having breakfast while she watches Nino get himself into a lather. He's confused further by Marco driving past in the Mercedes. Marco doesn't stop, but waves and beeps loudly, causing Nino to drop his phone, followed by an extended, ever more complicated, and explicit litany of ex-Yugoslav curses after it.

'I swear you will have a heart attack,' says Faida, having mercy on the old man. She gets up from the table, picks up the phone parts and carefully reconstructs Nino's technology back to its habitual form. 'And that's just from the swearing. And I don't need to remind you that there is a lady present.'

'Give me the phone, quickly,' says Nino. 'I'm going to deal with these bastards once and for all.'

'Take it easy, my dear,' says Faida, realising something is deeply troubling him. 'Nino – it's supposed to be holiday time. What can be so urgent that you can't sit down for breakfast with me just for five minutes?'

'It's these fucking Chinese. They won't leave me alone,' shouts Nino in frustration as he redials. 'Christmas, Three Kings – means nothing to them. Bloody heathens. They even invented their own fucking New Year.'

He taps angrily another number.

'And that lazy English bastard Dalrymple isn't picking up either,' he growls, frantically looking for something around the table, in his pockets, under the seat cover, before Faida opens her hand.

'Are you looking for these?' she says, holding up his keys.

'There they are. Why were you hiding them? Hand them over.'

'Where are you going?' asks Faida, worried.

'Brioni,' he says. 'And before you ask, yes – it's for a meeting of the Central Committee. And yes – I might be late.'

*****

It was one of his favourite 10k runs, as it took in some countryside, some urban vistas, a break at the Pazin Caves, and a tough uphill road run that really gave good burn. Marco parked up the Mercedes next to the churchyard of Saint Martin in Lindar and did some stretching as it had been a while since he had done a proper run. Again, as with almost everywhere in Istria, he was amazed that a small community of 130 people could sustain four churches celebrating five saints: Saint Catherine, Saint Sebastian, Saints Mohar and Fortunato, and Saint Martin. It demonstrated that the sweep of history had been resolutely Catholic, and the people had been controlled by the Papists for centuries. The churches' upkeep was the result of the same superstitions that were cultivated by the local clergy, making Croatia one of the most fanatically devoted Roman Catholic countries in the world. If Nino had been with him, he would have stopped in the Church of Saint Catherine to revisit the fresco of The Living Cross, which was unique among the numerous medieval wall paintings in Istria and an important part of Istrian cultural heritage and artistic history. But there was no time for that now. Perhaps on the way back.

Keen to get running and clear his head, Marco followed the country path down into the town of Pazin, which took him an easy couple of kilometres down around past the old Austro-Hungarian Railway station, the small supermarket, and the gas station. It wasn't ideal running with badly bruised ribs, but he took it gently and tried not to put pressure on them. He went into the pedestrian area, past the pharmacy, the hospital, the Middle School and the Courthouse, and the Pazin State Archive. All these were signposts on the road of his youth. He was headed for the iconic Pazin Caves where he would make his first and only stop, but as he came round the corner of the State Archive, in true *Groundhog Day* fashion, he almost bumped into Dalrymple, or Bonkers as he was now known to Marco.

'Can't stop, Marco, I'm in a hurry. By the way, have you heard from Nino? He's been trying to get hold of me all morning, but I had the old Beethoven on full blast and didn't hear the phone. Must be urgent from the frequency of his calls, but now I can't reach him.'

'Last I saw him he was at home in Draguć, having breakfast with Faida. Can't stop.'

'Me neither. See you at New Year – Nino at Ninety, don't forget. Oh, and remember to bring your *Youth*. Ha!' he quipped, rather pleased with himself.

Running on down the Prilaz Kaštelu and into Valvasorova Street, Marco arrived at the Pazin Caves, and despite the winter chill had broken a serious sweat. Looking at his watch he had made decent time over the five kilometres, but nowhere near his 13-minute record a couple of years ago. He decided to give up on the watch.

He loved this place in winter when there were no tourists around with their various zip-line and speleological aspirations, and he could concentrate on how Jules Verne must have imagined the caves from the descriptions of his young protégé Charles Yriarte back in 1875. Yriarte was something of an expert on the area following the publication of his book *Les Bords de l'Adriatique et le Monténégro*. It was he who brought Verne's attention to the story of the young Count Esdorff, a local dignitary in the town. He had gone down into the lake deep underneath the Pazin Caves in a small boat but couldn't get to the end of them. It was from Yriarte that Verne, who was a veritable magpie for snippets like this, picked up the local myth that the river Pazinčica flowed for miles underground through the caves and finally saw the light of day near the Lim Fjord on the west coast of Istria. The German writer Karl May had never visited North America, but his tales of the Old West about Winnetou and Old Shatterhand had regaled generations of young Germans from the 1880s onwards. Similarly, Jules Verne never visited Pazin, but he 'borrowed' the story gleaned from the travelogues of Charles Yriarte and his *Shores of the Adriatic Sea* and made it the centrepiece of his three-volume story *Matthias Sandorff*. Fiction is, indeed, thought Marco, stranger than truth.

Literature aside, the location, known as the *Foibe di Pisino* in Italian, was extraordinary, and even more amazing when viewed from the Vršić Bridge. This arches over the Abyss of Pazin, giving a stunning view deep into the unique hydrogeological phenomenon that goes down at least 130 metres and opens up to a trio of underground lakes. Verne's thesis that the waters flowed down to Lim was thought to be disproved early in the last century by a scientist who released marked eels into the waters. These eels eventually re-appeared in the Raša river on the eastern side of the peninsula flowing into the Kvarner. Marco was unconvinced by this experiment, claiming that the eels might have missed a turn. So, to this day no-one can be really sure where the underground waters of the Pazin Abyss lead.

Perhaps science fiction is more interesting than science fact. Verne certainly thought so, as did Marco. And Marco had another debt of gratitude to Verne: his passion for the classics. It was not only his father's influence that instilled this in him; it was also an early reading of Verne's *Journey to the Centre of the Earth* that made his 12-year-old mind fizz with imagination about the lava fields below the magnificent Snæfellsness glacier – another Verne story where a character drops down one hole and appears in another. Only that time it wasn't the few kilometres from Pazin to Lim, it was down the Snæfellsjökull volcano to Stromboli. When Verne explained that Axel, the professor and Mr Fridriksson could only converse in Latin as it was the only language they shared, Marco was inspired to go on to be the Latin scholar that he became.

The distance between Snæfellsjökull and Stromboli may have been 5,000 kilometres, but the balance of the five kilometres back up to Lindar was harder than Marco remembered. He used to be a master of uphill running, having cut his teeth on the hillsides of Istria. But being in London and Oxford had made him soft. There was a time that he used to seek out parts of London with hilly inclines, but they were few and far between. His favourite was Parliament Hill on the south-east corner of Hampstead Heath with its spectacular views over the city, and the name itself laden with the ideals of democracy, justice and fair play. His treatment at the hands of the authorities of the law of that country made him a bit more sceptical these days, but back then, before Brexit, England was for many people the litmus test of correct standards, where honour, decency and a man's word counted for something. How were the mighty fallen, he thought to himself, as he climbed the last few hundred metres of the main road to Labin and Plomin and emerged into the Italianate confines of the medieval village of Lindar once more.

★★★★★

Emina loved her small apartment in the centre of Pula. It was more like a loft, but with the added advantage of a big garden. Given the warren of houses and apartments in the old town, it was architecturally unusual as well as a rarity to have such a large outside space. And more than anything else she loved to live and spend time there alone. It was an oasis away from the madness of her activist world, which if she wasn't careful could become all-consuming. However, it was a beautiful morning and she decided to bring the tray with her *burek* and coffee *al fresco*. As an afterthought she picked up her phone and brought that as well.

Emina's claim that she lived alone was a bit of an exaggeration. There were five other inhabitants of her world, and they were feline. And if you counted the recently arrived stray tomcat whom she had taken a shine to, this otherwise all-female environment made six. Emina sat down at her terrace table, sipped her Turkish coffee and savoured the moment of peace with her *burek* and her cats. The cats decorated the garden variously – occasionally taking note that there was a tame human on their turf. It wasn't not long before an old blind cat, Siva, found her way into Emina's lap.

'Siva, Siva, Siva,' intoned Emina to her friend. 'What are we going to do with Siva now she's old and grey?'

She tickled Siva's ears gently and rubbed her throat softly.

'I know what you really want,' whispered Emina, 'and it's not only my love. You want a taste of home. Here.'

The cat took the flaky, cheesy remnants of the *burek* from the hand of her mistress, and all was right with the world. These two had come a long way together.

Emina rarely talked about her past. But beatings at the hands of brutal parents in her hometown of Srebrenica were so bad that she ran away from home when she was nine. This was as the war was beginning but she managed to get a ticket for a bus to Sarajevo and headed in the direction of her favourite aunt and uncle. Her timing couldn't have been worse. When she arrived in Sarajevo her uncle and aunt, Mariam and Selim, had already left for Croatia. She was left alone. She wandered for weeks around the desperate streets of the city trying to survive and was eventually taken in by the state orphanage. She told them her parents were dead, killed by Serbs, and that her only relatives were Mariam and Selim, now living in Pula. Two years later – two hellish years of abuse, lack of food and daily fear of death by bomb or sniper when the siege of Sarajevo was in full swing – Selim and Mariam finally managed to get her out of Sarajevo. They told her to pack one bag. That was the easy bit: she didn't have anything to put in it. So, she figured if she was going to be saved, she would save someone else from this living hell. When she entered the Sarajevo 'tunnel of hope' that night she had one small rucksack with a toothbrush and a change of clothes. Siva, the blind cat that now sat on her lap basking in the winter sun of another beautiful day in Pula, was underneath that change of clothes.

It was her nine-year-old's instinct that led her to leave the violent world of her parents in Srebrenica. It was what saved her life. Her parents, brothers and sisters were less lucky when Bosnian Serb nationalists finished off the work that they had started a few years earlier with the Srebrenica genocide. The entire family without exception were wiped out.

Putting Siva down on her seat, the grey began her grooming and Emina made her way over to the other beast that lay waiting in the corner of her garden. Her pride and joy. Her other favourite animal. The iron horse. Taking second position to the struggle, the activist's life, Emina's real passion was motorcycles. Her Triumph Bonneville T100 was a modern classic, and she prayed for good weather every day so that she could ride it. She ran her hands over the sleek petrol tank and wiped cat hairs from the seat where the felines had been taking the sun; and she made a decision.

She picked up the phone once more. Again, no answer. This time she decided to leave a message.

'Hey, asshole. I've got a plan. I'm taking you for a little excursion. The weather's perfect. I'll pick you up in Dragać at 4. It's OK, I have a spare helmet.'

*****

Nino is in a mighty hurry as he pulls into the Brioni hotel car park in Fažana at speed. He parks up, jumps out of his car, and makes his way over to the jetty where the ferry to the main island is leaving in a couple of minutes. Nino knows Brioni like the back of his hand, in the same way that he knew the ferry timetables – and not just from the time when he used to head tourism for the region in the eighties. It was something he didn't mention much these days, since Tito had fallen out of fashion, but his relationship to the Marshal went beyond the regular professional service Tito expected his top officers to provide. He wouldn't call it friendship, because Tito didn't really do friends, but Nino and Tito were close. If in his cups and pressed Nino could tell stories from the high life on Brioni, all-night poker schools with the actor Franco Nero flown in specially from Rome for whisky and cigar-fuelled weekends of card playing just one of them. Also, Tito was partial, as a bon vivant, to the occasional truffle, as was his wife, Jovanka: and thus their relationship was sealed.

Nino doesn't need to get a ticket; he knows all the captains and he walks straight on board. He goes up to the bridge where his old mate Marino is on duty. Nino hands over a bottle.

'Only a few passengers on board today – why not?' says Marino. His sailors cast off and he manoeuvres the vessel slowly out into the Fažana Channel and sets course for Veliki Brijun.

'*Orahevac*,' says Nino. 'You won't find better. Made by my neighbours, Ema and Pepi. She swears by it. She's nearly the same age as me. Made with walnuts from the tree of life.'

Nino looks as if his resolve needs stiffening. Marino swigs straight from the bottle. Nino does the same.

'Cheers,' they say in unison.

The first time that Nino had plied these waters was as a young officer after the war. He had been an aide-de-camp at the meetings led by Tito that eventually led to the foundation of the Non-Aligned Movement. In the years following Tito's famous split with Stalin in 1948, the world was a very polarised place. The wounds of the Second World War had barely started to heal when a Cold War began between the two competing ideologies and major superpowers of the time, the United States of America and the Union of Soviet Socialist Republics – the capitalism of the West versus the Marxist communism of the East. In the midst of these controlling orthodoxies, some of the biggest nations on earth which all happened to have super-smart and inspirational leaders who found themselves caught between the two camps came up with an alternative: the Non-Aligned Movement.

It was his memories of the Brijuni Islands when they became known as 'the islands of peace' that Nino was thinking of as Marino docked the ferry at the main jetty in front of the Hotel Neptune. It was here that the 'Brijuni Declaration' was made. Its key tenet was that peace could not – and would not – be achieved with polarised separation; the independence of nations could only be confirmed by the aspiration towards collective security in global terms and expansion of freedom. Some would say that its somewhat idealistic aim of terminating the domination of one country over another was bordering on the naïve. Nevertheless, the Non-Aligned Movement still exists today, while the Cold War is ancient history.

Nino believed Comrade Tito to be a good guy and a modernizer who used centralised power to transform Yugoslavia from an economically backward, largely agrarian society into a developed industrial nation. He could also control the forces of nationalism in his own lifetime; after his death these were unleashed because they could not be controlled by lesser men. This ultimately culminated in the disintegration of Yugoslavia.

It is a very United Nations delegation that meets Nino as he steps off the gangplank from Marino's ferry: waiting for him is a young Chinese businessman dressed in a suit, standing by a golf cart.

They shake hands, climb into the cart, and drive across the island to a large villa at the end of the southern promontory which commands a magnificent view of the Adriatic and the town of Pula.

*****

Emina makes sure that Siva is safe inside the house and locks the door. Her remaining cats scatter across the garden; they know that when she is dressed head to toe in black motorcycle leathers and has purpose in her stride that she means business. Strapping down the last of the buckles on her boots, she opens the back gate of the townhouse and wheels the Bonneville out into the alleyway at the back. Helmeted, ignition on, the 900cc twin-cylinder engine rumbles to life, sounding far grumpier than its sleek classic looks. It was this retro sound that Emina fell in love with when she first saw and heard it in the showroom. It was a world apart from the weekend-biker, business-as-usual, robotic tick-tick-tick sound of its German counterparts; nothing ladylike about this one – more like cheeky, verging on bad girl.

Once on the Riva coast road she roars past the Uljanik shipyards until she sees the Brijuni Islands rising behind the port and the marina, cluttered with gin palaces and fishing vessels alike but with very little action at this time of year. More of a boat park. Coming up to the mighty Roman arena on her right, she powers down and cuts a hard left just as she comes into the full majesty of its view. The arena was where she saw her first movies in Croatia when she arrived all those years ago. Watching films under the stars in an amphitheatre which seated 7,000 people was an amazing experience. It got even better when she could go there with her then-new boyfriend Marco, whom she had met at music summer camp, and there was no nagging uncle and auntie doing the morality police thing. Fortunately, Croatian cinema at the time was so abominably execrable that they didn't miss anything by climbing to the back of the ancient seating and spending their evenings drinking beer and making out. The summers were long and the days endless. Hugging and kissing in the back row of the movies.

But the fun she had in the arena isn't uppermost in her mind as she allows the Triumph to clear its metaphorical throats (it being a twin-cylinder beast) as it winds its way around the jetty for the Venice Ferry, down Saint Peter Street, past the barely functioning railway station, which was, given the dire state of Croatian Railways, a much more successful pizzeria than it was a point of transit. Emina has another place on her mind as she rides past Puntižela, down on to the main road to Vodnjan and on to the Ipsilon for an easy cruise up to Cerovlje then Buzet. The Triumph knows the way and she puts it on autopilot while thinking back to those the endless summers with Marco; first in Grožnjan, then Pula, and finally Motovun.

She adores the short and winding road up to Draguccio. In its honour she removes her helmet and lets her hair flow in the wind, held away from her clear-eyed face by a red bandanna. She loves riding with no helmet, and though aware of the dangers will do it on country roads from time to time; to feel in the moment, to feel completely in the frame of the road and the total contact with nature, the air, the fields, the trees and all its beauty. Riding without a helmet played to all manner of things in her; her outlaw spirit, her love of danger and, to a great extent, she simply found it one of the sexiest things a girl could possibly do on her own.

Faida and Marco are waiting as she pulls under the sign of the Stancija Mihailić restaurant.

'Are you completely insane?' shouts Marco. 'Riding without a helmet?'

Emina completely ignores him, parks up, jumps off, puts the bike on the side stand and greets Faida.

'Hello, my darling,' says Faida, kissing Emina on both cheeks. 'You will be careful now, won't you, my love?'

'Of course I will. As long as old sissy-pants here doesn't keep on moaning like that all day. I'm shaking in my leathers that he might write me a ticket. Or give me a good telling off.'

'I'm sorry, Emina,' says Marco, indignantly. 'I've seen too many road traffic accidents in my time. I promised myself that when I left the police I wouldn't ever scrape brain from asphalt again.'

'I've survived far greater risks than that already in my life,' says Emina, 'but I understand your concern, and I apologise. I won't let you see me doing it again.'

Silence. She nudges him: 'Come on, Marco! I said I'm sorry. I want today to be fun, so let's break the habit of a lifetime and not start off on the wrong foot.'

'You forgot to say, "as usual",' says Marco, smiling. The smile is a winner, and it breaks the ice.

'Now, come on, you two,' says Faida. 'You'll make me cry with your bickering. You remind me so much of Nino and myself when we were your age.'

'See? The age of romance isn't dead,' says Marco.

'Neither is the age of chivalry, I hope. You're buying me dinner in Motovun.'

'It's a deal.'

'Before you two go,' says Faida, 'I don't think it's anything, but I haven't heard from Nino yet. He often goes off all day without calling in, but this morning he was in such a state as he left, I was even worried about him driving. If either of you hear from him, just call and let me know. I've asked Zvonko to do the same.'

'It's OK, grandma,' says Marco. 'He's probably trying to sort out the dog thing. He told me they found another one running around the roads down at Novaki. But I'll keep you posted if I hear anything. Oh, and can you close up the Rose House? I left the door open, and Alen was hanging about there this morning.'

★★★★★

With Marco helmeted, on board the pillion and comfortable, together they sailed on the back roads over the hills of Istria in a haze of fading winter light. Grateful for the absence of summer bugs, they could at least ride with their visors up and take in the scenery. Oslići, Prodani, a hard left at Penićići to Vrh. For the first part of the journey the scenery was dominated by the brownish greens of Učka with its small white skull cap of snow; the winter, so far, had not been so hard. Then moving further inland, the undulating velvet greenery of the vine-laden hillsides below Vrh with Butoniga Lake stretched out beneath them; and just visible above it the great 'Big Joe' Tower of Motovun.

Marco remembered the story of Big Joe, read to him first by his father, then his mother, and then by Faida one time when his parents were away. She said it was a story that she had learned during the war, and she had used it to teach the men in her unit how to read and write in Croatian as they were Italian speaking. She encouraged them not to be like the men back in their home villages who couldn't even write their names, explaining that a new socialist age was dawning, and they needed to be a part of it. This was one of the very few times that Faida mentioned the war. Nino was full of it. The Partisans and the JNA. But Faida, who everyone knew was a senior officer by the end of the war on active service with Tito's High Command, let on little.

Coming down the steep hillside beneath Vrh with Brda to the north with their faded red Partisan graffiti, and Senjak below, Emina's skill as a motorcyclist became very apparent to Marco as she took what seemed like almost vertical hairpin bends with ease and safety. Never once did he feel uncomfortable as he often had when riding as a pillion passenger.

Turning right on to the small road that ran parallel to the Butoniga River, they were now deep in truffle country. The oak forest that flourished on the hillsides that ran down from Motovun to the confluence of the Mirna and the Butoniga and onwards towards the hot springs of Istarske Toplice was prime truffle-foraging territory.

But the forest had changed since Marco was a kid. In recent years it had become seriously overcrowded in the main September to December truffle season, with over 3,000 licences issued by the local authorities to hunters. Each 400-euro licence was cheap compared to the average annual earnings for trufflers which came in at around 15,000 to 20,000 euros for those locals with an ability with dogs and a nose and an eye for the right places to look. In the past the forest could provide a good living in a country where the number of jobs were shrinking, economic migration booming and the growth rate tumbling to heretofore unrecorded levels. But with the woods so crowded it was a different matter. Even that was on its way out as a way to earn a crust.

They crossed the Mirna just east of Istarske Toplice, where warm sulphurous springs have occurred naturally for millennia. Toplice was a byword for the healing properties of the waters, which had been known and used since Roman times and continued to flow into the Mirna even since its diversion in the nineteenth century. The Mirna ran in a straight line, and so did the road alongside it. As it was exceptionally clear of traffic Emina couldn't resist giving the Triumph its head and hammering all the way down to the end of the highway, bypassing the Motovun turn in the simple interest of enjoying the ride. She pulled up at the *konoba* at Ponte Porton, equidistant between Grožnjan and Motovun as the crow flies.

★★★★★

'Let's have drink here. I love this place. It's always so peaceful,' says Emina, sitting out on the terrace of the *konoba*. 'Why don't you go in and ask for drinks? They rarely bother to come out.'

Removing her leather jacket to reveal a homely cardigan underneath, Emina puts on her sunglasses and enjoys the weakening late afternoon sun on her face.

'I think I've just had a *déjà vu*,' says Marco, as he returns bearing beers and olives. 'A decade and a half ago. Maybe more. You sitting exactly there when we escaped from Grožnjan and the music lessons for a whole afternoon. Do you remember? We were in deep shit. Miss Pintar, the kindly but highly moral principal of the *Jeunesses Musicales*, was furious. Which wasn't really scary at all.'

She laughs at the memory.

'While Zvonko was off rutting with the flaxen-haired Ukrainian twins up in the spooky neo-gothic-looking dorm they called "Drakula". Only they were neither real blondes, nor real twins. They only told him that to give him an extra *frisson*, which he clearly didn't need.'

'Let the good times roll,' says Marco. 'Cheers!'

'Here's to new beginnings,' says Emina.

'Amen to that,' says Marco.

They sit and enjoy their beers in silence.

'You know this used to be the port in Roman times,' says Emina. 'It's hard to believe but the sea used to reach here. You would take a smaller boat along the Mirna down to Buzet, or Pinguentum as it was known back then. And that road going up to Grožnjan and Buje, that was the Via Flavia; and beyond that, Rome, and the western empire. We are literally sitting on a crossroads of history. And yet all that's really here is this pub, this beer, and us.'

'The good thing about global warming,' says Marco, 'is that it's very likely this will become a port again. Actually, I'm not sure that would be a bad thing. But I see what you mean about the tide of history. There's so much we take for granted.'

'I always thought there was something, weird, about Grožnjan,' says Emina. 'I don't know. Maybe it's something to do with being a refugee. I think it was great that those empty houses were given to artists and galleries and the *Jeunesses Musicales* and all that. But I could never stop thinking about the original owners. The people who lived in them and made them their homes, who had to leave in an earlier time, either semi-voluntarily in the *esodo*, or for economic reasons. There was something of the cuckoo's nest about it that always sat badly with the refugee inside me.'

'You see it as karmically challenged?' asks Marco.

'Something like that,' replies Emina.

'I know what you mean, but I have something different,' says Marco. 'Maybe something to do with my family being from round here. They stayed and have done quite well. I've been thinking a lot about the *foibe* recently. You know, as a kind of unfinished chapter of the Second World War. How many of those houses in Grožnjan belonged to people who just disappeared?'

Emina lets the question linger and then: 'We'll never know.'

*****

The last 200-metre walk up to Motovun from the car park at the church is always a bit steep. But Marco has a spring in his step this fine evening. Not only is he out on a kind of a 'date' with his ex-girlfriend and soulmate, but he is also re-visiting the scene of the happiest memories of his youth in Motovun – which he spent with Emina and Zvonko when they all worked as volunteers at the film festival every last week in July for about three or four years.

It was the scene of their teenage crimes. The Motovun Film Festival. What happened in Grožnjan stayed in Grožnjan. They were so young and so innocent at music school, but the games they played there were minor league compared to the rampant naughtiness of Motovun. What happened in Motovun everyone knew about and stayed in the folklore for years. What happened in Motovun was the stuff of legend.

'I was thinking earlier today, when I drove past the arena,' says Emina, 'of the fun we used to have not watching movies in Pula at that dreadful Croatian Films Festival. Then I remembered, as we pulled up the hill to come here, what a magic movie mountain it was for both of us.'

'I guess we really began to understand what art really was,' says Marco, 'why it existed and how it actually affected us – and how we could affect it. Anything else before was theory, but Motovun was the real thing.'

'Where art meets life 277 metres above reality,' laughs Emina.

'Some things remain eternally the same,' says Marco, 'whether it is the timeless magic of Motovun or the endlessly-disappointing, below-averageness of Croatian cinema.'

As they come through the Venetian arch, laden with its multiple Lions of Saint Mark, they see the three propellers of the Motovun Film Festival in their memories, spinning in the sky. In the distance are the salt marshes of the Antenal lagoon in the Mirna River estuary, and the propellers spinning to the memory of Josef Ressel, inhabitant of the town itself several lifetimes ago. Inventor of the propeller and who, as forestry commissioner, was also the man responsible for reporting to the emperor the value of the local oak forests for his navy's ship-building interests.

First out of Adriano's bar is Adriano himself, followed by his wife, Aida.

'Where have you guys been? It's been years.'

'I've been underground, she's been overground,' says Marco. 'Just like the Wombles.'

Adriano and Aida were the real heroes of the Motovun Film Festival, and the only people who did any real work, 24 hours a day during the event, dealing with dicks, assholes and jerks who used their drunkenness exactly for that: as an excuse to be a dick, an asshole, or a jerk.

'What do you think?' Emina asks Marco. 'A drink on the terrace here and then dinner at Luna?'

'Sorry,' says Adriano, overhearing; 'we're fully booked.'

Their faces fall. Then Nikola, the head waiter, appears from behind, saying: 'Don't listen to this bullshitter! You need a table? You come and see me. I'll take care of you, like always.'

Adriano, laughing, says: 'I nearly had you there! Listen. I'm so happy to see you, and happy to see you together. You look like you are on a date. Come on. Come down to the restaurant whenever you want – dinner is on me.'

They watch another Istrian sun go down. It's spectacular the way the disc dives into the sea giving off its purple-red flash. From their vantage point with a direct opening down the flood plain of the Mirna Valley they have a front-row seat.

Dinner is a joy. Truffles for starters, truffles for main course, and truffles for dessert. They reminisce about what happened at the festival over a couple of bottles of exceptional Kozlović teran. Marco reminds Emina of the time they were smoking pot at the back of the garden behind the Hotel Kaštel and suddenly the bushes started to move. After a few grunts and groans, out stumbled a leading international film director slightly dishevelled, behind him one of the young lads helping in the guest office. 'I've been to Cannes, I've been to the Academy Awards', he slurred, 'but they don't do hospitality like they do in Motovun.' Took the joint, smoked most of it, handed it back, and said, 'Thanks very much, old chap,' and wandered off into the night. Sadly, in the intervening years the festival had fallen into terminal, irreparable disrepair.

'Memories are made of this,' says Emina, leaning back in her chair.

'And I think we're too drunk to ride that beast home,' says Marco.

'Better book a room in the hotel,' says Emina.

'Better had,' says Marco.

'Single beds,' says Emina, slurring slightly. 'And no funny business or...'

'Or what?' says Marco.

'Or' says Emina, too tired to say anything else.

Chapter XIV

Taking Care of Business

Colonia Pietas Iulia, 81 AD

Severus's suspicions were aroused when summoned first thing in the morning to Pretty Boy Oceanus's quarters. It was rare that the sybarite roused himself before midday. His demands for Severus to appear before him were, more often than not, for the most spurious of reasons; and latterly he had become more insistent on knowing the whereabouts of Lucia and inquisitive as to the dates of her return. Severus was usually right when it came to his instincts, and his feeling was that Pretty Boy had Lucia in his sights to be the next Mrs Oceanus, the aims being: to make an honest man of himself in the eyes of the emperor; to quash any rumours (which everyone knew were true in any case) about his relationship with his sidekick, Seneschal; and to keep a close watch on Severus by holding a family member hostage. Pretty Boy did politics. Nasica's untimely death had given the impetus he needed, but now that a more or less decent time had passed since the death of Nasica, Severus expected Oceanus to up the stakes.

'Severus, my dear, Severus,' says Oceanus, effusively. 'Thank you so much for coming over to see me this early. I hope Seneschal didn't wake you.'

'Thanks, Oceanus,' says Severus, 'but I was already up and having breakfast with the men. Once a week I do the barley mash thing with them; it's not just good for morale, it allows me to check that the kitchen isn't short-changing the gladiators on their mess. They have healthy appetites and are growing lads. You remember what it was like yourself, Oceanus – it's not so long since you were a barley man yourself.'

'Indeed, that's true, very true indeed, the barmaid's choice himself,' he says, swapping a smile with the ever-present Seneschal. 'But it's not my career in the arena that I have brought you here so early to discuss, illustrious and glorious though it was. In many ways the trust in which the emperor holds me as *lanista*, *editor* and procurator of the games at Colonia Pietas Iulia comes from my hey-day in the amphitheatre. The one thing I do regret, however, is that my career was over before I could fight in the Coliseum in Rome. But who knows? Maybe he has plans for me there in another role – should things turn out well here.'

'I am sure the emperor has many plans for you, Oceanus,' says Severus blandly.

'Now, first of all, how is the delectable Lucia? My sources tell me she is no longer with your brother. Have you sent her away for ever?'

'She's travelling right now, sir, sourcing new dogs, talking to breeders around the provinces.'

'Is that right? I thought she was done with the arena. And if she is done with the arena, why is she sourcing new dogs?'

'You know Lucia, Oceanus, it's her passion, her life. She wants to start breeding herself, not for the arena, and she needs good breeds to get started with. But you'll have to ask her that yourself. As you know, she's very much her own woman.'

'Yes, I bet Lucia is a good breeder,' says Oceanus, another half-smile tripping around his thin lips. 'Please, let her come to me when she returns. I have a proposal for her that will be to both her and your advantage.'

Severus doesn't respond and looks at Seneschal as if asking if this was the reason he had been summoned from his breakfast.

'But now, down to business. We have good news. I wasn't expecting it so soon, but there seems to be method in the old man's madness.'

'Who do you mean by that?' says Severus.

'Why, the emperor,' says Oceanus, 'dear old Domitian. He wants us to hold another games this summer and he will come along in person again. Seneschal brought the message back from Rome. I am sharing this information with you so that you understand how important it is that these games go ahead. Even if you have to come out of retirement and fight in the arena again, I will have these games.'

'It would be murder if we allowed half of these young gladiators into the arena,' says Severus raising his tone to one of defiance, 'and it would be suicide if they chose to go.'

'I'm not asking you to turn out a full contingent of fighters,' says Oceanus, 'because I have other plans. Are you willing to hear me out?'

Without waiting for the answer, Oceanus explains to Severus that when Domitian was last in Pola for the games he said that as soon as he had established himself comfortably as Emperor, and judged himself to be fully in control of the mechanisms of state, he would begin the process of turning himself into a god. It wasn't unusual for an emperor to deify himself; since the times of Augustus the imperial cult had fully developed, especially in cities of the Greek east which had an extensive history of ruler worship and deification. Under Emperor Augustus, Istria – and, indeed, Colonia – had been incorporated as a discrete region within the Roman province of Italia, making it an integral part of the empire; nevertheless, Colonia Pietas Iulia was really considered to be the first city of the east which would incorporate the worship of Domitian into its public cults.

'Well, if he's a god then perhaps he could wave the old magic wand and accelerate the training of my boys so that they can be ready to fight professionally by summer – which, I'm telling you straight up, they won't be. God or no god.'

'You are not listening to me, Severus,' says Oceanus. 'I've spoken to the navy boys, and they believe that the amphitheatre can be ready by summer to stage a full-on sea battle. This will be my calling card to eventually open the arena directly to the sea. What I am proposing is that for the afternoon line-up – after the *venationes*, the executions and crucifixions, and the procession of the gladiators – we stage an epic sea battle on the theme of Jason and the Golden Fleece. It will be a fitting tribute to Domitian's deification that we present the Neptune show to end all Neptune shows. Then we will follow it by putting up half a gladiator roster, say of just the heavily-armed fighters, and – hey, presto! – we have entertainment. What do you say?'

Severus doesn't answer. He stands there in silence, shakes his head, looks at the floor in disbelief, and walks out back down to the training ground to finish his breakfast with his lads. Oceanus shouts after him: 'You've got to stop thinking like a pleb, Severus. The emperor released you from your fighting contracts, but if he hears you aren't co-operating to give him his deification games, I'm sure he will reverse that decision.'

Then, turning to Seneschal: 'If he and Lucia don't play ball with us, we shall play ball with them. Literally.'

'I've been thinking,' confides Seneschal, 'that we need to think of a good way to use those African elephants that arrived last week. Can't think of a better way to put them to use. Human *harpastum*. How the crowd will roar!'

*****

Spring is in full bloom at the Laime Channel. By the brackish, clear waters at the estuary that was no longer served by the river that carved it, the current occupants of the inn of Festus and Vita comprise mainly of the home team: Lucia, Thelos, Philumena and a small pack of dogs.

There are also a couple of pilgrim travellers heading by foot to Rome to the temple of Isis and a pair of merchants from Aquilea. This means it is quiet and allows Lucia and her energetic team of helpers, both human and canine, to perfect and refine the various methods of preserving, storing and ultimately transporting their tuberous treasures.

'Well?' asks Festus, entering the *sancta sanctorum* that is Vita's kitchen.

'Well, what?' replies Vita. 'Well, how about you get out of my kitchen,' she says, looking over at Lucia who is hard at work on one of her truffle preservation experiments. 'Rather, *our* kitchen. Strange, until we discovered the endless temptation of the tuber you showed zero interest in the kitchen except by eating whatever came out of it and never washing what went back into it.'

'She's a hard woman, Lucia,' says Festus, taking Vita's laying down of the law in good humour. 'I expect you are thinking what a tolerant fellow I am to put up with this harridan slave driver. Who will buy me my freedom, who?'

'I know why he's snooping around, Vita,' says Lucia, deliberately ignoring him. 'It's because he's afraid we are wasting or eating the last harvest of tubers from our recent visit to Pinguentum.'

'That has nothing to do with it. I'm just curious, that's all. And a bit hungry.'

Thelos comes running into the kitchen, his usual enthusiastic self.

'Here's the salt water you asked for,' says Thelos.

'Thank you, Thelos, and put it over here,' says Lucia. 'I'll give it a try but…'

'You know that water is salty, but it's not as salty as the water in Pola,' says Thelos. 'Maybe if you add some more salt to it afterwards it might be better for preserving the truffles.'

'You've just given me an idea, Thelos. Maybe the oysters and mussels, if taken out of their shells and put in salt water, might be a better way of preserving them than just drying or putting them on ice. There's never any ice anyway, and the season of ice from Mons Maior is always so short.'

Vita has had enough disruption in her kitchen and throws the boys out. 'OK, you two, go off and do your boys' experiments on the seafood,' she says, 'and leave us to do the proper work. The work that's actually going to make us rich instead of another of Festus's hare-brained ideas.'

When they are gone Vita and Lucia get down to business. Lucia thinks she has had a breakthrough with drying the tuber, but she fears that the flavour is much reduced after too much time. She's not too hopeful about the seawater or salt-water experiment, because the fresh-water experiment she tried on the black truffles ended in disaster as they just crumbled and floated around in a thousand pieces making a foul-tasting drink. She did find out, however, that if she uses that same water for cooking rice she can make some exquisite treats for the dogs; Philumena is at this very moment using them in her re-training of the arena dogs up in the forests above the inn. She will use similar treats to train the litter of first-generation truffle dogs that Britannica is currently carrying and would give birth to in six weeks or so.

Suddenly Lucia looks up from what she has been doing. She has a smile on her face: 'Vita,' she says, 'Come over here. I want you to try something.'

★★★★★

It was very quiet down at the forum that evening when Severus wandered down after a full day's training, looking to clear his head and refresh his mind. He also had to try to think straight after his one-way conversation with Oceanus earlier in the day. Severus had been plagued by a feeling he had in his guts ever since the emperor put his name down to set up the school. It was all well and good being freed from his obligations in the arena and knowing that he would live to see another day, but it was another thing being joined at the hip to someone as untrustworthy and double-dealing as Oceanus. This morning's meeting had revealed that not only were Oceanus's fantasies of pulling together another games with sea battles and argonauts an impossibility, but also that anyone who made a promise to deliver them and then failed would be first in line for the chop. It was fine to be Domitian's favourite in the good times, but he had a reputation as a ruthless and brutal killer should you fail to deliver his demands to the letter.

Severus had built up a good thirst as he wandered down past the Temple of Augustus and around to the port, looking for a small hostelry where he could quietly drown some of the horrors of his day so far.

After his meeting with Oceanus, Severus had taken over the training of the heavily armoured gladiators from the veteran Tetraites as a way of clearing his head.

A lifelong *aficionado* of the *palus*, Severus was a great believer that by concentrating on training with the *palus* and using a wooden sword you couldn't go wrong – and nothing was ever wasted. The *rudus* minimised the accidents that could take place in training, especially amongst the young tyros. Minimising injuries would ultimately allow his gladiators to fight more. Popular fighters could be sure they would make it to the amphitheatre in the best health possible, thus maximising their chance of survival and fame.

He'd spent most of the afternoon giving a masterclass to his students on to how to beat your opponent to death and survive by sustaining as few injuries as possible, while at the same time demonstrating techniques of how to get the fickle crowd on your side. He was also one to tell the gladiators how their life really would be when they got out into the ring. Today had been no exception, for as he beat relentlessly at the *palus* he had broken two wooden swords, such was his frustration after the meeting with Oceanus. The exercise was also a reality check for his students. In between blows to the *palus* he reminded them that after every bout their chances of survival would be more reduced and that most fighters didn't last for more than four years. 'Go and look at the numbers on the gravestones if you don't believe me,' he had screamed at them, before heading off down to the forum. 'If you can find me anyone older than 30, I'm buying drinks for the whole school.'

He was now in a small tavern down at the port drowning his sorrows in a bucketful of *setinum*, exactly what Lucia had warned him against doing if the going got tough. Severus's spirit was willing, but sometimes his flesh was weak, and tonight was one of those nights. As he knocked back goblet after goblet of a half-way decent *setinum* he heard a commotion at the table behind him. Someone had started a fight and he stood up to see what it was.

At a neighbouring table a squabble over a game of dice was taking place. Right at the centre of it was Apion the boatman. Severus stepped over to the table and his presence alone was enough to make Apion's attackers head for the door without a word. No-one was going to take on Severus the *murmillo*, drunk or sober.

Apion was several sheets to the wind, so drunk in fact that he wasn't even able to recognise the fact that it was Severus who had just saved his bacon.

'And you can fuck off as well, I won that one fair and square,' slurred Apion, picking up his dice and getting ready for a fight.

'Apion, it's me, Severus. Come here to my table and join me for a drink. I have some fine *setinum* here going to waste.'

'Severus. Severus. I know you Severus,' said Apion, stumbling over to the table, for he really was very drunk indeed. 'I'll take your wine.'

'Here, have a taste,' said Severus, 'but I don't think you should have much more.'

'I'll have as much as I like, Mr Severus the fucking gladiator,' said Apion. 'Finished me off, that did. That job with your brother. All gone. Seneschal told me I was no good any more after that last letter. Couldn't read a word of it, they said.'

Severus, who had been drinking pretty heavily himself, started to sober up.

'What was that you said?' he snarled, slightly disingenuously as he already knew of Apion's treachery. 'Have you been giving my letters to Seneschal? You double-dealing little son of a whore.'

He pulled Apion to his feet and on his way up slapped him about the head to loosen his tongue a bit more. 'Why, I have killed men for less than that,' he roared, giving Apion an unsavoury blast of his beans and *setinum* halitosis as he did so. 'What else did you tell them, you little shit? Come on boatman, speak up, or I'll drown you in the harbour out there.'

'I didn't tell them anything else. Honest, Severus,' says Apion, also achieving a swift return to some sobriety in the face of his imminent demise. 'But I can tell you stuff. I know stuff.'

'You had better talk – and talk fast, shithead,' Severus screamed in his face, upping the stakes and dragging him out to the harbour wall where there were fewer witnesses.

Apion hesitates, and in that moment, Severus has Apion's head under the stinking water of the harbour and holds him there for a minute, and then another minute; and only when Apion empties his bladder does he then release his grip.

'OK, now talk – or it's bye-bye boatman.'

Apion is on his knees spitting water, trying to catch his breath. Severus has managed to scare the living daylights out of him and is now worried Apion will have a heart attack before he spills his guts. 'Seneschal,' he sputters, hyperventilating and vomiting up more black water. 'He killed the gladiator. Lucia's man. Nasica. Followed him to Rome. Knifed him in the back in Ostia Aterni. That's all I know. Now let me go. I swear, that's all I know.'

Severus steps back from Apion, throwing him aside like a rag doll. Sobriety overcomes him like a dark cloak, and he makes his way with great purpose back to the barracks of the Legio II Adiutrix Pia Fidelis.

*****

'Come over here, Vita,' says Lucia. 'Thelos, go and get Festus. I've got something I want to show all of you.'

Thelos runs out of the kitchen and soon returns, bringing the querulous Festus.

'I wish you two would make up your minds: am I allowed in here or am I forbidden?'

'Shut up and listen,' says Vita.

'A few weeks ago, when we arrived back from Pinguentum,' says Lucia, 'I tried several methods to find the best way of preserving the flavours of the tubers. In my mind I wanted to combine this with the best way of transporting them back to Rome and around the empire.'

Lucia was well aware that Rome was the biggest market for such things, but places such as Alexandria, Carthagos, Pergamon, Antioch, Ephesos and even Byzantium were also where the rich and wealthy played, generating markets for such luxuries.

'As you know, I've tried various permutations. But now I think I have found the answer to our questions about preservation, transport and logistics.'

She opens one of the large jars in front of her and takes out a white truffle. It is dripping with olive oil. She cuts off two small pieces and gives one each to Vita and Festus.

'Tastes like it just came out of the ground,' says Festus, eyeing the rest of the truffle greedily, 'but even more intense. I know it shouldn't, but it feels like that.'

'And the texture doesn't seem to have been affected by being suspended in the oil for a long period of time.'

'That's exactly right,' says Lucia, 'but there is another by-product we must not forget.' She pours some of the oil onto a plate and asks Thelos to bring over some bread. 'Now, dip the bread in here.'

Simultaneously, Thelos, Festus and Vita dip their bread in the oil and bring it to their mouths.

'Mmmm. That is delicious,' says Vita, 'really, really good. Sometimes the truffles are a bit too strong for me, but this oil really has a lot of flavour yet is not so overpowering.'

Lucia leaves the kitchen and comes back in a couple of minutes later with a small wooden box. She opens it and inside are four single truffles resting on a bed of straw.

'Now, if you try these, you will see that they are of a very good quality and the flavour is good.'

They all agree.

'These are from the original harvest that Britannica and Brutus found when we first came here three months ago. I think therefore that we can draw a number of conclusions. In general, the truffle holds its flavour quite well, and because it is quite light we can even take significant numbers by road to Rome during the *mare clausum*. So we can capture our year-round market. Because the harvest is seasonal, we can release the product slowly through the year, so we keep up a regular supply to regular customers.'

'The only problem with such a valuable commodity is security on the road,' says Festus. 'I think we will probably need to disguise it as something else, something less valuable.'

'I'll come to security later,' says Lucia, 'but bear in mind we have a new contingent of guard dogs on the way. For now, let's concentrate on the summer months. When it is possible to go by sea we can send the *amphorae* full of oil and truffles. The extra benefit is the aromatic oil, because once the truffles have been removed after transportation the oil can be added to food to give the impression of the truffle, the ghost of the truffle. There are loads of things we can do with it. We could even just use and re-use some truffles to give the aroma to the oil. What I'm saying is that I think we have finally worked out how to make this business work.'

'Ladies and gentlemen, we ought to drink to that,' says Festus, reaching for his trusty cask of Falernian.

★★★★★

When Severus arrives back at the barracks he is, indeed, stone cold sober. The harsh reality of the truth that he had heard from Oceanus's own spy, Apion, had really hit home. Nasica had been on a mission of mercy to bring his family much-needed funds in Rome but had been killed on his return by Seneschal. With Nasica out of the picture Oceanus would be able to marry Lucia, control Severus and have a free hand not only with the amphitheatre and the games, but he would also have the future of the games, via the new school, under his rule. At the same time he would be able to keep his lover, Seneschal, close by while appearing to be living the decent family life of a good, honest, upright Roman citizen.

Keeping his legendary temper under control, Severus tells himself again and again that he needs to think like Lucia and be strategic – and not lose his head. First of all, he goes up to his own *tablinum*, his office, where he keeps his *arca*; in Severus's case this is a heavy chest, chained to the floor, containing his money and valuables. He selects the most important of his possessions and throws them into a hessian sack. He knows he will have to move fast and travel light.

He is on his way out of the *tablinum* when he sees to the left of the portal on the wall the two pieces of metal that make up his *manica*, the piece of armour that he had used throughout his fighting life, a sort of talisman of his career in the arena, so precious that he never left it in the armoury. This was the *manica* he had symbolically gifted to Nasica before his untimely death. He thinks hard before taking it and putting it in the already overfull sack. Lucia would want it.

Leaving his bag in his *tablinum* he slips silently down the stairs and along the corridor to the other end of the officers' quarters where Oceanus has his suite of rooms. Climbing the stairs, he hears voices: first, Seneschal's loud, drunken Roman accent, followed by girlish laughter that he doesn't recognise. Pulling aside the heavy drape that separates the rooms from the corridor he finds a party going on. Spiculus, the novice *murmillo*, is stripped to the waist and doing a dance for Oceanus and Seneschal, his back to the portal; he is shaking his hips in a sinuous and suggestive fashion whilst Oceanus and Seneschal are lapping it up, enjoying the show. All three are very drunk.

Oceanus sees Severus first and cries out, 'Severus, welcome! Come and join the fun.'

Spiculus stops his dancing, looks around and, seeing his chief Doctor, immediately tries to cover himself.

'We've just been doing a little extra curricular cramming with young Spiculus here,' says Oceanus. 'Domitian has quite exotic and eclectic tastes and we thought that the novices should be prepared in case they got the call after the next *ludus*.'

'It's a pity we could never get Nasica to play. He was always the prettiest of all you big barley men,' says Seneschal, not quite reading the situation.

'Get out of here now, you,' orders Severus. 'Now!'

Spiculus moves swiftly towards the exit without looking back.

'I'll deal with you tomorrow, if you are stupid enough to stick around,' says Severus, who then turns to Seneschal: 'As for you…'

Severus didn't wait for a response and swiftly gave a perfectly placed head butt to Seneschal's large Roman nose, making it crack and spray blood over both Seneschal and Oceanus whom he easily takes down with a simple elbow to the temple. Swinging back in the opposite direction he lifts Seneschal off the floor and brings his powerful knee forcefully into his groin and in a single motion turns him around, gripping his forearms around the major domo's neck and in a single powerful motion snaps it back.

Scrambling for the door, Oceanus tries to escape – but Severus is too quick and tackles him to the floor. With Nasica's killer dispatched to the next world, Severus turns his growing anger and bloodlust on to the real culprit, Oceanus. With just the sound of his own heartbeat throbbing in his head he brings his fist up and down and up and down repeatedly – as he practised earlier in the day with the wooden sword on the *palus* – in a rhythmic beat that almost forbids him to stop. Then, at one moment, he comes to and remembers Lucia's advice to think straight and be strategic.

Pretty Boy Oceanus's face looks back up at him, his mangled lip merged with his smashed-up nose. The whole visage, or what is left of it, is caked in a veil of blood pouring out of orifices in his face where, until then, there hadn't been orifices. In fact, he now barely had features. Severus stands up and looks down at his victim. He knows that Spiculus won't sound the alarm because he would be too afraid of the consequences of being implicated. So much for 'Pretty Boy', thought Severus, standing up straight and looking down at his own, broken, blood-spattered hands.

★★★★★

Such was the delight of Lucia, Festus, and Vita at finally cracking the truffle preservation and transportation conundrum that, on Philumena's return from her dog training trip, they all went down into the lagoon to bathe and enjoy the remainder of the beautiful sunny spring day. The woods and the forests of the Laime had suddenly burst to life after the long winter. The trees were full of birdsong, not just from the native local breeding varieties but also from some of the more beautiful visiting exotics such as the kingfisher, which found the semi-sweet waters of the channel perfect for fishing. In the evening the owls hooted out their eerie cries, but they were also wont to chirp, whistle, scream, screech, bark, as well as growl. Today, though, it was the usurping cuckoo and the rat-a-tat of the ubiquitous woodpecker that provided the backdrop to their swim, along with a carpet of large tortoiseshell, nettle-tree and Cleopatra butterflies that bedecked the steep slopes of spring-flowering trees all around them. It was like the Garden of Eden.

The children and the dogs bathed and played in the waters, while Vita and Lucia took the sun on the banks of the channel. Festus, perpetually hungry, foraged in his oyster beds for some fresh pickings for supper of clams, mussels, and scallops.

'I'm so happy that we have been able to make these plans together,' said Vita. 'It has been a whole new world for me, with you and Philumena and Thelos coming to live here. Finally feels like I have a family. I'll be sorry when you go back to the woods.'

'It will only be for the season, and Philumena and Thelos will come back and forth with our treasures.'

'You also need to get Festus involved in that as well, get his lazy fat arse out on the road and lose some weight.'

Lucia had spent all her waking hours since learning of the death of Nasica working on the truffle plan. She was convinced they could build a life away from the carnage of the arena that would allow Severus to retire with dignity and Philumena and Thelos to get an education and live decently in the country away from the madness and dirt of the town. This spring afternoon was a perfect example of the life she wanted for everyone. Carefree: no worries about safety, money, status, or food.

'Festus was right when he mentioned security earlier,' said Lucia. 'We need to keep the fact that we are working with precious commodities under wraps. First of all, we need to protect the secrets of where our treasures are buried. Then, like we said, we should transport them securely between the truffle forests and here. That's where Philumena and Thelos and some of the dogs who haven't taken to truffling will come in.'

'And Festus,' said Vita, 'it will be good to get rid of him for a few days, especially when one or other of the kids is around. They are just adorable. And hard workers as well.'

'It's true,' said Lucia, 'and they will be integral to what we do. But I've been thinking. We need some kind of excuse to be a family living in the woods. And I thought that if we presented ourselves as humble foragers or gleaners – or perhaps charcoal burners – it could provide a brilliant alibi to explain our presence in the forest.'

'Not a bad idea,' said Vita. 'And with all the black soot from the charcoal, you can add an element of disguise to it.'

'We need to work on the idea, but let's run it by Festus and Severus and see what they think.'

*****

Two days later Lucia's wish is answered. Just before dawn, a mere 36 hours after his slaying of Seneschal and Oceanus in the officers' quarters of his former legion at Colonia Pietas Iulia, Severus creeps up the hillside from the Laime Channel's waters and slips into the inn by the back door. He is sitting at the kitchen table when Vita appears, just after sunrise.

'Jove and all the heavens above, you gave me a fright,' says Vita, not expecting to find anyone, least of all Severus, sitting at her kitchen table working through last night's leftovers and about to start on anything else edible he could find in Vita's kitchen.

'I could eat a donkey's arse,' says Severus, a little tipsy from the Falernian he has also discovered from Festus's supply. 'In fact, I may have just done that. What's next, Vita? Bread? Olives? Honestly, I haven't eaten for a whole day, and I've just about had it.'

'What on earth have you done to your hands, Severus? Come here. Let me clean them.'

Vita pours water into a basin and starts to unwrap the dirty pieces of cloth that cover Severus's bloodied fists.

'Ahhh, don't pull too hard,' moans Severus. 'Maybe I need to soak them off. They are completely dried in. I used some of Lucia's spare silk material, as it helps open wounds heal well.'

'Severus, what are you doing here? What has happened? Why are your hands in this state?' Vita asks.

'You should see the other guys. They don't look so clever now. I'm not sure I like this real-life fighting, though, it's very painful.'

Lucia, hearing the commotion, joins them in the kitchen. Thelos follows swiftly.

'Severus – you're here! Talk of the devil, we were just speaking about you before we went to sleep,' says Lucia.

Seeing the state of Severus's hands, she sends Thelos up to her room to bring down her medicine box. 'Does it hurt still?'

'Not so much,' says Severus, slowly removing the crusty silk bandages from his fists. 'Oops, I think I just pulled out one of Pretty Boy's teeth. I think we're going to have to re-name him. In death he became "Not So Pretty Boy" after the thrashing I gave him.'

Lucia finishes off bathing Severus's hands. She applies a honey-and-poppy balm to them to help the healing and keep them free of infection as well as a way of killing some of the pain. Severus then explains in great detail the events of the last 36 hours to Lucia and Vita: Apion's confession, followed by the killing of Seneschal and Oceanus. By this time Festus has joined them in the kitchen and picks up the highlights.

'Are you sure you killed Oceanus?' asks Festus. 'Because if you didn't that man knows the first place you will run to is here. And from what you have told me hell hath no fury like a Pretty Boy scorned.'

'You're right, Festus. We can't take any chances on that,' says Lucia, 'we need a plan.'

'Whether I killed him or not,' says Severus, 'he is certainly not going anywhere for a while. And if he does, no-one is going to recognise him.'

'It's little comfort to any of us,' says Lucia, 'but at least we know now who it was that killed Nasica. Those two bastards; they have to control and own everything they see. You did the right thing, father, thank you for doing this. I just hope Oceanus has had his last ticket to the arena punched.'

'I don't think you two are safe here for now,' says Vita. 'We need to get you away from here until it all blows over.'

'Which may be some time, as Oceanus has the memory of an elephant,' adds Lucia.

'Not if he's dead,' says Festus.

'Yes, but we don't know that,' says Vita. 'I think we need to get started on your original plan, Lucia: the charcoal burners. Let's begin immediately. Tomorrow we will leave for the Porta Porton and the Aquilis forest. We'll make all the preparations today and leave at dawn tomorrow. Severus, you need to get some sleep and get those hands well again – you're going to need them.'

'This changes everything,' says Festus. 'I don't trust anyone, least of all Oceanus. We need an escape plan in case it all goes horribly wrong. First of all, the money we earn will be kept in the hands of our merchant in Rome until we need it. We can get it any time, but for safety, until everything settles down into a routine, we leave it there. Second, we need an escape route. And I think I have found one. There is a cave just to the south-east of Motovun, in a valley where there is a massive ravine. We came across it when we were on patrols from Pinguentum one day. Down into that ravine runs a river which disappears. That river runs straight down here to the Laimes and then to the sea. And that, my friends, will be our escape route should everything go tits up.'

*****

The next day Severus and Lucia had made their way up to the forest between Pinguentum and Montona and within the week had set up their operation on the south side of the Aquilis. They were far enough from Pinguentum as to be untraceable in the deep forest, and in the shade of the east side of the eponymous Montona as to be almost entirely invisible to the world. And then, for extra security, they had their alibi profession: the charcoal burner.

It wasn't the cleanest profession in the world. But it made great cover for the truffle-hunting family led by Severus and Lucia. The least suspicious people in the forest were the charcoal burners: outcasts who lived by choice away from urban communities. Disguised as such, Severus, Lucia, Thelos and Philumena began their new lives in exile in the profundity of the thick forest that ran between Pinguentum, Montona and the coast at Porta Ponton. The first thing they had done on choosing an appropriate clearing in the forest was to begin to dig a fire pit for the large wooden marquis-like framework that would look like it was ready for burning. But it would actually serve as their shelter and home for the seasons when they were based away from Laime collecting the tubers.

Ancient Rome was a fuel-hungry society and the daily need for charcoal in all parts of the empire was ubiquitous. Charcoal was a prized commodity. Individual households in Pinguentum needed heat and a way to cook their food. Businesses such as bakeries and bathhouses required supplies of wood and charcoal on a daily basis.

And then there were the industries like metalworking, refining and pottery which were absolutely dependent on a steady supply of fuel to heat forges and fire kilns; they often needed specialized types of charcoal made from a particular wood.

Throughout history, as far back as Greek times, charcoal burners were ostracized, shunned, and considered apart from society by the isolated way of life they lived and by the unclean way they looked. Their profession was considered dishonourable and they were frequently accused of evil practices because of their position as outsiders. They were an easy target to accuse. This suited Severus and Lucia fine enough, as they didn't want to be bothered by anyone in the woods. But like real charcoal burners, their seasonal stint in the forest was a job that was more arduous, lonely and, at times, dangerous than they at first imagined.

Lucia and Severus got lucky on their first few days when beginning to make their charcoal-burner's camp. As they dug into the earth to create the pit that would serve as their living area, they cut into the roof of a cave. Not only did it give them a dry living space to inhabit, but it also gave them a steady supply of the fresh water that they would need for their day-to-day living and working. It opened up into a small system of other caves that with the addition of some oil lamps could prove useful for storage as well as provide different chambers for living. In short, they had fallen through a hole (literally, in Severus's case as he was digging). The entrance to the cave was, therefore, disguised by the traditional structure that burnt the wood that made the charcoal.

The summer evenings were drawing in with the onset of autumn. Life deep in the forest was becoming a little danker, a little darker as the moisture from the atmosphere and the earth increased with the season, bringing about the chemical reactions which would hopefully result in a bumper crop of truffles for their first season; not enough to retire on, but sufficient to build a new business.

'At least we are away from the arena,' said, Lucia as they sat in their cave after dinner one early autumn night, 'and no-one will ever be able to find us here. Even if what they say is true and

Oceanus survived, I think the beating you gave him will make him wary of trying to get revenge.'

'I wouldn't count on that, Lucia,' said Severus wearily. 'That man's whole life was driven by revenge of some kind or other. I actually think he loved Seneschal. Probably the only person he ever loved in his life. And now he doesn't have that, well – idle hands are the devil's workshop.'

'Even if he wanted to find us he would have trouble tracking us down here,' replied Lucia.

'And if he did, I am ready for him,' declared Severus, who had taken to cleaning his old gladiator armour of an evening; the two parts that made up the *manica* were now gleaming like the sun as the fire glinted off their surface deep in the cave below the charcoal pile that covered their hide-out.

'I wish you wouldn't keep playing with that armour. Too many bad memories,' said Lucia. 'I never want to see any bloodshed like that ever again.'

Just then the door in the roof opened and down the ladder came Thelos and Philumena. As they entered the main living area where the fire provided the focus of the room, it was clear they were hiding something in their tunics from Lucia and Severus.

'Surprise!' they said in unison and produced as if by magic their hidden cache of puppies.

'Philumena, no! I've told you – no puppies in the cave. At least not until they have got used to being outside with their mother for long enough. They are our early warning system, our alarm.'

'Oh, but we wanted to show you something,' said Philumena. Lucia saw how tender she was with the little ones and how cute the puppies of Brutus and Britannica were – and she couldn't resist.

'What is it you wanted to show us?'

'Look, they are only four weeks old, but already they have a talent for finding the truffle. Go on Thelos, show them. Hide it.'

Thelos went into an obscure part of the cave and scraped away some earth, unseen by the puppies. When Philumena released the little bundles of fur they first of all had a curious sniff around the cave, but after a few minutes their little tails went up and they got the scent of the truffle. Soon after they were digging in the corner of the cave where Thelos had left a small piece of black truffle.

'These are very talented little babies already,' said Severus, scooping them both up in his big gladiator arms. 'And what might their names be?'

'The little girl is Bestia, because she is the smallest but the strongest. And she fights like a beast and is so stubborn.'

'And the boy is Strigo,' said Thelos, 'and he's mine. He's called Strigo because he is intelligent, clever and can outwit any of the other dogs or men. We named him in honour of the Strigo who was killed in the arena. He was such a good dog.'

At that moment they heared whimpering at the top of the ladder: a mother looking for her lost children.

'Quick, you two, take them back to Britannica. She is worried and we don't want her to lose her milk. They need to grow up big and strong like their mummy and daddy.'

'Come back quickly and get some sleep,' said Severus. 'We have a big day tomorrow. Festus and Vita are arriving soon with supplies, and we must complete our first quota of truffles. The orders have already started to come in from Rome and we need to fulfil them, so bedtime!'

Chapter XV

Trieste is Ours!

German Occupied Istria, April 1945

The journey back to base after the aborted attack on Ljotić's car took double the time of the outward trek and was at least twice as difficult. The ambush party had a pre-arranged rendezvous contingency for cases like this at Ustje. It was there an hour later after they had shaken off the last of their pursuers that Pino was able to take stock and estimate the damage suffered by his troop. By all accounts they had lost three men. All three members of the gun crew – Janez, David and Brdjan – hadn't made it, being the closest to the front line of attack. Two more, the *bombaši* that Pino was saving in reserve to finish off the Ljotićevci in the car, had been wounded: Boris, whose neck was still bleeding profusely, and Denis whose arm had been completely smashed by a spray of bullets and was lucky to be alive.

'Tomo, you need to do your best to get Boris's bleeding under control, otherwise…' Pino stopped himself mid-sentence.

'Yes, boss,' said Tomo, quickly intervening. Tomo was an experienced medic who had seen worse injuries in the field. 'I think it's getting less. We'll bind it tight and then see how it goes when we start moving.'

'In the meantime, I can clean and splint Denis's arm as best I can,' said Pino, taking time out to consult his map. 'And then we can make for Zalesje. The hospital at Šmagurje farm near Ostrožno Brdo. If we rest up here till dark, we can make it overnight.'

'I'm going to give you both something for the pain,' said Tomo, 'so you can get some rest. It's a long hike to Zalesje.'

'Then on the way over, I want all of you to give some thought as to who it was that betrayed us. We may have survived, but that God-loving bastard Ljotić, Mita Bogomoljac, did as well. If it's the last thing I do on this earth, I will find out who betrayed us and make them pay for this.'

And then there was also the lingering feeling haunting the back of Pino's mind that he had failed in his mission to carry out a direct order from Comrade Tito. His name would be known, and not in a good way.

★★★★★

The remaining Partisans at the camp back in Rašpor went about the daily round of their business and duties: collecting wood, maintaining the oil lights, cleaning their weapons, as well as attending the optional political education and literacy classes. Faida's literacy class was something that even the literate didn't want to miss, and today was no exception as she returned to her subject of the giants of Istria.

'There are so many legends about giants in Istria,' announced Faida to her group of twenty or so battle-hardened veterans. 'I thought today we'd try to make up some of our own. Mine is the story of the giant Ban Dragonja, who was one of the giants that created the caves that we are living in now. This is the story of the huge cave that connects to this one and goes all the way to the sea at the Lim Fjord.'

It was here that Faida stopped her story for dramatic effect and asked her audience to bring their chairs closer so she could see all their faces. They pulled their roughly hewn, home-made stools in, some reluctantly, and listened to her as she recounted her magical tale of days gone by.

'There was a time, back in the day, when giants walked the earth in Istria. The north of the country was blessed with rain and water and grottoes like this one where waters flowed, but the south was poor in water. Men, therefore, paid homage to the giant Ban Dragonja to bring them water. The giant agreed and took his gigantic oxen and his massive plough and drove the plough through the earth from the sea to the south and the water flowed. And he called this river the Dragonja. His wife, who was called Mirna, complained to him that she had no river named after her, so he went back down to the sea and furrowed another river down to meet the Dragonja in Pazin. This river he named the Mirna. Just as he passed Pazin castle a woman looked out at Ban Dragonja, and shouted, "You fool, can't you see you have not been ploughing straight. This river is crooked and bent. Idiot!" Dragonja, insulted, retreated with his great beasts and the water started to flood the town. He could hear the townspeople's cries as they drowned and called out to him for mercy. This made him even more angry, and angrier against the woman who called him an idiot when he was trying to do good. As he passed her window, he drove his foot as hard as he could into the ground and created the Pazin cave into which the Pazinčica river flowed down deep into the earth, disappearing forever into the ground.'

'I know the cave in Pazin – it's huge,' said Dino the cook. 'It makes this one look like a miniature. We used to go and swim in the underground lake in the summer with the girls' – and, with a sly wink and a smile – 'that's not all we did.'

'Thanks, Dino, for that,' replied Faida, handing around sheets of paper and pencils. 'Perhaps when we get to the "private diary" part of the literacy curriculum you can include a description of that as part of your contribution. But for today we are sticking with the subject, which is legends. Those of you who can write I want you to write down a legend that you know of. It doesn't have to be about Istria – it can be anything. If you can't, I can help you copy it down.'

'Does Comrade Tito count?' came a voice from the back.

'Comrade Tito counts because he is a living legend,' said Faida dutifully, 'but let's try to think of historical legends like the Jure Grande, or the Legend of the last Histrian king, Epulon. That kind of thing.'

'What about the Vampire of Kringa?' said one young raw recruit from the back.

The room erupted. The other Partisans shouted down the young man, who retreated into his corner.

'No, stop! What is this behaviour?' shouted Faida firmly, over their jeering. 'Comrade Šterpin? Come back here. Tell us. Is it true? You have vampires in Istria?'

'Of course,' said Šterpin, 'it's just we don't like to talk about it. We also have sorcerers. In the countryside. *Strigoni* and *vedaveci*. They suck the blood of children. Then they do other stuff. When they die, the *strigoni* go round the village and in the house whose door they knock on someone will lose their life. Soon after. Couple of days. They don't want to talk about it because their wives are at home alone. They go into the houses and into the beds of their wives when they are away. They especially like the young widows.'

'But this is a wonderful story, Šterpin,' cut in Faida, as she felt the tension in the room. 'You must write it down. You could publish it as an Istrian story like Comrade Nazor did with *Veli Jože*. It will make a great vampire legend.'

'What about the legend of the bastards who betrayed my operation?' came a voice from the natural doorway to the cave.

The voice belonged to Pino, who had staggered in covered in mud and barely able to stand.

'When I find the bastard who betrayed us, I will kill him with my own bare hands.'

Pino collapsed onto the floor in an exhausted mess as the remaining ten men of his decimated ambush team trooped into the cave, wearied, and overcome with the smell of failure.

*****

Pino and his men had made excellent time to the hospital at Šmagurje. The walking wounded managed the trip without too much trouble on the overnight trek and would survive. The onward journey back to Rašpor was more fraught with danger because the fog came down and it was impossible to navigate. Pino was determined to get his men back safely but he was also driven by the desire to warn the company that there was a potential spy in the camp. It took him an hour or so to recover from the exigencies of the 18-hour forced march that his men had undertaken.

Soon Pino managed to recover enough to face the officers in their cave and give his report of the disastrous events of the last two days.

'It was all too easy,' Pino told the Neapolitan, Major Gabrielli and Commissar Gasparini, who carefully listened to his account. 'As soon as we were set up and dug in they just started to pick us off one by one. Their positions were perfectly placed to be able to do that. If Janez hadn't asked for something to eat for sure it would have been me. We were lucky to get out with so few casualties.'

'Thank you, Pino,' said the Neapolitan. 'You and your men fought bravely, and you will be mentioned in dispatches. In the meantime, we will launch an inquiry into what breaches of security there could possibly have been. The most important thing is to find out if there is a mole in here or if the leak is further up in High Command.'

'I think it has to be someone here, sir, and I am going to find out. We lost three of our best men back there in Ajdovščina: we can't afford to lose any more to a traitor in our midst.'

'Hold on there, comrade Pino,' says the Neapolitan. 'There are any number of ways this information could have got back to Ljotić's men. The last thing we want to do is start a witch hunt here. You need to understand that there are wheels within wheels. This is a matter for our political commissariat, and they will take care of it.'

'For this reason,' continued the Neapolitan, 'the death of Ljotić would have been a major blow to the morale of the Nationalists, especially as now the Četniks and the Ljotćevci are essentially a single force. Our sources tell us that all 5,000 members of the SDS, SUK, Serbian Border Guard and the Special Police – as well as Đujić's and Dobroslav Jevdević's Četniks and Slovene collaborators – have now gathered on the Slovenian coast. Therefore, it's essential that we are part of the forces that liberate Trieste.'

'The chances of that are slim to zero right now,' chipped in the veteran Benvenuti, who until now had maintained his habitual taciturnity.

'What do you suggest we do then, comrade Pino? Interrogate all the men until someone confesses?' asked the Neapolitan. 'I have to admit myself that is not the way we do things, and that is not going to happen. We will make an immediate report to High Command. They will respond with regard to an internal investigation. Until then, you will do nothing. Have I made myself clear?'

'Yes, sir!' came the reluctant reply.

'Dismissed, comrade Pino,' said the Neapolitan.

Pino turned on his heels and was about to exit the officer's cave when Nino rushed in, swiftly followed by Vito, bearing a dispatch for the Neapolitan.

'Sir, urgent message from High Command,' said Nino, out of breath and bent over double with exhaustion. 'I've just picked it up from Comrade Armando at the meeting point, sir.'

The Neapolitan took the message from Nino and opened it immediately. The officers gathered around.

'Trusting you with the important messages, now, are they?' said Pino quietly to Nino.

'Here, it's in code,' said the Neapolitan to Benito Gasparini. 'Take a look at it and tell me what it says.'

There was silence while Gasparini sat at the communications desk and worked through the message with a pencil.

'I think I've got it all,' said the commissar. 'But anyway, here's the gist.'

LJOTIĆ DEATH CONFIRMED. CAR AND PASSENGERS DESTROYED HUBELJ RIVER. CONGRATULATIONS TO THE BATTALION. SPECIAL THANKS FROM COMRADE TITO TO LEADER OF AMBUSH AND MEN. WE MARCH ON TRIESTE. YOUR MEN WILL JOIN US. FURTHER ORDERS FOLLOW.

The Neapolitan looked at Benvenuti. Pino looked at Nino. Everyone looked at each other.

*****

The reality of the situation came to light later. Shortly after dawn Ljotić and his adjutant, along with a small security team, left the Miramar in between Trieste and Duino where he had been meeting with Hermann Neubacher, Hitler's special political representative for the Balkans.

The previous evening over dinner Neubacher attempted to discuss the harmless elegance of Rilke and the fact that he could be considered as un-subversive. But with Ljotić it was like talking to a brick wall; he was so lacking in culture he hadn't even heard of the *Duino Elegies*, let alone read them. After the coffee they moved on to more serious subjects, like the fact that Tito's 4th Army was advancing north along the coastal road from Novi Vinodolski in Croatia and would soon liberate Istria, Trieste, and all of central and western Slovenia. Neubacher took the opportunity to express his anxiety as to what would happen when Ljotić's Serbian Volunteer Corps, the SDK, and Mihajlović's Četnik forces in Istria came into contact with British and American units who were expected to move in that direction from Italy. Ljotić, of course, reassured Neubacher of the SDK's loyalty, but this gave Neubacher little comfort that the German retreat would be defended in every way possible. Neubacher realised that Ljotić was being unrealistic, indeed naïve as to just how close the Allies and the Partisans were to taking power. He put it to Ljotić that the endgame for the German armies in the Balkans and in Italy was a matter of days, or maybe a week. The dinner ended abruptly with Neubacher demanding to know Ljotić's plans for withdrawing and surrendering the SDK.

Ljotić was ostensibly rattled when he ordered his driver, Ratko Živadinović, to take the long road to Postojna because there were rumours of a possible ambush. Ljotić planned to meet up with General Đujić and, based on Neubacher's intelligence, they were to coordinate a general Četnik-SDK withdrawal towards Italy. At about eight o'clock, Ljotić, his adjutant and his driver stopped at a friendly inn at the village of Dobravlje to have breakfast prior to his crunch meeting with Đujić. They continued their journey to Postojna via Ajdovščina but when approaching a bridge on the Hubelj river Živadinović failed to notice that it had been partially destroyed by Partisan saboteurs. It was later established that he had very poor eyesight and so he accidentally drove the car into a hole that had been blown in the bridge. Ljotić's neck was broken, and he died instantly.

The news in the camp was greeted with amazement. After the initial confusion, happiness was followed by joy and then euphoria. The immediate sense was that the turning point had come; Tito's Partisan rag-tag army had not only become the victor against its own nationalist enemies – the Zbor, the SDK, the *Ustaša* the collaborationist Serbian State Guard and Mihailović's Četniks – but they had also beaten back Mussolini's Fascist army, as well as the Nazis. They could be proud of the fact that of all the European countries in World War Two the Yugoslav territories were one of only two which were liberated by their own forces. Of course, there was Russian assistance in the liberation of Belgrade and limited air assistance from the British, but at the end of the war no foreign troops were stationed on its soil.

★★★★★

Although the war is not yet won the Neapolitan and his fellow officers decide a celebration is in order. They crack open a few casks of wine they have been saving for such an occasion, and Dino the cook brings out a few bottles of the stash of *orahevac* that he has been saving to trade for cigarettes and suchlike.

The camp takes on a festive spirit. Faida has found a large broad red ribbon to put around Vito's neck. All the Partizanka have done their hair as best they can in the mountain conditions, and what little lipstick they have is shared between themselves.

'Well, if nobody else wants to dance with me then I'll dance with Vito,' says Faida to the general gathering. 'Actually, he's much better looking than most of you lot. Definitely smells better.'

Vito is a good sport and hops around the floor with Faida but soon gets bored and wanders off into the kitchen to look for scraps. Dino goes through his playlist of popular Istrian accordion classics and sing-alongs to the general delight of his audience who aren't used to these rare breaks in military life or access to half-way decent wine. The mood in the room is hotting up.

Pino isn't so happy. Even though his failure has turned into a success, his conscience and his pride cannot allow him to see it as such. Romano and Benvenuti had told him to take it as his success, ask no questions, and be part of the battalion of Partisans that will march into Trieste on May Day, the worker's holiday. The fact was that the *bombaši* had destroyed the bridge and that was what killed Ljotić. End of story. But neither Faida's entreaties, the Neapolitan's orders, nor Nino's friendly attempts to reach out can convince him otherwise. As far as he is concerned there is a traitor in the room – and he is going to find out who it is.

Pino moves on from the *malvazia* that Major Gabrielli had so generously supplied to the troops to Dino's *orahevac*. The volume of his intake, combined with a preternatural weakness for alcohol, has made him very drunk very quickly. Both Nino and Faida are keeping a wary eye on him as he moves about the room. The celebrations, however, are interrupted by Romano, who takes the floor: 'Thank you, comrade Dino,' says the Neapolitan, 'not only for your fine musical contribution but also for this excellent walnut brandy, the like of which I have not tasted since the beginning of the war!'

A cheer of gratitude goes up from the gathering of woodland warriors.

'As you all know, we are here to celebrate not just the success of the ambush and death of the bastard fascist, Ljotić.'

Another cheer goes up.

'But word has now come that we are very close to being able to march on Trieste,' continues Romano. 'We are no longer a small resistance group fighting in the mountains. We are part of a great army almost one million strong. We have defeated the armed forces of the Independent State of Croatia and the Wehrmacht, taken Sarajevo, and in the next few days we will finish off Croatia and Slovenia and march on Trieste.'

'It doesn't change the fact,' interjects Pino, 'that we have a fucking traitor in here somewhere. He betrayed us in Ajdovščina – and we lost three good men and true.'

Faida and Nino move in beside Pino and try to keep him quiet. Romano ignores the breach of discipline and continues: 'Tomorrow night, April 29th, we will join forces with our fellow Vladimir Gortan Brigade units at Erajavce and go from there to Slivija where we will meet up with the 20th Dalmatian Partisan Division around Kozina. Then we will take the *camionale* road and march on Trieste on the first of May. Trieste is ours!'

And so the chant began: 'Trieste is ours! Trieste is ours! Trieste is ours!' and lasted a full five minutes before Dino's accordion burst in with the unofficial Batallion song, a boy-meets-machine gun love story, attributed to their favourite Partisan and *Veli Jože* writer, Vladimir Nazor.

It's goodbye to Kata,
And Reza, and Anja too,
But I'll never break up with
My machine gun.

With it I will manage
A most fruitful marriage
So long as we can sing
Rat-a-tat-tat, rat-a-tat tat.

Hanging over my shoulder
Or resting on my chest
When it kills fascists
It makes me feel best.

Such warm metal
And light as a petal
Its throat yelling with joy
Rat-a-tat-tat, rat-a-tat tat.

My lovely machine gun
Knows all of the mountains
Each winding river
And ravine to the sea.

She drives all before her
Makes the black crows squawk
Shouting it out loud
Rat-a-tat-tat, rat-a-tat tat.

Everyone sings except Pino, who at this point is being led outside the caves to get some fresh air by the long-suffering Faida.

'Take it easy, my darling,' says Faida, humouring him in his drunken state. 'We have everything to celebrate. But you will only find out if there is an informer if you take things easy.'

'Take things easy?' slurs Pino, becoming agitated. 'When we are faking that we killed Ljotić? I was there and I know that we didn't kill him. Whatever way he died, it wasn't by a Partisan bullet. And here we are claiming the credit. This is wrong! And we still don't know who betrayed us. And who can still betray us.'

He pushes Faida away roughly, and Nino steps between them.

'Hey, hey, big brother, take it easy,' says Nino. 'Faida is only trying to help.'

Pino turns drunkenly on Nino, swigging deeply from a bottle of *loza* he has picked up.

'Oh, it's my little brother. My big man little brother. The pussy who couldn't take daddy's beating. Not good enough to come on the ambush because he's a little capitalist informer. I bet it was you, you little shit. You'll never make a Communist. Bastard.'

'Stop it, Pino,' says Faida, intervening between them, pushing Pino back. 'Nino is your brother – he would never do anything like that. He looks up to you and supports you. I know because he has told me.'

'My pathetic little brother,' says Pino threateningly to Nino. 'Who killed my mother. And killed his father. You may be able to fool my girl, but you don't fool me. I bet it was you who gave us away. Bastard.'

This is one step too far for Nino and he lashes out at Pino who falls to the ground. Dead drunk. He doesn't get up.

'Come on, let's get him to bed,' says Faida, getting hold of Pino under one arm. 'We need to save him from himself.'

'Let's go, big brother,' says Nino to the unconscious Pino, and then to Faida, 'I think he might be out for the count.'

They carry Nino back into the cave and directly to his sleeping quarters without having to go back through the party. They lie him down in his bed, take his shoes off, put a blanket over him and tuck him in. He's snoring before Faida and Nino can retreat. As they move beyond the exit, Faida turns to Nino: 'I'm so sorry. He's not usually like this.'

'He sometimes gets like this when he's drunk,' says Nino. 'But this isn't just bad drunk. Something else is eating away at his insides.'

'He wants to be a good Communist,' says Faida.

'Well, he has a strange way of going about it,' says Nino, turning to face Faida.

'I know,' she says, 'I know. Come here.'

Faida opens her arms and embraces Nino.

'I'm so sorry, Nino,' repeats Faida. 'It's nothing to do with you. I promise.'

And she holds him close.

*****

Pino opens his eyes. The morning after the night before. He remembers nothing about it. Nothing. Except that he had behaved extraordinarily badly. That overwhelming, underwhelming feeling on waking from a drunk. He was still trying to piece together in his mind the various bits of subconscious images while grappling with the fact that his throat was as dry as the sandal of a desert hermit and the blood in his head was thumping against its sides as if looking for a way out and unable to flow around his body. All the lovely effects of the various alcohols had been replaced by the terrible ones. The incisive ache along the brow, and the inability to have any clarity in the thought department.

Nino appears beside him and hands him a cup of water.

'I thought you might be needing this,' says Nino, whose words are barely audible to Pino, as if Nino is speaking to him through a wall of invisible cotton wool.

Pino gradually pulls himself up from his sprawl on the bed and scrambles for his watch.

'What time is it?' he asks Nino. 'And where has everybody gone?'

'It's just after midday,' replies Nino, 'and everyone has headed off to Kozina where the battalion is due to meet up with the Dalmatians and march on Trieste.'

'Oh fuck. I've fucked up again,' says Pino, putting his head in his hands.

'You haven't. It's exactly as it should be.'

'What do you mean? I should be with the rest of the brigade on the way to Trieste.'

'That's not what the Neapolitan decided this morning,' says Nino. 'After your behaviour last night he said that he couldn't trust you to stop your wild goose chase for an informer in the presence of other battalions and within the troops of High Command who are joining in the liberation of Trieste.'

'So what about us?' says Pino. 'Those of us who are left?'

'We have to mop up some local dissenters and then make an escort of prisoners of war to Buzet. Then we march on Pula.'

'On Pula,' says Pino, derisively. 'We march on Pula.'

'Yes, we will be the liberators of the capital of Istria. And if that's not good enough for you, Pino, maybe you should think about some of the thousands of Partisans who won't be liberating anything. Because they are dead.' And, as an afterthought, he hands Pino a piece of paper. 'By the way, Faida left this for you.'

Pino lies back on his bed and takes a deep breath. After a few minutes, he sits up again, takes a deep draught of the fresh spring water that Nino has brought him, and reads.

Dear Pino:

When the Neapolitan and Gasparini came to me this morning and gave me the choice of staying here to mop up or marching on Trieste, I knew I had no choice. That was before they told me that you won't be coming. I believe in us, Pino, and I have loved you as I have never loved someone who wasn't my family. I loved you like my family because you are the only one I have. But your behaviour since Nino arrived here has shown me that you love the revolution more than you love family, and for me that's the wrong way round. Yes, I know we should never say it, and I know I am taking a huge risk writing this down. But I can do it because I really do believe in the revolution and believe in love. You need to embrace your brother and love him. The things you said to him last night were unforgiveable. I am sure he will find it in his heart to forgive you if you just ask him. Meanwhile, I think it would be good if we spent some time apart and for you to reflect on what is important and what isn't important. What is good and what is bad, what is real and what is compromise. If you can love me first and Tito second, we can have a future together. They are calling me to join the ranks. I'm taking this chance as a Partizanka to march on Trieste. I've stood at the back and been a good nurse for long enough. We are as strong as the men, if not stronger. And, as Tito says, we will take our place in Yugoslavia alongside the men after the liberation. I send you my love.

Faida

P.S. One thing you were right about. You were betrayed. Dino the cook overheard the officers talking about the ambush when he brought them their fuži a few nights ago. He slipped away during the night. He won't get far.

Part Six

Chapter XVI
The Reckoning
Istria: December 30th, 2019

The daylight that appeared gradually through the slats of the shuttered windows on the third floor of the Hotel Kaštel dappled the covers on the single bed that held two bodies joined fast together in embrace. One, female, was sound asleep; the other, male, stared at the ceiling wide awake watching the dawn light slowly move across the room. As the grey morning rays seeped through the windows from the east, Marco, the male, dared not move for fear of waking his lover, Emina.

When they arrived at the hotel after midnight looking for a room, they were lucky that they knew the night watchman from their festival days but also they were lucky to find a room, because normally the hotel was fully booked. A cancellation, however, had just come in and Emina's specific request for twin beds could be fulfilled. Both a little drunk they giggled their way upstairs to the ominously numbered room 101 and after some fumbling of the key in the lock they opened the door and went inside. Marco made immediately for the bathroom, while Emina flopped on one of the beds.

Taking his time, Marco did his business, showered, towelled himself off and reflected that this day was probably the best so far since his return, in that he had the sense of another life being possible and the edge of the London history began to fade slightly and not take up every waking hour. Putting his watch back on he went back into the main room to find Emina out cold, still fully dressed, and emitting a gently feminine *renflement*. Bitter experience had told him never to associate the 'snore' word with the female of the species, even in thought. That way madness lay.

Turning off the light, he slipped past her, gently discarded his towel and slid naked into bed.

Twenty minutes later and fast asleep Marco felt another warm body slip in next to him in the narrow cot and slide her leg over his.

'You men are fucking useless,' Emina had said, squeezing him tight. 'I was only pretending to be asleep, so you could seduce me.'

'But you were snoring,' said Marco, immediately regretting it. He felt Emina stiffen.

'I do not snore,' she said with some insistence.

Pulling herself onto Marco, she folded herself into him in one movement; at the same time her mouth found his and they kissed and began the tentative process of rediscovering each other and the familiar physical landscapes now made more mellow with the passing of time.

The next thing Marco heard was the loud tick-tock of his watch in his ear and then the five o'clock chime from the Big Joe bell tower not 30 metres away. Emina was curled around him, her head on his chest. She somehow managed to sleep through the bells (and, indeed, her own extraordinary snoring). But that was another matter. For the first time in months Marco had slept through the night untroubled by nightmares, and had woken, as he had done in his previous life, with the first light.

Afraid to move lest he disturbed Emina, Marco wanted to savour being in the moment before reality would begin to bite again.

This was the time of day he loved the most, when pure thoughts had the best chance of becoming real, however much they faded as the travails of the day erased them. For now, grateful musings of having survived the past and with a new world of possibilities opening unexpectedly up, he felt himself to be a lucky man. At the same time he also experienced the flicker of desire as Emina ceased her breathy grunting, moved lazily in her sleep, and muttered one word.

'Coffee.'

Snuggling down in the bed beside her, Marco found her face; a face that, after all these years, he still found endlessly fascinating.

'Coffee,' whispered Marco gently, 'is on its way,' as he moved down her lithe body to kiss the tips of her breasts as gently, they made love for a second time, lazily, as if they had all the time in the world.

*****

'You said coffee was on its way, bitch!' shouted Emina in his ear, shattering his post-coital haze as she jumped from the bed and headed for the bathroom. 'You are a lying bastard. You took advantage of me!'

'Only because you wanted me to take advantage of you,' said Marco, reaching for the house phone. 'And as for the coffee, I'll get on it right away!'

By the time Emina had finished her shower and coffee from room service had arrived, Marco took over the bathroom in order to perform his morning ablutions. Meanwhile, Emina found her phone and fired it up. It immediately started to beep and squeak and buzz as she was inundated with messages.

The first was from Zvonko. The second from Faida. The third from Zvonko again. Then the WhatsApp messages.

Call me. Nino missing overnight. Remaining dogs slaughtered at Grimalda Kennels. Faida going crazy. For fuck's sake where are you both?

Emina dialled Zvonko. 'Where are you now?' she asked urgently.

'Grimalda, with the police,' replied Zvonko.

'We'll be there in half an hour,' said Emina. 'Don't go anywhere. Is Faida with you?'

'No, we'll go to Draguć after. But you need to come here. If your fucking animal liberation people had anything to do with this, they have a fucking weird way of liberating animals.'

Gathering her things, she knocked open the bathroom door and explained to Marco the urgency. He threw his clothes on, picked up his helmet and phone, and they both dashed down the stairs. In ten minutes Emina's Triumph was negotiating the winding road down the Motovun hillside, the Venetian battlements behind them, and roaring along the Mirna straits heading down to Butoniga lakeside, then up the Grimalda hillside to the village where Nino kept a number of his working dogs in sheltered kennels at the back of the old priest's house.

*****

A crazy dog appeared in the road from the house on the left on the way up as they entered the village. Marco lashed out with his boot and just missed the savage mutt on the side of the head, as Emina struggled to keep control of the bike. Having done so, she made a dignified entry into the already crowded, tiny village square.

The police were out in force: two squad cars and four uniformed officers were around the back of the priest's house. No-one lived in the place, and the church had allowed the once beautiful edifice, which had been there as long as there had been a church, to fall into complete disrepair. There were, in fact two churches in Grimalda, both named after Saint George: one from the nineteenth century and one from the thirteenth century. The village had no inhabitants. The last one, some random foreigner, had left, driven mad by the seemingly random electronic bells from the ancient steeple of the Romanesque edifice.

Zvonko came running up.

'It's pretty bad,' he said, kissing Emina and hugging Marco. 'In fact, it's a bloodbath.'

'Let's go and have a look,' said Marco, walking down the hill behind the priest's house.

Nino kept his dogs in Grimalda precisely because it was uninhabited. Any potential barking would not bother any neighbours, and the anti-social church bells that rang out around the clock gave the dogs something to howl at – the dogs all being anti-clerical good Communists, according to Nino. It was also away from other hunting dogs, so they didn't bother each other with their howling. The pens were insulated against sun in summer and cold in winter and, as Emina confirmed, the conditions Nino kept his animals in were better than anywhere in the county.

Emina wasn't quite ready for the shock of seeing Vito, Nino's favourite, hung in a noose and hanging from the roof of the cages as if as a warning to all dogs. Five other dogs we simply finished off with bullets to the head. Another four dogs had been found badly wounded when the police arrived and had to be finished off by the policemen's service revolvers.

'What kind of cruel bastard would do this to these poor beautiful animals?' sobbed Emina, who had turned to Marco and put her head for a moment on his chest. 'Who the fuck would do such a fucking thing? Let me get my hands on the bastards who did this and I will kill them with my bare hands.'

'I've seen enough here,' said Marco.

'Do any of you know who might have done something like this?' asked one of the young policemen who had been doing all they could to help.

'No,' said Zvonko, firmly, 'we have no idea. All we know is that these dogs belong to Marco's grandfather, Nino, who I am sure you know. And he is going to be very upset.'

'Is Mr Mihailić on his way?' asked the policeman.

'Not yet,' replied Marco.

'We've called the municipal vet to take the dogs away.'

'I think that's for the best. Nino shouldn't see this bloodbath. It would finish him off,' said Marco.

'He will want to bury Vito at home,' said Emina.

'We'll sort that with the vet,' said Zvonko. 'If we try that with these jobsworths they'll just read the rulebook at us and say it's illegal to bury animals on private ground, etcetera, etcetera. The vet is the person to play ball with later.'

Standing on top of the freshwater cistern that until a couple of years ago was the main water source for the village and in the shade of the old school – which had, like the priest's house fallen into disrepair – the tinny electronic bell system suddenly burst into action. A random selection of ding-a-lings squawked through a cheap and fuzzy Tannoy-like speaker which went on for five minutes and had little rhyme, reason, or logic.

'Look, I don't know about you guys,' said Zvonko, 'but these fucking Chinese have to have something to do with this. Their human rights record is bad enough, let alone their animal rights.'

'Dalrymple told me that Nino was trying to reach him yesterday about the Chinese,' said Marco. 'Emina told me she thought he was joking when he said he was going to Brioni for a meeting of the "CPC-CPR central committee".'

'But if they had him on Brioni, why would they do this to the dogs?' asked Emina.

'To scare the shit out of him? That this would be him or members of his family next – and that they are capable of anything? I honestly don't know. But if we don't get down to Brioni as soon as possible and find out, we may be too late. These guys mean business.'

'OK, I'll go back quickly to Dragać to check on Faida and see if there is any news,' said Emina. 'You guys go on to the olive mill at Fažana. I'll meet you there in an hour, hour and a half.'

'Sure,' said Zvonko. 'By that time I'll have sorted out a boat and found which villa they are in. I don't think we should take the regular ferry; we may need to make a fast escape. Depending on what we find.'

*****

Marco took the wheel of Zvonko's car as his buddy got on the phone to get the loan of a small boat to go out to the islands. As a designated National Park they could only be visited by the general public in official groups on the time-tabled shuttle transfer, which was limited at this time of year. Zvonko knew his way around Fažana and how to circumvent detection and any red tape that might be involved.

'If these Chinese bastards have touched a hair on Nono's head I swear that I will fucking kill them,' said Zvonko. He had just been on the phone to a friend who worked as a manager at the Hotel Neptune to find out where exactly on Brioni they were staying. The island had three hotels and numerous private villas, and it turned out that there were three Asian gentlemen staying in the Villa Lovorka, an extensive property in a secluded bay on the east side of the island facing Forta Punta Christo.

'I know that place,' said Zvonko. 'One of those gangsters with a Tito complex – but without Tito's negotiating skills – who wanted to invest in the olive oil business stayed there when we were trying to do a deal. It's impossible to approach from the Fažana or Valbandon side because a small-engined boat would be immediately spotted from the terrace. As the islands are protected by being a National Park, they would sense immediately something was up.'

'Thinking about it, why don't we just go in the regular way, through the front door, and ask politely if Nino is there?' asked Marco, rationally.

'You saw what they did to the dogs back there,' replied Zvonko. 'This is serious stuff now. They started off with a warning, then it got serious, and it's about to get real with Nino.'

Marco shrugged and carried on driving down the Ipsilon Road, past the small shepherd's *kazun* that served as a kind of folkloric rest stop on the last stretch of the road to Pula where the landscape became flatter in the rugged plain that stretches down to the coast. This area provides excellent conditions for the finest Istrian olives and produces some of the best oil in the world.

The micro-climate between Vodnjan and Fažana has allowed the growth of the noble olive for thousands of years. Ever since the time of the Emperor Claudius, Istrian olive oil was to become the backbone of the local economy as it was exported not only to Rome but also onwards to the Danubian Limes and upwards towards Germania. Now it was the Germans who packed into Zvonko's olive-oil workshops to taste the best he had to offer. Aside from original ancient techniques that Zvonko was reviving, he was also dependent on a combination of rich soils, the sea winds that blew in from the Adriatic and the *Kvarner*, as well as a blend of gentle rains and the right amount of sunlight. These were the bits he had little control over.

It was around noon as Zvonko and Marco pulled into the public car park on the other side of Fažana near the municipal football pitch. Marco was itching to get to Brioni, so a change of rendezvous with Emina had been made to the sports ground. Zvonko pulled out a map from the glove compartment.

'Look, we need to bring the boat into Verige Bay,' said Zvonko. 'There is a quiet cove there from where we can go overland. We skip down through the Roman villa and go about a hundred metres across country. Then we can hit the Villa Lovorka from behind and take the fuckers by surprise.'

A couple of minutes later the pair in the car heard the familiar throaty rumble of the Bonneville's four cylinders come round the bend into the car park and pull up next to them. Emina pulled off her helmet and her hair fell loose onto her shoulders. She immediately put it back up under a woollen cap, brought for that express reason.

'How is Faida?' asked Marco. 'Is she OK?'

'She's furious,' replied Emina, 'and she knows it's not helpful. I spared her the gruesome details of the dogs. She has no idea where Nino might be other than over there on the island. She just repeated that he hasn't been sleeping and that he has been acting very weirdly.'

'He's been acting weirdly for weeks,' said Zvonko. 'He hasn't been anything like his usual self.'

'Oh, one other piece of useful information,' said Emina. 'Their bank accounts have been cleared out. All of them: Kuna, euro, pounds, the lot. Nothing left in there.'

'Right. That is interesting,' said Marco, 'especially as Dalrymple says that he has also been taking large sums of money from the Chinese.'

'There's more to this than meets the eye,' said Zvonko. 'So let's get going and see what these Chinese gentlemen have to say for themselves.'

Zvonko led off down to the coastal path that came out of the south of Fažana and through a break in the woods that took them to the shore. A dinghy with an outboard motor awaited them, tied to a small concrete jetty. They climbed in and Zvonko fired up the engine. The dinghy chugged out into the Fažana Channel, and after a brief forward run Zvonko pulled it around to port and headed for Verige Bay.

After about a quarter of an hour the bay came into view. It was easy to understand, even on a sunny winter's day, why the Romans chose to build their Villa Rusticae on this sheltered part of the archipelago. The bay possessed probably one of the most spectacularly beautiful aspects in the empire. The waters were a limpid turquoise blue and the white stone beaches led into verdant pine forests that smelled of pure health itself.

The virginal exclusivity of the islands had been treasured for over two thousand years. Over the centuries man had been kind to the islands, respecting their natural beauty, their historical charm and importance, and their sheer elegance and grace. Before the acquisition of the islands by the socialist state of Yugoslavia, it was late in the nineteenth century that the archipelago took on its more or less modern aspect when Paul Kupelwieser, a wealthy industrialist and steel baron, took the islands in hand and combined a closeness to pristine nature with a few modern conveniences. The first thing he did was enlist the aid of the German scientist Robert Koch to rid the islands of malarial mosquitoes. He bore Brijuni no ill will after Koch contracted the disease himself there on his first visits. The next 20 years saw the islands being developed from what was essentially a pile of old rocks and a few cypress trees into one of the most fashionable and upscale resorts in the Austro-Hungarian Empire. Koch spent two years on the islands between 1900 and 1902, and Kupelwieser was so indebted to Koch that he commissioned a sculpture in honour of him which still stands near the fifteen-century Saint German's church on Great Brijun Island.

But it wasn't malaria or the ancient Romans that our trio had in mind as Zvonko manoeuvred the dinghy into Verige Bay. The remains of the Roman villa seen from a distance gave an expansive idea of how magnificent the modestly named 'rustic villa' must have looked and felt like, with a bit of imagination.

'This is how olive-oil merchants in Roman times lived,' said Zvonko.

'Still could live, if you carry on growing the business and turn it into an industrial process. You could make millions,' said Marco, testing his friend's mettle.

'Get thee behind me, Satan,' replied Zvonko with a chuckle. 'There's nothing he likes more, Emina, than to play the devil's avocado.'

'I know, I know,' said Emina. 'I don't know why we bother with him. I guess if we exorcise our devils then our good angels might disappear as well. So I reckon we are stuck with him.'

'Is it just me, or does this whole island feel like a film set? Like a backdrop that has been painted to perfection, but isn't quite real?'

Before anyone had time to answer, Zvonko cut the engine and let the little boat drift towards the small jetty. Once everyone was ashore and the boat was tied up, Zvonko took charge. 'Follow me,' he said. 'We'll follow the bay around and cut up through to the villa.'

Emina and Marco followed Zvonko. He had adopted a semi-commando style of running: keeping close to the ruined walls of the villa and running low along the porticoed walkway that led back into the recesses of what was once a magnificent *peristylium* and into the pine forest behind. Here they stopped and caught their breath. They could now just about see the stone rear walls of the single-storey, bungalow-like edifice. Presumably built in the fifties, the stunted design spread wide over much of the inlet below them. Its bland retro ugliness was far more suburban than the lavish magnificence of the Roman architectural antecedents on the islands.

'I suggest that I take the back entrance on the landward side. You two come in via the terrace on the opposite side of the building and we meet in the middle. In exactly two minutes from now we should all enter at the same time. Got it?'

Exactly two minutes later Zvonko kicked down the main door into the open-plan sitting area of the Villa Lovorka causing minor damage to the door and scaring the living daylights out of three Chinese businessmen who looked up from their laptops – not only in shock, but also too surprised to move at all.

Emina and Marco appeared seconds later as Zvonko screamed, 'Put your hands in the air and get over against the wall.' He was pointing a small Croatian-made HS 2000 pistol at the businessmen.

The three Asian gentlemen calmly and dutifully obeyed.

'Hey, Zvonko!' shouted Marco. 'Nobody said anything about weapons. Put it down.'

'What – and let these bastards get the better of us? Not a chance.'

The tallest of the three Chinese, who stood between his two colleagues, spoke first. 'To what do we owe the pleasure of this visit, gentlemen? We were not expecting guests. Usually, the reception calls to inform us, and we collect by golf buggy.'

'Zvonko, put down the gun,' said Marco. 'Leave this to me. I know what I'm doing.'

Marco looked at his opposite number, standing there in shirt sleeves and tie, and looking every inch the antithesis of the Chinese gangster Zvonko had led him to believe was there.

'Excuse us for the unorthodox entrance,' said Marco. 'And please, gentlemen, you can put your hands down. There's no danger here. We need your help.'

Zvonko looked to Emina, as if to ask, 'What's going on?' Emina signalled to him to calm down.

'We're sorry about frightening you with our crude entry,' explained Emina. 'But we were looking for the grandfather of our friend Marco, here.'

'And what,' asked the taller of the Chinese, 'would be the name of the gentleman in question?'

'Nino,' said Marco, 'Nino Mihailić. My grandfather.'

The three Chinese exchanged looks, and the taller of them made a gesture suggesting that they sit around the table. 'My name is Feng,' he said, reaching out to shake hands before sitting down. 'This is Mr Chen, and this is Mr Zhang. We know your respected grandfather and we have been doing business with him this last year.'

'Do you know where he is?' asked Marco.

'I am afraid we do not,' replied the younger of the three, Mr Zhang. 'Yesterday I took him back to the boat at 16.00. That was the last we saw of him.'

'Do you mind me asking,' asked Emina, 'what was the purpose of his visit here?'

'Please, young lady, sit,' offered Mr Chen. 'Can I get you all some tea?'

All six sit around the dining table of the Villa Lovorka and try to get to the bottom of the mystery of Nino's disappearance. Mr Chen prepared the tea.

'That is a good question,' said Mr Feng, 'and I will give you a good answer. The purpose of his visit was to deliver to us approximately eight kilos of truffles. As you know, the shortage of good truffles made the prices rise and everyone got nervous. We have worked for a number of years with your grandfather, and so we took a risk and gave him up front the €25,000 he was asking for the eight kilos in question. The reason for his visit here was to tell us that the delivery of the truffles had been delayed. He thought it would be another couple of days. He begged us to bear with him while he resolved the situation.'

'We have no problem with Mr Nino,' said Mr Chen. 'He has always delivered for us. But this time it has been problematic. We have very much respect for your grandfather. But this has been – how to put it? – somewhat difficult. Because we have taken a risk on behalf of our clients and advanced the money.'

'We represent a consortium of businessmen in Hong Kong,' said Mr Zhang, 'and we have done so every year since they purchased as a publicity stunt what was purported to be the world's biggest-ever white truffle from Italy for $96,000. The price of this exceptional truffle did not correspond to the market price, which back then was around 350 euros for 100 grams. They paid over the odds because the sale was for charity, and also because of the rarity of an 850-gram truffle. The bigger the truffle the more valuable it is deemed to be in truffle circles back east.'

Mr Zhang went on to explain that since that purchase in 2014 their charity event had taken off so well that it didn't need publicity stunts, it just needed truffles. It turned out that Mr Zhang's father had met Nino in his foreign office days back in the Yugoslav era when stationed at the Chinese embassy. Gifts of truffles were a regular and memorable event in the mundane life of a Chinese officer based in dreary Belgrade.

'It is for this that we share your worries about comrade Nino,' said Mr Chen. 'Usually, he is in a much better mood. Something was troubling him, and he wasn't his usual self.'

'Gentlemen,' said Marco, standing with Emina and Zvonko. 'You have been more than understanding. I can only apologise for the strange nature of our appearance here today and thank you for your courtesy, solidarity, tea, and duty of care for my grandfather. If we could exchange cards and numbers, I would like to keep in touch with you until we manage to regularise the situation here. Our first worry is for my grandfather and his well-being, over which there still seems to be some question.'

'The second duty of care we have,' said Zvonko, 'is to you as guests in our country. I give you my personal guarantee that if this situation cannot be resolved by supplying you the truffles you paid for, I will make sure that your funds are returned to you.'

'The funds are the least of our worries,' said Mr Feng. 'We have made commitments to our investors, and they have made commitments to charities and restaurants to deliver truffles by the time of the Chinese New Year in late January. We would be grateful for your help to fulfil this demand.'

'We will do our very best, gentlemen,' said Marco. 'Thank you and goodbye.'

*****

As they walked down the main pathway of the villa towards the olive and tangerine groves, waving back at the smiling Chinese, Zvonko remarked, 'Well, those were the most civilised James Bond villains I've ever come across.'

Continuing their exit on the more conventional coast road around Verige Bay back to their dinghy, they took it easy and enjoyed the gentleness of the landscape and the cornucopia of exotic smells, including the distant whiff of elephant dung from the nearby safari park. This was the work of Lanka, the remaining elderly Asian elephant gifted originally as part of a pair by Indira Gandhi in 1972; Lanka's 80-kilo a day veggie habit had been making a mark on the quotidian Brijuni biosphere for nigh on half a century.

'OK. This is all well and good,' said Emina when they reached the dinghy. 'But it doesn't get us any closer to knowing where the hell Nino is.'

'Look, we have to try to piece this together from what we have,' said Zvonko, yanking the pull rope on the recoil starter of the outboard motor. 'Let's go back to my place and make some calls.'

'We don't have a signal here,' says Emina, 'but maybe there is some news from either Faida or Dalrymple. Nino's been gone more than 24 hours now, so we need to start to think about informing the police as well.'

They pulled out into the bay and saw Fort Punta Christo rise above Saint Jerolim Island on the right and, straight ahead, the harbour at Valbandon. Zvonko pointed the little dinghy towards the Fažana coastline and, as he did so, he had an idea.

'Let's drop in to Fažana itself on the way,' said Zvonko. 'Perhaps one of the ferry boat captains can give us some information.'

'I've got a bad feeling about this,' said Emina, when they docked at Fažana. 'You don't suppose he could simply have got lost? You know how fragile he is getting; he's 90 years old and his memory has started to go. It's what happens when you get to his age.'

'I suggest that while Zvonko goes to talk with the ferry boat people,' said Marco, 'you stay here by the mooring and phone Faida to find out if there is any news. I'll go and check if his car is in the Brioni parking lot and have a wander through the town and ask if anyone has seen him. Let's rendezvous back at the olive mill.'

Brioni was a car-free zone, so all hotel guests and VIPs left their vehicles in a purpose-built car park a few steps from the jetty. Marco took a look around but couldn't see Nino's car, and there was no-one around to ask. So he took a walk through the town to see if there was someone he knew to ask if they had seen Nino. It was then he realised that he really had been away for too much time and no longer knew anyone. Istria was a very small place and there was usually someone whom you knew – or two degrees of separation, minimum. Back in the day he was more likely to see Leonid Brezhnev or Liz Taylor in Fažana as they made their way over to Tito's idyll. As he walked through the balmy streets of Fažana he could admire the extraordinary beauty of the Brijuni Islands from where the water gently brushed against the harbour walls and the pastel-coloured fishing boats like a scene from Bizet's *Pearl Fishers*. Finding no trace of Nino, Marco turned back soon after he crossed the main square. He passed in front of the campanile of the fourteenth-century church of Saint Cosmas and Saint Damian and made for Zvonko's office.

The place was a-buzz with action as Zvonko and Emina worked the phones.

'I drew a blank,' says Marco. 'But his car wasn't there, so he's definitely not in Fažana.'

'There's also something suspicious about him not parking in the official car park,' said Zvonko. 'Usually he parks here and saves himself a few Kuna. Oh, and by the way, I spoke with Marino, the duty ferry boat captain that day. He said nothing suspicious on the way out and Nino was picked up by our Chinese friend in the golf buggy. But on the way back, he had to delay the boat departure as Nino was having a flaming row with someone on his mobile and didn't want the boat to leave because he would lose the signal. He said he waited as long as he could, sounded his ship's horn as loud as was polite, and sailed for Fažana. He was none too happy. Nino didn't come up on the bridge on the return journey like he always does.'

'I've also spoken with Faida,' said Emina. 'She has heard nothing. I asked her about going to the police, but she wanted to think about it. I said we'd speak in an hour. She did say that there was one weird thing. She went down to clean your room, and – you remember you left the gladiator's arm plate, the *manica*, on the coffee table?'

'Yes,' answered Marco. 'Dalrymple and I decided to do a bit of code busting, which we had more or less done. Except the information just stops suddenly – the sentences don't complete. So, you could say we're halfway there.'

'Well, it looks like you're not even that far now,' says Emina, 'because Faida says that it isn't there anymore. Gone. She thinks it might have something to do with Nino's disappearance.'

'What on earth could that have to do with it?' asked Marco.

'No idea; we'll have to ask her. If she can know anything, which I doubt.'

'Anyway, it's at least another piece of the puzzle. Something to go on,' said Emina.

Zvonko's phone rang. He answered it on the first ring. Aside from the pleasantries, he did the listening.

'OK, looks like we have a lock on him,' said Zvonko, putting his hand over the mouthpiece.

'What? How?' asked Emina.

'I called the BMW dealership,' said Zvonko. 'Beppo's going back through the paperwork. All their leased cars have an anti-theft tracker. I explained the situation.'

Emina high-fived Marco,

'Yes! Gotcha!' said Marco.

'And you what? You fucking what?' said Zvonko into his phone, rising in anger. 'You will fucking tell me where his fucking car is or I will come round there now and rip you a new asshole so that you'll be even more of an asshole. What do you mean he's somewhere around Pazin? Everything in Istria is somewhere around Pazin.'

Zvonko turned to Marco: 'The bastard is refusing to tell me where Nino is. He hung up on me. Pillock. Data protection. He says I need to get Nino's permission to let me know where his car is. And that, as I was a friend, he could tell me it wasn't far from Pazin. Bastard.'

'OK, it's a start,' said Marco. 'Let's head to Pazin. And on the way – I've just had an idea: if we can do this with the car, we can do it with the person if his phone is switched on. Come on, let's go. I'll make some calls when we're on the road, I think this might be the way to trace him. It's a long shot, but...'

They had only driven a short distance when Zvonko suddenly pulled over. The car screeched to a halt. Marco and Emina exchanged looks. Zvonko got out of the car and started dialling. He walked up and down about 20 metres from the car, gesticulating wildly. After about five minutes he returned. Calm. As if nothing had happened and started driving again.

After about one kilometre of driving in silence Zvonko's phone rang again. He put the phone on speaker. 'OK, tell me,' he said.

'Go to the Cerovlje turn-off, take the Buzet road. When you get to Oslići take the Kotli road and the car is somewhere there just before Benčići.'

'That the best you can do, Beppo?'

'Fuck you, Zvonko, you are a fucking piece of work.'

'And fuck you, too, Beppo – or I suppose you can't hear that because of your punctured eardrum.'

Zvonko hung up. 'Little shit,' said Zvonko. 'He dodged the draft in '93 by getting his mate to puncture his eardrum for him with an ice-pick.'

'Ouch! Painful,' said Marco.

'Yeah. Not quite as painful as death,' mused Zvonko. 'Anyway, I called him on it, and he caved immediately.'

Emina stuck her head in between them. 'So, what's the plan? We head to Oslići?'

*****

Nino steps out of his BMW and walks down the lane that runs between Oslići and Benčići. He's looking for something. After walking on for half a kilometre or so he stops, out of breath, and looks closely into what appear to be bushes. Hidden behind brambles and juniper is a small white road. Around 50 metres in front of him, obscured from the lane, is a small shepherd's *kazun*. As he walks towards it he is taken aback, as if seeing it for the first time, but also by its humble beauty. It is made by hand, simply of dry stone; no mortar, just stones horizontally piled but slanting downwards and outwards – both the walls and the roof. It looks to Nino like the most perfect, simple place of refuge. However, as with many wonders of the past in newly composed Croatia, its disappearance has been on the cards for decades. The art of building the *kazun* has all but disappeared, kept going on life support by various municipal and regional heritage projects but not by the shepherds and stonemasons who originally crafted these desirable objects of beauty. This particular *kazun* had stood the test of time. As Nino reviews his life, made complicated by his greed and mistakes, it is thrown into ironic relief by the purity of this Istrian symbol of simple perfection. He wants to revert to the simple life. Before it all got so complicated;

before he killed his own father. He picks up his pace and starts to walk quickly towards it, driven on by something he has seen. Behind a wall in the brush, completely overgrown, he spots the handlebars of an old bike. He drops down on a crude lichen-covered stone bench next to the *kazun*, puts his head in his hands and begins to sob.

*****

'As Faida says, it's as if he came back to the restaurant to pick up my Roman arm guard, the *manica*,' says Marco as they pull past the Žminj turn-off on the Ipsilon road. 'That must have something to do with the shit that Nino is in. There is no way that, in his current state, Nino would have gone all the way back to the restaurant, picked up the artefact, and then disappeared again without this being somehow at the centre of things. It must have something to so with the *manica*, but I'm damned if I can think what it could be.'

'You said earlier that the markings on the back of the arm shield were in a kind of code,' says Emina, 'and that Dalrymple had managed to break it in some way?'

'Yes. It was the old Caesar cypher – as used by Julius Caesar to disguise his battle plans,' says Marco. 'My dad had been making a beginner's mistake in thinking it was something more complicated when the answer was staring him in the face. Me, too, come to that.'

'OK, OK. Get to the point,' says Zvonko. 'What was the code saying? What was the message?'

'Well, that's sort of the point,' says Marco. 'It's inconclusive. It stops halfway through. Dalrymple thinks that the other half of the message reveals where the prime truffle-bearing land is. That half is actually on the companion piece of the *manica*, which came in two pieces, one for the upper arm and a more complicated series of slats for the lower arm.'

'Well, it looks like we need Dalrymple,' says Emina. 'Maybe he has told Nino he cracked the code, and it means something to him. Maybe he is thinking he can use it to solve his little Asian problem.'

'It's not a problem,' says Zvonko. 'We can stop at the Gymnasium on the way through Pazin and pick him up.'

Five minutes later they have paid the toll at Pazin and are sweeping down the hill into the town centre, above the Pazin abyss, past the

Istrian Regional Governor's office. They meet Dalrymple, pulling on his coat and coming out of the front door of the Gymnasium. He jumps in the back with Emina.

'This had better be important,' says Bonkers. 'I was in a final rehearsal for Nino at Ninety – do you know how hard it is to get those little bastards to come in to practice out of term time?'

'There is sod all else to do in Pazin,' quips Zvonko. 'The little fuckers should be grateful to you for giving their sad provincial lives some meaning.'

Which, as an icebreaker works, and everyone laughs.

'Now, Bonkers,' says Marco. 'What did you tell Nino about the code of the *manica*?'

*****

Still leaning against the back of the *kazun* and wiping the tears from his eyes, Nino stares into the distance. The last time he was in this spot was during the occupation so many decades before. Nothing has changed. It looks as if no-one has been there since then. The only signs of life are a few empty beer cans, an old pair of Y-fronts, and a littering of ancient and slightly soiled prophylactics. The *kazun* stood as solid as any hand-made, dry stonework would after almost a century of existence. It was here that, having shot his father, he had made his getaway from Draguccio on his father's bicycle, now just about visible through the undergrowth. Dumping the bike in the brush he had walked the rest of the way across country via Kotli and Hum and made his escape to his uncle Armando, his mother's brother, who ran the *konoba* in Buzet. Lost in reminiscence, he is startled back to reality by the ringing of his mobile phone. He looks to see who it is and answers.

'Yes. I am here. Where are you?' says Nino. 'OK. From Buzet take the main Pazin road. The rest is on the link I sent you. You'll see my car. Brown BMW. On the right is a white road and an old shepherd's *kazun*. I'm waiting for you there. No-one knows I am here. Yes. I have the arm guard. You can have everything. It's yours.'

He ends the call. Stares out into the distance, down to the village of Hum and the Aleja Glagoljaša between Roc and Hum. It brings back memories of Mr Valli teaching him the Glagolitic alphabet and their school trips to Hum.

The thought of Valli, Pino, and the revisionist history of his Partisan heroics brings Nino back to earth with a bump. He picks up his phone again, finds Faida's WhatsApp connection, presses the 'Record message' icon, and begins to speak.

'Dear Faida: I got your message about the dogs. About Vito. I don't know what to say. I'm….I don't have the courage to speak to you directly about this and so many other things because it concerns something that happened way back. When we were Partisans. When we were barely out of childhood. Back before you and I fell in love. When you and Pino were still together. You remember: May the first, 1945. The day you marched into Trieste with the massed battalions of Partisans, with you in the vanguard. This was a great day for our country, and for you. For me history turned out differently…'

*****

'Nino called me a few hours ago. He gave me a good bollocking for not being available to go with him to the Chinese,' Dalrymple explained. 'Then in his confused kind of way started talking about the *manica* and the code. He told me he was going to give the piece back to its rightful owner and he needed to know what the code signified. The rest you know. I told him that the code referred to a great trove of truffles that was in the region between Montona and Pinguente but couldn't be located exactly because the message stopped halfway through. I told him that whoever had the companion piece would simply be able to decode whatever is on the other arm piece. They simply need to use the Caesar cypher. Did I say the wrong thing? Should I have told him? He was very insistent.'

'It has to be something to do with knowing who has the companion piece,' says Zvonko. 'The question is, who is it and are they the ones responsible for all the carnage?'

Before anyone could interrogate Dalrymple further Zvonko's phone rang again, just as he sped down the straits on the road between Cerovlje and Buzet, heading towards Nino at Oslići. Zvonko responded on speaker. 'Hello? Faida! What's new? We are about 10 minutes from your place'

'You'd better come quick, Zvonko,' said Faida, distraught in a way he hadn't heard before in her voice. 'It's Nino. He has just sent me a message. It's not good, Zvonko. Come quickly. He's going to do something completely crazy; I am sure of it.'

*****

A large black sedan pulls past Nino's car and glides to a halt in front of it. Three men exit the car: two younger ones in their forties wearing suits and an older one whose morbid obesity obliges him to wear a shell suit for convenience and who walks slowly, carefully balancing on two sticks. The two younger gentlemen walk either side of him as they move carefully down the lane and through the bushes on to the white road that leads to Nino's *kazun*.

'Enzo, take the back of the shepherd's hut, just in case,' says the old man as, step by step, he makes his way down the track towards the *kazun*. 'Maurizio, stay close; this path is making me unsteady.'

As Enzo disappears into the bushes to circle behind the *kazun*, Nino appears from the entrance of the hut and calls out to his visitors. 'You see I am alone. I have got what you want. Here.' Nino holds up his part of the *manica*.

'It is 75 years since I have seen this piece,' says the old man. 'My father's legacy. The only heirloom that remains from the time of the *esodo* and the *foibe*.'

'Is this your son?' asks Nino.

'Yes, this is Maurizio. And he will take over my business from me when I am no longer here,' says Mario.

'I lost my only son. In the Homeland War. He is never coming back,' says Nino.

The two men remain silent. Nino holds up the *manica*.

'This was my gift to him. When he was a boy. It inspired him, so much so that he became an archaeologist. And a teacher. He was a good boy. When he died he left it to his son. For some reason his mother kept it from him until she died very recently. I found this news out only yesterday. A day too late to save my beauties.'

'Now all you need to do is tell us what the code is. Then with the two parts we can solve this mystery and see what it leads to,' says Mario. 'My father always said that legend had it that it held a secret that could bring us great riches. Now we have the two parts we can put this story to rest.'

'I have never forgiven myself for the death of your father,' says Nino, with genuine regret in his voice.

Mario interjects: 'Oh, spare me the sob story. What about the 120 other victims that day at the Bertarelli *foibe*? As far as I know, I was the only one who got away. So don't give me the self-pitying whinge. Enzo, go and take the artefact from him and we can get on with our business.'

'Hold it right there, both of you,' says Nino, pulling out his father's old Beretta 1915 from the back of his belt. 'This might be an old one, but it's beautifully oiled and works just fine.'

*****

Marco, Zvonko, Emina, Dalrymple and Faida stand around the stone table on the terrace at Stancija Mihailić and stare grim-faced at the phone that Faida has placed at the centre. Nino's cracked and tearful voice comes across faintly, but clearly.

'…so, a year ago I got a message from a man in Trieste to say that he wanted to meet up. I had no idea who it was. Turns out he had seen my picture in that lifestyle piece they did about the restaurant in *Gloria* magazine, as well as the historical pictures of us back when we were Partisans. I knew it was a mistake to release those photos. When he told me what it was about, I agreed to meet to try to settle the matter. I had been the witness to the murder of his father. By Pino. My brother. Your fiancé. And, also, he accused me of being a part of the massacre of over a hundred people at the *foibe* of Bertarelli – something, Faida, I swear to you I had no part in. Anyway. That was when the blackmail started. Small amounts at first, then bigger, then amounts that I could never repay. I took the advances from the Chinese to keep them away. Now I am at the end of it. A couple of weeks ago he started to talk about the other part of the Roman armour. I ignored it. Played dumb. When I heard your message about the slaughtered dogs, that finished it for me. I knew I had to do something. Then I realized that we had it, that the other part of the arm guard was in Marco's possession. I knew at that moment that I had to take this chance to get rid of him once and for all. I don't know, Faida, how this meeting that I am now waiting for here will turn out. I know I have to end it. But if I don't come back. If I don't come back....'

The message ends abruptly.

Zvonko looks at Marco who looks at Faida and says, 'OK, Oslići.'

*****

'Drop the gun, old man: put your hands in the air, turn around slowly, and kick it over here. Or I will kill you.'

Maurizio's voice comes out of nowhere and Nino freezes in fear. Maurizio has circled the *kazun* and approached from the rear in case the whole thing had been a set up. Nino drops the gun and kicks it to Maurizio. He picks it up, looks at it with some admiration, keeping his gun trained on Nino. When he sees the terror in the old man's eyes and understands there is no danger, Maurizio lowers the gun and moves slowly towards Nino.

'We don't want to do you any harm. We just want the armour. Now, hand it over.'

Nino moves towards Maurizio, holding out the artefact.

'You old fool, how did you think you could cheat us like that? Same way as you have been cheating people all your life,' shouts Mario, hoarsely.

'I want no trouble,' says Nino in trepidation as he moves towards Enzo, holding out the object of their desire. As he gets close to Enzo, Nino takes a step back, swings his arm as hard and as fast as he can and cracks the armour against the Italian's skull with some heft for a nonagenarian. Enzo goes down and Nino makes a break for it, still hanging on to the armour.

*****

Zvonko takes the right turn in the sleepy centre of Oslići at speed, scaring the living daylights out of an old Istrian sheepdog asleep by the side of the road and only slows down to a stop after the corner when he sees the two cars about 100 metres down the lane.

'Looks like there's not so many of them, four or five max. We should be able to handle that between us, shouldn't we?'

'Don't look at me,' says Dalrymple, 'I'm a pacifist.'

'I am looking at you, Bonkers, directly at you,' says Zvonko, rising to the occasion. 'Just how bonkers are you, Bonkers?'

'Is this part of your "repeat until funny" game, you two? If so, I am not playing.' With that, Dalrymple does up the remaining buttons of his duffle coat and gets out of the car. The others follow.

'OK. Here's the plan,' says Zvonko.

'Keep your fucking voice down. If this GPS signal is correct, he's about a hundred metres away down that white road on the right,' says Marco.

'Perfect. Now, Emina. Bonkers is your grandfather. You are out walking the dogs together. Only the dogs have run off chasing a rabbit. You are going to walk after your dogs, down the white road. Meanwhile, me and Marco will approach from the north and south. Marco: swing down to the south of the road now; I'll give you three minutes to get into position. Then we all move in – you two openly and Marco and I under cover. We'll take it from there.'

*****

Nino doesn't get far. About 50 metres down the path his legs just give way, and he buckles.

Maurizio has picked himself up, dusted himself down. Patting the cut on his temple from Nino's *manica* attack he walks down to the old man. He checks Nino is OK and carefully helps him up, then walks him back down to the dry-stone seat outside the *kazun*.

'You were a young fool then and an old fool now,' says Mario, hobbling up on his two sticks and sitting himself down next to Nino. 'How did you think you could get away with it? You've been watching too many Partisan movies, old man.'

'I don't know,' says Nino, catching his breath. 'Maybe because I have always got away with it. I thought I got away with killing my brother. Until you came.'

'He… was your brother?' asks Mario, the gravity of Nino's confession slowly dawning on him. 'You killed your brother for me? So that I could escape to freedom?'

There is a long silence.

'I made a promise to your father.'

Mario and Nino face each other and stare into one another's eyes.

As the two elderly gentlemen turn, they sit in silence side by side. Enzo and Maurizio look closely at the two pieces of armour, studying the markings on the inside.

The silence hangs in the air until Nino breaks it. 'Why did you have to kill the dogs? The dogs hurt no-one,' he says.

'It was the only way to get your attention. You were ignoring our calls. You didn't respond to the dogs simply being released. Stronger measures were called for. You broke your promises. But now you can rest easy. To have my father's relic back in one piece, this is enough. Worth more than the money. The reparations. My work here is done. I can go to my grave in peace. I'm sorry about the dogs. They were an expedient necessity. But what I now regret more than anything else is that the death of my father caused you to kill your brother. This, I can never repair.'

'Your father was a good man. My brother was not. He was turning into my father.'

'My father said you were a good boy. That you would take care of me. He did his best to reassure me that day that everything would be all right. Strangely, it was.'

A silence falls between them once more. It's an unusually comfortable one, eventually broken by something inside Nino. 'Your father was a great man. He taught me so much. About things which have remained important to me all my life. The things my father could never give me.'

Another long silence ensues.

'I am so sorry,' says Mario.

'But what about the code? What about the truffle forest? With the two pieces we can solve the riddle and find its location,' says Nino, reviving.

'Steady on, old man. You and I have enough money. I have it from my wine business in the Veneto,' says Mario. 'You have it from your truffle business and restaurant. I can only wear one pair of trousers and one shirt at a time. It's nearly the end of the road, Nino. We are in our nineties, for heaven's sake. Where does the greed end?'

'You are lucky to have been in the wine business,' says Nino. 'It's honest labour at least. The truffle is something else. It exerts a power over you. And it is a power and an urge that is hard to shake off. Even now we are coming to the end.'

'Don't be so naïve about the wine business being honest labour. It's one of the most cut-throat and fraudulent businesses there is. The survivors often don't have very clean hands,' says Mario.

Enzo and Maurizio alert their father: 'Someone is coming, papa – what shall we do?'

'Who is it?' asks Mario.

'And old man and a girl. Out walking.'

'Let them pass. We are just friends here, having a rest outside our little shepherd's hut,' says Mario. 'Waiting for the lambs to come home.'

Around the bend in the white road appear Dalrymple and Emina.

'It is my granddaughter and my friend,' says Nino, standing.

'Tell them to come,' says Mario; 'Enzo, Maurizio. It's OK.'

Nino waves.

'Emina, Dalrymple, over here!' shouts Nino, dusting himself down, trying to make himself a little more presentable.

'Your son had a daughter?' says Mario.

'No. He had a son. It's complicated. Sometimes children and grandchildren are the product of love and not of biology,' says Nino.

Emina comes running up. 'Nono! What the fuck? We have been worried sick,' she says. 'What on earth have you been doing – and who are these people?'

'This is a…' Nino hesitates, and looking to Mario, who nods, 'this is an old friend of mine. From the war.'

Enzo and Maurizio move towards the group each holding a piece of the *manica* as Zvonko comes crashing clumsily through a nearby hedge, almost falling over, with his HS 2000 trained on all six of them.

Maurizio replies by whipping out Nino's Beretta and letting off a warning shot above Zvonko's head. Zvonko drops the gun immediately and raises his hands above his head.

'Don't bring a pussy pistol to a gunfight, dickhead,' says Maurizio. 'Hands up.'

'All right, all right. Enough!' says Mario. 'We are all friends here.'

'Zvonko, what the fuck were you playing at?' shouts Nino. 'You could see we were just talking.'

'How was I to know what the fuck you were talking about?' pleads Zvonko, his hands high in the air, looking like he is in a bad western or TV cop show.

'It's OK, it's OK. All good,' says Marco, coming through the bushes on the other side, completing the group. 'I'd just like to apologise for my trigger-happy friend, Zvonko.'

'It was Chekhov who said...' begins Zvonko.

'Just shut it for once, Zvonko,' says Emina.

'And let's hear what the gentlemen have to say,' says Marco.

Nino looks at Mario, who looks back at Nino.

'This is my grandson,' says Nino, 'and this, is Mr Valli. Mario Valli. The son of my high school teacher. From the war. His family left Istria during the *esodo*.'

'Your father and I met at a very difficult time during the war,' says Mario. 'As you know, the *esodo* is a glamorous biblical word for what you would now call ethnic cleansing. Yes, I know. It's not just the Serbs who did it. The Croats were pretty good at it, too. And the Partisans. Your father was a Partisan. But one of the good ones. He saved my life. He tried but failed nobly to save the life of my father, his teacher. And in doing so made a great sacrifice for me. He is a hero.'

Emina, Marco and Zvonko exchange looks.

'Sit, Mr Mario. Please sit here on the stone bench,' says Emina, taking his arm. 'And tell us everything.'

'To be perfectly honest,' says Mario, 'there is not much more to tell. Your grandfather's brother killed my father in cold blood. Nino allowed me to escape. He had nothing to do with the *foibe* massacre. I could see that he was confused about what was happening. He also thought we were going to the re-education camp, but no – when we got to Bertarelli the machine gun was set up ready for us. He tried to help me and my father escape, and in doing so took an enormous risk. We both live to tell the story. And to lay it to rest. Before we two are laid to rest.'

'But it's you who have been blackmailing him, isn't it? What about the dogs?' asks Emina, genuinely curious.

'Sometimes, my dear, our memory betrays us,' says Mario. 'Sometimes it is distorted. By time. By hate. Sometimes the urge for revenge is irrational. It stops being personal. Over time it grows like a beast out of all proportions. It becomes for the collective. When I saw a picture of your grandfather in a glossy magazine, with his big house and successful restaurant looking as if he had a charmed life, something in me cracked. Some weird kind of envy, even though I and my sons have enough. Sometimes this dish that they speak of, "revenge", becomes very tempting. Even cold. Seventy-five years cold. The human is a strange beast. It wasn't until I saw Nino that I recognized him. I saw what time has done to him. And to me. The body contains the life story as much as the brain. And I saw that inside him there was still the spirited young boy who saved my life. It was like having my whole life revised and turned upside down in a second. I had got it so wrong. We have so much more in common than the things which separate us.'

The group has gathered around the *kazun*: Marco and Zvonko sitting on the ground; Enzo and Maurizio, not wanting to ruin their suits, crouching. Emina sits between the two old men, holding their hands. Off by the door of the stone hut, Dalrymple studies intently both pieces of the *manica*.

'Nino, I know it's hard to look back on all this now,' says Marco, 'but at least one good thing has come out of all this chaos – that you have some kind of resolution. You don't have to carry this around with you alone any longer. That's why we are here. We are family.'

'It's not all there is, Marco, my boy,' says Nino, standing and making as if to leave. 'There's more. A lot more. And it will be hard for anyone to understand. But it has made me who I am today. Three-quarters of a century ago I came to this very spot. I was on the run. I needed to get to my uncle Armando's in Buzet. I had stolen a bike, and because it would incriminate me I hid the bike here.'

He goes over to the place where he hid the bicycle all those years ago.

'This was my father's. It was his status symbol. No-one else had such a bike in the village. I threw it in here after I shot him.'

There is a silence.

'He was a terrible man. He brutalised my mother – I know this from her brother, my uncle Armando, God rest his soul. Every day of my life he cursed me and blamed me for her death giving birth to me. One day he beat my brother Pino to within an inch of his life, and when Pino could stand again he used his legs to walk off into the woods to join the Partisans. And I did, too, the first chance I could. The first place I came was here. After I killed my father. With my first dog, Vito. Vito…'

He trails off. The group look at each other and at Nino, waiting to see if he has finished. But he starts up again.

'I didn't kill him because he beat Pino and me, or because he hated me. He was at least nice to Vito. I killed him because he was a collaborator. One day the Germans came and collected the men from all the villages around. They needed 64 men. Sixteen locals for every German. My father and the local priest, Father Frane, chose the men who were to die. Like gods, they made the selection for the Germans. I saw it with my own eyes. Vito was with me. When I saw the men being sliced apart by the machine guns in the square in Grimalda, in front of that bastard priest's house, I ran like the wind back to Draguć. I went to the cellar and got my father's service revolver. Yes, Maurizio, the one you have in your hand, the Beretta. I made sure it was loaded. And after my father came cycling back up the hill and came into the house, I shot him. Right in the middle of the head. I took my things. And I left with Vito. And ended up ditching the bike here and walking the long way round to Buzet to try to cover my tracks'

Emina moves towards him. He raises his hands to stop her.

'Emina. No, I haven't finished. I need to come back to Mario's story. He is right. I knew nothing about the planned killings at the *foibe* until we got to Bertarelli. I do not have that on my conscience. But the image of watching over a hundred people being sent to the most brutal death in the ravine will never leave me until my dying day. The screams are still alive in here. Every time the lights go dark, they start again.'

He points to his own head.

'They are going nowhere. Like my brother, Pino. He went nowhere after that day. Mario knows this. Despite all the troubles we have had these last weeks, he has not gone so far as to tell you my darkest secret. You remember I used to take you to see the frescoes at the Church of Saint Vincent in Svetvinčenat, Marco?'

'I remember, grandfather, like it was yesterday,' says Marco. 'You wanted to show me the frescoes painted by Master Ognobenus from Treviso. You told me they were the best of the remaining Istrian cycles of Romanesque frescoes painted under the Byzantine influence.'

'They were, and they still are. Beauties,' continues Nino. 'You remember the triumphal arch and the scenes of the Annunciation and Cain and Abel's Offering. Cain spoke to Abel his brother. And when they were in the field, Cain rose up against his brother, Abel, and killed him. This is what brought me there. My penance. Pino would have hated it. He hated the church with a vengeance. But what Mario isn't telling you was that when Mr Valli, his father, went onto his knees and begged Pino not for his own life, but to spare his son, Pino put a bullet in the back of his head. And before Pino could get Mario into the *foibe* I myself had pulled the trigger. And killed my brother. I killed Faida's fiancé.'

The silence persists. Nino makes a move to walk away. He gets a few steps down the white road towards his car and turns.

'And this, to my eternal shame after seventy years of marriage, is something I have never told my wife. And that, my friends, is what now I must tell her now. She will know who I really am.'

*****

As much as the temptation was to run after Nino and accompany him home, there was an instant understanding between the three – Zvonko, Emina and Marco – that Nino needed to go home alone. Mario made the first move: 'Maurizio, I think you should return the antique to Marco, here,' he says. 'I mean, of course, the Beretta.'

Mario chuckles to himself and says wearily, 'What to do with the Roman artefacts, now that they are reunited, seems to me to be less clear. God knows what their journey has been throughout history, but they have brought no luck to my family. Although I can at least be grateful to have escaped with my life from the *foibe* on the *esodo*. And, unlike my poor father, I have lived a full life and have the blessing of a healthy family. Perhaps, however, there is some kind of curse upon these metal plates to whoever holds them.'

Dalrymple looks up from his studious analysis and gets to his feet. 'You know, I think I've got it,' he says.

'What do you mean?' asks Zvonko.

'I've cracked the code. I know where the motherlode is,' he replies, and laughs, a slightly deranged Dalrymple kind of laugh, which ends in a coughing fit.

'Oh, no – the curse of the *manica*,' says Marco. 'Whosoever shall discover the secret of the truffle forest shall also simultaneously spontaneously combust.'

'Lucky that Nino is otherwise engaged right now,' says Zvonko. 'I'm sure his old ticker wouldn't be able to take the stress.'

They all laugh.

'You may laugh, but you'll be laughing on the other side of your face when you see where I'm going to take you now,' says Dalrymple. 'Gentlemen, Emina: follow me. I shan't take up much of your time.'

★★★★★

Fifteen minutes later the two cars are travelling at speed down the perfectly straight stretch of road that runs between Buzet and Ponte Porton, following alongside the unnaturally direct line of the Mirna River.

Coming around the corner after Veli Mlun they slow down to a snail's pace and take a right turn. After five minutes' further meandering, they pull up in front of what looks like an old Communist compound, originally intended for some kind of military use. The large unlit sign displaying the word 'Wellness' seems like a paradox: in the first instance because of the grim martial-like aspect of the buildings, and second because of the foul sulphurous smell that seems to emanate from everything.

The Anglo-Italo-Istrian group gather in the shadow of a very large rock around the professorial Mr Dalrymple who obliges them by going into full pedant mode. 'In my humble opinion, after a superficial study of the artefact that Mr Mario has brought from Italy,' says the professor, 'and a more elaborate study of the code used in the *manica* that has been held in Istria, its partner piece, the original owner has used them as a way of remembering and re-locating truffle areas, mainly in the oak woods between modern-day Buzet, Motovun, Ponte Porton and Oprtalj. Nothing new there. These lands have been, throughout history, prime oak-bearing territory.'

'Of course, this is what gives us the naturally occurring truffles that have been the driving force for so much of the recent wealth in the area,' says Marco.

'And the greed,' chips in Emina.

'Throughout history these oak forests have been prized,' continues Dalrymple. 'The Montona Forest was rich with wood. These were most valued by the Venetian Republic on the one hand, and later by the subsequent principalities, namely the Austro-Hungarians, who wanted power over this natural resource. Wood was so important for the construction of the Venetian fleet that even Goethe wanted to see the famous Istrian oak which contributed to the glory of the Venetian Republic.'

Dalrymple gets into his stride and picks up the pace. ' "I have seen worked the finest oak from Istria and have made my observations in return upon this valuable tree" remarks Goethe in his *Italian Journey*.'

'This I remember from my father,' says Mario. 'He would refer to it very often. Especially with regard to the building of the Venetian fleet that dominated world trade – all thanks to the Quercus of Istria.'

'Yes, but what about the motherlode? Is there one? How can we find it?' interjects Zvonko. 'Are we rich yet, Bonkers?'

'I'm coming to that. Everything comes to he who waits, Zvonko,' says Dalrymple. 'Be patient. Oh, and it's Professor Bonkers to you.'

'Who is the one driven by greed now?' says Emina.

'Until the Middle Ages these forests covered the whole of Istria, even beyond. From Krk to here in the north and across most of the peninsula the *Quercus pubescens* and *Quercus ilex* were ubiquitous, along with other species in the high forests of beech, fir, spruce. By the time the Austrians arrived the forests had almost been stripped bare to build ships for Venice. This was the reason why Austrian foresters were forced to manage the forests dedicated to the supply of the navy in a sustainable way. The long and the short of it is that without people like Josef Ressel there would be no truffle business here today: because there would have been no sustainable foresting.'

'This is all very interesting, Mr Dalrymple,' says Mario. 'But it is the Roman people who have left this coded message for us in the metal of the *manica*. Before I return to Italy please tell us, simply to end this mystery, what the message is.'

'I believe from the little information that is here,' says Dalrymple, 'and other bits and pieces which I have gleaned over the years from Marco and his father, Ivo, that this *manica* belonged to a man named Severus. He was once a gladiator in the arena at Pula. He had a daughter, Lucia. Together they retired from the fight business and became truffle hunters deep in the forest between Montona, Pinguentum and Ponte Porton. The markings show in code where the prized trees and fertile areas are to be found. It is an attempt to leave it as a record for future generations of his family in order that they might reap the harvest. It is far more than an heirloom, a memento from his fighting days; it is his inheritance to his daughter and grandchildren.'

'That is so sweet,' says Emina.

'Oh, it gets even sweeter, Emina,' says Dalrymple, 'and here I come to my point. The great irony of it: most of the information is, alas, now common knowledge. *However*: Severus has given specific directions, with distances and pointers, to the motherlode of all motherlodes of truffles. The location of the greatest crop he ever discovered. The white truffle, happy hunting ground of them all. Situated in the forest "under the great rock, to the north of the river, where the land smells of sulphur and the healing waters run hot". This, my dear friends, is the stuff of legend. This is where the myth comes from that the *manica* holds a secret of great wealth. It is here, staring us right in the face.'

Dalrymple points to the miserable concrete buildings that cover several hectares spreading out before them, ruining the beautiful countryside with their seventies ugliness. 'This is the great forest that will yield the untold wealth. Or, rather, *was* the forest of legend.'

In the dwindling twilight the sun begins to set behind the Gorostas cliff, towering 100 metres above them and silhouetting Saint Stephen's Church. At that very moment a neon light on the front of the decrepit spa building crackles into life. It displays the word, in big red letters.

'W E L L N E S S'

Almost: only six of the letters on the sign light up, spelling 'W E L L E S .'

Chuckling to himself, Dalrymple comments, 'I wonder what the master of illusion would have made of this story. But that's enough local history from me. It's always the historians that boringly look to the facts and not the "human story" as, indeed, the great maestro Orson Welles would have done. By the way, the name "Orson" is of Latin origin, meaning "bear cub". And there is a little bear cub in this story. But what does the story really tell us? Well, it comes down to this. Once upon a time there was a family who escaped from the circus and became hunters. Hunters of the Istrian black diamond. The truffle. The father was called Severus, the daughter was called Lucia, and Lucia's young boy cub was called Nasica. And, if my deductions are correct, they all lived happily ever after.'

The group laugh and give Dalrymple a round of applause as they begin their friendly farewells.

Chapter XVII

Severus Unbound

Central Istria, AD 81

The most lucrative part of the truffling year was gearing up. For reasons of efficiency and expediency Lucia and Severus had decided to start going out into the woods in two teams – two people and two dogs. The main reason for this was to maximise potential; the other, quite important, to was train up Thelos and Philumena to go out on their own, if required.

Now that they knew the forests were, for the most part, safe, their confidence had grown. Lucia and Philumena would take the flatlands on the other side of the Aquilis river, following it down to the hot springs towards Bastija harbour at Porta Porton. Britannica would be taken away from her puppies for the first time, so Brutus would accompany them. Severus and Thelos would take the less experienced but younger and more energetic couple of dogs: Aello, who was fast like the whirlwind his name suggested; and Agre, who also lived up to his name and was a keen-scented hunter. Their happy hunting grounds would be the damp forests beneath the hill of Montona on the south of the Aquilis.

They set out at dawn, each team in a separate direction. The distinct aim was not only to collect as many truffles as possible, but also to fully map the areas so they could remember the most fertile areas and note for which kind of truffle and at what time of year the area was at its best. Severus, strangely, was the more scientific of the two about meticulously setting down his findings at the end of every day and storing his notes carefully. In fact, he often had to squeeze Lucia for her findings, but she, exhausted by the day's hunting and finding of truffles, was very often too tired to hand over the information. However, Severus was a stickler for this and wouldn't let her rest until he had collected the details and marked them down on wax tablets.

They had worked out that there was a tendency for white truffles to appear on the north side of the Aquilis in the beech and hazel forests not so far from the flood plain; the black truffles came from the oaks further up on the hillsides around Montona. They also discovered that whilst the dogs could be used for all kind of truffles, Aello and Agre had more of a nose for black truffles. Slowly and surely they were picking up the information they needed and sharing it on a daily basis with Thelos and Philumena.

It was a grim, foggy October morning when they set off. The damp in the air chilled Philumena and Lucia to the bone as they wound their way along the southern banks of the Aquilis. They found the shallow crossing point they habitually used before turning left and heading towards the sea. The sky was a dark grey colour, and no-one had much enthusiasm for the water, least of all Britannica and Brutus, as they forded the familiar stream. The heavy fog could be cut with a knife and hung around them at this early hour. Their going was slow because they kept on losing their way as they trudged up the slopes of the hazel and beech forests under which, they hoped, lay their fortune.

The dogs ran on ahead, forcing their mistresses to keep up the pace. Soon all four were moving through the forest, maintaining a good rhythm whilst keeping a wary eye out for other foresters and signs of the tuber. They were now 20 or so minutes into a particularly dense part of the beech wood, overgrown with ivy and covered with damp leaves. It was a part of the forest that had rarely, if ever, had contact with the human species. All of a sudden, Britannica started to whimper as if she was hurt in some way. Soon after, Brutus followed suit and they circled in ever-diminishing concentric circles with their noses not stuck to the ground but held about a foot off the forest floor. Then Brutus started to dig; about five metres away Britannica began to paw at the earth.

Philumena took Britannica in hand and gave her a treat of hard cheese, as it was her favourite. Lucia did the same with Brutus, and in typical male style he was more aggressive in wanting to eat the truffle until he remembered that he would get a nice sausage treat (his choice) and then everyone would be happy. Each hunter had a small, trowel-like wooden spoon – fashioned by Festus back at the inn – and scraped away; first at the leaves, and then at the moist humus that held in its protective cradle the object of their desire. In this case, a small crop of white truffles, six pieces, adding up to somewhere between a *dextans* and a *deunx*, which both Philumena and Lucia agreed wasn't a bad start to the day.

'OK, Philumena,' said Lucia. 'Make a careful note on the wax tablet of where we are and how far from the river and that sort of thing, otherwise Severus will give us a good scolding again when we get home.'

Onwards they went deeper into the forest, zigzagging through the undergrowth where possible. Occasionally they followed small paths made by heavier forest animals such as deer and foxes which, up until now, had shared the forest only with other wild animals and birds. The human was a new arrival and something to be feared.

*****

Back on the other side of the river over towards Montona, Severus and Thelos were finding it even harder going. The younger, less experienced dogs were not only getting tired after the first few hours, they were also getting bored; for Thelos it was more and more difficult to keep their attention. He hoped they would discover something very soon so he could reward the dogs and inspire them to get through the rest of the day with vim and energy. Severus was glad of the rain when it came early on; it cleared the air for the dogs to be able to concentrate on the smells that were important to their job. There weren't so many odours of other people, although that could happen, but they could detect rabbits, squirrels, and even snakes. A bad snake bite would be a major setback. Severus himself had experienced one a few months previously when his foot had swollen to double its size after he had stepped on a viper in the woods. This had happened just after he had recovered from his swollen hand experience after having beaten Oceanus to a pulp. As his foot continued to swell and blister, he got weaker. Lucia made good use of her pharmacopoeia and administered to him as best she could, given the circumstances, and prayed to the gods that his fever would subside. Five days later he recovered, but it was a lesson well learned. Severus said that he felt it was like his foot was a sausage on a grill with the skin about to burst and the flesh on the verge of exploding. It was then that Lucia came up with the idea of tying bells to the dogs' collars so that any wild animals or predators would hear all of them coming and would run away.

These truffle pioneers were learning as they went. For the first time in Severus's life, after 25 years in the legions and ten in the arena, he felt that in some ways he had begun to give his life some meaning. Not just in the provision of a living via the truffles, but by sharing the whole experience with his young family; he wanted to give them the opportunity of living off the forests so as to have a better life. It was a small sacrifice to live in nature as a charcoal burner for a few months of the year and live the good life for the rest of the time. If they learned the ways and mores of the forest then it could be an inheritance to pass down the generations. Hence his obsession with keeping records about everything. In this sense he was a true son of the empire.

However, collecting the secrets of the truffle forest and guarding them carefully were furthest from his mind when he was deep in the hunt. Truffle hunting, he soon discovered, was an arduous task. Just trying to find them was a dawn-to-dusk affair as the truffler slowly moved across country looking for the tell-tale signs, trying to control often anarchic dogs – as Agre and Aello were proving today. Patience was the best friend of the truffler – and hope. They found all kinds of signs to follow. Cracks in the earth where a truffle was expanding, small flies buzzing around in groups under the canopy and above the roots of the mighty oak; all manner of signals could be found. But no signal was stronger than when the dog got a scent; and the problem was then, especially with these younger dogs, not the truffle, but protecting the truffle from the dog. There was also discipline: picking a truffle too early before it had reached its full size was something to think carefully about. Then the copious notetaking came into its own.

'Let's go over here,' said Thelos, pointing up a fairly steep slope. 'We had some luck there a couple of weeks back, and perhaps the area has matured.'

'Or perhaps it has just been cleared,' said Severus, envious of his young charge's boundless energy and goat-like agility.

They walked upwards, each with a long stick in their hands scraping the ground in front of them to better see the tell-tale flies that accompanied the tuber. If a stranger had been watching they would appear to be a couple of sightless beggars moving through the woods with their blind-man sticks and guide dogs. In many ways, the truffle hunter and his dog represented the perfect symbiosis between man and canine, both working together to mutual advantage. One discovery of Thelos's came about by accident when he had forgotten to feed his dogs before taking them out with Philumena. However, Philumena had remembered to feed her pair. Thelos's dogs fared much better in the hunt than Philumena's, and yet again another lesson of the hunt was learned by experience. From then on there was no breakfast for the dogs prior to going out into the forest. Their appetites were keen for treats, and that inspired their noses to be more aware of the scent of the elusive tuber.

Thelos put a small distance between himself and the more sluggish Severus, trying to catch up with Agre and Aello who had finally stopped playing with each other to relieve the boredom. Now they seemed to be on to something. They had run ahead, stopped, and were circling. On his way up the hill Thelos saw hundreds of dainty little hoofmarks leading up to where the dogs were circling, confused. They could smell something but couldn't find anything, however much they dug. The wild boar had got there first.

'Look, at this, Severus,' shouted Thelos. 'This is where we had good pickings a few weeks ago. The wild pigs beat us to it.'

'Looks like they had a party,' said Severus, observing the scene of utter devastation of the vegetation, down to the roots of the mighty oak, where the boars had feasted, 'Luckily the little pig, the hedgehog, doesn't do so much damage. OK, let's make a note of this and bring the records up to date. We'll make sure to revisit towards the end of the season to see what it looks like.'

'Let's hope the pigs aren't taking notes too,' quipped Thelos.

The pair of dogs ran on happily down the other side of the autumnal slope, the trees already red and yellow with the season and looking magnificent in the late afternoon sun as it dropped down towards the Adriatic near Aemonia. They cut down a ravine towards the Aquilis; the stream there had been swollen by heavy autumnal rains and the young dogs happily splashed through the waters to the other side. Aello, true to his name, was swift and beat Thelos to it. He dug hard and fast and in a second he had the tuber above ground. Thelos thought it was a fairly chunky white one, but it was dispatched in seconds, also to Agre's disappointment. Severus and Thelos examined the area to see if there were any further treasures, but no: just the longing, lingering smell of the white truffle, elusive, magical, and currently on its way to being digested in Aello's stomach.

'You win some, you lose some,' said Severus philosophically, 'just like in the arena. But at least we have learned a few things here today. Lots to put down to experience, and experience is what makes us better next time.'

*****

Brutus and Britannica headed back down the Aquilea in the direction of Pinguentum. The team was heading home after a punishing day in the day in the Montona truffle forest. Unusually for this part of the forest there were only slim pickings to be had under the hazels and the beeches that dominated this side of the river.

'Severus is right,' said Lucia. 'The forests are very mercurial. But, in the end, there must be some kind of logic as to why and where the truffles appear when they do. I think we should try to be more co-operative when he is asking for details from us. It's also good for your letters, you and Thelos. From now on you two can alternate in giving details to Severus about our days in the forest. Does that sound like a good plan?'

'I'd prefer it if we could just tell him,' said Philumena, who found writing difficult to knuckle down to even on the nice new wax tablet Festus had brought exactly for that purpose on his last visit. 'But I'll do my best.'

'Good girl,' said Lucia. 'You're not going to be stuck in this forest in these charcoal-burner clothes and black-faced for the rest of your life. Although I do think that this charcoal is doing wonders for my complexion underneath. Maybe we can sell it to the wealthy patrician ladies of Rome as a miracle skincare cure.'

'Don't be silly,' laughed Philumena. 'The fashion in Rome is to have light alabaster-like skin which is whiter than white. It's a sign of nobility, they say.'

'Looks unhealthy if you ask me,' said Lucia. 'Anyway, don't change the subject. You need an education so you can read and write well. Then you can move about, see places, learn things.'

'You were the one who changed the subject.'

'Shh. Wait,' said Lucia. 'I think they may have found something.'

Up ahead on a small rise they could see the two tails of Britannica and Brutus up in the air and wagging as they pawed the ground and dug. Lucia broke into a trot to get to the pair before they started to get greedy if it turned out to be a good find.

'Finally!' shouted Lucia back to Philumena, who had fallen behind.

Lucia got to the top of the rise, and just as she reached the dogs, she heard a rumble as a massive wild boar charged out of the undergrowth and smashed her to the ground.

Brutus and Britannica immediately reacted and formed a defensive cordon around Lucia. The extremely angry male turned and came back for a second charge. Philumena ran in between, thrashing with her stick at the moment that a female boar making an infernal noise shot across her path with eight squealing piglets behind. The dogs went insane and gave chase, leaving Lucia on the floor and barely conscious after being badly gored.

Seeing the male turn to charge again, Philumena threw aside her fly-truffling stick and grabbed a handy log of wood about the size and heft of a *rudus* from the arena that she used to play with as a kid.

'Come on you bastaaaaarrdddd!' she screamed at the boar and pre-empted it by charging as fast as possible towards it. Surprised by this turn of events, the animal, which must have been about a metre high and weighed 100 kilos, skipped on its nimble hooves into reverse, turned on a *sestercius* and rumbled back into the forest to find his family.

'Philumena,' said Lucia, briefly coming to life, 'that was very foolish and very, very dangerous,' before passing out once again.

★★★★★

'Where the hell have you been?' shouts Severus as Lucia, Philumena and the dogs come back into the cave encampment. 'We have been worried sick.'

Seeing the state of Lucia – and also the dogs, who are in none too good a shape – Severus and Festus take Lucia in hand and make her comfortable in front of the fire in the open air. She has been gored in the thigh quite deeply and lost a lot of blood. Though severely weakened, Lucia remains very much in charge.

'Boil some water, quickly,' she says to Philumena. 'We'll need to clean the wound on my leg and treat the bites on the dogs before they become infected.'

They would have been back earlier, but the dogs had got into a major fight with the sow, who, protecting her piglets to the last, put up an extraordinary fight. With no large protrusive tusk-like teeth, which her male counterpart could brandish, the female of the species had to bite her way out of trouble. Although Philumena didn't see who came off worst, Brutus and Britannica – no shrinking violets in the fight game – had come off pretty badly. Not surprising, considering the sow's notorious protective spirit of its young and also the fact that Philumena said it was about the size of a small cow. They had begun their journey back to camp as night had started to fall. At least Lucia was able to begin to put some weight on the leg as it had been bound with leaves, herbs, and forest plants that Lucia and Philumena knew to be good antiseptics.

'The problem is possible infection,' says Lucia, reaching into her medicine bag.

'Festus, give me the wine flask you brought with you,' says Vita, who had arrived with Festus a couple of hours before to pick up the latest crop of truffles to take back to Laime. 'Pour some of this on. The alcohol is a good cleaner, too.'

'Thank you, Vita,' adds Lucia, indicating that she is down but not out. 'It will also save Festus from himself a bit later on. Don't worry, Festus, we won't use it all.'

'Give me some over here,' says Philumena, who has begun to clean the wounds on Brutus and Britannica. They aren't happy about this, and growl and groan in agony. The phrase, licking their wounds, could have been made just for them in this moment. To err on the side of caution, Philumena muzzles them with some pieces of tough rope she keeps specially for such occasions.

This initial emergency work completed, Vita descends into the cave to prepare the evening meal as Festus, Severus and Thelos gently lower Lucia into the protective womb of the cavern and to her sleeping area. Philumena finishes up with Britannica. Now that the dog is comfortable and has stopped bleeding, Philumena fetches the young whelps from their pen and reunites them with their mother. Before she does so, she carefully rubs the diluted truffle solution onto the teats of the bitch so that the puppies continue their training as future trufflers.

Meanwhile, Festus has begun his debriefing of Severus. He gives a full report on the truffle situation and provides a rough estimate as to how many truffles he thinks they can harvest in the four months they believe will be the season, based on their intelligence and basic understanding of the conditions.

'It may be that after the season of the white tubers,' says Severus, drinking liberally of the re-supply of Falernian that Festus has thoughtfully brought with him, 'we may have more black ones. Maybe the white ones turn black? This is all stuff we do not know and so we have to keep an open mind. For sure, we know the black truffles are pretty much everywhere in summer, even down in the Arsa basin.'

'All right. We'll deal with that situation when we come to it,' says Festus. 'Now that we have our contacts in Rome sorted, I'm more concerned about the transport logistics for the winter. I've put together a small team of ex-soldiers; they reckon it takes between 20 and 30 days to reach Rome, and slightly less on the return. They'll take a week's break and go again. They'll dress as pilgrims and carry the truffles in their kit bags. They'll also have the dogs in tow for extra security. Bodyguards for the bodyguards. The belt and braces approach. It's the safest way. By the time we pay their expenses we'll still be in the money.'

'Sounds like a plan, partner,' says Severus, raising his cup in a toast. 'When we were in the legion, we were carrying 75 *libra* on our backs. Plenty of room there for profit. Here's to the Istria gold. Long may it keep us in Falernian!'

'I'll drink to that,' says Festus, offering his hand to his partner as Vita appears bearing a bowl of hot soup for Lucia.

'I'll just go in and see how she is doing.'

Lucia is well tucked into her bed and looks at the roof in the gloom provided by the oil lamps around the cave. The pain has been assuaged by some of the poppy mixture that she always carries with her. She is grateful for the soup, for although the medicine has taken away her appetite, she knows she must eat.

'Drink this down,' says Vita. 'Nothing like a bit of broth to get you well again.'

'Oh, that is ambrosia,' says Lucia, 'it's heavenly. Thank you, Vita, this is just delicious.'

'I put some truffles in the stock, to give it an extra kick.'

'Just like that wild boar gave me in the forest,' says Lucia, slightly woozy. 'You should have seen the little piggies. Mummy Pig, Daddy Pig, and all the baby pigs. Poor little babies don't have a mummy.'

'Hush, hush, Lucia,' says Vita. 'Give me the bowl. You'll spill it. Here, let me feed you. I think the poppy mixture is working.'

'Oh, yes, it is. It's working alright,' slurs Lucia. 'But what about my baby? Did I not tell you, Vita? I'm going to have a little baby. Little Nasica. Here. Inside. It's my secret.'

The effects of the opiate finally kick in and, aside from the transparency it induces in Lucia, it has now induced its ultimate soporific effect, which was her ultimate goal.

'Good night, sweetheart,' whispers Vita, tucking her in and giving her a kiss on the cheek. 'It will be better in the morning.'

Vita makes her way back into the main cave and joins Severus and Festus around the fire. Thelos and Philumena, exhausted, have fallen asleep in their corner of the cave. The men are continuing their business discussion.

'Now that Lucia is essentially out of action for a while,' says Severus, 'I think it would be great if one of you at least could stay and help us with the harvest. Normally I think we could cover, as Thelos and Philumena know the job, but as you saw from yesterday's pig incident there's some safety in numbers and the forest isn't exactly a harmless place.'

'I think it makes sense,' says Festus.

'I think it does, too,' says Vita, cutting in. 'And I think it should be me, because when we aren't in the forest I can be looking after Lucia. Her wound won't be too much of a problem if it isn't infected, but the chances are that it is. We'll know more when she wakes up. I think she'll be out for a good 12 hours, so let's see what she's like in the morning.'

'OK, I'll check on her during the night,' says Severus. 'I haven't been sleeping too well since we got here.'

'And another thing: give me that wine, Festus, I think I need a drink,' says Vita. 'And you two are going to need a top-up as well – because I have news for you.'

The two men look up.

'It's Lucia. She's going to have a baby. Cheers!'

Festus and Severus look at her wide-eyed with surprise and break into laughter.

'Ha, old man,' says Festus, 'looks like Nasica has made a grandfather of you. I'll drink to that.'

Severus's face breaks into a big, wide soppy smile, and then into joyfully loud and uncontrollable laughter. He clicks goblets with his brother and sister-in-law before starting to shed tears of happiness. After a pause it is Festus who speaks: 'Sorry to break up the party. But in the light of this good news there's something else you should know. We need to talk about Oceanus.'

'What about him?'

'He hasn't gone away.'

Severus looks at Festus and again at Vita in total surprise. 'But I could have sworn – I could have sworn I did for him. I couldn't be completely sure, but…'

'Well, he survived,' says Festus. 'Just before we came here, we had a little visit from a few of his boys. We woke up one morning and they were snooping about the place.'

'I could go back to Pola and finish the job. In fact, that's what I think I need to do, Festus. Otherwise we'll never have any peace, knowing that he'll come and ruin everything for Lucia and the kids.'

'Hold on, hold on. It's not as bad as all that,' says Festus. 'I told them you had come to our place, but that you were going to Rome to plead your case to Domitian and were probably there right now. That seemed to satisfy them.'

'OK. Well, that buys us some time, I guess. Let's hope they don't catch on to what we are doing down here, otherwise it's bye-bye truffle business.'

'The good news is that they don't call him Pretty Boy any more,' says Festus, 'or Barmaid's Choice. In fact, his lads took great pleasure in telling me that he wears a mask most of the time now, you disfigured him so badly.'

The news is cold comfort to Severus, who realises he made a perilous mistake in not finishing off Oceanus.

*****

Much to Lucia's frustration her recovery takes longer than she expected. After two weeks she is only just able to get up and about and climb the ladder to the camp outside. The boar's tusk had gone in deep; it had sliced through the hamstring at the back and reached the adductor muscles on the interior. A pretty big mess had been made on pulling it out. Lucia is grateful for all mercies, big or small, and the fact that she doesn't get infected is a tribute to her skills as a pharmacist and also to her general state of health, being a very fit young woman. And, as everyone now knew, a very fit young pregnant woman.

For the first couple of weeks Festus stays so there can be two teams going into the forest daily. Vita takes care of the domestic and nursing arrangements with Lucia. They discuss taking Lucia back to Laime so that she can recover there, but Lucia's response is blunt: 'I'm five months pregnant, my leg is healing. What am I going to do, sitting alone at the inn?'

'There's plenty,' says Vita. 'You can set up your kitchen to experiment with the truffles, and you can have more time to do the research with the herbs and plants that you love so dearly. After seeing you with the poppy seed mixture, I wouldn't mind having a try at that. You seemed very happy for a few days, despite having had half your leg ripped apart.'

They laugh.

'How is the leg now?' asks Vita. 'You seem to be able to get about a bit better these days.'

'I need a little more time, but I think I should be able to be back in the woods in a couple of weeks.'

'Oh, I'm not sure about that. You need to be really careful otherwise it won't heal properly, and you'll end up going lame. Then you won't be much use to anybody.'

The rustle of the dogs through the undergrowth signals the arrival of the first team, Festus and Philumena, back from the hunt.

'You're early. How was the day?' says Lucia to Philumena.

'It was fine, but in the afternoon it got a bit slow,' says Philumena. 'I'm not sure if it's the weather conditions or something with the dogs. Maybe there are fewer scents to be found. For sure, we did well in the morning with the whites.'

'We had run out of material in any case,' says Festus, 'so there was no other way of marking the trees other than with a few pebbles around the bases.'

They had recently started to mark the trees that were producing and went back regularly to the same spots to see if tubers matured at different periods of time, and it looked as though that was the case. The teams now had regular routes which they would alternate in the mornings; and then in the afternoons they would scout new areas to try and find fresh patches. With Severus's keen eye for information they soon had a solid and regular supply of truffles coming in. They waited to see if these would keep coming or if they were finite in nature.

★★★★★

As they sit round the campfire and eat a wild boar stew cooked by Vita and particularly enjoyed by Lucia, Severus regales them about how he had killed the animal with a slice of his dagger through the jugular after finding it in one of the animal traps he left around the camp – and which everyone was very aware of and careful to avoid. The forests were rich in game, and a boar or a deer could keep the charcoal burners in meat for a good few weeks.

'I was thinking,' says Thelos, who has entered into the intellectual spirit of the truffle hunting game as well as the rest of them. 'Very often we arrive at what must have been amazing truffle grounds but the wild pigs have beaten us to it.'

'You're right,' says Festus. 'My heart breaks when I see the damage they've done. But worse, I think about the sheer amount of truffles that must have been there.'

'What if,' says Thelos, 'we could somehow capture one of the pigs and train it to find the truffles?'

'What, and put Britannica and Brutus out of business?'

'Noooo,' says Thelos. 'We'd never do that. But it wouldn't hurt maybe to have a different kind of nose for different kinds of locations, or even types of truffles.'

'It's not a bad idea,' says Lucia, encouraging the boy. 'Maybe if we find a young one, we could try. But we'd have to prepare for when it got big; some of them grow to extraordinary sizes and controlling a beast like that could be tricky. Unlike the dogs, who are relatively obedient.'

'Well, I had better turn in for the night,' says Festus. He is due to take the next consignment back to Laime for shipping to Rome.

'Thelos and I will be off at dawn. I am going to take the Aquilis route up the valley south below Montona to the cave, just to secure that as the escape route. If we have time, we'll make a raft and hide it in the cave, because we'll be sitting ducks if there is any trouble, and we have to go down the Aquilis to the Flavia every time.'

★★★★★

November came, the nights drew in, and life in the forest became a dank, dark, depressing affair. Lucia grew and grew, and in her seventh month, although she was back on her feet, everyone agreed that on Festus's return from Laime in the next few days she would return with him, leaving Severus, Vita and the kids to do the truffling. The harvest was steady, yet often they were stopped by powerful autumn rains and the wild *bora* winds which sometimes accompanied them. In the aftermath the pickings were substantial, especially if followed by some strong Istrian autumn sun. And often there was.

On such an afternoon after the rains Lucia and Philumena are on their familiar turf, not far from the hot springs, when the dogs start to act in a strangely irrational way. They are trying a new combination of old dog/young dog, so Brutus is paired with Aello in very much the same way the old and young combo of human teams worked. They are just within striking distance of the hot springs; the ferrous, sulphurous odour can be felt on the air by humans, let alone by dogs, when both animals literally go into a tailspin. Round and round under a massive oak which must have been several hundred years old. Its root system stretched far and wide, probably to the water table fed by the hot springs.

'Quick, Philumena, run,' says Lucia, struggling up the slope and out of breath. 'I can barely walk any further, let alone keep those two under control.'

Philumena arrives half a minute behind them as they paw at the earth extravagantly. Taking them by their collars she pulls them back, gives them their favourite treats and tells them to sit. They dutifully obey.

'It looks like it's a big one,' says Philumena. 'They were scratching everywhere.'

Two hours later, having spent the whole time digging around the root system of the oak, they return to camp bearing at least three kilos of white tubers. It is the most they have ever found in one tree by a long chalk. And they could even return for more. Aello and Brutus have never had so many treats in their lives, and Philumena is careful to give them some of the truffle itself. As ever, they appear to be eternally grateful, tails wagging furiously.

When they reach camp after their trek across the river, they realise immediately something is wrong. Severus and Festus are building barricades around the entrance to the cave through the charcoal burner's structure.

'Quick, inside. All of you, dogs as well,' says Severus.

'What's happening, what's wrong?' asks Lucia.

'Festus just arrived, and hard on his heels is Pretty Boy and a delegation of armed barley men from the arena. He spotted them on the Via Flavia and then cut across country south of the Montona hillside. He reckons if they take the boat down to Pinguentum they could be here within the hour. Assuming they know where we are, which looks highly likely.'

'That's right,' cuts in Festus. 'I reckon that one of his boys must have followed me the last time I came and got a sighting of where we were and reported back. There were four of them and heavily armed.'

'I'm not going anywhere,' says Lucia. 'I can stay and fight with you. The dogs can take at least two down and you two can take the others.'

'Lucia, you're seven months pregnant. You can't do that. It wouldn't be right. To the child – or to the memory of Nasica. You and Vita take Philumena and the dogs out through the cave system and down to the Aquilis as soon as we know that they are near. We'll set fire to the charcoal pile once you're away. Then we'll finish him off.'

'Severus is right, Lucia,' says Vita. 'If he doesn't kill Oceanus now this could go on indefinitely and we'll be looking over our shoulders for the rest of our lives. And you are in no condition to be any part of this.'

'Come on, Lucia,' says Philumena, leading her to the entrance of the cave. 'Let's pick up our things and get ready to leave.'

Severus comes running over with his armour, the two-piece *manica* he has been working on every night, carving his little symbols and maps into the inside of the metal.

'Lucia, here,' says Severus: 'you need these. Keep them. Guard them well. It has your child's inheritance on it. The legacy of Nasica. All the information of all the places where we gather the best crops of truffles. Use the code. The usual code. And the trick is that you need both parts of the armour to ascertain the secret, like two halves of a puzzle. When the danger has passed, we will come back together and this *manica* will secure all of our futures. You see, the smaller section has the maps of the area and the larger has the instructions on to how to get there. The code reveals all.'

Lucia takes the two parts of the arm guard. Then she holds Severus close. For once in her life she doesn't dispute the wisdom of what he is proposing.

'Father, I love you,' says Lucia.

'Now go, my child,' says Severus, 'and take with you all the dogs. They are our irreplaceable precious resource.'

They go down into the cave and see that Vita has already packed everything ready to leave.

No sooner is the wood structure closed off at the top than a spear comes flying out of the woods and embeds itself into Thelos's right shoulder. Thelos goes down with a scream, and Festus and Severus, now heavily armed, drag him to cover. Festus dives for the entrance to the cave and shouts down: 'Get going, immediately! We'll rendezvous at Laime. The gods willing.'

*****

Philumena as the smallest of the team leads the way deeper down into the limestone cavern and the dogs follow her. In a basket over her shoulder she carries the four puppies. In her left hand she carries a torch specially prepared for this eventuality, which they have rehearsed numerous times. Behind follows Lucia, cursing to herself, with Vita fussing and trying to take her arm, having mother and child's interests at heart in case she falls further into the cavern. Two hundred metres along they see light at the end of the tunnel and Philumena picks up the pace. When they reach the riverbank they have a choice: go east and pick up a boat from Pinguentum down to the Via Flavia, or cut their losses and just head for the Via Flavia.

Lucia chooses neither option.

'I don't know about you, but I'm not going to let those three die up there on their own,' says Lucia, calling Brutus and Britannica over to her. 'I'm going back.'

'Don't be so stubborn! You can't do anything in your condition, and it's not fair to the child.'

'It's not fair to the child that he doesn't have a father, and I'm not going to allow him not to have a grandfather, either. The dogs are coming with me. You two stay here. Here, take these – guard them for me, they are precious. Don't worry. I will be back.'

Philumena looks at Vita and hands her the basket with the puppies and the torch, now extinguished. She takes a long, large knife, more like a crescent blade from the east, from her other bag and follows Lucia up the hill to circle round on the encampment.

'Lucia, wait – I'm coming with you,' shouts Philumena. She runs as fast as her teenage heels can carry her up the banks from the Aquilis to take the long way round behind the attackers.

★★★★★

Oceanus steps out of the forest into the clearing before the charcoal 'pile' in front of him. In bodyguard formation are three other men: one of whom is the boy, Spiculus, armed with a short *gladius* and shield; the two others each carry a *hasta*, a short spear used in close combat used for thrusting, as well as a full-length legionnaire's *scutum* shield. Oceanus sports a black leather mask with holes for eyes and mouth. He carries a *sica*, a curved scimitar, and has no shield, just a *manica* on his left arm and greaves. Clearly, they haven't just dropped in for tea.

'Come out, come out, wherever you are, Severus,' taunts Oceanus sinisterly through his leather mask. 'Come and see your handiwork. Before I return the compliment, send out the dog woman Lucia, because I want you to see her suffer as Seneschal suffered before we finish you off.'

Severus steps out from behind the barricade they have made in front of the entrance to the cave and where Festus tends as best he can the spear wound in Thelos's shoulder. Severus has lit a torch, which he carries in his left hand and his trusty *gladius* in the other.

'I would rather Lucia was dead by my hand than ever be contaminated by such a piece of low-life shit as you, Pretty Boy. Oh, sorry, they probably don't call you that any more. I bet the barmen are crazy for that mask. Gives them an extra little thrill down in the tavern. Oceanus, the arena's colonial leather-face man of mystery.'

As he says this, Severus turns to the straw-covered charcoal edifice and sets fire to its outer covering with the burning torch: it bursts immediately into a massive conflagration.

Spiculus and his two friends exchange nervous looks as Oceanus steps forward and says, 'Come on, Severus, come and fight me like a man. Just the two of us, one on one.'

'OK, fair's fair. I don't have my *manica* – it's being used for a higher purpose. I don't have any armour. My brother Festus will tie some wadding to my arm to give us an even playing field. Not that I need it – I can beat you with one arm tied behind my back.'

'Ah, this idiot brother Festus,' says Oceanus. 'I heard he's begun to drink all the stock in his own inn. I'm surprised his fingers are so dextrous as to tie a *manica*. At least another member of your tribe I will make watch you die.

'Kill the bastard for me, if not for yourself, Nasica and Lucia and your grandchild,' says Festus to his brother.

As Festus ties the makeshift *manica* Severus leans close and says, 'I can take him and one of his boys – the one on the left, who seems like a bruiser but will run a mile if challenged. If it looks as if I'm going down, take the other two – whatever happens, I will take the not-so-pretty one with me. You need to get away with Thelos and help the girls escape.'

'If one of us goes down, brother, we all go down,' says Festus.

They grasp each other's forearm and hold each other's gaze in solid confirmation.

Severus steps forward to face Oceanus. In his mind he hears the roar of the crowd as if hearing it in the arena for the very first time. It's now he realises that the unfinished elusive dream that he has been chasing through the early hours every single night since he left Colonia Pietas Iulia will finally be completed, because this is the point at which he always wakes up. He decides to go for it.

Severus fills his lungs to their full capacity and charges Oceanus, who although a fool in real life is nobody's fool in a fight. He has been expecting this opening move from the big man and neatly steps aside, almost sending Severus tumbling as his scimitar rips down through his opponent's *manica*, rendering it useless as protection. Seeing he has drawn blood Oceanus looks over to his acolytes for support and praise, and they cheer dutifully. Severus returns with a big handful of earth in the face, temporarily blinding the masked man and leaving him open to Severus's *gladius*, which he just avoids by swinging around with his shield wildly and knocking his opponent, temporarily at least, aside.

'Come on, Severus,' shouts Thelos, 'do for him! He fights like a poor man's Samnite.'

'I bet the young lad is a good fuck,' says Oceanus to Severus as they square off against each other one more time. 'Because that's what I am going to do to him when I have finished with you.'

Severus swings out in anger as Oceanus had hoped, and misses, while the former pretty boy swings his scimitar down over Severus's head, just missing his ear and leaving there a tinnitus ring that acts as a wake-up call. And wake up he does, with a massive roar and comes out again, blades clashing. Oceanus skilfully dodges the bigger man's heavier sword, looking for the chance to get in at some flesh.

Oceanus blocks the repeated thrusts of Severus, whose fitness is seriously challenged by the younger man and weighed down as he is by his heavier weaponry. He is also losing blood from the wound in his upper arm. Oceanus then re-doubles his attack, thrusting and parrying like the serious and brutal killer that he is at heart. Sensing he has Severus on the run he charges one more time, slashing the older fighter across the chest in a long deep wound that immediately spews blood. In doing so, Oceanus drops his sword as Severus falls to his knees, clutching his chest.

'Throw me your spear,' shouts Oceanus to Spiculus. 'This is going to be fun.'

Unseen until this point, Lucia, Philumena and the dogs move forward from their cover in the woods.

'If only your little bitch girl Lucia was here to see this,' gloats Oceanus, moving in for the kill. 'I would have made her eat your balls for breakfast while I buggered your little boy. Maybe when I find her I will do that, because you don't think that I believe she is in that fake charcoal pile there.'

The charcoal pile blazes higher and higher and is now in its full raging glory as it burns in on itself, creating the charcoal it was originally intended to make.

Severus looks up and, just before he passes out, he shouts, 'Oceanus, look: your wish has come true. Lucia. She's behind you.'

Oceanus laughs derisively and says, 'Oh, good one, Severus. Your famous dumb last words turn out to be the oldest trick in the book.'

'Go!' says Lucia to Brutus and Britannica, and in a second, they are on Oceanus and his throat is ripped out moments after he looks around and sees her standing there, her knife at the throat of one of his bodyguards.

Spiculus, brave gladiator, runs off unarmed into the forest as Lucia and Philumena cut the throats of the other two bodyguards and leave them for dead.

Festus heads into the woods to deal with Spiculus. He returns in a few minutes, having made quick work of the treacherous young tyro.

In the centre of the clearing the charcoal fire blazes down as the wind drops and begins to smoulder in the dusk that is now beginning to envelop the family. Vita appears from the woods, bearing all of the baggage they originally intended to bring with them. She is completely out of breath.

'Someone take something,' she says. 'Philumena, take this damned *manica* – it's killing me,' as she falls to her knees from sheer exhaustion.

'Well, what now?' says Lucia, smiling at Severus, as the burning wooden structure falls in on itself.

'Well, I was thinking,' says Severus, 'there's good money to be had in charcoal. Let's re-group, devise a new strategy and set up a new base, because this one is over now. I hear they pay good money for high-quality coals in Tergeste and Altinum, as well as in Pinguentum and the municipium of Flumen.'

'Great idea,' says Festus. 'And in between I think a trip to Rome is in order to shore up our future contracts for the tubers with the merchants there for the winter and summer seasons.'

'Oh, my God!' shouts Vita, rousing herself. 'Philumena, boil water. Now. Immediately. And take these sheets.'

They all turn and look at Lucia, who is bent double in pain and being held up by Vita. The front of her tunic is soaked. Severus rushes to find a stool for her and Festus supports her on the other side. The fire burns bright in the background.

'The waters have broken,' says Lucia. 'I will have my boy.'

Chapter XVIII

The Bertarelli Foibe

Partisan Liberated Istria, May 1st, 1945

With the tide of the war having changed radically in favour of the Allies and Tito's Partisans, so the ways and means of warfare changed with it. The battalion was now divided between the units who were to join the victorious march of liberation into Trieste, mopping up any patches of resistance on the way, and a detachment that would apparently escort a number of prisoners of war and undesirable aliens to the Partisan re-education camp above Rijeka, on the other side of Učka. They would then join up with the rest of their group in the First Partisan Battalion Pino Budicin and formally liberate Pula.

It seemed as though the whole of Istria was on the move, not only the ethnic Italians who were becoming part of what would be known as the *esodo* or exodus, but also local collaborators who had made themselves useful to the Germans and Italian Fascists before them, and anti-Communist agitators – anyone who had something to fear from the Partisans. There were masses of armed and unarmed men, women and families on the roads, all trying to reach the Allied forces and gain protection from the Partisans who would be seeking retribution for all and any crimes against the Yugoslav people.

The unit that had marched on Trieste had word that a vast column of Četniks 20,000 strong were also on the road and heading from the Postojna region where Ljotić had been going just a few days before his untimely demise. Their goal was the Italian border at Gorizia where they would seek asylum with the Americans or the British, whoever they could reach first before the Partisans got them. Most of these were Serbs, but they also included Montenegrins, Slovenians, and Dalmatians of all kinds of political colours, but held together by the fact that they were loyal to King Petar II, Mihajlović, or Ljotić. The Nationalists were ruthless as they came through Gorizia, sacking houses and attacking defenceless citizens. The local *carabinieri* and members of the local National Liberation Committee could do little to prevent them.

The rape and pillage stopped after three days when the Četniks set up camp near Palmanova, just east of the British lines.

The First of May celebrations at the Rašpor caves were muted, with many of the battalion off liberating Trieste. Still, the remaining troops managed to rouse their spirits having found Dino the stool-pigeon's accordion, a few bottles of *loza* brought up by Armando from Buzet, and some men-only *kolo* dancing. This traditional, collective folk dance was performed by dancers who were interlinked to form a chain, usually moving in a circular line holding hands with their arms down. It usually required women, but all the girls were part of the liberating force that would be dancing the night away in Trieste following their triumphant entry into the Italian capital of the Julian Marches. The *kolo* that was being drunkenly and lethargically danced by those left behind in Rašpor had been specially composed for the unit.

'Come on, Pino, cheer up,' says Nino. 'It will all work out. This is just a temporary punishment. They will come round later, after we march on Pula.'

'It's already fucked up. I'm fucked,' says Pino, drinking water only. 'You have no idea. You only get one chance in the Partisans. And I have blown it. Everyone else – Faida, Gasparini, the Neapolitan – are all part of the liberation army of Trieste, marching heroically on the International Day of the Worker. But here we are celebrating May Day in our dark hole in Istria with only the escort duty of prisoners of war on the roster for tomorrow. I don't know how I managed to do it, Nino, but I have managed to fuck things up – not just with the High Command, but also with Faida.'

'Don't worry, brother,' says Nino. 'She's an honest girl – she'll forgive you. Don't worry.'

'Fuck off, Nino,' says Pino. 'I don't need your pity.'

Vito has had a rapid rise in the Partisan ranks since his arrival and has become the company's mascot. There was talk of taking him on the victory march into Trieste, a discussion that was brought to a rapid conclusion by Nino who refused to go if his brother was to be left behind. For all his faults, he understood how much being a Partisan meant to Pino, far more than it ever meant to himself. Faida was another matter; she was under strict orders to go and had no choice. Tito was keen to demonstrate that there would be a new world order after the departure of the Germans, and this would have women included as an active part of the vanguard.

'Come on, Pino, let's at least celebrate a bit. It isn't all bad,' says Nino.

'It might not be for you, now you're in with the *bourgeois* elements of the top brass as their supplier of luxury goods,' says Pino.

'Me giving the truffles to the officers is no different to giving them to Armando. We're all on the same side,' says Nino.

'I wouldn't be so sure of that, Nino, if I were you,' says Pino. 'The revolution lasts a long time. You have to choose which side you are on.'

'But we're family,' says Nino. 'So is uncle Armando. Why are you being like this?'

'You saw how it is with family,' says Pino. 'Dad was family, but he betrayed everyone. And look what happened to him. Look where that got you. You had to kill him.'

'That was different,' says Nino. 'It was justice. It was a clear case. After what he did in Grimalda. And to you. I did it for you.'

'And there was me thinking you did it as some kind of political revelation. That you'd finally realised who the oppressor is. Get away from me, Nino, and take the ugly dog with you. I only have one family. It's called the Party.'

And with that Pino retreated to his sleeping bunk on the other side of the cave and took no further part in the festivities.

While Pino was sleeping crucial information was relayed back to the Rašpor caves. Two nights previously the battalion had joined the other Gortan Brigade units and marched down the *camionale* towards Trieste. As it made great progress heading for the city marching at double time the battalion was ambushed, this time by German forces already in flight towards the Austrian border. But despite this its vanguard made contact with the 20th Dalmatian Partisan Division near Kozina. Everything was looking good for the battalion's march into Trieste with the liberators. It was then that the battalion commander's request to march down to Trieste was refused. However, four battalion members, one of whom was Faida, were attached to other Partisan forces and entered Trieste with them on May Day 1945.

★★★★★

The detachment of Partisans that Benvenuti sent down to Buzet met no resistance on the way, just significant numbers of people on the road from central Istria towards Fiume in the opposite direction. People on foot, people with horse and cart or wheelbarrow in the manner of refugees who all over Europe at this time were on the move. It reminded Nino of the floods of refugees he had seen after the Italians had moved out following the Armistice of Cassibile in 1943 when not only the Italian army but also vast swathes of the populace discharged themselves *en masse* in the direction of Italy. Technically speaking, Fiume and Pola, being military and naval strongholds, were still occupied by the Germans, but in name only.

The Italians had been moved in after the end of the First World War in 1918. Their emigration back to the Venezia Giulia region started after the Italian capitulation. Some had withdrawn from war-affected areas; some Italians who had come to Istria during Italian rule now left; others who fled were those individuals who had compromised themselves during the Fascist regime.

★★★★★

It is the second day of May, and Pino and a detachment of 15 men march down the hill from Rašpor and up into the ancient walled city of Buzet. They are to take charge of a group of prisoners and undesirables who have been told by the political officer, Gasparini, that they would be taken to the 13th Division based just north of Fiume for re-education.

It is a ragged group of individuals who await the Partisans in the main square of Buzet old town. There are about 120 of them: men, women, children, old and young, Italian and Croatian speakers. Numerous professions are included, some of them still in uniform like the postman and the policeman, as well as a couple of nurses and a forest ranger.

Armando appears at a certain point, and it is the first time that Nino has seen him in uniform. He addresses the prisoners: 'Listen up, because I will only say this once. The local tribunal has found you all guilty of collaborating with the enemy. The usual penalty for this is death, as you may have heard. You are the lucky ones. We believe that you can be re-educated and re-integrated into society as good anti-fascists. Who knows, maybe one day you could become good Communists. I doubt it, but I've been ordered to give you a reprieve. You are now in the hands of comrade Pino, whose men will take you to our camp just outside of Rijeka for re-education and rehabilitation. Disobey him or try to escape and you will be summarily executed. Carry on, comrade.'

They exchange the single-fisted Communist salute and begin to march the prisoners, whose hands have been bound with rope tightly behind their backs, down the hill and out onto the Lupoglav road. They march in single file, with the 15-man guard spread out alongside the line. As he passes Pino, Nino questions him: 'Where are we taking them?'

'Back up to Rašpor,' says Pino. 'It's on the way to Rijeka where we'll spend the night.'

'But the 13th Division isn't there. And there is no space for all these people.'

Pino laughs at him disbelievingly and shakes his head, saying, 'Just obey the orders and guard this fascist scum until I tell you not to.'

As they move the bedraggled convoy out of the town, the various inhabitants appear on the street to throw things, call names and spit at the passing column of undesirables. One thug comes right up to an old man in the line and simply kicks him in the stomach. The old man falls down and brings the whole column to a halt.

Nino goes to help him up. Vito, who has been running alongside them, growls at the perpetrator, threatening him not to do it again.

'I see you have a fascist-loving dog there; maybe he should be executed, too.'

'Shut the fuck up, Pajkić,' says Nino. 'You were a coward in school, and you are still a coward.'

It is only then that Nino recognises the broken old man as his teacher from high school – Mr Valli, who had taught him about the Glagolitic language and the paintings, as well as the ancient Mediterranean history that had inspired him so much. When he began truffling with Vito it was Mr Valli who told him that the Greek philosopher Plutarch wrote that truffles were born in violent storms when a clap of thunder coincided with a bolt of lightning. Mr Valli had also carefully explained that Plutarch shouldn't be confused with Petrarch, the fourteenth-century Italian poet who also wrote of the tuber.

'Mr Valli,' says Nino. 'I am so sorry. There must be some mistake here.'

'If you know what's good for you, pretend you don't know me,' says Valli, 'and hit me with the gun for good measure.'

Nino hesitates, but Valli looks at Nino and nods, as if he is expecting it of him, so Nino hits the old man in the shoulder.

'Next time you get a bullet, you old bastard,' says Nino, finally understanding and putting on a show for his comrades.

Pino leads on and takes them off the main road and up the slopes to Sveti Martin in the direction of Rakitovec. Clearly the intention is not to draw any further attention to the column than is necessary. They move the motley group deeper and deeper into the anonymous countryside around Počekaji, and from there across open country to Slum before picking up the road again up to Brest.

Along the way Nino takes the chance to try to talk with Mr Valli. The old man is reluctant at first, but when it becomes clear that the other guards aren't taking any notice they manage to have a couple of exchanges. Valli explains that as a teacher in the Italian and German occupation he is now *persona non grata* with the new regime, especially as he is an ethnic Italian. He explains that he is with his son, the 14-year-old walking behind him, and begs Nino to do what he can to help the boy. Nino tries to put Mr Valli's mind at rest and says that after re-education his uncle Armando would make sure that everything was OK.

'I know your uncle, Nino. Armando is a die-hard,' says Valli. 'I don't expect to come back. But Mario, my son – he's young, he has a chance.'

'I will do what I can when we get to camp,' says Nino.

As they reach the far side of the village of Slum, Pino calls the column to halt and gives the order that they can drink at the spring by the side of the road. 'Fifteen-minute rest stop,' he shouts.

By the time each of the prisoners has knelt by the spring and lapped at the stream like dogs it is time to move on. For those who don't manage to get a drink Pino tells them it is their own fault and they should have been faster. Nino is confused at this attitude and behaviour as he had supposed that the Partisans would be gracious in victory. He wishes Faida was here to intervene with him.

As they line up again by the side of the road, the angry clouds that have been gathering over Učka become even darker. The trees around them start to pirouette as they do before a storm. The column is about two hours' march from their base camp in the caves at Rašpor.

'Looks like there is a *bora* storm coming up. It would be a pity to lose any of these bastards on the way,' says Pino, as he passes another long wire through the bindings of each prisoner, making sure that they are all tied together; no-one can make a break for it without dragging the person in front of them.

'I'll take up the rear,' says Nino, ensuring himself a position from which he can continue the conversation with Valli. 'I'll shoot any bastard that tries to make a break for it.'

'Good thinking, comrade Nino,' says his brother, winking at him. 'That's the spirit; we'll make a good Partisan of you yet.'

Meanwhile the *bora* is building and blowing a heavy north-north-easterly as they move out of Slum and onwards and up to the camp. They slow their pace considerably as the powerful wind whips into the line of prisoners. Pino has taken charge at the front as he knows the off-road terrain better than anyone. Nino lags behind, giving him the chance to speak a bit more with his former teacher, Mr Valli.

'Why did they arrest you?' asks Nino, the wind and rain now lashing his face. 'I don't understand. You were just doing your job, teaching.'

'There's nothing to understand. All public servants are collaborators in their eyes. Especially if you look, sound and have an Italian name.'

'It's madness. I will speak to the commandant, the Neapolitan, when he gets back. Gasparini, the political commissar, will also have something to say about this.'

'Don't be naïve, Nino; you will get us both and yourself in bigger trouble than we are already,' says Valli. 'Forget about me. I'm finished. But do something for my son, Mario – he has his whole life in front of him.'

The *bora* chose that very moment to increase its speed and therefore the intensity of the rain. The column of prisoners and Partisan guards appears to be leaning into the storm and moving, but not very quickly. With gusts of up to 150 kilometres per hour it is particularly powerful, but Pino insists on keeping going rather than taking shelter. It is also the weather that Vito loathes, and he tucks himself in between Professor Valli and Nino, fearful of the constant rumble of thunder and occasional lightning that bursts out of the now coal-black clouds over Učka. The *bora* at its worst could reach hurricane strength – today it satisfied itself by simply storming down the mountain protector of Istria, Mount Učka, and down the coastline of the Adriatic, bursting through gaps in the highlands to fall angrily upon the islands of Cres and Lošinj.

'It's funny, ironic even,' said the professor, 'that this wind, the *bora*, should be blowing today. It was my nickname, you know, when I was a child, no more than Mario's age. I was always considered a bit of a tearaway when I was young. And they call the *bora* the *enfant terrible* of the Adriatic. Surely, I taught you that in your classes – I did it every year.'

'You taught us that no good ever comes of it, that's for sure,' says Nino. 'I wondered why I woke up feeling weird this morning. I could feel the *bora* in my bones.'

'Listen, Nino,' says the professor, 'I know you are an intelligent boy. And I know from your uncle Armando that you have the taste of the truffle in your blood now. Look here,' he says, pointing to a silver plate inside his coat. 'This is a treasure from the Roman Empire. It is the armour from a gladiator – a *manica*, worn to protect the arm. There is a smaller piece for the upper arm and shoulder which Mario has. The legend has it that the code in the inscriptions on the pieces contain the secret to the location of a great lost truffle forest somewhere between the Mirna and the Raša. Take it. It's more use to you than me. But do what you can for Mario.'

'Professor, I can't take anything from you,' says Nino. 'It is not the Partisan way. Even out in the forests when we are on missions, we pay the peasants for everything. Listen, hold firm for now. When we get to camp we will sort everything out with the Neapolitan. But listen, what I'm going to do is loosen your shackles, if I can, and those of Mario. And if you see a chance to disappear into the woods when I am not looking, you take it.'

'I know what is going to happen, Nino,' says the professor, 'and I don't blame you. But this will be like in '43. When your man Gasparini and Ćiro Raner were on the special tribunal in Pisano before the Germans came. They did the same to Norma Cossetto, who was a student of mine. They threw her violated, abused teenager's body into the *foibe* near Villa Suvani up by Piran.'

While Mr Valli has been talking through the haze of the passing cloud, Nino has managed to loosen the wire around both the professor's and young Mario's hands. But at the very moment he completes his task Pino, as if by magic, appears at Nino's side. The rain once again begins to come down in bucket loads, and as they climb higher up towards Trstenik and Lanišće a heavy fog descends and envelops the column of prisoners. They walk in an ethereal haze, moving in and out of each other's sight as they effectively move through a cloud.

'A bit too much fraternising with the enemy back here,' says Pino. 'I'll bring up the rear for a bit, and you and the ugly dog can lead the way. This is your *petit bourgeois* truffling route, so you know it best. And it will stop you getting too cosy with the *dottore* here.'

'I'll see you in Rašpor,' whispers Nino to Mr Valli, as he puts Vito on the leash. 'And don't worry. Everything will be fine.'

As he moves to the front with Vito in tow, Nino thinks to himself that the one thing he cannot abide about Pino's new-found Communism and loyalty to the party is that he seems to take on with it the village peasant's fear of the dog. He can forgive most other things, but this change in heart towards animals clearly demonstrates to Nino the profound and possibly irrevocable change that has come about in his brother, the change that Faida told him about during the long night of celebrations up at the cave complex.

*****

In a break in the clouds Nino leads the column closer and closer to the Rašpor caves, which had become the home of his Partisan battalion for the last few months. He catches sight of the ruins of the Fortress of Rašpor, high above the village. Versions of this fortress had been there since Roman times. For over a century in the Venetian period it was the most important village in Istria, known as the *Clavis totius custodiae Histriae* – holding the key to the whole of Istria. It controlled all roads that connected central Istria with all points north towards the foothills of the Alps. As such it was first from here and then later from Buzet that the Venetian Captains of Pasenatico, known as Rašpor's Captains, managed to control all of Istria and its communications.

But it is not the fortress that is on Pino's mind as he comes running to the front of the column to take control of it again.

'We're not going to the camp, you idiot,' says Pino, diverting his brother to the left-hand turn. 'We're headed to the ravine, to the Bertarelli abyss. So take them up there, this way – now. I'm right behind you. By the way, your professor friend just tried to offer me a bribe. I should have shot him there and then, but his son was watching, so we'll keep a close eye on him and make sure he joins the 13th Division as soon as possible.'

The clouds come and go, but the wind and the rain has stopped. As Nino comes up into a clearing above the Bertarelli abyss he sees a group of gunners from the Pino Budicin Battalion, waiting as if for a pre-arranged meeting.

'Ciao, Nino,' shouts one of the gunners, 'and ciao, Vito – how are you, little fella? Let's see if I have something for you.'

They are gathered around a small fire in an oil can next to their truck, trying to get such warmth as was possible in the damp, foetid atmosphere of Učka's foothills.

'Here, Vito,' says the gunner, slipping him a treat, 'as Epicurus said, "Give me a piece of cheese and I shall have a feast". And, no – there is no more. Now, fuck off you little mutt and bring me back some truffles.'

They all laugh, the dog bringing a modicum of humanity to the general mood of wartime depression.

Pino takes control. 'OK, you lot. Now all line up over here and face away, looking up at the fortress,' he says, disappearing into the back of the truck.

'I thought we were supposed to be meeting the 13th Division,' says Nino to the gunners, who have begun to follow Pino to the back of the truck. The gunners look at each other, wondering whether to let Nino in on the secret, but then think the better of it.

They jump up on the back of the truck and pull away the tarpaulin to reveal its awful contents.

Before the column of 'undesirables' know what is happening, Pino not only gives the order to fire but also carries out some of the firing of the Maxim gun himself. Starting at the right, the first few are simply cut down into the Bertarelli abyss in front of them. Once the these have begun the 500-metre-deep fall, those who had been tied together drag the others with them. The screams of terror that cut through the air pierce the heart of Nino, and in his confusion, he screams at Pino to stop.

In a split-second Nino understands what the '13th Division' is. He dashes towards the left of the line and shouts to Valli and his son to run for their lives back the way they have come. The noise of the machine gun is terrifying, and the stink of cordite makes the victims panic, only hastening their fall into the depths of the abyss beneath them. The gun jams and there is silence.

Pino takes his rifle and jumps down from the truck. He begins to finish the remaining victims off, one by one, with a single bullet to the back of the neck. Then he sees the two escapees disappearing down the mountain track.

'Carry on here, gunners,' shouts Pino, as he watches his men roughly shoving the remaining victims by hand into the ravine.

'Why waste the bullets? Save those for the Germans in Pula,' shouts one of the gunners after Pino, but he has already begun to chase after the *bourgeois* professor and his son.

In the chaos behind them Nino, unseen by his comrades, slips away after his brother and his teacher. Pino has discarded his rifle and with his revolver is taking pot shots at Valli as he descends into the forest. It is at the fording of a fast-running stream that Pino catches up with Mr Valli.

'Stop there, you fascist bastards!' yells Pino. 'Stop or you both get the bullet.'

Mario is trying to pull his father up the other side of the bank, having fallen in the stream. He raises his hands in the air, letting his father slide down into the freezing water.

'OK, both of you, come here – come towards me. We're going back up the hill. I'd prefer not to have to waste any more bullets on dirty fascist scum like you. You are not worth the metal. But we are following orders, so we need to dispose of you as instructed.'

'Drop the gun, brother,' comes a voice from behind his head. 'Drop it, or I won't hesitate to kill you.'

Pino turns and snarls at Nino, 'Now it becomes clear. Now it becomes clear who the traitor is – who has allowed these collaborators to go free. It was you who untied their bindings. Traitor. I'll have you shot for this.'

'What would Stjepan Filipovic think of you now?' asks Nino of his brother, referring to the hero the story of whose execution he had kept so faithfully in his bedside cupboard. 'These are the people. These are the *real* people. Have you forgotten who they are? Or, like Dad, have you never really had any contact with humanity? They have done no harm. Or maybe you got your slogan mixed up, "Death to the people, freedom to fascists"?'

'What would you know about it, truffle boy? If I had an extra bullet, I'd put it in the dog as well.'

'I have a full cartridge here, and I have all the time in the world.'

'You don't have the balls,' says Pino, who turns and puts a bullet in Professor Valli's forehead, spraying the contents of his skull over his son behind him.

Pino turns to Nino with a big shit-eating grin and says, 'Go on then, your turn.'

Nino turns away, puts a bullet into the breach of his rifle. Locks the bolt. Takes aim.

'You haven't got the balls,' laughs Pino.

Nino pulls the trigger and shoots his brother. Pino falls to the ground and his head drops into the stream, his blood flowing fast like the water.

'Now you, Mario,' says Nino to his teacher's son, 'you need to run – run fast, run far, and run away from Buzet as far as you can. And don't come back.'

The boy takes the *manica* out from his jacket, as his father had done with its counterpart earlier, and offers it to Nino.

'No, I told you,' shouts Nino, aggressively, and shoots over his head. 'Now run. Quick, before I change my mind.'

Mario runs off down the forest path and into the unknown.

Nino looks at his old professor whose body lets out a groan as he rolls over face down into the fast-flowing stream. His overcoat opens, revealing the metal of the forearm *manica* and all its secrets that he had previously offered Nino. The body is picked up in the current, light as it is from wartime malnutrition, and slips away downstream to the sea.

Nino watches his old professor disappear in the water. After he does so, he reaches down to his brother's corpse, drags him into the centre of the stream and lets the current take him.

Leaning forwards into the water, Nino sees that the *manica* has stuck to the riverbed. He retrieves it and places it safely in the knapsack he has on his back. He walks back up the hill to the Bertarelli abyss.

Part Seven

Chapter XIX

Oh Youth!

Istria: December 31st, 2019

The day remaining until New Year is sober one at Stancija Mihailić. The restaurant remains closed. Faida has retreated to her room. She has taken Nino's confession very badly and left strict instructions that she is not to be disturbed. She has eaten very little of the simple food and drink brought by her loyal and trusted restaurant staff and, from time to time, her old friends, Ema and Marija. Faida is not someone to be messed with, so these orders are observed by all – including Emina, whose special relationship cannot cut through the stone wall of silence that has descended on the property overnight.

Nino is distracted beyond belief. He arrives at dawn after a night alone, bearing coffee and wakes Marco at the Rose House. Marco wipes the sleep from his eyes and shakes the weariness from the last days' efforts out of his bones and joins his grandfather on his little terrace. There are occasional roses on the walls of the small cottage that have survived the winter cold and are struggling, holding on to dear life as the winter sun beats down on the house and its inhabitants. These signs of life in nature, however small, are of some comfort to Nino as he observes them.

Hands shaking, Nino pours the coffee into two small cups, adds sugar, and hands one to Marco. He lights up a Marlboro.

'You're back on 40-a-day now, I see,' says Marco. 'So much for the double bypass surgery, stent and new valve. I wonder if you'll make it to the "Nino at Ninety" celebration tonight.'

Nino says nothing. He drinks his coffee, pulls on the cigarette, and exhales extravagantly the sweet smoke.

'When you get to my age little things like smoking don't matter anymore,' says Nino. 'Something's going to get you and it may as well be something that gives you pleasure. That's an easy one. But what really matters are the big questions. Did I live a good life? What could I have done better? What can I do to be better? How should I end my days?'

'When I was in the police my partner got shot by a burglar,' says Marco. 'When he lay there waiting for the ambulance to come, me putting pressure on the wound to stop the blood, he looked up at me and spoke. "Marco I've made a mess of my life. But, then again, I've made a mess of all my shirts." When he made it out of intensive care, I brought him half a dozen beautiful Van Heusen shirts. He saw the funny side.'

Nino laughs.

'I guess what I mean is that it's never too late to start again,' says Marco.

Nino takes another long drag on his cigarette and another sip of coffee, stands, and stares intently across the valley to Grimalda where a single church bell has begun to ring anomalously between the hours, a sure signal that someone local has died in the night.

'When I go I want you to bury me near my frescoes, here in Saint Eliseus's graveyard; but I want you to ring the bell in Grimalda. Not just for me, but for all the men I saw murdered in the square by my father, the priest and the Nazis all those years ago. I will be the last eyewitness to go, and I pass the memory along to you, lest we forget. We need to remember with all the shit that's going on in this country right now.'

Emina emerges from the house, towelling her long black hair wet from the shower.

'I thought I heard you two out here, setting the world to rights, cheering yourselves up with doom and gloom,' says Emina, pouring herself a cup from the *ibrik* pot. 'Look at the view, breathe in the air. It's good to be alive.'

'Oh, yeah,' says Marco, kissing her on the forehead, 'we were just getting on to the juicy business of burials, reprisal killings, and death. You can chip in on the ethnic cleansing side if you like. Cheer up, it might never happen, Nino.'

'Nothing like starting the day with a good hard giggle,' says Emina, sitting down next to Nino and taking his hand. 'Is she still taking it badly?'

'She hasn't spoken to me since,' says Nino, 'I'm not sure I can bear it much longer. This will finish me. You know, this isn't the first time… that she has come close to leaving me.'

'Give her time,' says Emina, stroking his arm. 'Imagine how it feels for her. You have been holding on to that knowledge for 75 years. It's become part of your flesh. She, on the other hand, has had only a few hours to come to terms with it. And Nono, you know I love you, but it isn't all about you.'

'I know, I know. I need to be patient,' says Nino. 'But it also brought it all back to life for me, too; Mario, the *esodo* and the *foibe*. Those were hard times. Times best forgotten. But still must not be forgotten. I've forgotten all the Nazis and collaborators I killed. Except one. The first one. But to kill your father, and your brother. And mother as well. This is not natural.'

'I know it's not the same,' says Marco. 'But I knew a couple of guys on the force in England who accidentally killed a victim in the line of duty. I know from them, from accidental killers, the guilt they feel, in spite of everyone telling them it wasn't their fault. We have some deep, primitive instinct in us that somehow a life must pay for a life.'

'It wasn't an accident, Marco,' says Nino. 'I wanted to kill him. He deserved it. And all these years I've been keeping a seat for him at our Christmas dinner. The ghost of Christmas Past. The empty chair was really an empty chair for my hypocrisy and guilt.'

Marco looks over to Nino and feels his pain. Then to Emina. And feels for her, too. He knows what she is thinking. The guilt she feels for leaving her family behind in Srebrenica. Not a day goes by when she doesn't feel that she would have given her life to have her parents back. But they both turn to Nino, whose pain is growing by the minute. Every minute that Faida's love is withdrawn is another minute closer to death for him.

'I keep having the dream,' says Nino. 'Tomislav, my father, comes to me like some Old Testament God. Like one of the frescoes in Beram or Poreč. Pointing his finger: "Where is Pino?" he shouts. Like God asked after the murder, "Where is your brother Abel?" and Cain replies, "I do not know; am I my brother's keeper?" And I shout back, "I don't know, he's the oldest one, he should be looking after me." But Cain *does* know where Abel is – he murdered him. And I murdered Pino.'

Faida has been standing at the top of the steps listening to Nino's monologue. She has a patient look on her face. No-one else has noticed her yet.

'But the worst of it has been living with the guilt, hiding my secret,' says Nino, beginning to shed tears. 'The nightmares. The sleepless nights. I felt sick in the stomach most of the time. I couldn't look Faida in the eye. But I knew how much she suffered, too. And I cried and cried and cried. I drank in secret, just to forget. I went to Italy and saw so many doctors, counsellors, psychologists, psychiatrists. They told me I had depression and then they invented this new thing – this post-traumatic stress disorder. All the kids were coming back from the recent war with it. They were all strung out on drugs they didn't need. That was when I knew I needed to end it and the thoughts of suicide began.'

'Sounds like you spoke with everyone,' says Faida, walking down the steps. 'You gave everyone the sob story everywhere you went. The shrinks, the counsellors, the doctors – not telling them the truth, though. I followed it for years. The highs. The lows. The drinking. The pills. More pills. How did you think I wouldn't notice that something was profoundly, basically, deeply wrong with you? You told all these people *almost* everything. But it took Mario, Mr Valli's son, returning from the dead and threatening your very existence, your livelihood, and your reputation – oh, yes, your blessed patricidal, fratricidal reputation – for you to tell the truth to me. Your wife. Your best friend. A life shared.'

'You don't understand…' says Nino.

'Oh, Nino, spare me the "don't understand",' says Faida. 'I've been understanding everything for the last 75 fucking years. You just didn't notice that I was understanding.'

Emina and Marco exchange a look as Faida says: 'You two – Marco, Emina – go in the kitchen and make yourself some breakfast. I need some time with this one. It won't take long. Make some pancakes. Feed the dog. Do something. Go.'

The couple leave solemnly, hand-in-hand, to the kitchen.

'Look at them,' says Faida to Nino, 'such a beautiful couple. Just like Ivo and Maja were. They remind me of you and me when we came back from the war. Everything seemed possible. And it was. For such a long time. The socialism I dreamed about and the society you knew you wanted were all possible and became a reality. And we made it happen. We did make it happen. Then they took it apart. Piece by piece.'

Nino makes a move in Faida's direction. She stops him.

'No, Nino, now you need to listen. I'm going to say this once. I know, and you know, that there was something not right with Pino. I had started to realise it even before we came here that day in Dragué to celebrate the founding of the battalion. The day you showed me the frescoes in the Church of Saint Rocco. I thought that by going to his hometown and meeting his family I could try to get to the bottom of why he was like he was. I should have realised when his father didn't appear. Why he was becoming, and eventually became, a fanatic. A fanatic of the dogma. I guess it gave him a safe place. A place of solace and order to go to when everything else was chaotic and disordered. A home. I thought I could give him that. You need to understand, Nino, that if you hadn't have killed him someone else sooner or later would have. So you didn't actually just do Mario a favour, you did the world a favour. I'm not saying this to forgive you for hiding this from me. But imagine if Pino had been like that in Russia, working for Stalin? He would have given Beria a run for his money. No – that's not fair. But you know what I mean. It's like he had been fitted with an empathy bypass.'

She looks into his eyes.

'What was unbearable, and what is unbearable, is that you have spent the whole of your life with me, from day one till yesterday, lying to me.'

Faida, dry-eyed, stops, and her words hang in the air.

'Now I have to dig deep inside myself and find a way of living with that and living with you for the rest of my natural days, brief though they may be, without hating myself and without hating you. Without hating our memories. And right now, Nino, I am not sure that I have it in me to do that. I'll do my best. I promise. I love you. I have spent my life loving you and I know that deep down you are a good man, but sometimes it has been just so hard. If you trust me, Nino. I'll do my best. I promise. Now come here.'

Nino, weeping, falls into her open arms.

Faida stares out over lake Butoniga and wonders what the rest of her days hold for her.

Then, rousing herself, 'Come on old soldier,' she says, 'we have a big party for the Central Committee tonight. In honour of someone very special to us all. It'll be just like old times – seven and a half decades, give or take, since we first met at a party in Draguć.' She pauses for thought: 'And, by all that is good, we are still here.'

*****

The blaring of the first notes of the *Colonel Bogey* tune, from the air-horn feature of his recently pimped new ride, is the first indication that Zvonko has arrived at Stancija Mihailić. It is this wake-up call that causes Marco to rouse himself from his siesta slumber, roll over to kiss Emina, only to find her side of the bed empty. Before he has time to work out where she might be Zvonko and Emina burst in through the bedroom door, bearing costumes, props, and various bits of kit.

'OK, you two, I've worked everything out,' says Emina. 'We have a few hours before we are needed to help with the final preparations for the party. We can rehearse down in the old barn – it's perfect, I've just been down there. Come on, sleepyhead, let's go.'

'I spoke to Dalrymple,' says Zvonko.

'Surely you mean "Bonkers",' says Marco.

'Yes. The very same. Bonkers. The old fart will be here in an hour.'

'Perfect,' says Emina. 'Then we can run through the music.'

*****

Up at the restaurant the finishing touches are being put to the *mise-en-place* by the regular waiting staff. They are being helped by Zvonko's kids, eleven-year-old Dado and fifteen going on thirty-five Marijana, who are doing their best to make the festive table.

'It may not look like it,' says Faida, 'but making a table beautiful to eat from is the easiest thing in the world. It just needs some love and care. It's the same with making your bed. I once read in a magazine that in an average life we spend nearly 50 per cent of it eating and sleeping. These are the two things you know you will do every single day of your life – so it's worth making sure you do both of them really well, because you spend so much time in that.'

Dado yawns and plonks down a few more bits of cutlery in roughly the correct order.

'I totally get it, grandma,' says Marijana. 'I love my bed. But with the table, it's like everything needs to be in the correct place and aligned and in order; then you can give it the feeling and mood that you want by adding different things, depending on the occasion and the people. But if you don't have the basics then you're going nowhere.' And to Dado, 'And doing it with love is a basic, dickhead, so straighten that setting out and then we'll bring some decoration.'

Marijana the thirty-five-year-old has more or less taken charge of the restaurant now and goes off to join the waitresses who are preparing the room for the evening's special event.

'You, young man,' says Faida, 'come with me to the kitchen. I want to show you something.'

'Are we going to cook something, Grandma?'

'No time for cooking today, Dado,' says Faida. 'We're supervising, which can be equally tiring.'

They enter the kitchen where everything is in full swing for their New Year's Nino at Ninety celebration.

'Dinner for thirty coming up, Mrs Faida,' shouts the head chef, Adis, from the heart of the operations room as he conducts his orchestra of cooks into the regular order of chaos that is a professional kitchen.

'Dado and I have come to test the *fritule*,' says Faida, with a laugh. 'You know what General Major Nino is like about his New Year's *fritule*.'

'Crisp on the outside and hot in the middle,' says Dado confidently, as Adis the chef ruffles his hair and whispers, 'Even we Slavonians know how to make *fritule*. Don't worry, my man.'

'Here's the batter we prepared earlier,' says Adis. 'It's Armando's original recipe, except I substituted lemon zest for lime zest this year, as I think it gives an extra zing.'

Faida looks at him doubtfully. 'Are you sure you should be experimenting so near to the deadline?'

'Let's try them and you can see,' says Adis. 'If you don't like them, I can make some new ones, no trouble. Everything is under control.'

'OK, let's try,' says Faida. 'But you know what the old bastard is like.'

'Let me just heat up the oil,' says Adis. 'Stand aside there, young Dado, I don't want any accidents. I need to control the oil temperature. Too hot and the little *bastardo* will burn; but if the temperature is too low it will soak the oil up like a fatburger. OK. We try with these three.'

'If you put the right amount of *rakija* in the mixture it will prevent too much fat being absorbed,' says Faida. 'Well, that's what my grandfather used to say. My younger brother and I used to watch our Nono make *fritule* and we always argued about who was going to have the biggest in the batch. But that was many years ago. I'm glad to see these are all the same size.'

'Your father was right, Faida: the *rakija* works perfectly and adds a little extra lift,' says Adis, fishing the three fried dough balls out of the oil. 'Let's sprinkle some icing sugar on. And… what's the verdict?'

'I'm not quite sure,' says Dado, trying his luck. 'I think I need a few more tries.'

'The lime is a great idea,' says Faida, 'like all your ideas, Adis. Brilliant. You are the best.'

She kisses him on the cheek.

'I love you too, Adi-baby,' says Dado, and kisses him on the other cheek.

'And remember, everyone,' says Faida, shouting out to the whole kitchen, 'NO TRUFFLES ON ANYTHING TONIGHT!'

'Well, even if I wanted to,' says Adis, 'there are none. I don't know what is happening with Nino's suppliers but there isn't a single truffle in the whole kitchen.'

'Good,' says Faida. 'Maybe he has finally given up the ghost.'

'Oh, and I brought my camera,' says Adis. 'I'll take some shots. We need to record this for posterity.'

★★★★★

'I'm going to kick your ass,' shouts Zvonko as he chases Marco out of the old barn and into the rear courtyard behind the kitchens. 'You are one sorry, sad sack son of a bitch.'

'Pack it in, you two,' shouts Emina, 'you are scaring the dogs. The poor things. They've been through enough.'

'They're scaring the shit out of me, too,' says Professor Dalrymple as they walk towards the burning embers in the corner of the courtyard. 'If I may put it so bluntly.'

'Oooooh, lucky Marco – saved by the smell,' says Zvonko, turning his attention to the huge spit-roasted hog that is slowly turning above the coals just outside the kitchen. 'My god, is there any better smell on earth?'

'Speaking as a lapsed Muslim,' interjects Emina, 'no, there isn't.'

'As for me,' says Dalrymple, 'much as I agree, I need to go and change and be ready for when the kids arrive for the surprise performance and walk them through the songs. We'll rendezvous back at the barn after the food is served.'

'OK, maestro,' says Marco. 'See you there – and… thanks.'

'This is what makes life worth living,' says Zvonko, salivating. 'Look at the skin, how it crackles and glows in the dark. This will taste like heaven!'

'Go on Ante, let's have a little taste before Adis comes out,' says Marco.

'Sorry, mate, strict orders. No picking. Even for family,' responds Ante. 'But I do have some primo Istrian home-grown weed at bargain basement "family" prices if you are interested?'

'I think you've just made me an offer I can't refuse,' says Zvonko, 'it being New Year and all. I'll drop by after dinner. As for now, watch out – the big man is on his way.'

'I knew there would be some awkward customers out here disturbing my staff,' says Adis, embracing Zvonko and Marco. 'You have no fucking idea do you, you two, that this man Ante is a fucking artist and you are disturbing him at his very important work. Isn't that right, Ante?'

'If you say so, chief – you the man!' says Ante.

Ante is simultaneously turning the spit slowly and basting the animal with a variety of oils and marinades, making sure the whole beast is kept in perfect condition right up until the moment it reaches the table in three hours' time.

'As you two knuckleheads should be aware,' says Adis, 'this is a very ancient method of preparing food. Imported to these parts from the East. Yes, yes – even naughty Muslims like me do it. Tonight, we do it the traditional way – normally, with the full-sized beast. This business with the young animals is OK for the city and the suburbs, but it's not the real thing. In the old days because the scarcity of meat it was usual that an animal should reach its full adult size before being slaughtered. In Slavonia, where my mum comes from, we still use this ancient tradition to spit roast the full-size pig, particularly for popular festivities like this one. But here I'm using some Istrian touches. This marinade is made from wild salvia – or regular sage – which gives it a real taste of our region. The baster is made from the biggest branches of rosemary we could find. Inside it's stuffed with a very rough poultice of lemon thyme, ordinary thyme, bay leaf, marjoram and oregano.'

'Look, Adi, I came over here to have a taste of the pig, not to get a lecture on what you've stuffed up its arse,' says Zvonko. 'If you're not putting out, then me and Love Rat Boy here are fucking off.'

'Well, you'd better fuck off then,' says Adis, and blowing him a kiss, 'I'll save you a big prime choice piece for later, big boy.'

*****

It's 8pm. It's New Year's Eve. And it's show time. The guests have just begun to arrive at Stancija Mihailić and the place is beginning to buzz. Marco has been out front with his torch, directing the guests to the overflow car park below the property. The thirty or so close friends, neighbours, great and good, are arriving as instructed, on time and dressed to kill.

Nino is suited and booted and on best behaviour at the top of the steps of the restaurant welcoming everyone personally as they come in. Faida, resplendent in an emerald-green dress and hair freshly styled by Emina, flits by his side between welcoming and kitchen duties, keen to make sure that everyone from the Prefect of the region to her neighbours down the street are treated properly, as well as checking that all is well with the pig roast, the timing of which is essential to get right.

'Oh, ho, ho, welcome, welcome,' says Nino to the Prefect and his wife, who both hug and kiss him with the familiarity of family.

'It has been a long time, Nino,' says the boss of the region. 'I'm sorry to hear about the dogs, but I understand the problem has gone away. Let's talk later. I have something for you.'

'Let's talk then,' says Nino.

Coming up behind them are three Chinese men in suits, accompanied by an expansive and beaming Zvonko.

'Greetings, greetings,' says Mr Feng, the spokesman for the three, bowing respectfully. 'Thank you so much for the invitation, Mr Nino. And thank you for the part-truffle, part-cash settlement you sent with Mr Zvonko. Everything is clear now; we thank you from the bottom of our hearts.'

'My pleasure, Mr Feng,' says Nino, 'Mr Chen, Mr Zhang. Zvonko is a good boy, like a second son to me. You know you are always welcome; my home is your home. Please, come this way.'

As Nino shows the Chinese delegation to their seats, Faida and Emina take over the welcoming duties inside the lobby as the weather has taken a little turn for the worse and a light snow has started to fall.

'If this snow keeps up,' says Emina, 'it looks like everyone will be locked in for the night.'

'I wouldn't have it any other way,' says Faida. 'We've come this far. We had better make the New Year and the next 90 years go with a bang.'

'Let's drink to that,' says Emina, grabbing two classes of prosecco from a passing waiter. 'Cheers. I'm glad you're back with us.'

'Cheers to you, my dear; I could say the same,' says Faida. 'Now I can sleep again at night. And, who knows, Nino permitting, I might die a happy woman. Knowing that you and Marco have found each other again.'

'What about you and Nino?' asks Emina.

'We've come too far together for it to be anything different,' says Faida, 'whichever way you look at it. What is done is done. And if we all stand together maybe together we can find a way to go on living with it.'

They hug. As they do so, Mario, Enzo and Maurizio arrive at the bottom of the steps.

'Who are these people?' asks Faida to Emina in a whisper.

'These are the Valli's. The father is the man Nino saved at Bertarelli.'

'Welcome here in our house Mr Valli, please come in,' announces Faida in her most welcoming and charming manner. 'My husband has told me about you and your boys. Thank you so much for coming.'

Faida kisses them all, on both cheeks, as does Emina.

'It is I who should be thanking you,' says Mario, as he recovers his breath from the steps. 'I owe my life to your husband. I'm only sorry that…'

'Stop right there, Mr Mario,' says Faida. 'You have nothing to be sorry about here. Marijana, be a good young lady and show the Valli family to their seats.'

'It will be my pleasure, Nona,' says Marijana, leading the Italians to their places of honour near the *Župan*, and opposite the Chinese.

'They seem such nice people,' says Faida.

Suddenly Dado appears, ringing a very loud bell and ushering everyone to their seats. A single table has been laid out in a horseshoe shape, with the top table just within shouting distance of the kitchen. At the other end is a small stage. As the guests sit down, Mr Dalrymple, in crumpled seventies-style evening wear with large bow tie and red velvet cummerbund, lurks in the offstage area. He looks like a refugee from a TV snooker programme made in 1982.

Zvonko has been entertaining the Chinese guests, while Emina and Marco have been getting to know the Valli's a little better. Nino and Faida have been catching up with the Prefect and his wife. Adis in his chef's outfit moves discreetly around the table taking photos.

'One two, one two, one two,' says Mr Dalrymple into the microphone. 'Now, can everybody hear? Good. I'm not sure why anyone would want an old gringo like me to be master of ceremonies this evening, or on any evening come to that, but I seem to have drawn the short straw, so let's get on with it.'

Cheers and applause from the cheap seats, noticeably Zvonko and Marco. 'Bonkers!!! Go on Bonkers!!!' they cheer him on as they slip backstage behind him.

'When I first came here,' he continues, 'God knows how many years ago, as a young, idealistic socialist, I thought I had found the promised land. Yugoslavia. Istria. It was a far cry from what was going on in the seventies in England. You had a just and fair society, jobs, housing and food for all, and a lifestyle that was the envy of anywhere in the west. And *joie de vivre* – a way of enjoying life that, growing up in the fifties in suburban England, was but a dream for a young man. And there was equality for all. OK, some people were more equal than others, but they had earned their place in a small hierarchy in an egalitarian society. And those who were more equal were only a little bit more equal than everyone else, not like the disparities you see today. Anyway, I became the English teacher to the man who sits in front of us at the top of the table. Yugoslavia was opening up and Istria was the place that was becoming very attractive to holidaymakers the world over. To my eternal shame he is the only pupil in my 40-year-long career to whom I have failed to teach English in a meaningful way. But, having said that, it was I who learned something from Nino. I learned what the value is of a thing called friendship, a thing called loyalty, a thing called kindness. He picked me up under his arm and gave me a life here. So I want to start the evening with everyone standing with me, filling your glasses with *rakija*, and toasting the great man whose ninetieth birthday we celebrate here tonight: Nino Mihailić!'

*****

True to his word Adis had not served a single truffle shaving on any of the *hors d'oeuvres* which were now presented to the table. The platters contained a wide range of Istrian specialities, ranging from brodet, a fish soup made from at least seven kinds of different local fish, to shells, crab and shrimp from the Lim Fjord, *buzar*-style; then there was *peškafonda*, line-caught Adriatic squid – the royalty of all Istrian cephalopods. Alongside that there were scallops from up the road in Novigrad, special because of their provenance from the brackish waters there, as well as the majestic Lim Fjord oyster – the local delicacy that has been appreciated since the Roman times – served raw, with a few drops of lemon juice.

'Adis,' calls out Nino over the growing babble of the feast, 'what's going on? This *Novigrad capesante* would be perfect with a few shavings of white, don't you think?'

'Sorry, Nino, Faida's orders,' says Adis, taking a break from his photographic duties. 'No truffles allowed on the table tonight. On pain of severe castration.'

'Is there any other kind?' says the Prefect, overhearing and joining the conversation.

'Me or you?' ventures Nino.

'Both!' affirms Adis.

'It was that French chef,' says the Prefect, 'who said that whilst the truffle is not a positive aphrodisiac it can from time to time make one more tender and more apt to love.'

'It was the same one who claimed that whoever utters the word "truffle",' adds Nino, 'uses a great word which awakens both gastronomic and erotic notions.'

'Now don't you go giving him ideas,' chips in Lydia, the Prefect's wife, with a naughty chuckle.

'Nino,' says Faida, breaking off from her tête-à-tête with Lydia, 'I said no, and I mean no. And, anyway, it's going to be a while, I think, before Nino is going to be feeling "apt to love" anywhere near me. Tread carefully. You aren't out of the doghouse yet.' And she turns back to her conversation with Lydia, a smile playing across her lips. The two women laugh conspiratorially.

The Prefect leans in to Nino. 'I don't know about you, Nino, but it's a dish that is rarely served in my house anyway, so I don't know why I bother.'

At that moment, Mr Feng appears at the table between the Nino and the Prefect. 'I am happy to make your acquaintance, sir, and, please, my card,' says the businessman with tact and diplomacy. 'Now, I could not but help hear of your current predicament with the truffles,' continues Mr Feng. 'I think perhaps I can help you. We always carry them with us just in case. So many of those Istrian restaurants are serving cheap Chinese truffles these days.'

The three laugh collusively while covering the tubers from Faida.

'Well, if you can – just don't let her see you,' says Nino.

'I met your charming wife earlier, Mr Nino. And in Chinese we would say she is "Yīgè hen jiānqiáng de nürén" – a very strong woman.'

'I like your style, Mr Feng,' says the Prefect, 'and also your perfect use of the understatement. Now, about the truffle: do you have some?'

Discretely Feng takes a small box out of his pocket, which contains a fine white truffle, the *tuber magnatum pico*, as well as a small silver blade which he uses to slice slivers of the beauty on to the delicious *capesante*.

'Your New Year would not be the same without it!' says Mr Feng.

'Try telling her that,' says Nino. 'I thought this was to be my birthday celebration.'

'Come on, Nino – looking for special treatment?' says the Prefect. 'It's only your ninetieth. Pull yourself together, comrade.'

Dalrymple appears at Mr Feng's side. 'Ah, Mr Feng; honoured to meet you again.'

'Mr Dalrymple, the pleasure is all mine,' replies Feng.

'I couldn't help but notice,' says Dalrymple conspiratorially, 'that you have what Rossini termed the "Mozart of Mushrooms" in your pocket. Do you think I could… ?'

'With pleasure, Mr Dalrymple,' says Feng. 'And thank you for all your help on the deal with Mr Nino. We couldn't have done it without you.'

'My pleasure, Mr Feng. Call on me any time.'

'Speaking of Rossini,' says Feng, 'he was a great lover of – as you say – the black princess. He once said that he had only cried three times in his life: when his first opera failed; the first time he heard Paganini play violin; and thirdly when a truffled turkey fell overboard at a boating picnic.'

With a flash of the blade, he shaves a flourish of *magnatum pico* over Dalrymple's *coquilles Saint Jacques* and re-joins his party.

They laugh. As do many of the joyful collective as they feast on the best seafood the Adriatic and *Quarnero* has to offer and some of the finest hospitality in Istria, courtesy of the Mihailić's.

As the gathered chosen few work their way through more grilled sardines, raw prawns, and slithers of *Savudrija švoja* – a kind of a sole fish, and one of the traditional culinary symbols of north-west Istria – a strange-looking fellow in bizarre costume takes to the stage and walks towards the microphone. A hush comes over the room.

'Ladies and gentlemen,' comes the stentorian announcement, indicating that it is indeed Mr Dalrymple beneath the costume, 'as you know, Istria was an important part of the Roman Empire for centuries. It became an official colony 178 years before Jesus Christ and was famous for its oil, its wine, and its beautiful women.'

There is a round of applause for 'the ladies'. Emina, also dressed in an exotic costume, has installed herself behind the piano, and is playing the odd dramatic chord to add emphasis and to punctuate Mr Dalrymple's presentation.

'Now, you may very well ask what has the Roman Empire and this ridiculous costume I am wearing got to do with General Major Mihailić's ninetieth birthday? Be patient. All will become clear. This costume is an accurate reconstruction of what an *Umpire* would be wearing in the Roman arena towards the end of the first century AD. This striped tunic, which looks like something my mother would have worn to a funeral of someone she didn't like, would be the symbol of fairness and justice in the arena. And I don't want any jokes about the "Fall of the Roman Umpire" – keep them to yourself.'

The audience laugh at this last gag as Emina plays a 'boom-boom – ta daaaah' chord to punctuate the laugh, at which point two fully-dressed and masked Roman gladiators come onto the stage. Obviously, Marco and Zvonko, who receive rapturous applause from the audience.

'Ladies and gentlemen, in the blue corner,' says Dalrymple, adopting the style of a latter-day World Wrestling Federation referee and pointing to Zvonko: 'is the defending champion, Pretty Boy Oceanus. As you can see from his attire, he is a Thracian, or *Thraex*, with his small rectangular shield and very short sword. In Roman times he would have been the "baddie".'

The audience play along with the charade, and hiss and boo. Zvonko moves intimidatingly towards them, his hands in the air and waggling his tongue lewdly as they continue to boo and hiss. Lucia plays 'baddie' music on the piano. Zvonko waggles his tongue at her, and with his back to the audience lifts his tunic in time-honoured pantomime fashion.

'Boooooo! Boooooooo!' shout the audience.

'And, in the green corner, we have the great local boy made good: Severus the *murmillo*!'

Marco moves modestly centre stage, one arm in the air. He is sporting the classic *murmillo* helmet with a stylised fish on the crest (the *mormylos*, or sea fish), as well as an arm guard (the *manica*), a loincloth and belt, and a gaiter on his right leg.

The audience cheer Severus the *Murmillo* to the rafters. Marco steps forwards and says: 'My name is Severus Decimus Meridius, Commander of the Armies of the North, General of the Felix Legions, loyal servant to the true emperor, General Major Nino Mihailić. Father to a murdered son, husband to a murdered wife. And I will have my vengeance, in this life or the next.'

He steps back to a huge round of applause.

'OK you two,' says Dalrymple, 'as it's before the watershed we have given you wooden swords because live killing is banned onstage in Croatia before 9 pm. The only exception is metaphorical "dying" onstage, which is clearly what this act is here. I want to see a fair fight. Two falls, two submissions, or a knockout. The bell, please.'

Emina rings the bell to start the bout.

Marco and Zvonko, dressed in their authentic gladiator outfits and with their short wooden *rudus* swords, set about each other with a vengeance. But it is more Buster Keaton than Spartacus. To that end, Emina's repertoire changes to silent movie chase-type music as they beat their *ruderi* against each other in time to the beat, whipping the audience into a frenzy. Severus, *rudus* aloft, chases a terrified Oceanus through the audience, around the table and back up onto the stage where he is knocked to the ground *à la* Harold Lloyd. The audience are in paroxysms of laughter. Finally, Severus is about to impale Pretty Boy who begs for mercy.

'Ladies and gentlemen, this is where the audience participation begins,' says Dalrymple.

'Oh no it doesn't,' pops up Zvonko from his horizontal position.

Dalrymple corpsing badly: 'This is sadly not a decision for the Umpire – if it were I'd let them both have it. BUT if we want to let him go, shout *Mitte!* If we want Severus to kill him, shout *Iugula!*'

The audience cries out in one voice: '*Iugula! Iugula! Iugula!*'

Severus drives the *rudus* home mercilessly under Pretty Boy's arm to cheers from the crowd. Severus/Marco removes his *murmillo* helmet and has his arm held aloft by Bonkers. As the cheers subside Marco steps forward to the microphone and starts to remove the *manica* from his arm.

'That was a lot of fun. And many of you will be disappointed to hear that I didn't really kill Zvonko – so a round of applause for our designated baddie of the evening, Pretty Boy Oceanus.'

The dinner guests, getting more and more drunk, cheer wildly the pantomime baddie that is Zvonko. Marijana, his daughter, runs on stage and gives him a kiss and runs back again.

'Strangely enough, this armour that I am now removing, which is called a *manica*,' continues Marco, 'did once belong to a gladiator called Severus who fought in the arena in Pula. Over the years it changed hands, many times, until it ended up in the hands of the father of the man I will introduce now: Mr Mario Valli.'

Mario is assisted onto the stage by Enzo and Maurizio who step to the side, ready to help him down again.

'Good evening,' begins Mario. 'None of you here know me. My name is Mario Valli. I want to thank Nino for inviting me and my sons to this wonderful gathering. It has been over 70 years since I was last in this village before my departure from here during the unfortunate exodus of some of the Italian community in the 1940s, during and just after the war. My father was a much-loved teacher at the Gymnasium in Pazin like your great poet and statesman Vladimir Nazor before him. Nino, whose life we are here to celebrate tonight, was one of his pupils. I would like to ask Nino to join me here on stage.'

Nino moves from his place of honour at the head of the table and joins Mario at the microphone.

'Nino was a boy soldier, a Partisan when I met him. He was, unbeknown to him, sent with his detachment to take a group of Italians to their deaths at the Bertarelli *foibe*. Already on the journey to what he thought was going to be a re-education camp he had tried to help us by loosening our shackles so that at a certain point we could run free. That moment only became possible as the slaughter began at the *foibe*. Nino tried his best to save my father, but his efforts were in vain, and my father was shot. Nino, at great personal risk to himself, allowed me to escape in the chaos and panic of that day. I shall be forever in his debt. Today is the day that I get to express my thanks to him personally. Thank you, Nino, for giving me life.'

Nino and Mario both shed tears and embrace. Faida looks on, tears in her eyes. Emina, Marco and Zvonko all hug each other.

Dado and Marijana join in their scrum. The audience applauds, respectfully. Mario breaks the embrace.

'Now, there is a reason why Mr Dalrymple started the entertainment with the mock gladiator combat,' he continues. 'It's a part of the story. When we were being led to the *foibe* my father was carrying the *manica* of a gladiator, a *murmillo* like Severus today. It was his most treasured possession. He wanted to smuggle it back to Italy but in the end tried to use it as a bribe to get us away. One part was with my father and one part with me. When we were separated by his death, I took one piece with me. The other piece remained in Istria. He had offered it to Nino, who refused accept anything. But when father was killed Nino found it in the river and took it with him. A few days ago, these two pieces of history were reunited.'

'These pieces were made in Istria and stayed in Istria for the best part of two millennia, except for one brief excursion to London,' says Nino. 'They contain a very special story. The story of our truffle. The truffle that has become the symbol and byword for our part of Istria, something that is deeply rooted, literally, in our patrimony. We would like this story to be told. To that end the County of Istria would like to officially commission our expert, Mr Dalrymple, to write this story, the story of this amazing artefact. Mr Valli – Mario – would like in memory of his father to donate this valuable relic to the Ethnographical Museum in Pazin. He would like to present it now to the Prefect of Istria, who will accept it on behalf of the museum.'

The boss of Istria, a real pro, is on stage in a flash and accepts the *manica*. There are hugs all round. 'Ladies and gentlemen, thanks so much to the Valli family and the Mihailić family for returning this piece of our national history to where it belongs. Our Roman roots are all around us – we live with them every day – and this *manica*, with the story that it tells hidden in a coded message carved onto the inside of its metal slats, is a fundamental part of all of our histories. Which is why, as Nino mentioned, the office of the Prefect's cultural department would like to commission a book from our scholarly expert, Mr Dalrymple, which commemorates the precious story of Severus, Lucia and Nasica and how they found their liberty through the truffle. He was the man who solved the puzzle, and he knows all the war stories of Nino and Faida – so I am interested to see what kind of tale he will tell.'

'Thank you, Mr Prefect. And now, ladies and gentlemen,' says Nino, 'before we raise our glasses to Mario Valli and his father and family, our *chef extraordinaire*, Adis, will introduce you to someone I know you all have been waiting for all evening. Ladies and gentlemen, I give you The Pig!'

Adis and all the kitchen staff parade from the restaurant, through the dining room, past the stage, bearing a huge pig on a bier at shoulder height: resplendently golden, hot, succulent, simple and traditional and with a perfume to die for, the classic cooking apple holding its large mouth wide open. They lay the main course on a reinforced guéridon in the centre of the table and begin serving. The guests fall upon the piggy buffet with gusto, heads down, plates filled. No nonsense.

The room is abuzz with conversation, chat and laughter and the sound of feasting. The Chinese are deep in conversation with Mario about the wines of the Veneto, with Enzo turning out to be a pretty good translator of English. The Prefect and Dalrymple discuss the commission to write the story of the Istrian truffle through the prism of the *manica*, the arena, the truffle, and Nino's wartime story. Zvonko, Marijana and Dado are huddled together at the corner of the table, eating, drinking and making merry as only a happy family can. Adis acrobatically clambers between the chairs and the tables and the buffet, finding the best angles and snapping away on his state-of-the-art camera.

As New Year approaches the excitement in the room has grown tangibly greater. The litany of the endless drinks menu has already taken into account local prosecco to start with, followed by an appetite-sharpening grappa from Nino's own distillery; this is succeeded by a very crisp *malvasia* from the western part of the peninsula, and then by a powerful red from the central highlands. They are the perfect accompaniment to the locally sourced products turned into simple culinary masterpieces by maestro Adis.

'If you think all this has been good,' says Faida to Nino as they enjoy a rare private moment together at table, 'you should wait till you taste the *fritule*. He has done something with lime zest instead of lemon zest and it gives it an extra something.'

'Oh, no – he hasn't been messing with uncle Armando's original recipe?' says Nino.

'Yes, he has, Nino,' says Faida. 'And take it from me, it's an improvement. Armando's was good, this is better. You'll see. After all, it's New Year. We need to be open to new things, new ideas. We have the whole of the rest of our lives to look forward to.'

The piano stirs to life and is just about heard above the conversation playing a few gentle bars of a ballad. Nino looks at Faida, who looks back at him straight in the eyes.

'No, it isn't. You haven't?' says Nino.

'I asked Dalrymple for it,' says Faida. 'He said he would do a special arrangement. For your birthday. Our special song.'

The lights come up on stage and Dalrymple is at the piano.

'Ladies and gentlemen, as New Year is almost upon us,' says Mr Dalrymple as he toys with his nimble fingers a few gentle chords. 'We have had a special request from a very special lady to play a song for her and Nino. Their song.'

A low light at the back of the stage finds Emina and Marco, now changed out of his gladiator outfit, hand in hand, walking downstage to the opening bars of Arsen Dedić's *Oh Youth*, exactly as they had rehearsed: the long intro, the G minor, C minor 7th, then D7; ready… one, two, three, four…

Faida and Nino kiss each other and jump to their feet, alive, vibrant and a world away from their demeanour of the last days. They look at Emina and Marco, their younger selves, with hope and longing. The young couple begin in unison. As a small choir of a dozen young adults from the school slowly walk forwards from the back of the stage and join the lovers, boys on Marco's side, girls on Emina's side. They all sing refrain of youth:

You gave it to me, but you it stole back
And so unfaithful you were to me
It wasn't so much you gave, no, just
Youth, oh youth
Oh my youth.

Smiling through the tears, Faida and Nino look straight up at the youngsters and mouth the words along with them, also joining in the chorus.

The sun had barely set upon
That sorry love, those fleeting dreams
For memories that is but little
Oh youth, oh youth of mine.
Just take it easy, and give me strength
At least the time to say farewell
And let my friends finish the song
And let me finish my drink.

By the finale of the song no-one can hold back, and it is a free-for-all that everyone has joined in; tears of joy on every face, unable to survive the power of the poetry.

Still full of hope, what shall I do now?
And we are only halfway there
But this morning is new youth here
Youth, Oh youth
Oh my youth.
So, goodbye, be better with the next one
Try a bit more tenderness
What I'm losing is not the whole thing
Oh youth, youth….

A cheer goes up. Rapturous applause, for the song, for the singers, for Faida, for the birthday boy, Nino. Someone starts a chant, 'Ni-no, Ni-no, Ni-no.' Dalrymple plays some martial-sounding music on the piano. It sounds like a marching song. A Partisan song. The youngsters all have their Partisan hats on. They tramp in time to the music as the words begin. It's a war-time anthem. Adis is wearing a Partisan hat. 'Everyone, face this way, group photo,' he shouts above Dalrymple's piano intro. 'OK – everyone, hats on!'

Everyone in the room has revealed they have party Partisan hats with the single star, and they put them on. The Pazin Gymnasium Choir gives a rousing rendition of *Mitraljeza*, the song by adopted local boy Vladimir Nazor, the former President of the Socialist

Federal Republic of Croatia within Yugoslavia, about the story of a man who takes his machine gun as a girlfriend. It's a crowd pleaser. By now everyone has their hats on and are facing the camera. Adis shouts out again: 'PARTISANS! SALUTE!'

Clenched fists are held to the temple, a flashbulb pops, and the moment in captured on digital celluloid for eternity.

Bibliographical Note

Istria Gold takes in a wide-ranging sweep of history and topography and therefore a broad span of reading was not only helpful, but absolutely necessary in order to accurately inform the fictional depiction of contemporary underground policing in the UK, life in the Roman arena and Partisanship in the peninsula. Gladiators, truffles, Partisans, and undercover cops in the eco-movement are unlikely bedfellows, but fascinating subjects and there is a vast array of excellent material out there to wade through and wallow in, thus my initial need was to be as selective as possible. In this, I occasionally failed.

On the subject of gladiators and the Roman arena, I am indebted to the eminent Dutch historian Fik Meijer for *The Gladiators – History's Most Dangerous Sport* (2003), which remains the go-to in depth book on the subject, with eyewitness testimonies that aren't for the faint-hearted. Meijer is an epic historian and a great writer. Equally vivid and colourful was Robert Knapp's ambitious and informative *Invisible Romans – Prostitutes, Outlaws, Slaves, Gladiators, Ordinary Men and Women… The Romans that History Forgot* (2013); his scholarly approach, combined with explicit revelation, is a million miles away from the dry-as-dust histories on the period. Susanna Shadrake's *The World of the Gladiator* (2005) knocks on the head many of the popular myths about life in the arena and gets to grips with the gruesome realities of this deadly 'sport'. Her experience in gladiator re-enactment spectacle gives an unusually authentic insight not usually present in serious academic studies.

This having been said, Alan Baker's *The Gladiator – The Secret History of Rome's Warrior Slaves* (2000), whilst light in academe and scholarship, is indeed a work of history that reads like fiction, bringing to life a number of memorable players of the nearly thousand-year-long gladiatorial era. On a slightly lighter note, Philip Matyszak's *Gladiator – The Roman Fighter's Unofficial Manual* (2013) uses an amusing and sometimes irreverent tongue-in-cheek humour to paint the harsh life of gladiators in vivid detail while maintaining a scholarly depth. Stefan Mlekar's *The Amphitheatre in Pula* (1984) a pamphlet which provided a dry-as-dust description of the extraordinary physical edifice of Vespasian's Istrian architectural masterpiece, including a history of viticulture, olive husbandry as well as casting required locally for the shipping of oil. *Gladiator – Rome's Bloody Spectacle* (2005) by Konstantin Nossov, as well as reinforcing the notion that all books about the arena written in modern times require a dramatic subtitle, is a well-researched, highly-readable evidence-based analysis of the gladiatorial industry of ancient Rome.

Finally, love her or loathe her, Mary Beard's seminal and masterful history of the *Roman Empire, SPQR – A History of Ancient Rome* (2016) relates the story of an empire, which is not only engaging, but scholarly and page-turningly readable. Appositely, she gives her last word to the Greek historian, Polybius: 'Who could be so indifferent or so idle that they did not want to find out how, and under what kind of political organisation, almost the whole of the inhabited world was conquered and fell under the sole power of the Romans in less than 53 years, something previously unparalleled?' I know that this is one of the key things that drove my fascination with the period.

I add, *passim*, original source literary texts accrued over a lifetime's fascination with ancient culture inspired by my Latin and Greek master, Pete Whitton, who would be tickled that I had carried forward my youthful passion for the classics into later life: Petronius's *Satyricon liber* (*The Satyricon*), Seneca's *Apocolocyntosis (divi) Claudii*, (*The Pumpkinification of (the Divine) Claudius*), Suetonius's *De vita Caesarum* (*The Twelve Caesars*), Plutarch's *Parallel Lives* (*Bíoi Parállēloi*), as well as Tacitus's *The Annals of Imperial Rome* (*Annales*). There is no better original version/translation than the Loeb Classical Library (Harvard University Press), 'the crib' as Pete used to call it, which aside from providing the standard texts with excellent parallel translations are things of beauty in themselves.

When it came to delving into the history of Istria during the Second World War pickings were far fewer, but of no less a higher standard than that of the research material available on the ancient times. Velimir Vukšić's trim but excellent monograph for Osprey, *Tito's Partisans 1941-45* (2003), provided a crisp, succinct insight into the daily lives of some of the bravest fighting men and women in history. Basil Davidson's excellent *Partisan Picture* (1946) gives an unrivalled account of his time with the Yugoslav resistance and extraordinary insight into the daily lives of Tito's guerrilla force. Equally, the American OSS point of view is superbly put in the witty and scholarly *Beacons in the Night* (1993) by Franklin Lindsay and is also an illuminating introduction to the contemporary Yugoslav tragedy. Similarly, Peter Wilkinson's *Foreign Fields* (1997) covers the SOE's hazardous attempt to penetrate the soft underbelly of the Third Reich in co-operation with Tito's Partisans.

Invaluable in understanding the importance of women to the Partisan struggle was Jelena Batinić's incisive and scholarly *Women and Yugoslav Partisans. A History of World War II Resistance* (2015); best were the veteran reminiscences throwing into relief changes in gender norms caused by the Partisan struggle. In David Martin's *Ally Betrayed, the Uncensored Story of Tito and Mihailović* (1946), it was interesting to see the period from a pro-Četnik perspective, however unconvincing the argument and however bizarre Rebecca West's foreword. Alec Brown's *Diaries from Yugoslav Liberation* (1946) published in *The Slavonic and East European Review* brought me face to face with the war of key Partisan frontliners Vladimir Nazor and Vladimir Dedijer.

Dedijer's 1953 biography of Josip Broz, *Tito*, is a masterpiece of the genre. Clearly not unbiased, this analysis is infused with a sincerity completely unusual in Communist hagiographies. To understand Yugoslavia, and therefore Istria, it is crucial to understand Tito, and Dedijer understood him better than anyone else. His *The Beloved Land* (1961) demonstrates a solidarity with the Partisan cause and the Yugoslavian resistance during which he forged a friendship with Tito, but where I found it useful was how Dedijer's ancestral history threw light onto the religious and social conflicts that have beset the region since time immemorial. For a more balanced view Richard West's excellent *TITO – and the Rise and Fall of Yugoslavia* (1994) skilfully unravels the conundrum of why after forty years of Tito the country could cease to exist so easily, and civil war could descend with such comparative ease.

The limited repertoire of literature and non-fiction books on the subject of Istria in general has meant re-activating the little Italian that remained from my school days to approach the wide range of material on the subject, the daddy of them all being Gologorica's Carlo di Francheschi who in 1879 made the very first attempt to chronicle the peninsula from its earlier times in *L'Istria Note Storica* (1879). Equally inspirational was Darko Darovec's *A Brief History of Istria* (1998); with rigorous methodology (and in a mere 120 pages) Darovec's digest from pre-history to the present day is a solid and reliable source.

Early on in my research it became clear that most material on the subject of Istria is urban centred on the littoral and the major centres. Dario Alberi's excellent *Istria, Storia, Arte Culture* (1997) takes us to the heart of the region where *Istria Gold* mostly takes place, remarkably covering the 1,500 hamlets which make up the often-forgotten vast majority of the peninsula. Another essential point of reference is Bernardo Benussi's *L'Istria ne suoi due Millenia de Storia* (1924), scrupulously researched, it is a treasure trove of Istrian historiography from prehistory to irredentism. I owe a debt of gratitude to the excellent Openstarts programme of the Università Degli Studie di Trieste, whose digital repository which hosts and indexes the faculty's regional documentation is second to none, and open access to boot.

The crucial twentieth century events that marked Istria's Italian speaking community for better or for worse are chronicled ably in Arrigo Petacco's *A Tragedy Revealed – The Story of the Italian Population of Istria, Dalmatia and Venezia Giulia, 1943-1956* (1999), a crucial book which broke the great silence of the subject of the *foibe*. On the fictional side of things, of the slim pickings available in English, easily the most moving and impressive was Fulvio Tomizza's *Materada*, the chronicle of a man with a regional identity who has no state to represent or defend him. The book is imbued with a love for a native region that drew me to Istria in the first place over 40 years ago.

Staying in the land of the literary for a moment, Istrians, on the other hand, should be grateful that James Joyce after his disastrous sojurn in Pula didn't write anything about it or its inhabitants. (I write this as his fellow Irishman, who has had an entirely different experience.) A debt is owed to the 'local' literary legend and Partisan, Vladimir Nazor, in my paraphrasing of his paen to freedom, *Veli Jože* (*Big Joe)* (1908), and his *Istarske priče* (*Istrian Tales*) (1913); hailing from the island of Brač he is very much considered a son of Istria. Other Croatian literature worth a look was the short but excellent travelogue *Istrian Journeys* (1919) by Franjo Horvat-Kiš which deserves to be mentioned as a very singular work in Croatian literature.

Incidentally, I didn't read *Matthias Sandorf*, Jules Verne's Mediterranean adventure set partly in the Pazin Caves; instead I dipped into Charles Yriarte's lacklustre *Les bords de l'Adriatique et le Monténégro* (1878), which was the source material from which Verne pillaged much of his information about Pazin.

On a slightly more macro scale the *Istarska Enciklopedija* (2005) has been a constant companion, fact checker and full partner when it comes to the truth, the whole truth and nothing but the truth. Whilst truth and fiction have little to do with each other, I pay respect to the editors Miroslav Bertoša and Robert Matijašić, as well as the Lexikografski Zavod Miroslav Krleža that, surprisingly, still engages in accurate scientific and scholarly study on behalf of the Croatian government.

Equally important, but from the private sector, is Svein Karl Mønnesland's encyclopedic, yet utterly accessible, totally readable and beautifully researched *Istria and Kvarner Through Foreign Eyes* (*Istra i Kvarner očima stranaca*) (2019). Slightly more esoteric is Roman Latković and Ranko Dokmanović's *Bewitching Istria – A Never Ending Story* (1994), a exotic monochrome miscellany of Istriana that opened my doors of perception.

And while we are on the subject of 'bewitching' there are few things more bewitching that the intoxicating lure of the truffle. It has been my pleasure to explore the alpha and omega of the underground empress via a number of reliable sources. It was best to start with the hard facts and those were provided by Ian R. Hall, Gordon T. Brown and Alessandra Zambonelli in their unrivalled *Taming of the Truffle – The History and Lore and Science of the Ultimate Mushroom* (2007); they manage to eloquently elide the art and science of cultivating the fungus that is worth more than gold in a most comprehensive and practical treatment of this gastronomic treasure to date. Elisabeth Luard's *Truffles* (2006), with exquisite photography by John Heseltine, provided a passionate culinary perspective. Patricia Welles backed that up in *Simply Truffles* (2011), capturing the essence of and reverence for the Black Diamond, both in the kitchen and in the field. Both works hold a vast array of anecdotes and quotes which, combined with menu suggestions and wine pairings, all conspired to arouse an extraordinary appetite in the unsuspecting reader. *A propos* of which *The Physiology of Taste – or Meditations on Transcendental Gastronomy* (1825) by Jean Anthelme Brillat-Savarin proved a welcome and amusing companion.

On the fiction side, Gustaf Sobin's elegantly slim volume of crisp prose, *The Fly Truffler* (2000), opened my eyes to the world of fly truffling, an almanac of magic realism, gently evoking the heretofore unknown technique, and incidentally providing a mildly erotic, kind of gothic handbook to support it. And on the journalistic side of things, Ryan Jacobs' *The Truffle Underground* (2019) is excellent investigative journalism in the dark underbelly of the fungus, except he didn't make it to Istria and could also use an index in the next edition.

On the subject of police infiltration of activist groups, *Undercover: The True Story of Britain's Secret Police* (2012) by *Guardian* journalists Rob Evans and Paul Lewis proved to be a seminal example of good, old-fashioned long-haul journalism that has brought to book and held to account the murky, ugly, hidden forces of the establishment. A perfect example of why a free press is essential to any democracy.

Finally, we need to acknowledge the tomes that gave significant in-depth overview to the region, and the best starting place for this is Dame Rebecca West's *Black Lamb and Grey Falcon: A Journey Through Yugoslavia* (1941), not simply the most in-depth analysis of its kind of the region ever done by a Westerner, it is a portrait of Europe on the edge of war. Tim Judah's *The Serbs: History, Myth and the Destruction of Yugoslavia* (1997), is not merely a polemic to counter local, mutual, demonisation, but an impartial study that continues to be a benchmark in historical analysis. The natural partner to Judah's piece is Marcus Tanner's brisk, no-nonsense *Croatia: A Nation Forged in War* (2010). Their respective accounts perfectly collect the baggage of history carried by the Yugoslav ethnic groups and analyse how they arrived their contemporary destination.

Acknowledgements

Istria Gold is my first foray into fiction, written in precious stolen moments over the last few years. During this time I have been scrupulous in telling as few people as possible of my literary ambitions, living in mock terror of the apocryphal Peter Cook story, who, when sat next to someone at a dinner party, that person announced, 'I'm writing a novel, you know,' to which Cook replied in his habitual fruity deadpan, 'Oh, really? Neither am I.'

It was therefore crucial that when I 'came out' to place the manuscript it was into the right hands. I am thus grateful to the ever-patient 'safe pair of hands' that belong to Nick Marston at Curtis Brown for his enormous encouragement and belief in me as a writer. His initial response gave me the courage and energy to embark on a major re-write, without which *Istria Gold* would never have seen the light of day. A huge vote of thanks is also due to German *über* agent Petra Hermanns of the eponymous Literaturagentur Petra Hermanns GmbH who was an early champion of the project and whose sound advice and generously proffered experience helped me to bash on when the task in hand looked threateningly sisyphic.

A debt of gratitude is owed to Julian Friedmann of the Blake Friedmann Literary Agency for helping me keep on track with his incisive comments on the final manuscript as well as confidence inspiring pep talks. Thank you, Julian. The same goes to my old chum, Steve Williams, who put the finished book through its paces and provided some detailed criticism, much of which was incorporated. The same goes for my loyal first reader of the manuscript, Rudolf Biermann. On the Croatian side of things, master translator Duško Čavić provided much-needed guidance not merely on the local literary and linguistic side of things; his encyclopaedical knowledge of the historical, political, and topographical gave me some crucial indicators, especially regarding the authenticity of certain aspects of my story.

This book would have been impossible without the advice, encouragement and editorial talents that are owned by Jonathan Preece. He has performed miracles born from a lifetime in copy, text

– the written word itself. His work on the manuscript has been a vast exercise of editorial skill and vison; his long-suffering but utterly invaluable literary input has been nothing short of heroic. For this I give him the most profound thanks.

No less thanks are due to the extraordinary publishing team at MPress Media and distributors Calm Productions and their perennially helpful, positive, and supportive role in getting this book to press and market. Publisher Cliff Moulder and I go back a long way (to the days of hot metal typesetting and letterpress printing), and without his enthusiastic backing and the fabulous work of his creative team led by Paul Moulder and Tony Moulder this book would still be languishing in the proverbial bottom drawer. Alongside Jonathan, Cliff, and Paul stand a small but very committed army of proof-readers, copy editors, designers, publicists, printers, marketeers without whom we'd all be in trouble. And then there are the booksellers, librarians, and book clubs who bring them most crucially to you, the reader. To all the unsung heroes, I give thanks.

I should add, however, at this point, that all mistakes herein are mine alone.

My dear friends and acquaintances from my connection of more than 40 years with the region all in some way contributed to this book, whether they like it or not. Maja Volk first introduced me to the peninsula in 1979 and I spent three blissfully lonely months in her parents' house in Premantura writing my master's thesis for L'Université de Paris X (Nanterre). I have known since that time that the 'terra magica' that is Istria would play a big part in my life. After the war Rajko Grlić invited me to lecture at the Grožnjan Imaginary Film Academy where Ana Grlić thankfully insisted that I have a coffee with the quondam director of the *Jeunesses Musicales Internationales* programme, Marijana Pintar. It was a good job I accepted because, as it turned out, twenty-something years later Marijana remains the great love of my life. Thank you, Ana.

That Grožnjan sojurn proved to be the catalyst for my friendship with Boris T. Matić (and eventually Lana Matić *née* Ujdur) who, along with Rajko, Olinka Vištica, Nikola Zinić and myself, created the once legendary, now lacklustre and disappointing Motovun Film Festival. The welcome you gave me into your community and friendship endures personally and professionally to this day. Motovun was responsible for so many inspirational encounters, whether with photographer and gallerist Hassan Abdelghani, or restauranteurs Klaudio and Leila Ivasić. The Venetian hill town was once one of the major cultural hubs of the region. Sadly, no more. Equally, I'd like to thank my colleagues Tanja Miličić and Hrvoje Pukšec who during the artistic directorship at the Pula Film Festival with me helped to make what could have been a difficult tenure as creative and positive as was possible under the circumstances. I include Gordana Restović in that as well.

Nevertheless, it was my encounter with legendary Istrian designer and artist Željko Burić that proved the game changer in my Istrian existence, and I owe a vast debt of gratitude to Željko for being my guide and mentor with regard to most things Istrian. He not only found me the magnificent edifice which eventually became my home, but the three short years we spent designing, adapting, and rebuilding were a baptism of fire into the region, the culture, the wine, the cuisine, the music, the art, and the sheer sense of the importance of quality of life that marks the Istrian spirit. How we laughed. Still laugh.

Time spent with an extraordinary number of people, in a bizarre array places, positions, situations and arrangements are too many to mention. And if I've forgotten anyone, don't worry, there will be a sequel – but here goes. Thanks also due to: Zorica Pintar, Ivica Matosević, Djurdjica Orepić, Tomislav Popović, Mariam Abdelghani, Marko and Silvija Burić, Branka Abdelghani, Armando and Mariella Lušetić, Dušica Radojčić, Salih Sadiković and Desanka Virant. Srdjan Karanović's encouragement over the years has been a source of much inspiration. The old Grimalda gang to whom I am more than grateful as friends and neighbours and the completely welcoming people of Central Istria for providing such a perfect place and inspiration to write more specifically: Ema and Pepi, Marija and Misha. And a little further down the hill but still close to heart, Irena, Drago, and Karolina. The stepchildren, Rudolph Herzog and Nerma Mehadžić and all of our other offspring – as a wise old man once said to me, and as Nino reiterates in the novel, 'Children are the product of love, and not of biology.' How right he was. Is. Blood, however, is thicker than water, so here's to the Downeys – Anne, Brian, and dearly departed Tommy, Bridie and Peter, as well as Mike and Dawn – whether you like it or not, you're family now. Same goes for you, Stephen Daldry. Thank you for a lifetime of friendship.

But I return as always to the warmth of spirit and the heart of kindness which has driven so many things in my life for the last two-and-a-half decades, my partner and love, Marijana. If I were to list all her qualities, and her contribution to not just this book, but my entire world, you would, like Olivia in Shakespeare's *Twelfth Night*, 'condemn it as an improbable fiction'. Improbable a fiction as this book is, I dedicate this book to you, Marijana Pintar: thank you for giving meaning to my reality and making it all, I mean all, worthwhile.

Mike Downey
Grimalda, Istria, May 1st, 2022

A Note on the Type

Caslon is the name given to serif typefaces designed by William Caslon I (c. 1692–1766) in London. Adobe Caslon Pro is a smooth, easy reading text face rooted in the typefaces of this notable eighteenth-century printer. Carol Twombly designed this Caslon revival for Adobe in 1990, after studying Caslon's own specimen sheets from the mid-eighteenth century. This elegant version is quite true to the source and has been optimized for the demands of digital design and printing. Considered the first original English typeface, it shares many characteristics of the Dutch Baroque type fonts of the era and may be a variation on the Dutch Fell type fonts cut by Voskens or Van Dyck at that time. From 1725 through to 1730 three books printed by William Bower used roman and italic fonts cut by Caslon. The fonts were popular throughout the British Empire including the American Colonies, where they acquired their distinctive appearance from the exposure to salt air during the voyage from Britain. Indeed, it was in the U.S. that Benjamin Franklin used it extensively and in fact it was the font used to set both the Declaration of Independence and the U.S. Constitution.